FORMULA 2000,
the Dream

JOE BARFIELD

CreateSpace Publishing

FORMULA 2000, THE DREAM

Copyright 2015 by Joe Barfield
All rights reserved

No part of this book may be used or reproduced by any means, graphic, electronic, or mechanical, including photocopying, recording, taping or by any information storage retrieval system without the written permission of the publisher except in the case of brief quotations embodied in critical articles and reviews.

ISBN:1511869518
ISBN-13: 978-1511869515

DEDICATION

To my son Beaux Barfield and the wonderful adventures we had racing on and off the track.

FORMULA 2000, THE DREAM

TABLE OF CONTENTS

	Prologue	i
1	WATKINS GLEN	1
2	MOSPORT	44
3	IRP	65
4	DALLAS GRAND PRIX	85
5	SEBRING	100
6	Pepper Automotive	135
7	MID-OHIO	139
8	PHAR Motorsports	155
9	CHARLOTTE	160
10	RUAN GRAND PRIX	176
11	ROAD AMERICA	194
12	ROAD ATLANTA	210
	Hot Laps – Video Links	236
	About the Author	238
	Other Books by the Author	239

Prologue

Sometimes I think I was born in a racecar. Many times I've asked a person's first memory of their being. Always it was an accident, a trip or punishment...something stamped on the memory.

My name is Charlie Pepper and in all my 55 years my first conscious memory was that of sitting on my father's shoulders when I was four--and watching the start of the 1947 Indy 500. My second memory was sitting behind the steering wheel of Mauri Rose's winning car in the same Indy 500 after the race. My father was a mechanic for that team and Rose's Deidt FD Offy. I remember the next year Rose won the Indy 500 again.

I didn't miss an Indy 500 until 1992.

My father told me one day I would be a racecar driver. I thought I wanted to be a driver but over the years, I found making the cars perform at maximum capabilities interested me the most. From that day when I could first remember the Indy 500 I fell in love with the sweet thunder of the exhaust, the high rpm whine of the engine and the lightning quickness of the racecars. The fact was I could fix a suspension next to none, but I was better at building engines. Somehow I always managed to pull at least one more horsepower from an engine than anybody else. Some accused me of voodoo with cars...it was time. I think I had heard every engine imaginable and when an engine went sour, I could pinpoint it and usually find the exact problem. I loved to make an engine perform.

When it came to racing, I'd been to most kinds. I first started racing circle track and dirt track but not long after my dad died I started wrenching for a variety of teams. First was the circle track circuit with a friend of mine, Richard Graham. But old Rich, who was nine years older, found a woman and got married. Rich settled down and quit the racing scene. I stuck with racing and went on to NASCAR, GTP, Formula One and the Indy series. Building engines for all.

Not too long after Rich married, I met Mary Ann and got married. She was a fine woman and I probably screwed up, but Mary Ann gave me an ultimatum--her or working on cars all across the country. How could I tell her she was my second love--working on cars was my first. Not to mention I had a mistress. They say a mistress is the ultimate in excitement--a thrill like no other! Well my mistress was just like that. My mistress was racing!

Mary Ann was gone. Sometimes I think of her and wonder if I did the right thing.

With Rich and Mary Ann out of my life I found a permanent companion in '75 when I worked a race at Texas World Speedway before it was abandoned. After the Indy race, a couple of my racing friends and I went to the Mexican border town of Reynosa and stayed in a two dollar a night hotel for a week. One night I almost married one of those Mexican beauties when I tied a wild one on. She talked about kids and settling down with her "Gringo." Suddenly I saw racing disappear and I sobered instantly. She was gone. Or to put it more correctly, I hauled ass from that little hotel. Two hours later, I met my permanent companion, Tex.

Now, Tex was the best old Amazon Parrot you ever saw and went with me to LeMans, Indy and some NASCAR. Tex became part of me. Wherever I went, so did Tex.

Before I forget, some of my friends in NASCAR use to call me, "Popeye." Well, let me set the story straight. Popeye was a cartoon character. I'm not. Granted, I have a small forehead and a big chin, but I don't look like Popeye. Besides, I have black hair, kinda thin and a little grey. I know I squint one eye but that's because of the sun. True, I wear suspenders, baggy coveralls and big industrial boots, but those shoes come natural after dropping a few carburetors and crankshafts on my feet. I know I have small biceps and large forearms with stubby fingers but that comes from years of wrenching. I don't look like Popeye. And another thing, I wear one of those girdle things around my waist to help my back. Shamed to admit it but it really does help. Popeye, I'm not.

Anyway, back to my story. Racing brought me my finest memories…and my saddest. I worked with drivers like Foyt, Unser, Petty and Andretti. Petty was a legend and the nicest man you could meet. Definitely a fan favorite. Old Foyt was ornery as hell but a heck of a driver. He and I had a clash of personalities, but I admired him. Even saw him win all four of his Indy 500 races in '61, '64, '67 and '77. If ever a driver could make a car win, it had to be Dale Earnhardt. He could bang up a car more than anyone I've ever seen and still bring it around to finish or even win a race. Dale was uncanny but a kid came along and knocked him off as king of the hill--Jeff Gordon. At the opposite end of good drivers was Mario Andretti, who should have won more than one Indy race but couldn't buy a win at the track if his life depended on it. Mario won in '69 and never won again. Talk about not being able to buy a race, Michael Andretti sure paid his dues when he went to Formula One. Al Unser Sr. was one of the best drivers I ever watched and Little Al had the same push as his father. When I think of kids, I always think of Little Al and Michael Andretti. Hell, I remember seeing Little Al when he was no bigger than my foot. Thing is, they now call Little Al and Michael the old men on the circuit. Just seems kinda hard for me to accept. Maybe one day when A.J. Foyt quits fielding a team, I'll believe it.

Thinking back, if I had to choose two drivers to run for me, I'd pick Rick Mears and Darrell Waltrip with Little Al and Jeff Gordon a close second. They were easy on the equipment, and you could count on them being around at the end of the race. Both had the fire--the look in their eye! You could always tell a real racer by the look in his eyes...a look you couldn't touch and you couldn't describe. But I could see it.

The sadness almost took me out of racing. I'd seen too many young men die. The death of a driver at Indy in '92 made me quit and go back to my shop in Atlanta. I wanted no more racing. About that time, I started seeing my old friend Rich again. A year later, Alan Kulwicki died then Davey Allison. What a loss! Right after Kulwicki died so did my friend Rich. Rich always worked a 9 to 5 job, or more accurately was paid for one, when in reality, he worked a dozen hours a day for more than 20 years. Rich always talked about the places he wanted to see when he retired. He died with a lot of money, never having fulfilled his dreams. That's when I realized I had lived a lifetime each year on the racing circuit. So had all those others who died while racing. Kulwicki, Allison, all tragic losses but living life to the fullest.

The time had come to continue living with my mistress, so Tex and I hooked up with a team out of Birmingham, Alabama, called BRM. Anthony Benson, a wealthy computer mogul, set a team up for his son, TJ, while I prepared the cars.

I coached TJ Benson for two years. The third year was about to begin. I was hoping to see the fire in his eyes like I had in Waltrip and Mears. TJ certainly had the ability to win, even the intensity and he almost had the look in his eyes--but he lacked the fire. I hadn't seen the fire in years...until!

WATKINS GLEN

The legendary Watkins Glen lay nestled in the Eastern New York woods. The Glen, as those familiar with the road course called it, offered an interesting combination of turns and elevation changes, challenging even the most experienced race driver. The Glen offered two options, a short 2.4-mile version, which eliminated the boot, or the longer, much more challenging 3.38-mile version, which included the three-turn boot.

Watkins Glen, where men came, again and again, to check their nerve and boys came to test their mettle. The Glen, a track some said was as old as cars. When men first sought the dangers and excitement of speed, they came to the Glen. Possibly the most exciting and legendary racing spot in the country, the Glen, offered one of the first 24 hour endurance races in the United States. A track where men tempted and cheated death, challenging the road course with only their skills and equipment. They raced for the fun, the glory, and occasionally, the stupidity of it all.

The early May race would provide an unusually cold testing ground for the opening race weekend of the highly touted U.S. Formula Ford 2000 National Championship series, sponsored by the Sports Car Club of America (SCCA) and the United States Auto Club (USAC). Another step on the ladder for Indy racing hopefuls. This was usually the third step of a long frustrating ladder most failed to climb. Many started in Go-carts, then advanced to Formula-Vee or Formula Ford. The next step was to Formula Ford 2000 or Formula Continental. Some also called the sleek racecars, "The Continentals" or "FC," while others affectionately called the speedy cars, "Formula 2000."

Previously three organizations offered Formula Continental series; SCCA with the American Continental Championship (ACC) series, the United States Auto Club (USAC) with the USAC 2000 series and Hooters F2 SuperCup oval series. When Hooters exploded on the racing world in '94, it forced USAC and SCCA to join forces and merge their Formula 2000 series in '95 to make a single series more competitive against Hooters Supercup. Both SCCA and USAC offered a unique opportunity with a variety of professional racing series, which were both challenging and relatively inexpensive. Inexpensive--that is compared to some series that ran in the tens of thousands per race. Formula 2000 could be run in the thousands and even with a team, could come in less than $10,000.

Often televised, the three series gave the competitors an opportunity to find sponsors and more important, be noticed across the country. For those with racing ability, the most insurmountable problems were money, obtaining adequate equipment, and time. Time they needed to devote to their dream, and time their jobs demanded. Many times their jobs were the only means of providing money to follow the elusive dream. The young and the rich came to these races to prove themselves. They came to live their dreams. Some came hoping to fulfill them. Some barely scraped along, while others used unlimited funds but all with the same dream-- WINNING!

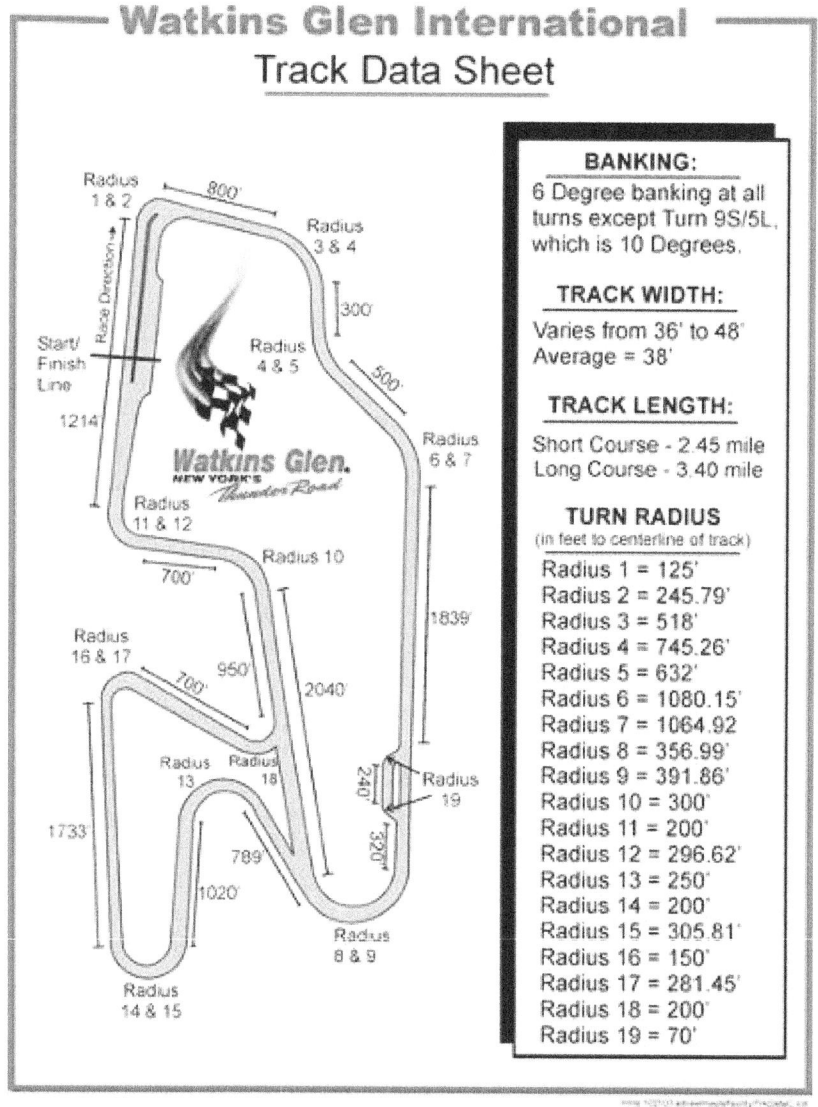

Watkins Glen International — Track Data Sheet

BANKING:
6 Degree banking at all turns except Turn 9S/5L, which is 10 Degrees.

TRACK WIDTH:
Varies from 36' to 48'
Average = 38'

TRACK LENGTH:
Short Course - 2.45 mile
Long Course - 3.40 mile

TURN RADIUS
(in feet to centerline of track)

Radius 1 = 125'
Radius 2 = 245.79'
Radius 3 = 518'
Radius 4 = 745.26'
Radius 5 = 632'
Radius 6 = 1080.15'
Radius 7 = 1064.92'
Radius 8 = 356.99'
Radius 9 = 391.86'
Radius 10 = 300'
Radius 11 = 200'
Radius 12 = 296.62'
Radius 13 = 250'
Radius 14 = 200'
Radius 15 = 305.81'
Radius 16 = 150'
Radius 17 = 281.45'
Radius 18 = 200'
Radius 19 = 70'

FORMULA 2000, the Dream

The Formula Continental used a modified two-liter, four cylinder, Ford engine boasting 140 horsepower. Including the driver, helmet and fireproof suit, the small open wheel Indy type racer weighed in at a minimum 1175 pounds. Some tried to build their own engines, but most preferred to rely on proven engine builders like Ivey, Elite, Quicksilver and Atwell. The price tag varied but usually cost around $6000 for a complete engine. All Formula Continentals used 4-speed manual transmissions and changed the four gear sets to fit each individual track.

Previous winners in the series ran Swift DB-8 and Van Diemen RF95 chassis while some relied on the Crossle 95SF, Citation 95SF, or Reynard 95F. And still others gambled on new chassis setups like the Vector TF95-C, Stohr F3, Spirit F291, and BRD AFC-04. A new season for me, Charlie Pepper, as the mechanic for Anthony Benson's son, Tony Joe. Anthony Benson was well known and an exceptionally rich man who rose quickly in the computer field during the 80's. Now his son, TJ, pursued lofty aspirations of becoming a professional driver. Anthony wanted to start TJ in a lower series and let him progress on the condition that each time TJ won a series, he could advance to the next. After Formula Continental, the next step up on the ladder was Formula Atlantic, INDY Lights and then to the INDY cars and CART.

This was TJ's year, and I knew it. For two years, I had taught and watched as TJ learned and improved. I tolerated the idiosyncrasies that seemed to follow wealth as TJ occasionally proved stubborn and hard to deal with. But I had what I wanted; involvement with my first and only love, RACING.

Here I was in my mid-fifties, already having built cars for INDY, even crewing in the legendary race, and I was still getting a charge out of the sport like I was a kid. Outside the van, it was still cold. I looked at my hands, cut from two day's previous preparation on the racecar. Eternal grease was still under my fingernails

Using my jacket, I covered my small companion of twenty years, "Tex," a small green and orange parrot. I jumped from the vehicle and darted to the building to register for the race.

"Jesus, Jesus," I mumbled with each chilling stride until I reached the building. Quickly, I closed the door behind to lock out the cold. "Jesus Christ," I yelled, rubbing my arms together trying to warm myself. "To think I left Atlanta and came north to the cold of "The Glen." I must be getting senile in my old age. You'd think the people scheduling these races would think about people like me when they do that."

From behind me a familiar voice suddenly spoke up. "Aw, stop your bitchin', Charlie," said Wesley O'Brien.

O'Brien also worked as a mechanic for an opposing team run by Bob Dotson of Dotson Racing. With him was another mechanic, Rusty Thomas, who worked for a friendly racer, Guido Pepin. Both O'Brien and Thomas wore jeans, tennis shoes, and jackets covered with team logos and colors.

"Hey, Wesley. Ready for another year?" I asked, extending my hand.

"Yep. Where's Tex?" O'Brien asked, wondering about the parrot he always expected to see with me.

"Kinda chilly for my fine feathered friend, so I left him in the van," I said. I took an open bag of lemon drops from my pocket. Lemon drops that were as familiar around the racetrack as my parrot, Tex. I popped one in my mouth, then offered one to Wesley and Rusty, but both politely refused. "Rusty, where's the rig and Guido?"

Thomas pointed outside to the large black and white eighteen-wheeler with the word, "GO," tilted slightly forward, to appear as though moving. The block letters "Racing" followed the "GO," which stood for Guido's Operations, and was painted on both sides of the lavish semi-trailer. Guido Pepin, who also raced, owned GO Racing and was closer to Pepper's age than the much younger O'Brien. The trailer housed Guido's car and two other team members' Formula Continentals. Each racecar also carried the insignia. The setup attested to the wealth Guido had amassed in the restaurant business. Now Guido played and spent money he earned, and Guido's game was racing.

Guido was physically unfit for racing. In simple terms, he was fat and nearly incapable of finishing each race. But as big as Guido was--he had a heart to match. He was an average driver and he knew it, progressing to the highest level he intended, content to rub shoulders and visit with the likes of Pepper, O'Brien and the up and coming 'wanna be' racing drivers. The slogan, painted in script across the back of his tractor trailer, showed Guido's feelings toward racing: "Behind these doors lies an obsession even a woman can't cure."

"Guido will be here in a little while," said Thomas.

"Almost missed it with all those rigs out there."

"Well, I better get the rig inside," said Rusty. "See you guys later."

Wesley nodded and I waved when he walked away.

"I hear we're the Saturday prelim for the Sunday SCCA Endurance race," I said.

"Yep. You staying?"

"Hell, no. I gotta get back to Atlanta."

"You usta stay, Charlie."

"Yeah, but it doesn't hold the interest it used to," I said. "You haven't stayed for the Sunday race since you came back from the INDY circuit."

"Things are different, Wesley," I said. "Do we still practice today and qualify Friday and Saturday?"

"Yep, and race Saturday afternoon. Only difference is "The Glen" is charging an extra three hundred dollars to practice today."

"Shouldn't hurt most drivers."

"Only the ones with limited funds."

"Boy, howdy! Not a sport to try with limited funds," I retorted.

"Maybe, but the budget racers give us drivers like Moses, Patches, Turtle, and Murf," snapped O'Brien, who always angered at watching talent passed aside when money could buy its way on the track. "The young guys without money don't have a chance!"

"Boy, howdy."

"Where are Les and Marty?" Wesley asked, referring to the two young mechanic helpers who also worked for TJ Benson or actually worked for me.

"Hopefully, they're already inside waiting for me."

Wesley and I talked about the new season while we stood in line waiting to register for the race. We showed our credentials, signed the release forms, and had new picture ID's made.

Outside, two rows of incoming traffic paused as drivers, crew and racers parked and took time to fill out their registration forms. Also adding to the congestion were Stewards of the event and helpers. The all-important Sports Car Club of America corner workers, the life support system for drivers involved in life threatening wrecks. Patches from previous events sewed on the white uniforms easily distinguished the Corner Workers. The patches literally covered a few uniforms, attesting to the desire and participation of the corner workers. All waited in the appropriate lines ready for the event to begin.

With registration completed, Wesley and I paused at the door near a bulletin board, filled with posters and information, to look at the previous year's final standings of competitors. Neatly typed additions of rookies at the bottom completed the list of drivers competing in the coming season.

"How's Flash?" O'Brien asked. In the past, Wesley had his encounters with my driver, TJ. And if not for me, I don't think Wesley would ever have ventured near the BRM team. "Flash" was a derogatory term Wesley and a few others used when they spoke of TJ Benson. TJ had everything done and never worked on the cars. That was something I intended to change and felt would speed up the learning process if TJ had hands on experience.

"If he can control his temper, this will be his year," I said, shrugging my shoulders as we studied the list.

For me, the list offered a comprehensive quick check, not only of the drivers, but also of the racecars each driver intended to compete with and their team names. Those with money usually joined a proven team, which consisted of six, as varied as the rainbow of colors used to represent them. The six major teams were identified by large eighteen wheel diesel rigs or diesel crew cab pickups and long trailers all splattered with teams' logos and sponsors' names, each with crews and mechanics.

The independents relied on Ford, Dodge, or Chevy crew cabs usually powered by diesel or large V-8's with most pulling shorter trailers to satisfy their personal needs. Some chose to pull smaller trailers with motor homes from elaborate to simple cabover. Many had their own personal team names even though they were the only team member. The dreams never stopped.

Those without money fended for themselves, although many independent drivers tended to group together. All offered each other assistance and help whenever necessary.

Including my BRM team, there were six major teams: Wesley's team, Dotson Racing; TART, a Canadian team run by Ron Leclair; PACE, a French Canadian team Ian Poirier owned; Spratt Racing owner, Phil Spratt; and, GO Racing with Guido Pepin. Only Spratt and TART relied on something less than the large eighteen-wheelers. They used diesel Cummings, 1 ton crew cab Fords to pull their 42 foot fifth wheel trailers. Although not as impressive as the larger teams, they still came well prepared. I scanned the impromptu drivers' list, a copy from the previous year's standings with new drivers added at the bottom. The number 1, 4, 5, 12 and 13 positions, marked through with a wide black marker, showed five previous competitors who either advanced to another series, fulfilling yet another step in their dreams, or reached another temporary stopping point along their rough road of dreams. They would surely return another time or another place. I continued to survey the summary sheets:

```
                        SCCA/USAC
            U.S. Formula Ford 2000 National Championship
                       Final Standings
           Name                   Car                   Team
    1.     ----------------------------------------------------
    2.     TJ Benson              VanDiemen RF95        BRM
    3.     Ian Poirier            Swift DB-8            PACE
    4.     ----------------------------------------------------
    5.     ----------------------------------------------------
    6.     Ron Leclair            VanDiemen RF95        TART
    7.     Bob Dotson             Spirit                Dotson Racing
    8.     Freddy Mercury         Reynard 95F           Dotson Racing
    9.     Phil Spratt            Reynard 95F           Spratt Racing
   10.     Gordon Chappel         VanDiemen RF95
   11.     Alan Reckert           Stohr                 TART
   12.     ----------------------------------------------------
   13.     ----------------------------------------------------
   14.     Jude Dionne            Swift DB-8            PACE
   15.     Mark McGrath           Swift DB-3            M&M Racing
   16.     Bill Murfy             Swift DB-8
   17.     Cliff Roe              VanDiemen RF94        GO Racing
   18.     Neil Kray              Swift DB-3
   19.     Tom Craig              Swift DB-3            TC Racing
   20.     Rex VanHorn            Reynard SF91
   21.     Rick Henry             Swift DB-8
   22.     Darrell Pollard        VanDiemen RF95        BRM
   23.     Guido Pepin            Swift DB-8            GO Racing
   24.     Ben Cifelli            Swift DB-3
   25.     Art Grindle            Swift SE-3
   26.     Barton Springs         VanDiemen RF91        BS Racing
   27.     Will Jones             Swift DB-8
   28.     Augie Zuehl**          VanDiemen RF95        BRM
         **Partial Season
          * First Year

          * Hanna Lee             Swift DB-8            Dotson Racing
          * Claude Marcoux        Swift DB-8            PACE
          * Steve Smagala         Swift SE-3
          * Roberto Cruz          VanDiemen RF94        Spratt Racing
          * Shannon Kelly         Crossle 71F           DAD
          * Chase Wilder          Reynard SF90
```

O'Brien reached into his back pocket and pulled out a black billfold, took out a five-dollar bill, and held it in front of my face, "Let's see if you can do it three years in a row. Go ahead, Charlie, pick the winners again."

As though in thought, I rubbed my chin and smiled, knowing the top three vacated positions moved to other more lucrative series in their quest to win and rightfully so as they proved themselves well. If TJ Benson had shown more humility and tact at the proper times, he also would have advanced. TJ let his temper and attitude beat himself, something I hoped to correct. I also intended to teach TJ the proper preparation for a racecar.

"Well, TJ should win the series hands down, but Ian Poirier will give him a run for the money."

"Aw, come on, Charlie. Don't you think anybody else has a chance? What about Reckert, Mercury, Dotson, or Spratt?"

I shook my head and continued to scan the sheet attached to the wall. "Sorry. They're all good, but I still say TJ. After all he does have the Van Diemen. Dotson's still screwing with the Spirit chassis, and Reckert with the Stohr. Both would be more competitive with the Swift or the Van Diemen. Mercury should do well with the Reynard, but I don't think any of 'em can touch TJ or Ian."

"Look Charlie, I don't care who wins as long as it isn't Flash or the Dwarf. TJ needs to learn some manners and Ian . . well, he's dangerous. I swear if Ian's mother was in front of him, he would knock her off, just so he could win--and he'd never look back."

The year before a young racer had dedicated the song, "Cold as Ice" to Ian Poirier. Ian had knocked the driver out of a race, without seeing Ian's expression change. Ian was cool all right. Yes, maybe even cold. Occasionally, when Wesley got mad at Ian, he would refer to him as the Canadian Dwarf, because Ian was only five-foot-five and wore two-inch heels when he didn't race. Everyone knew about Poirier's inheritance and the two million dollars he collected from his trust fund each year. Still, I held hope for TJ. Obviously, TJ had the ability. And true, TJ was arrogant and occasionally short with me; but hopefully, he could be molded into a fine racer. I had almost quit in the middle of the previous year, but when TJ sincerely apologized, I stayed on, even though the same problem reoccurred when TJ won the last two races.

"Give the kid a chance, Wesley. He'll be okay, you'll see," I said.

"It's not fun for you, Charlie. It's not like working for Mercury or Dotson. I really look forward to the race weekends with them. You should with TJ," said O'Brien.

A voice from behind me said, "Who do you think will take the series this year, Pepper?"

Neither I nor O'Brien could mistake the French Canadian accent as we turned to face Ian Poirier. Poirier wore the familiar two-inch heels enabling him to reach all of five foot seven. His long black hair was tied back in a ponytail with a rubber band. His arrogant and confident tone was supported with an ability to race with the best. Standing beside Poirier was another French Canadian with flowing black curly hair even longer than Poirier's. He was obviously unable to speak English when Poirier appeared to tell his much taller companion what was happening. Poirier wore a jacket with the lime green and white team colors trimmed with the dark green letters, PACE, on the back. Those letters stood for Poirier Automotive Competition Enterprises.

I laughed, "TJ will win because he has something you don't have."

"And what is that?" Poirier challenged more than asked.

With a fist, I slapped my chest, "Me!"

Poirier retaliated, "I have Shea LaForche."

Again, Poirier appeared to translate to his companion, which brought a nod and a smile--but not a smile from Poirier.

"Yeah, LaForche is good--but he's no Charlie Pepper," I laughed, to Poirier's immense irritation.

"I intend to take the series," said Poirier. "We'll see when the races start."

"Boy, howdy--that we will."

The two Canadian teams were as different as night and day. Poirier's team usually consisted of French Canadians, while The American Racing Team, or TART, boasted two fun-loving Canadians, Ron Leclair and Alan Reckert, who spoke better English than me.

Poirier said something to his companion who looked at me and smiled. They spun around, walked away from the building, and returned to their rig, so they could enter the track.

"You were kinda rough on the Dwarf," laughed O'Brien. "I loved it."

Again, I smiled, "Might as well start the mind games early."

"Well, ya sure got under his skin," O'Brien added.

"Who's the guy with Ian?" I asked.

O'Brien pointed to the bottom of the list to the rookie, Claude Marcoux.

"Let me clue you in on Marcoux," said O'Brien. "He was suspended from a Canadian series for dangerous and reckless driving. The Canadians took his license away, but he was able to get another racing license with SCCA. Poirier put him on his team, and that looks bad. I don't like it."

"Wesley, you're too suspicious. I doubt if anything will happen. And don't forget the Stewards will come down hard if he does anything dangerous."

"Just suppose Ian has a chance to win by putting TJ out."

"People don't do that--besides I thought you didn't like TJ."

"I don't. I think TJ is an asshole. Just a cocky, little rich-kid, but he doesn't drive dirty . . . I'll give him that."

I smiled and clapped my hands in mock celebration, "Will miracles never cease." "Yeah, but even if the Stewards catch Marcoux doing something dangerous, once he's done it, it will be too late."

Wesley had a point, but I passed it off and continued checking the list, "With the new Swift and Van Diemen chassis this year, you're gonna see every track record fall."

"Every track record?"

"Yep . . . unless it rains. If that happens not only will the times be slower, but the rain will also make all the cars equal . . . and few drivers excel in the rain. It's a driver's race in the rain," I stated, remembering the many previous rain races I had seen.

"Well, I hope it doesn't rain," said O'Brien. "The rain sucks, and Poirier never loses in the rain."

"Look, Wesley," I said, pointing far down the list to the rookies, "a woman . . . Hanna Lee in a Swift with your team."

"Yeah, I know. Everyone says she's related to the Lee Jeans' people. They say she's a looker and only twenty-three. Looks like she's got the money, if she's with Dotson," said O'Brien. "Say, the last year you were at INDY, there was a woman racing, wasn't there?"

"1992 . . . quite a woman. Lyn St. James won rookie of the year. A tough legacy to live up to for our new little Miss Blue Jeans."

"Didn't somebody get killed in that race?"

For a moment I stood there, my smile vanishing as I was transported to an INDY practice session in '92. Practice. A crash. A death. After a long pause, I answered. "Marcelo got killed in qualifying." O'Brien couldn't hear the last words I mumbled as I remembered, "Just a kid . . . a real swell kid."

Marcelo's death was my reason for dropping from the INDY circuit. Only at Anthony Benson's insistence had I returned to racing to train young TJ. No one really knew the reason I had dropped to the lower bracket of Formula Continental racing. But racing was my number one love and I was unable to stay away. Still, INDY and Marcelo were as fresh in my mind as though it were only yesterday. Killed at INDY. The kid in his prime . . . his whole life ahead of him.

O'Brien saw the instant transformation and I know he tried to change the subject quickly, "You think the other rookies have a chance?"

I blinked my eyes as I came out of my self-induced trance, and turned my attention to the list, "Obviously, Claude Marcoux from what you said. Roberto Cruz has the right chassis and a good team, but no matter who they are, I don't think they will touch Ian or TJ."

Then I spotted the name Shannon Kelly and his old Crossle 71F. "Well, this Shannon Kelly is dead meat, if he's driving that antique Crossle. No one can win with a Crossle. He can't be a serious contender."

Suddenly, Wesley's words haunted me when I remembered what he had said about what money could buy. Maybe the kid had all he could afford. I thought about Murf, Patches, Turtle, and Moses. Murf the Smurf, Bill Murfy, who painted his car blue and white, and when his car was in the pits, always had a stuffed Smurf in the driver's seat. Patches, Tom Craig, who somehow always seemed to ding his car in practice and qualifying. He did his own repairs, which were painfully obvious to everyone. His horrendous craftsmanship got him his nickname "Patches," but he took the teasing good-naturedly. Then, there was Will Jones, who almost always managed to finish last. Turtle wasn't a hard name to stick on Will. Still, he loved to get out on the racetrack. When you talked old nobody beat Gordon Chappel, who was in his fortieth year of racing and would soon celebrate his seventy-first birthday. Everyone called him, "Moses." Not only did he enjoy racing, he consistently finished in the top ten and even at seventy was a very competent and competitive racer, still capable of winning.

"Think he'll win?"

Suddenly, I was pulled from my thoughts. "What?"

"This kid, Shannon Kelly, do you think he'll win?"

"No way. Not with that old Crossle." Across from Shannon Kelly's name under the column for teams were the letters, DAD. "What the hell race team is, 'D-A-D'?"

"Dunno." O'Brien laughed, "They say this Kelly kid wants to race at INDY. He just turned nineteen, and he'll be the youngest obstacle we'll face on the track."

"What's he won?" I asked.

"I don't think he's won anything. Least ways, nothing anybody knows about."

"Great, now we gotta worry about lapping a kid every race. As if Ian and those Canadians won't be enough. Shannon Kelly doesn't have a prayer."

A moment later, someone tapped me on the shoulder and I twisted my head around. Before me was a kid slightly over six feet, forcing me to look up. The boy had thick black hair and was extremely muscular, evidenced by the tight T-shirt he wore. He, too, seemed unprepared for the cold weather. His smile was infectious and the grey piercing eyes never strayed. Just like the kid at INDY . . ."Man, this sure isn't like the weather in Texas. Good thing my Dad told me to pack a coat," said the kid.

"Boy, howdy. I'm from Atlanta, and I wasn't ready for the cold either."

"Say, could you tell me where I sign in?" the tall kid asked.

"Yeah, the workers are over there," said O'Brien pointing to the other side of the room.

For a split second, I froze, I couldn't move . . . I could see the spark in the kid's eyes--the fire!

The kid laughed, "That's probably where I should be, but this weekend I'm racing." He stuck his hand in my direction, "I'm Shannon Kelly."

"Charlie Pepper," I said, still searching for the fire and feeling the confidence in Shannon's handshake.

"Wesley O'Brien."

"Nice to meet ya." The smile was contagious as was the youthful enthusiasm, "Man, have you ever seen so many cars. I can't believe we're gonna race the day before the Showroom Stock Endurance race. I'm staying to watch, are you?"

"I don't know yet," I said, which got an inquisitive glance from Wesley. "Say, what kind of a race team is D-A-D?"

Shannon laughed, making the dimples and the cleft in his square jaw more prominent, "Shoot, they asked if I had any sponsors, and I told them my Dad. I don't have a race team, and if it wasn't for my Dad, I wouldn't be here."

Nodding my head, I said, "Oh."

Shannon held the series racing schedule in his hand and had a puzzled look on his face. He moved it, so I could also see the schedule:

```
                    SCCA/USAC
             U.S. Formula Ford 2000
                  Season Schedule

       1.  Watkins Glen         (April 23)
       2.  Mosport              (May 14)
       3.  IRP                  (May 28)
       4.  Dallas Grand Prix    (June 12)
       5.  Sebring              (June 26)
       6.  Mid-Ohio             (July 9)
       7.  TBA                  (July 23)
       8.  Ruan Grand Prix      (Aug. 14)
       9.  Road America         (Aug. 28)
       10. Road Atlanta         (Sept. 11)
```

The sheet contained a list of the ten races for the US Formula Ford 2000 National Championship series. Many tracks to pick from but only ten were chosen. Tracks not chosen were Shannonville and Trois-Rivieres in Canada, Limerock, Daytona, Laguna Seca, Firebird Raceway Park, St. Louis International Raceway, Sears Point and Charlotte. Each track had legends and stories of their own.

Shannon pointed to race number 3 and asked, "Maybe you could help me, and I hope this doesn't sound dumb, 'cause I've never raced in a real series before. I know IRP is for Indianapolis Raceway Park, but TBA . . . where is that?"

O'Brien could not suppress a laugh. I smiled, but realized the kid was serious.

I waved a hand, "There is nowhere, TBA means, 'To Be Announced.'"

Shannon turned slightly red and half laughed to himself, "Ohhh."

"Hey, I never would have known if somebody hadn't told me the first time. Remember, this is all a learning process. You aren't born with the knowledge, and if you don't ask, you'll never find out. What I will tell you is race seven will be either at Charlotte Motor Speedway or Daytona."

"Daytona? Like the Daytona 500?" asked Shannon, the awe evident in his voice.

"Yep," I said. Again, Shannon pointed to the list and the number 8 race,

"Where is Ruan?"

"The Ruan Grand Prix is held on the streets of Des Moines, Iowa. You'll get to race seven road courses plus the oval of Indianapolis Raceway Park. The other two races will be tight street circuits. The one you just pointed to, Ruan Grand Prix and the Dallas Grand Prix, will make this a hellva race season."

"Wow! Well, I better get signed in," said Shannon. "Hope to see ya later."

We nodded to Shannon as he moved to the driver's line, then Wesley and I walked away from the registration area.

"Sure as hell seems like a nice kid," said O'Brien. "Hope he didn't hear what we said. TBA--now, that's a classic."

"Boy, howdy . . . and he wants to run INDY. Humph."

* * *

Thursday's last practice session, for the U.S. Formula Ford 2000 National Championship event, was nearly finished. I took times on all the cars along with my crew, Les and Marty. All the Formula Continentals registered for the series and three locals made at least one session on the track--all, that is, except Shannon Kelly. Curiosity had the best of me. Earlier in practice, Gordon "Moses" Chappel and Will "Turtle" Jones mentioned a polite kid parked next to them in a motorhome and said the kid even made them lunch--an excellent lunch. The comment said a lot for Turtle because he was known for being as picky an eater as he was slow a driver. They said the kid's car was off the trailer and ready, but he had made no effort to run. They couldn't remember his name but said his old Crossle looked beautiful. Well, I knew where Moses and Turtle were parked; and after the session, I was determined to talk more to this new rookie, Shannon Kelly.

When TJ came in for his last tire temperature checks, I was almost happy that young TJ was more interested in the new racing beauty Hanna Lee. She was pretty but I hoped TJ would remember to concentrate on the following day's qualifications. TJ's one and only complaint was about the throttle not being fully engaged on the last lap. Other than that, TJ was completely satisfied.

The day's practice had Ian Poirier first, followed by Freddy Mercury, Ron Leclair, and Phil Spratt with six more drivers ahead of TJ; Bob Dotson, teammate Augie Zuehl, Claude Marcoux, old Moses and surprisingly, the rookies, Roberto Cruz, and the woman, Hanna Lee. With close to thirty entries, three rookies were in the top twenty, including Hanna, but practice didn't bother me. Adjustments needed to be made to TJ's car's suspension that would surely give him the half second difference from his position and Poirier, not to mention temperatures in the 70's predicted for Friday. Hotter tire compounds would quicken Friday's pace more than two seconds. Already it felt warmer, and I even had Tex hanging just inside the door of the red, white and blue BRM 40 foot semi-trailer, strutting his feathers.

When I arrived at the trailer, I told Les to remove the computer from TJ's Van Diemen and get a full printout for each of TJ's laps.

Perched on my shoulder, Tex's yellow head bobbed about while I took a quick look at the racecars. I removed the rear cover to the Van Diemen and checked the throttle linkage. The vertical throttle clip, braced back to the manifold at another point for rigidity and attached to another clip carrying the throttle cable was loose. The threaded bolt holding the two clips in place had worked out and stripped. While I tried to rethread the hole, TJ walked from the dressing area of the BRM trailer.

"What's the problem?" TJ asked.

I shrugged my shoulders and told him, "The throttle cable."

"Listen," said TJ obviously on edge, "This new car has had problems every time we've taken it out. I want my old car back."

I put my hand in the small of my back and tried to stand erect. Even with the girdle-type brace, it was hard. I looked over my half-moon reading glasses and said, "It's something to expect with a new car. The kinks should be out of it now."

"I don't care. I'll use this one for my spare," said TJ. "Get the old Van Diemen out, and I'll run it."

"The chassis dyno in Atlanta showed this one to be the fastest," I told him, while rubbing the rollbar affectionately.

TJ laughed, "I won the last two races last year in my old Van Diemen. I know that car, and personally, I'd rather have it. Besides, the suspension and gears are already set for here, just in case we needed it." TJ pointed to the new Van Diemen, "The new one is jinxed. It'll never be a winner . . . besides, it has the engine you built. No offense, Charlie, but my old car has a new Quicksilver engine. I want my old one."

I conceded to his demands, "All right, we'll race the old one."

TJ smiled and walked away. I wanted to argue for the new car because I knew it was better and faster although the older Van Diemen was just as good. Most important it was important for a driver to feel good about his car. If TJ felt the newer car was not as good, then he was likely not to do as well. The newer car was better but I would give TJ what he wanted.

The new racer was ready and I knew it. I patted the rollbar and shook my head, "Well, it looks like you don't get to show us your stuff. What a shame. After all the work I did to you." The new Van Diemen was prime, and I knew it. I was anxious to try out my first engine since the Indy series. Even the chassis dyno had proven my touch with engines still existed when it registered one more horsepower, and better torque than the new

Quicksilver. But it looked like I would have to wait to see what it could do.

Again, I patted the car, then ordered Les and Marty to remove TJ's old Van Diemen from the trailer and perform a complete check.

First, I would check out the old racer and make the few minor adjustments necessary for the race, then I wanted to talk more with the kid, Shannon Kelly.

* * *

Gordon Chappel was near the end of the third row of campers. All were allowed space for their camper and a similar sized space beside the camper for the race car. With space limited, teams usually parked tow vehicles outside the pit area. The way the campers crammed in never ceased to amaze me. Chappel and those who raced in the Formula Continental class were lucky because they were afforded the luxury of camping on the asphalt or paved area. Those who ran the SCCA Endurance Series were forced to settle for the unpaved area since the endurance cars suspensions were so high. The low clearance on the Formula cars gave them the advantage of a paved area, at least at this track, since each track was different. Those who stayed at the track told stories of the practice and compared notes. Others cooked or barbecued on grills outside their trailers. Some remained in their trailers watching videos from their RCA, Panasonic, or other in car video cameras. Still others, Pepper did not envy, busily repaired broken race cars.

On the way, Jolit Torres, a racing reporter for series from Trans-Am to Endurance and all those between, stopped me. A slight woman who always carried a shoulder bag with a word processor, recorder, and other paraphanalia required to report on racing.

"Hey, guy," said Jolit when she saw me. "When you headed back to INDY?"

"I'm happy here."

"That's not what I hear about the ever demanding Benson," chided Jolit.

"He's not so bad."

"Any scoops for a reporter?" asked the ever inquisitive Torres.

I hesitated, "No . . . nothing yet."

"Ooohhh, Charlie, you know how to make my blood race. You have something--I can tell," smiled Jolit.

"Not really."

"That means yes."

"No, Jolit. If I do, you'll be the first to know," I promised.

Satisfied she would find out later, Jolit continued in the opposite direction.

Three more times I was stopped for idle chat and helpful advice before I finally found Gordon Chappel. He was sitting in a lounge chair sipping ice tea beneath the roll-out canopy of his self-contained Ford Tioga. In front of the motor home, resting on jack stands was Moses' white number 71, Van Diemen RF95. Next to Moses' trailer sat Patches in a lounge chair, relaxed, and for once not doing his familiar repair work. Each had a helper and a mechanic as did the other drivers. Without a mechanic and help of some type, the drivers would tow the vehicles great distances alone, set the suspension and do all the mechanical work and repairs, including changing the gears in the transaxle for each race. To go it alone was next to impossible.

"Moses, how's the car?" I asked.

"Fine, Charlie. How come you're not back at the hotel taking a hot shower?"

At seventy, Moses was a wiry man, doing a young man's work. His skin was dark and leathery like mine and he kept his thinning gray hair cut in a burr. Two inches under six feet, his bright blue eyes were full of life of a man half his age. Large strong hands were part of his deceivingly small frame. Moses could load and unload his race trailer and do all the work on his race car. He still had the desire and the spirit to race--and win!

"Aw, just thought I'd look around and see the competition," I said, while staring at the beautiful shiny yellow Crossle with the blue and red trim and dark blue number 44.

"Pretty car, huh?" Chappel asked.

"Boy, howdy, but it's not a winner."

"Kid did all the work himself. Some real fine work." Chappel stood up, "Come on, Charlie, let's go be sociable."

Moses led me to an old tutone blue '79 Ford, 1-ton, extended van parked on the other side of Will Jones who was parked across from Moses. Behind the old van was an open trailer with an overhead tire rack fabricated from one-inch pipe. On the front of the trailer, stretching the width of the trailer, was a tool box used to carry accessories. The trailer was obviously as old as the Ford van and well maintained.

Attached to the side of the van was a blue plastic tarp supported with an aluminum tube frame. From the two outside poles hung a tire and rim, to keep the cover down in quick wind gusts.

The Crossle was on jack stands with the cover to the transaxle removed, revealing the missing gears, which were being replaced. Shannon was sitting inside the open sliding door on the passenger side of the van.

Immediately, I knew Shannon and his father were "poor boying" their dream. Still, I was impressed with the showroom new appearance of the antiquated racer. For a moment, the old Goodyear tires caught my eye, but Shannon diverted my attention.

When Shannon saw Moses and me, he came to meet us. "Mr. Pepper," said Shannon, extending his hand in a friendly, sincere handshake, somehow I expected. "Please, call me Charlie."

"Yes, sir," said Shannon. "Your guys sure looked good."

"Thanks. How come you weren't on the track?"

"Didn't have the money to rent the track," Shannon smiled.

We moved to a white fold out table with bench seats where Shannon opened an ice chest and offered me a soft drink. Shannon momentarily disappeared into the van and came back with a plate full of cookies. Peanut butter cookies! My favorite and still warm. I took one and was hooked. A half dozen cookies later, I stopped.

"These are great, who made them?"

"My dad" said Shannon with a prideful smile.

"Not bad," I said. I wondered where his father was because it appeared Shannon was alone. "Why don't you show me your racer. I'd like to see it."

Shannon jumped to his feet, pleased I wanted to see his race car.

The first thing I noticed was the lack of power tools and instead of an air compressor, only a five-foot tall cylinder filled with air. When we went to the Crossle, I looked over the tires and found what I thought I had seen earlier. The tires were old--very old, showing the first signs of dry rot, while the outer carcass was covered with continuous spider webs of cracks. From a pocket in my coveralls, I took the black, half moon, reading glasses and visually inspected the tires. The tires appeared to be older than two years, which might have been fine for street use but not tolerable in a race car. If the tires survived, they would give no traction due to the hard rubber compound.

To be sure, I pulled a durometer from my other shirt pocket and pressed the gauge into the rubber. The spring operated durometer was designed to give a reading when pressed into the rubber. The farther the shaft pressed into the rubber compound, the higher the number. A low number would indicate a hard compound. Racecars ran tires with a softness of 65 with the worst being 50. The durometer indicated 35, slightly harder than a regular street tire, which meant Shannon would be better off qualifying on street tires, than the aged hard rubber slicks.

"What's that?" Shannon asked.

"A durometer. I'm checking the softness."

Wrinkling his nose, Shannon asked, "Not good, huh?" "No, not good. Do you have other tires?"

"On the trailer," said Shannon, turning toward the trailer, with me close behind.

I found two at 40, but the others were even worse than those on the car. I showed Shannon the tires he should use, then said, "Put those two good ones on the left side. The Glen is run clockwise, so most turning will be to the right. Especially the downhill Turn 5."

"Hey, thanks."

From the appearance of Shannon's setup, he really was alone, "Say, where's your father?"

"He couldn't afford to come. He's still back in Dallas," said Shannon. "But you'll meet him at Mosport."

"I'm looking forward to it," I said. The comment and tires only verified the fact Shannon operated with minimal funds. "Who's helping you this weekend?"

"Nobody."

"You drove here by yourself?" I asked.

Shannon nodded and Moses interrupted, "Not only does Shannon do it all, he just finished driving to Seattle to pick up his Crossle. Arrived in Dallas and immediately came here."

"Amazing. Well, I'll give you credit for desire and determination," I said. "And I see you're doing the gears."

"Yes sir," nodded Shannon.

"Sure you got the right one?" I asked.

Shannon shrugged his shoulders, "A guy named Baytos said these were the right ones."

"Jon Baytos with Primus," I said more than asked, which got a nod from Shannon. "Well, if Baytos says those are the right gears, then best you put them in. You see ole' Baytos owns Primus and comes from Atlanta like me. He comes to all the races giving support to all the Van Diemen racers since he is the dealer for the Van Diemen chassis. You know, he backed former Formula 2000 champions Chris Simmons, Anthony Lazarro, and Ernest Sikes. The man knows what he's doing."

"Wow! You mean Ernest Sikes, the champion in '93?"

"Boy, howdy," I confirmed. "Or you can get gears from Taylor Engineering owned by Craig Taylor who won the USAC series in '91. Have you ever been on this track?"

"No, just what I've seen on television and that wasn't much."

"Well, it's time you got a good look at the track." I pulled out the bag of lemon drops and offered one to Moses and Shannon. Shannon took one and I popped one in my mouth, then said, "Let's go back to BRM, get two of the four wheelers and drive around The Glen. The track is closed, so it'll be okay to take a closer look."

We said goodbye to Moses and proceeded to the BRM trailer, where we found TJ prancing around Hanna Lee like a hot puppy. For the first time, I saw Hanna without a race suit. She wore tight jeans, a tucked in white t-shirt and clearly no bra. The shirt was covered with a thin red windbreaker. In her white tennis shoes, she was only a few inches shorter than TJ who was five foot eleven. I mused to myself when I realized Wesley would still be able to call Ian "Dwarf" since Hanna was taller than the small Canadian. Hanna was a looker.

I made a quick introduction and told TJ I was taking Shannon and two of the four wheelers to show him The Glen. For a moment, I didn't recognize the seemingly deep voice that wasn't really TJ's. It also seemed to me that Hanna was sure looking at Shannon a lot.

"Sure, Charlie, anything to help a rookie." TJ turned to Hanna, "Maybe you'd like me to show you the course and give you a few pointers?"

"That would be nice," said Hanna looking at Shannon, who seemed oblivious to her attention.

A few minutes later, we were rolling through the pits and onto the rough track. We moved down the main straight to the uphill curve at Turn 1. We dismounted from the four wheelers and walked to the inside right turn, near the theoretical apex.

TJ caught me and whispered in my ear, "Charlie, let me coach them on this turn. I think I can help. After all, I am the racer and you're just the mechanic."

At first, I was taken back with the last words but I controlled my temper and said, "Sure, be my guest."

TJ motioned for Hanna and Shannon to join him at the apex. I followed and listened intently. TJ, was a real piece of work, I thought.

"This is the second longest straightaway, going downhill, then climbing uphill, and leading into the longest straightaway. Don't break too late." TJ looked around, as though searching for something, then walked to a point on the turn, "Let your right tires hit the apex about here."

Instantly, I realized why TJ was having trouble earlier. The apex would be much earlier, and the breaking would be late and quick, taking maximum speed up the hill. Almost undetectable on the curve, about fifteen feet before the apex TJ picked, were a few traces of yellow paint, marks probably made by a previous school instructor who taught driving at the Glen. The true apex would be near the yellow marks. I was about to interrupt when Shannon move toward the true apex.

"I don't know," said Shannon. He looked down the straightaway then up the hill that made Turn 1. He moved along the turn and stopped four feet on the other side of the yellow marks I spotted. "It seems like the apex would be here."

Well, that's a better spot than the one TJ picked, I thought.

As though reading my mind, Shannon moved closer and stood only a few feet from the yellow spots. "More like here. And I think you need to break quick and hard and climb fast."

I smiled. Shannon apparently knew his geometry.

"No, no, no," admonished TJ. "At least you're moving closer to me, but I'm standing in the right spot. Where you're standing would be apexing too early."

"I think this is it," said Shannon with a positive tone.

TJ shook his head and sighed, "Look, Shannon, have you ever raced here before? No. I've been running this series for two years. I know what it takes." TJ looked at Hanna, "Both of you are rookies, so it will take time. You can't expect to win it all in one race. More than likely, neither of you will finish in the top ten this year anyway. Learn your cars and be patient."

I almost busted out laughing. The words were almost exactly like the ones I had used the first year TJ started racing, but the poor track advice TJ gave the rookies concerned me.

"If my spot isn't right, then tell me why it's not," Shannon said.

TJ threw his hands up in the air, "Because I know. I was second in the series last year, and I'm gonna win it this year. Besides, Shannon with your car, you should concentrate on learning and not worry so much about winning. You will be racing against nearly thirty experienced drivers who have equipment far superior to yours. That Crossle won't finish higher than twentieth. At least, Hanna has an outside chance of finishing in the top ten with her Swift."

I concurred with TJ. If Shannon were an excellent driver, he might finish as high as fifteenth--but no higher because everything TJ said was true. Still, I didn't like the way TJ came down so hard on Shannon. Now was the time to finesse the rookie drivers and not break their spirit like TJ appeared to be doing with Shannon. Again, I was about to interrupt.

"You won't win them all, " said Shannon with a confident grin.

"Maybe not but what makes you so sure?" TJ asked.

Shannon smiled, "Because I'm gonna win one of them."

For a moment, I thought I died and gone to heaven, and could barely hold back a laugh. No one talked to TJ like that and got away with it. Maybe Hanna's presence and TJ's need to impress her kept him in line. Then again, what did TJ have to worry about against this unknown rookie?

"What experience do you have?" TJ asked, somewhat perplexed at Shannon's confidence.

"I've raced Go-carts and I ran a Spec Ford last year."

"Oh, yeah, SCCA's, Spec Ford class where all the cars are sealed and equal. How many races did you run?"

"Three."

"Only three? Did you win?"

"No."

"You didn't even win and now you expect to move to a car with slicks and speeds near 150 mph. You need more than confidence, you're gonna need a lot of luck," snapped TJ almost sarcastically. Just as quickly, TJ laughed, "Try to help someone and they know it all. Well, at least you're comfortable with your concept--even though it's wrong." TJ looked to Hanna, "Come on, let's go to the next turn. At least, I can help you."

As they walked away, TJ approached me and whispered in my ear. "Charlie, this rookie is hopeless. Maybe you can give him some helpful advice. I just don't think he will listen to me."

I was so surprised, I had no comeback, "Yeah, sure." Listening to TJ was like hearing me talk to TJ when he first hired on. Only TJ still refused to listen to me, which worked to TJ's detriment.

TJ and Hanna were gone before I reached the four-wheeler. As I turned the key, Shannon pulled alongside. "What do you think about the turn, Charlie?" Shannon asked.

"You're sorta right," I agreed.

"Tell me why?"

I smiled, explained the corner and the way I felt it should be run, explaining a dozen drivers would run the same turn differently. We continued to Turn 2. TJ and Hanna left, leaving Shannon and me, for the most part, alone.

Their departure didn't appear to matter to Shannon, so with TJ and Hanna gone, I explained each turn carefully to the eager youth. Turn 2 was a right-hand sweeper going up a steep hill. The driver stayed to the right and hit the esses under full speed. The esses consisted of a left, then a right taken under full speed. The right led onto the back straight, which was slightly uphill until it crested and dropped to Turn 5. "Gotta watch the bad spots down this straight," I warned Shannon, "to prevent bottoming out so be careful and try to drive around them." Explaining the track to Shannon was fun.

After the crest, the Continental came under heavy downhill breaking going into the right-hand chute loop at Turn 5, a near 180 degree, off camber, downhill turn, pushing the car to the left edge of the track. The driver stayed on the inside. Next came Turn 6, the beginning of the boot; a banked, left hand, increasing radius downhill turn with a late apex and more speed than first estimated. The "toe," or Turn 7 was a downhill right turn with a late apex, which most drivers approached with too much speed. The car tended to slide forcing many drivers to compensate. A steep, uphill climb led to Turn 8--the heel of the boot, a steep, downhill, 120 degree right then Turn 9, a flat lefthander with poor traction and a long late apex. Turn 10, a left followed with Turn 11, a right, both with fairly normal lines, carried the driver back onto the start\finish straight away.

We went to each of the 11 turns and with each successive turn, I became more impressed with Shannon's ability to read the corners. Sometimes Shannon was off but not by much and when Shannon disagreed with me, it was followed by "Why?" Shannon listened intently, to my explanations and never interrupted. If only TJ could listen half as well.

I told Shannon all I knew about Watkins Glen, while TJ said very little about racing and gave small tidbits of advice to Hanna. Where Hanna was concerned, TJ's ideas were not related to racing.

After a little more than an hour, we arrived back at the BRM trailer. I left the three competitors arguing about the best way to attack the course on Friday and went to my hotel, took a warm shower, and promptly fell asleep.

* * *

Watkins Glen always remained open during an event. A guard kept vigil, checking credentials, and giving easy access to those who remained in the track area. Qualifying normally started at 8 a.m., unless specified in the supplementary regulations supplied with the entry form, or delayed due to bad weather. The Glen was no different from most race tracks. Those who stayed in hotels were usually up before 6:30 a.m., giving them time to shower, eat and make it to the track by 8 a.m., unless they were the first practice session, and then they might wake up thirty minutes earlier.

For the BRM crew, it would be a normal morning. For me it would be different. I didn't rise with the customary call from the hotel's front desk. Instead came a knock at the door, and a voice I recognized as Marty's.

I rubbed my face and made my way to the door. My wristwatch read 7:30 AM as I opened the door to Les and Marty. "What the hell happened?"

Marty shrugged his shoulders, "The automatic room dialing machine is on the fritz. They knocked at our room and I told them I'd come get you."

"TJ, Darrell, Augie?"

"They're up, and boy, is TJ pissed," snickered Les.

"Well, so am I. This means no darned breakfast," I snapped.

I always ate breakfast, and at least a couple cups of coffee. If I didn't eat three regular meals, I became irritable, and downright angry. Les and Marty had learned to keep a can of peanuts handy to calm me down should I miss a meal. They were thankful I carried the lemon drops.

"We're gonna get coffee and donuts. Okay?" asked Marty.

I calmed down knowing Les and Marty were doing the best they could and were not responsible for the incident. Besides, having TJ mad would be a big enough problem once they reached the track. I hated donuts, "Sounds good boys. Get what you can. Fuel up the cars, check the air in the tires. It's kinda cool, so let's start out with a few more pounds of air than usual . . . say, seventeen pounds of air front and rear."

"Okay, Charlie," Les and Marty said in unison as they turned to leave.

With them gone, I dressed quickly and headed for the track, arriving shortly before 8 a.m. Everything would be fine, only no breakfast. If I could just find one cup of coffee. Once at the track, I made a slight detour, to tell the Goodyear people to hold three new sets of tires for BRM. On the way to the Goodyear trailer, I passed Shannon's van and caught a strong whiff of buttermilk biscuits. My mouth started to water. Shannon saw me and waved. "Charlie." Momentarily, I paused, "I've got to check on some tires."

Shannon smiled, "Les told me if I saw you to tell you he already did. He said you didn't get any breakfast."

"Aw, it's okay," I lied.

"Want some buttermilk biscuits and coffee?"

"No thanks . . . ," the smell of biscuits was so overwhelming that I lost my will power, "Aw, hell, a couple won't hurt. Yeah, I think I will. Thanks."

"No problem," said Shannon, handing me a cup. "Pour yourself some coffee while I take the biscuits off the stove."

I poured a cup and sipped the strong coffee, "Good coffee. I like it strong."

"Yeah, my Dad said a good jolt in the mornin' would get ya. He says the watered down stuff is for wimps," said Shannon. He pulled biscuits from a covered pan laying on top of a green gas powered Coleman stove. "Boy, howdy. Your Dad hit the nail on the head. I already like the guy and I haven't even met him."

Shannon took another pot and poured gravy over the biscuits, "Oh, you'll like my Dad, he's the greatest." The fluffy biscuits melted in my mouth.

"If you race like you cook, this is sure gonna be a long season for the rest of us." My mouth was full, "You cook the biscuits?"

Shannon shook his head, "My dad baked the biscuits and bagged them for me. He also did the gravy and put it in Tupperware."

"Now that's the kind of father to have."

"I know."

I gobbled down the remaining biscuits and apologized for rushing off. Shannon poured another cup of coffee in a small cup and gave it to me, then told me to hurry back to my team. "I can't take your cup," I said.

Shannon smiled, "Bring it back at lunch."

I hesitated but the thought of another hot cup of coffee changed my mind, "Okay."

A few minutes later, I was at the BRM trailer, my stomach full and satisfied.

TJ stepped from the trailer, dressed in his race suit, ready for the first qualifying session. "Hurry up," he demanded.

Tex, my friendly ten-inch tall, green, yellow headed Amazon parrot, screamed and spread his wings in the cool morning air.

* * *

Beside the concrete barrier separating the fast pits from the track, I stood snapping my old stopwatch, while Marty simply hit a pre-keyed button on the expensive Compaq color laptop. After the qualifying session, we would be able to hook up the computer to a printer in the BRM trailer and have a printout of each driver and all his laps, or all the drivers and their fastest lap.

To my left I watched and waited for TJ to round Turn 11, and come down the rough straight in front of the pits, take the right of Turn 1, and up the hill. TJ came around Turn 11 bouncing down the straight throwing sparks from the expensive titanium skid pads as the Van Diemen rode the humps along the straightaway. The low clearance caused racecars, like the Formula 2000s, to bottom out many times on the rougher race courses like Watkins Glen. Smoother tracks might only have a few spots on the track where cars would throw sparks. Not all were sparking. TJ passed three cars down the straight before entering Turn 1. The main reason for the lack of sparks might be a higher clearance from the road, or the fact they used the cheaper, non-sparking steel skid bars beneath the frame of their race cars. Also, the skid pads might have worn down and needed replacing. I made a mental note to check the thickness of the three titanium pads beneath all three BRM racecars.

The checkered flag waved bringing an end to the timed qualifying session. Lunch followed the second session.

With the old Goodyear tires, Shannon was unable to break into the top twenty. I watched Shannon, impressed with his ability to control the Crossle even with the old tires. The straightaway speed was much slower than most of the other cars, which could be attributed to the much slower exit speed due to the tires. I was pleased with Shannon's approach. He went in as deep as any driver only to lose speed to the old tires as he tried to maneuver the car through the turn. A few times the car broke loose, but Shannon appeared to have "the touch," and somehow managed to pull out each time. When the session ended, I returned to the trailer.

Inside the BRM trailer, I had Marty run copies of the times, distributed them to the three drivers and kept one. TJ was first and Ian second. The new driver, Marcoux, was fifth. Although he would be considered a rookie, his position was somewhat expected since he had run the much faster Canadian series. Even with his experience, he had to contend with equal or better skill of at least a half dozen drivers in the U.S. Formula Ford 2000 National Championship series, one of which was my own prodigy, TJ Benson. I scanned the times. Hanna Lee had done well, as had TJ's teammate Augie Zuehl, both placing in the top 15. I continued down the list until I found Shannon, fifth from the bottom in the 25th position.

Not bad, considering the tires Shannon used and the fact he drove the old Crossle.

During lunch I returned the coffee cup and Shannon insisted I eat lunch with him. I hurried with lunch, then went back to the BRM trailer to make adjustments for the afternoon's final qualification.

As I cleaned the carburetor on TJ's Van Diemen, TJ approached.

"Are those the same tires we used Thursday?"

"Yes," I said.

"That's three-heat cycles. I don't want my final session on tires with any more than one-heat cycle, because I intend to race on those. Replace Pollard's tires too."

"Three cycles are fine TJ," I said, while thinking about the kid whose tires were dry rotted.

"No," TJ said flatly. "I want new tires."

Then I remembered Augie's tires, "Augie has three cycles, what about him?"

"He's not a contender. His tires will be fine," snapped TJ.

I smiled, and thought about a kid who would love tires with three cycles. "There's another set of your tires with three cycles in the trailer do you want me to get rid of them?"

"Yes," said TJ, staring down the pits to the Dotson Racing rig. As an after thought, he added, "That kid, Shannon, will be lucky if he breaks the top twenty."

I smiled, "I think he'll break the top fifteen."

TJ laughed, put his hands on his waist, and continued watching for Hanna. "Five bucks says Shannon doesn't break the top twenty."

"I'll take it, and also bet he qualifies in the top twenty and finishes in the top fifteen."

Again TJ laughed, "You may be a good mechanic but you sure don't know how to judge a man's racing ability. If you're that big a fool, I'll take the bet."

This time I actually chuckled, "You may be right about judging a man's racing ability--after all, I did pick you to win this championship."

TJ glared at me, then noticed Hanna in the distance, "Shannon has about as much chance of finishing in the top fifteen as he does making time with Hanna."

Hanna stood next to her light blue Swift with the black number 16. She wore a brown fedora to protect her from the sun, along with a long sleeve shirt and tight faded jeans.

When TJ saw her, he immediately started walking toward Dotson Racing.

If TJ wanted new tires, then new tires he would get. I had Marty finish the carburetor while he and Les jacked up Pollard's and TJ's racers and removed the tires. From beneath BRM's semi-trailer, I pulled out a small, hand trailer. I attached it to one of the Honda four-wheelers, then stacked the three sets of tires and rims on the trailer.

I took the tires to the Goodyear tent, told them to mount new tires and bill BRM. Then gave an additional instruction: Shannon Kelly would arrive soon, to take the three sets of used tires, and change them with his old ones. I also asked the Goodyear technicians to take tire temperatures and pressures, for the number 44 Crossle.

FORMULA 2000, the Dream

After I finished I passed Kelly's van, where I told Shannon to go to Goodyear and replace his old tires with some extras they had. I also told Shannon to let Goodyear take his temps and pressures. Shannon was extremely grateful, and when I was able to break away, I returned to BRM.

For me everything was ready for the last qualifying session. Loud speakers blared, gaining all drivers' attention, with the message that drivers entered in the U.S. Formula Ford 2000 National Championship were to meet with the Stewards of the race in the Drivers' Lounge immediately after their last qualifying session. The meetings were a normal procedure at every race and one was held for each race series.

* * *

All drivers were on the grid for Watkins Glens' final session of qualifying. Five SCCA member-workers walked the line of waiting Formula 2000 cars lined-up on the grid checking to see that all drivers were ready at the one-minute warning. All of them were women and they all offered a smile and a helpful hand for every driver.

The Grid Marshall, Cindy Hunt, stood ahead of the lead qualifier. Once a former corner worker, she opted to wear the all whites of the corner workers. Her long blond hair was shoved beneath the dark blue cap with the SCCA logo and sunglasses protected her from the sun. From Charlotte, North Carolina, Cindy was one of the many workers who unselfishly volunteered her time to make SCCA racing a success. Many times spending her own money for hotels and travel expenses, she managed to attend most pro-series races during the season. For the excitement and thrill, she gave all of her spare time. Without women like her and the other countless workers on the Grid, Timing and Scoring, and each corner filled with the life saving Corner Workers, SCCA would have been unable to put on any of their Professional or Amateur races. She pointed to Ian Poirier and motioned him to the track. The last Formula 2000 rolled to the track but I saw no sign of Shannon Kelly. Halfway through the session, Shannon sped through the fast pits, only to be stopped at the end of the pits by the Grid Marshall. Before gaining access to the track, Cindy made a quick inspection of Shannon's harness, gloves, arm restraints, and helmet. Satisfied with the check, she waited for a clearing, then waved Shannon on the track. Immediately Shannon was on the throttle, turning up the hill, into Turn 1, and aiming for Turn 2.

The Goodyear man, Carl Law, jogged to where I stood taking times. "It took a while to mount them and get them on, but Shannon seems as pleased as punch you gave him those tires. Never seen such a case of tire rot in my life. Oh, and I'm gonna have someone do temps and pressures, like you asked. Can you believe that kid is doing this whole thing by himself? Man, I'd be beat. No way, I could race too."

"Yeah, I know. Uh, thanks," I said, trying to pass it off as nothing, but I had a guilty look on my face when I looked at Les and Marty. Both had broad grins. Both waved "shame on you" fingers at me, then clapped their hands silently.

Marty looked at Les and whispered, "I can't believe someone would give their competition old, three-cycle tires." Les and Marty knew and understood. TJ Benson paid them but they would have done anything for me. They knew I liked helping underdogs--those who needed help. Shannon was more than a driver who needed help. He had potential and I knew it.

For the last half of the session, I watched Shannon. He tore into the corners and exited far faster than any of the others. His approach and exit speed helped him knock seconds off his qualifying, still he lacked straight line speed--and the others were also getting faster.

When the session was finally over, Les, Marty, and I checked Augie, TJ, and Darrell for tire temperature and tire pressure. I watched Shannon pull in and saw Goodyear take tire pressures. Quickly, my attention shifted to the matter at hand. We finished the checks and the three cars rolled from the fast pits and back to the BRM trailer. From there, Pollard, Zuehl, and TJ hurried to the mandatory driver's meeting.

Each event had a Chief Steward and each race series had a Race Chairman. Coincidentally, Andy Cobb was taking on dual roles for Watkins Glen. Already permanent Race Chairman for the Formula 2000 series, he was also serving as Chief Steward. Although in his fifties, Cobb, with black-greying hair and a full beard, presented an intimidating figure at six-foot-four. A former driver, his countenance was intense.

Cobb raised his hands for quiet and attention. His voice boomed, over the loud, idle talk of the drivers, "Listen up! I'll make this short and sweet. All of you have raced before, including the rookies, so I don't wanna hear any whining about the rookies."

A groan came from the whole group. "I want this series to run smooth. I don't want anybody to get cute with your cars like they do in that damn showroom stock series. Anybody caught cheating will be dealt with severely."

"Aw, come on, Cobb," yelled one of the drivers.

"This isn't a knock on anyone. It's just an early warning. Let me add that this series has been run clean for a quite a few years. I just want every driver to know what I want. Oh, yeah and don't anybody get caught with the fuel. We might check it after qualifying or the race. I don't wanna hear any driver bitching about their car being under weight. Tech will be open all day at every race. Weigh your cars before the race. If it's too light--it's your fault! I won't listen to any excuses, but I will weigh you again and double check the scales. Any questions?"

Shannon Kelly raised his hand, "Where will the TBA race be?"

I smiled and I heard someone laugh. I think it was Wesley.

Cobb said, "We've been in final negotiations and I think the location has been confirmed for Charlotte." Cobb's eyes scanned the drivers until he found Poirier. His eyes locked on and he said, "Other than cheating, there is only one more thing I want to make perfectly clear. Don't go banging around on your competitors with your racecars. These aren't bumper cars. It's deadly! You not only could kill somebody, you could also kill yourself. If I think anyone is doing it intentionally, I'll have them removed from the series and SCCA racing." Again Cobb peered at Poirier. "I won't tolerate it!"

The drivers started to mumble to one another, instantly rising in volume. Again Cobb got their attention. "Listen up!" Cobb smiled, "We're having a barbecue for the Corner Workers and would like each driver to contribute a couple of dollars at the door. Remember without them, you'd have no races." Cobb shrugged his shoulders and added, "That's all I have. I want to wish you all luck in the race."

The drivers milled slowly from the Drivers' Lounge, with almost all contributing to the Corner Workers' dinner. Some remained behind renewing old acquaintances from the year before.

TJ hurried to the BRM trailer where he removed his racing suit, slipped on jeans, tennis shoes, and a red, white and blue, monogrammed BRM shirt. He grabbed a bottle of Gatorade and eagerly waited for Marty to print out the fastest times on the drivers. I stood to the side and waited.

Marty pulled the sheet out, "Looks like TJ is first and Ian second."

"I know that," snapped TJ, grabbing the sheet. "But where is Shannon." He quickly scanned the sheet for Shannon's time and position, "You've made a mistake Marty, you have Shannon in 19th."

"There's no mistake," said Marty.

"Boy, howdy, the rookie broke the top twenty," I smiled.

"Wait till the race," sneered TJ, shoving the qualifying sheet at me.

After TJ disappeared to the front of the trailer, Les shook his head, looked at me, and said, "We got enough trouble with TJ, without you egging him on over this Shannon guy."

"Don't worry boys, it's my problem," I said, with a mischievous grin.

An hour later Les returned from the Hospitality Building with official grid sheets, confirming their preliminary times. Augie, Darrell, and I took time to look at the official grid:

```
                    SCCA/USAC
        U.S. Formula Ford 2000 National Championship
                    Official Grid
                     April 22
                   Watkins Glen
                Watkins Glen, New York
                    (3.38 miles)

        Car    Name             Model            Time       Time
        No.                                      1st        2nd
  1.    (1)    TJ Benson        VanDiemen RF95   1:57.15*   1:57.05*
  2.    (5)    Ian Poirier      Swift DB-8       1:57.28*   1:57.35
  3.    (7)    Ron Leclair      VanDiemen RF95   1:57.42    1:57.36
  4.    (34)   Claude Marcoux   Swift DB-8       1:57.67    1:57.41
  5.    (33)   Bob Dotson       Spirit           1:57.55    1:57.44
  6.    (11)   Alan Reckert     Stohr            1:58.40    1:57.47
  7.    (43)   Jude Dionne      Swift DB-8       1:58.33    1:57.53
  8.    (71)   Gordon Chappel   VanDiemen RF95   1:58.43    1:57.58
  9.    (8)    Freddy Mercury   Reynard 95F      1:58.46    1:57.63
 10.    (69)   Phil Spratt      Reynard 95F      1:57.68    1:58.50
 11.    (54)   Guido Pepin      Swift DB-8       1:57.83    1:57.73
 12.    (21)   Rick Henry       Swift DB-8       1:59.01    1:57.78
 13.    (55)   Cliff Roe        VanDiemen RF94   1:57.99    1:57.82
 14.    (47)   Darrell Pollard  VanDiemen RF95   1:58.25    1:57.89
 15.    (27)   Roberto Cruz     VanDiemen RF95   1:58.92    1:58.11
 16.    (22)   Augie Zuehl      VanDiemen RF95   1:59.15    1:58.23
 17.    (16)   Hanna Lee        Swift DB-8       1:59.23    1:58.51
 18.    (39)   Art Grindle      Swift SE-3       1:59.60    1:58.85
 19.    (44)   Shannon Kelly    Crossle 71F      2:02.48    1:58.87
 20.    (27)   Ben Cifelli      Swift DB-3       1:59.45    1:59.21
 21.    (88)   Barton Springs   VanDiemen RF91   2:00.74    1:59.53
 22.    (30)   Bill Murfy       Swift DB-8       2:00.45    1:59.88
 23.    (00)   Tom Craig        Swift DB-3       2:02.50    2:00.53
 24.    (74)   Mark McGrath     Swift DB-3       2:03.43    2:00.99
 25.    (60)   Rex VanHorn      Reynard SF91     2:01.27    2:01.34
 26.    (62)   Neil Kray        Swift DB-3       2:01.73    2:01.30
 27.    (13)   Steve Smagala    VanDiemen RF89   2:01.42    No Time
 28.    (25)   Chase Wilder     Reynard SF90     2:02.45    2:01.47
 29.    (3)    Will Jones       Swift DB-8       2:02.81    2:02.01

*Better than track record
```

* * *

As the sun started to set, TJ and Darrell went to the hotel while Augie went to visit his new friend, Shannon Kelly. Augie paused in front of me as he tucked his shirt in. "Can you believe Shannon drove all the way here by himself?"

"No. The trip's tough enough without having to prep your racecar and drive."

"He's a tough dude," said Augie. "Man, I'd be beat."

"Boy, howdy."

With the work on the race cars finished, Les and Marty covered them and departed for the hotel. I strolled casually to Kelly's van.

The Crossle was covered. Augie was gone. Shannon was inside the van changing clothes and getting ready to leave with Augie when he returned after cleaning up at the hotel.

"Want a Coke?" Shannon asked.

"Got a diet?"

Shannon nodded, got two drinks, returned to the table outside the van, and gave one to me.

We chatted for a while, then I asked for a pen and piece of paper and jotted down a few things for Shannon to do to the car before the race; new fuel filter and a few suspension checks and settings.

While I wrote down the items to check, Shannon asked, "Why do some of the cars spark so bad when they go down the straights?"

"Skid pads under the car," I said matter of factly. Then asked, "Have you checked yours?"

Shannon shrugged his shoulders and shook his head. "I didn't know there were any."

Realizing the answer appeared to be more of a question, I smiled and said. "Got a quick jack?"

"Sure."

Shannon turned around, and pulled a six-foot tall vertical aluminum bar with two tubes attached to four more horizontal tubes rolling on four two-inch steel wheels. At the end was a six-inch square plate. He slid the horizontal bar under the nose of the Crossle, and pushed the vertical bar back and down to the ground where it locked in place. Just a simple lever to quickly lift the racecar from the ground. Something all the teams carried to make quick checks beneath the car and for changing tires.

I bent to my knees, put both hands on the ground, laid my face on the asphalt, and looked up under the nose. I motioned Shannon down and pointed to a plate, eight inches square and attached to the front portion of the frame beneath the nose. The plate was approximately 1/8" thick and showed scrapes across the whole surface. Then I repeated the same thing at the rear of the Crossle where I pointed out two similar plates. Each of these was only one inch by three inches and again well worn.

"Does it look bad?" Shannon asked.

"No," I said, with a smile. I pulled a rag from the back pocket of my coveralls and wiped my hands off. "They look fine. When the plates are new, they're about 3/16 inch thick. Just keep an eye on them, 'cause you don't want them wearing out and grinding away the frame."

"Thanks," said Shannon, as I continued on the list I was making for Shannon. "When TJ passed me and hit one of the bumps there were so many sparks it looked like fireworks."

I laughed, "Boy, howdy. The titanium really throws out the sparks, but those old steel bars of yours will also spark."

Shannon shook his head in amazement.

Before leaving, I asked Shannon, "Why are you trying to race?" "It's a dream I've always had and my Dad said he would help me with it. You'll like my Dad when you meet him."

I sighed, "This may be a dream, but it's an expensive one. Can your Dad handle it?"

"I don't know. I don't want him to spend everything but he's determined to help me since he promised." Shannon shrugged his shoulders, "We tried to find sponsors, but they all want you to do something first, so my Dad said, 'Let's do something.'"

"Racing is tough and will cost more than you ever dreamed," I added.

"Well my Dad sold the house and is getting a motorhome and enclosed trailer next week." Shannon's eyes brightened, "He plans on coming to all the races."

"That's great," I said, but thought differently. I wanted to tell Shannon to leave. Tell his father to keep his money, because at the end of the season all that would remain would be an empty checking and savings account and just memories, but I said nothing.

"I've done everything with my Dad. He's been to all my go-cart races and even the SCCA Spec Ford races. I can't wait 'til he comes to the races."

"Looking forward to meeting him."

Shannon told me his father, Grant, was a teacher, and how they had moved from Laredo to Dallas, Texas. He went into more detail about his racing, and we talked until Augie arrived. I arrived at the hotel still wondering how I could dissuade Shannon and his father from racing.

* * *

While the ten o'clock news droned on, I paced about. Although the dream was none of my concern--I was concerned. It was obvious Shannon's father didn't have the funds to race Formula Continental, so if I could dissuade the two from spending their money on such a hopeless venture, I would. Trying to convince a man to stop racing would be like telling a heroin addict to stop taking drugs.

Suddenly, Jolit Torres entered my mind. I would ask for her help to see if Shannon pursued a hopeless dream. Since the Holiday Inn was the race headquarters, I assumed Jolit might be at the same hotel. After all, reporters seldom ventured far from the news and most of the racers were at the Holiday Inn. I called the main desk and sure enough Jolit Torres was registered. A moment later, I was connected to her room and she answered. "Jolit, this is Charlie Pepper. I need you to do something for me," I said.

"Is this a story?" Jolit asked.

"I don't know," I said truthfully.

For a few minutes, I explained Shannon's story and the raw talent I had seen in him. I told her about the Go-carts and the SCCA Spec Ford and that Shannon had lived in Laredo, Texas, but moved to Dallas.

"Should be easy, Shannon must have been a member of SCCA's Southwest Division. I was once a member of the same division and the

Houston Region. Shannon had to be a member of the Texas Region in Dallas. I have some friends I can contact. Texas doesn't have much racing except at Texas World Speedway, so it should be easy to find out what you want," said Jolit.

"I'd appreciate it," I said and hung up the phone, switched off the television, and went to sleep.

* * *

The Formula Continentals waited on the false grid for the start of the first race of the new season. The temperature had warmed at The Glen rising into the low 70's. The sun peeked through partially cloudy skies. The initial race for the U.S. Formula Ford 2000 National Championship series would be run under ideal conditions and would be followed by SCCA's popular Shelby CAN-AM race.

Spectators filled Watkins Glen, jockeying for the ideal view much like a racer did for position on the race track.

All 29 racing entrants were already in position on the grid awaiting the five-minute warning. TJ was giving Hanna last minute instructions. Shannon and Augie relaxed by kicking a hacky sack between them. Tom Craig made a quick inspection of the body work he had done to the nose on Friday and seemed content. Some drivers sat in their cars and waited while crew members shielded them from the sun with multi-colored umbrellas that often matched the racecars colors. In the second position, Poirier planned strategy with teammates, Claude Marcoux and Jude Dionne. Near the back of the line, Neil Kray nervously squeezed the steering wheel of his purple number 62 Swift DB-3. Neil would not be in many races with his terrified attitude. Having raced in other classes, he obviously had advanced beyond his ability. This race would tell. Other than TJ, Poirier and Marcoux, the most competitive drivers of the series were clustered around Freddy Mercury's white and royal blue number 8 Reynard 95F. Mercury sat on the asphalt, leaning against his car, asleep in the spring like weather, while the others talked about the off season and the start of a new.

Standing in the group were Gordon Chappel, Bob Dotson, Ron Leclair, Alan Reckert, Guido Pepin, Phil Spratt and of course nearby, Freddy Mercury who was asleep. All had the potential and expectations of winning and beating TJ and Poirier. Only a few in the small cluster would end the season with a win. Only one in the small group, Guido Pepin, could not expect to win.

Already flushed, and the season not even in the severe heat of summer, Guido joyfully engaged in idle talk and waited for the race with the others. His brown hair and face appeared greasy as always. With his red cheeks, bright face and rotund body, all he needed was white hair, beard, and a red suit to be a perfect Santa Claus, which he willingly played each year during the Christmas season. One thing Guido possessed, along with his fellow competitors, was an intense love of auto racing. He pursued his racing with the same desire and determination that had built his restaurant empire.

Leading the stories as usual was Bob Dotson, with only Chappel and Pepper able to tell more outlandish stories than he. When his teammate Mercury was not sleeping, the two men standing next to each other were complete opposites, identical only in height at an even six feet. Standing side by side, they looked more like the team of Laurel and Hardy. Although overweight, Dotson was not fat--he was a large man. At 230 pounds, he gave away 40 pounds of ballast to often younger and quicker competitors. He could ill afford to sacrifice the weight to smaller and lighter drivers although he took pride and reveled in his ability to beat those same drivers. Of all the others, Dotson was most likely to beat TJ and Poirier.

Mercury was slim but not skinny, and appeared to have no butt. He had a long thin face and he kept his wavy, black hair cut short. A wide gap was prominent between his two front teeth. From race to race, he grew a small trim moustache, occasionally shaving his upper lip clean. Presently he wore the thin moustache. He also had the next best shot at victory. He had an uncanny ability to relax and sleep anywhere. When awake, he challenged Dotson for the humor of the moment like he challenged Dotson on the race track. More than likely he and Dotson would each come away with a victory in the U.S. Formula Ford 2000 National Championship series. Both he and Dotson were known around the circuit as extreme party animals and practical jokers, but more so for their efforts in helping fellow competitors. Dotson had once said, "I'd rather help someone race and lose--than win alone!"

Leclair and Reckert were a pair of young, wealthy, Canadians, more American than most of the Americans who raced with them. Reckert was built like a fireplug, had red frizzy hair and was covered with freckles. Leclair had the build, dark hair and good looks of a daytime soap opera star.

In his late thirties, Phil Spratt had a medium build and owned a chain of auto parts stores. His good looks, blond hair, and blue eyes got him as far in business as it did with the women.

And, of course, Chappel, the oldest, had more experience and cunning.

Any of those six drivers were capable of a win during the season and all of them were a joy to be around. They seemed to be the most popular and friendliest, always offering helpful hints and aid to new and old drivers alike. For those very reasons, drivers would congregate about them and listen intently.

Others drivers clustered in smaller and smaller groups, with some electing never to mingle with others--either through shyness, desire or intimidation. A few of the drivers faces remained nameless due to their fraternizing with only a select few. They would come to race . . . then go home. Many could be remembered more for a car, a number or a color, than a face or a name. Some would be replaced with others the following year.

Shannon and Augie were definitely not shy. They easily formed friendships with the elite six and were now busily engaged in a kicking match of hacky sack to pass the time before the five-minute warning. Augie had wavy brown hair and brown eyes and although one of the shortest drivers, he took pride in his daily physical workouts including rigorous aerobic exercise.

Augie and Shannon were quickly establishing a friendship that would carry them both through the season.

TJ stood next to his old Van Diemen.

Poirier stood next to his lime green Swift DB-8, along with fellow French Canadians, Dionne and Marcoux. When together the three spoke only French.

The five-minute warning sounded and the drivers filed to their respective racers. Shannon wished TJ luck and then walked Hanna to her car, which intensely agitated TJ.

TJ mumbled as I helped him in his racer, "That kid should pay more attention to his racing and a lot less to the women."

"I think you speak wisely," I said, suppressing a smile. A whistle sounded, alerting the drivers to the three-minute warning. A Grid Worker walked down the line of cars holding her hand high and showing three fingers. Engines started and revved to a deafening crescendo.

I reached above the small dashboard and grabbed the steering wheel while TJ slid the wide portion of the black arm restraint down his arm to his elbow, leaving the half inch wide strip, with a loop at the other end, dangling freely. He repeated this with the right arm, then took the small right loop, at the other end of the arm restraint, slid it over the end of the right seat belt strap and pushed it into position on the five point harness. TJ did likewise with the left, then clicked the strap between his legs into the harness. Next, he pulled a 3 inch wide strap over each shoulder and clicked them into the final positions of the harness near his waist. I tugged at the waist strap while TJ pulled each shoulder strap snug. With the harness secure, I handed TJ the steering wheel. TJ then snap locked it in place on the steering column.

The dashboard held warning lights, starter button, water temperature gauge, an oil pressure gauge and a tachometer positioned so the 7000-rpm redline would be visible between the top center of the steering wheel. Behind the driver's right shoulder was the power switch. TJ started the engine and when the Van Diemen was running, I turned the switch behind TJ so the engine would run off the on board battery. Next, I reached behind and below the engine to disconnect the cable from the starter then tilted the starter cart and pulled it away.

TJ pushed the small radio earphones in each ear and slid the fireproof sock over his head. I handed TJ the blue helmet with a star on each side and the letters TJ scripted in each star. TJ pulled the helmet over his head and secured the chin strap.

I plugged in the radio cable to TJ's helmet and switched on the remote radio. The FM radio was activated with a small switch on the steering wheel. I checked the harness again, pulled the headphones from around my neck, and clicked the button on the radio strapped to my waist.

"Can you hear me, TJ?"

"Loud and clear," came the response.

Les carried a similar system for Augie, as did Marty for Darrell. Down the line of waiting anxious drivers, 25 other pairs worked similar rituals. Only Shannon Kelly strapped in alone. Bob Dotson had sent an extra crew member to start Shannon's Crossle at the three-warning. When the Crossle roared to life, Dotson's crew member flipped the red power switch and disconnected the battery starter placing the battery on the pit wall where Shannon would once again retrieve it after the race. Shannon was truly alone--no crew, no help.

The whistle blew and the Grid Marshall held up one finger, letting the drivers know one more minute remained before the pace lap started. The drivers held up their left hand making a fist; the signal they were ready. Crews backed away from the cars and moved to their position on pit row. At the one-minute warning, I was already halfway down the line of cars when I noticed Shannon sitting in his Crossle. No one was near.

I smiled, and moved to the side of Shannon, held a thumb up, and yelled, "Good luck, Shannon."

Shannon responded likewise, and I could tell he was smiling. Shannon flipped the visor down and checked the multiple, clear plastic tearaways covering the protective face shield on his helmet as the Grid Marshall signaled the cars to leave.

I knew Shannon had no crew: no one to make repairs in the pits; no one to show a pit board with times and laps; no one with a radio to communicate problems; no one to listen to his needs. I admired Shannon for his sheer desire, determination, and effort, but knew he could not mount a challenge "poor-boying," as Shannon and his father apparently needed to do.

Although my heart was filled with admiration for Shannon, I could not help him in the lofty pursuit of his elusive dream. Thirty yards ahead of the first car, the Grid Marshall, Cindy, stood in the center of the track ready to set their position. Unlike most racing, SCCA was abundant with women workers whose enthusiasm permeated every aspect of racing. From Timing and Scoring to the corner workers, women were an integral part of the racing. Without their participation, many races would be unsuccessful. Women played a major role in all aspects of SCCA racing--including racing as Hanna proved.

TJ had the pole, so Cindy pointed at TJ, then pointed to her left giving TJ the inside right for turn one. She pointed to Poirier, then motioned to her right. She did the same for each of the other 29 entrants, until the grid was clear.

I knew it would be a long season for Shannon and Grant.

The cars came around the last turn in two perfectly lined rows. TJ accelerated and Poirier matched him, as did the others who jammed in closely.

The green flag waved. The Formula Continentals thundered down the front straightaway, the whine exciting as they went through second and third gear. The roar of the 29 engines near start/finish was deafening. TJ and Poirier heeled and toed and flipped the throttle as they downshifted from third, to second, to first. They went into Turn 1, side by side, followed by Marcoux and Reckert. They wound through the gears to fourth. Leclair and Dotson both made a foolish move trying to pass four, but Dotson was pinched and pushed off the track as the others raced past dropping Dotson to last. Shannon got a great jump at the start and moved to 12th place.

At Turn 3, Poirier jumped ahead of TJ and held it until the back straight. TJ out braked Poirier, down shifted to third and dove to the inside of the inner loop before Turn 5. Hugging their exhaust came three Canadians, Leclair, Marcoux, and Reckert, followed by the old man, Moses, with Mercury and Dionne close behind. The first eight broke away and were one second ahead of the next group, which was led by Phil Spratt. Dotson was still at the rear and was having handling problems with the suspension after his off road excursion, but he was closing on the back markers.

Down the long, high speed, back straight, it was painfully obvious Shannon did not know the proper setup for the wings. He was out powered by the faster team cars and was quickly pushed back to 25th. Shannon remained in 25th position as the second lap started and was unable to improve his position until he reached the toe of the boot where he went from fourth to first gear passing two racers as he went through the gears. He passed two more in the uphill, right hander, in the heel of Turn 8, dropped to first gear and took Turn 9. Now in 21st, he faltered down the straightaway where the straight line speed he lacked hurt. A Continental passed him at Turn 1 but he held off the other three and through the esses took his position back plus one. Shannon came out of the esses so much faster than those who trailed. He managed to hold them off down the long back straight but the straight was enough to have them close the gap and again be on his tail. Dotson moved up quickly almost touching Shannon's exhaust at Turn 5. Dotson smiled and thought it a good time to test the young friendly rookie and he felt he could, even with his car acting so poorly. From Turn 5 to Turn 11, Dotson got a lesson in driving as Shannon put one second on Dotson. At first, Dotson thought he had major problems until he realized he too was pulling away from those behind. Shannon managed to pull away from him even quicker than he had out distanced the others.

On lap two TJ relinquished his lead to Poirier at Turn 5. At Turn 1 of lap three, TJ took Poirier and started to stretch his lead as both drivers pulled away.

At the end of the back straightaway, Neil Kray slid off the track hard crashing into the Armco steel barrier. He jumped from the car and with the help of the corner workers, climbed the embankment to safety. Neil turned around and looked at his car, fell to his knees and rocked back and forth as though a loved one had died. Another face, another number, another car . . . gone. Neil Kray's short racing season finished and another dream ended.

Still on lap three, the four Canadians broke away from the pack and diced for third. Marcoux, Reckert, Dionne, and Leclair fought hard for third. Seventh was a tossup between Mercury and Chappel. Far behind them followed Spratt, Pollard, Guido, and Rick Henry.

On lap seven, Steve Smagala broke too late, downshifted to first too hard, then his car broke loose and left the race course at Turn 9, bounced across the rough terrain and when he reentered the course at Turn 9, his right front tire no longer touched the pavement. Smagala limped into the pits, his race day finished and his position relegated to that of a spectator.

After ten laps and the race barely half over, Shannon passed Ben Cifelli for 18th. Dotson was falling back but still clinging to Shannon. On the next lap Shannon passed Murfy, the following lap he took Hanna. In the boot, on lap thirteen, he passed Augie. On the following lap in the boot, he passed Roberto Cruz, the rookie from Mexico. He passed Darrell Pollard as he went through the esses on lap fifteen. With three laps remaining, he joined the group with Henry, Guido and Spratt, where the four fought back and forth for the next two laps.

On lap seventeen Shannon overtook Henry's number 21 Swift DB-8 through the toe of the boot, Guido in the heel of Turn 8, and Spratt coming out of Turn 11. Going into Turn 1 on the last lap Spratt passed Shannon and blocked Shannon through the esses. Shannon came out of the esses so underpowered that Henry and Guido took him down the back straight. Far to the front, TJ cruised to victory on his final lap with Poirier controlling second. Leclair pulled away locking down third position and leaving the others fighting behind.

Somehow Shannon closed the distance on Henry and Guido through the boot, passed Guido in the left hander at Turn 9 and closed on Henry through Turn 10 with Guido tight on his back. Shannon took Henry to the inside of Turn 11. For a moment, he raced onto the straightaway toward the checkered flag, and holding tenth position. I found I was cheering Shannon much to the chagrin and enjoyment of Les and Marty. After all, TJ had walked away with a win as expected. What Shannon was doing was racing, and it was a hell of a lot of fun to watch.

Shannon came out of Turn 11, giving enough room to Henry on the outside. Henry had the position and speed and slowly pulled away. Guido, like the experienced driver he was, watched the situation unfold and if not for the power of his Swift DB-8 and the new Quicksilver engine, he would not have beaten Shannon to the finish line, nor would Henry. Henry barely finished one length ahead of Shannon and Guido marginally by only a nose. Shannon finished a hard fought 12th.

Whether first or last, the spectators' zealous cheers for the drivers were proof they approved of the mid-pack race.

Unable to catch Shannon, Dotson managed to move into 16th, just behind Cruz. Augie was behind Dotson, and Hanna in 18th.

The top six drivers reported to "Impound" for inspection: (1) Benson, (2) Poirier, (3) Leclair, (4) Marcoux, (5) Reckert and (6) Dionne. Before they moved to Impound, the first three went to the Winner's Circle, near start/finish, for pictures and an interview.

The other 21 cars returned to the pits to celebrate or whine depending on where they finished. All prepared and started thinking about the next race, three weeks away at Mosport, Canada.

I waited to give a thumbs up to Shannon as he drove past, then I went directly to Impound where I relieved TJ so I could do whatever the Stewards demanded. Les and Marty walked back to the BRM trailer to check on Pollard and Zuehl.

The Stewards decided on a light check for the first race, hooking a sun machine to the six cars in Impound, checking only timing.

I went straight to TJ, and held out my hand, "Five bucks."

"What?" asked TJ as he chugged from the plastic Gatorade bottle.

"The bet. Shannon finished twelfth," I smiled.

"He was lucky," sneered TJ. "He'll never be a front runner."

I shrugged my shoulders, "Five bucks is five bucks."

To further add to TJ's insult, the talk in Impound was about Shannon's race, which only angered TJ more.

Thirty minutes later, after all six Continental cars passed inspection, they returned to their respective paddock areas.

I took time to pass Shannon's paddock space and congratulate him for his great race. Shannon once again thanked me immensely for the tires. The ear to ear grin had not disappeared since his race, the excitement still shown on his face. A few minutes later I returned to the BRM trailer to pack and leave the race track.

Marty and I, with the help of the others, loaded the BRM trailer. An hour after Impound Les went to Timing and Scoring and came back with a copy of the final result, giving one to each of the three drivers and one to me:

```
                        SCCA/USAC
            U.S. Formula Ford 2000 National Championship
                     Official Race Results
                          April 23
                        Watkins Glen
                    Watkins Glen, New York
                         (3.38 miles)


        Car    Name            Model           Time      Speed    Laps
        No.

  1.    (1)    TJ Benson       VanDiemen RF95  1:56.97*  103.72   18
  2.    (5)    Ian Poirier     Swift DB-8      1:57.42   103.45   18
  3.    (7)    Ron Leclair     VanDiemen RF95  1:57.64   103.35   18
  4.    (34)   Claude Marcoux  Swift DB-8      1:57.75   103.15   18
  5.    (11)   Alan Reckert    Stohr           1:57 81   103.10   18
  6.    (43)   Jude Dionne     Swift DB-8      1:57.67   103.33   18
  7.    (71)   Gordon Chappel  VanDiemen RF95  1:57.88   103.05   18
  8.    (8)    Freddy Mercury  Reynard 95F     1:57.78   103.13   18
  9.    (69)   Phil Spratt     Reynard 95F     1:58.10   102.80   18
 10.    (21)   Rick Henry      Swift DB-8      1:58.50   102.50   18
 11.    (54)   Guido Pepin     Swift DB-8      1:59.61   101.40   18
 12.    (44)   Shannon Kelly   Crossle 71F     2:01.11   100.60   18
 13.    (47)   Darrell Pollard VanDiemen RF95  1:59.45   102.55   18
 14.    (55)   Cliff Roe       VanDiemen RF94  2:00.29   101.10   18
 15.    (27)   Roberto Cruz    VanDiemen RF95  2:00.43   101.02   18
 16.    (22)   Augie Zuehl     VanDiemen RF95  2:01.80   100.20   18
 17.    (33)   Bob Dotson      Spirit          1:57.84   103.08   18
 18.    (16)   Hanna Lee       Swift DB-8      2:02.45    99.63   18
 19.    (30)   Bill Murfy      Swift DB-8      2:03.13    99.29   18
 20.    (27)   Ben Cifelli     Swift DB-3      2:03.00    99.39   18
 21.    (25)   Chase Wilder    Reynard SF90    2:03.75    98.98   18
 22.    (39)   Art Grindle     Swift SE-3      2:03.85    98.87   18
 23.    (00)   Tom Craig       Swift DB-3      2:04.00    98.79   17
 24.    (74)   Mark McGrath    Swift DB-3      2:04.63    98.35   17
 25.    (88)   Barton Springs  VanDiemen RF91  2:09.45    96.11   16
 26.    (60)   Rex VanHorn     Reynard SF91    2:10.73    95.75   15
 27.    (3)    Will Jones      Swift DB-8      2:10.98    95.63   14
 DNF    (13)   Steve Smagala   VanDiemen RF89  2:00.33   101.15    7
 DNF    (62)   Neil Kray       Swift DB-3      2:12.73    94.58    3
      FASTEST
        LAP
        Car    Time            Speed
         1     1:56.97*      103.72 mph
      *Track Record
```

I looked at the final results. TJ started on the pole, set a track record, and won the race.

Already dressed, with bags outside the trailer waiting for the return trip home, all three drivers scanned the results.

"All right," said TJ.

Pollard and Zuehl congratulated Benson on his performance, then sped quickly away in their rented cars to the airport and to flights that would take them home.

TJ stood next to me, outside the BRM trailer. He bent over his duffel bag and removed a high tech expensive cellular phone. With a snap of his wrist, he flipped the cellular phone open and punched a preset number with the authority and coolness of Captain Kirk waiting for Scotty to beam him aboard the Enterprise.

When the party on the other end answered, TJ said, "Anthony Benson, please . . . Pop, I took the pole and won! . . . Thanks. Pop you gotta come to Mosport, and watch me win it for you." TJ paused, his face overshadowed with sadness.

The conversation was easy to follow, even without hearing Anthony Benson speak, just by watching TJ's face.

"Japan? . . . Can't someone else go . . . Pop, you haven't seen a race in almost two years. You said you'd see one this year . . . I know you're busy, but which race can you make? . . . What? . . . Sure, if you're busy, I understand. I'll tell you about the race when I get home."

TJ flipped the phone shut and stood there for what seemed like an eternity, while Marty, Les, and I worked steadily loading the trailer. After a brief moment, he sighed and put the phone back in his bag. He picked up the bag and looked at the three still working.

"See you guys later. I'm outa here," said TJ.

"Bye, TJ," said Les and Marty.

"Great race," I said.

Somewhat surprised TJ said, "Thanks, Charlie." He walked to his rental car and a moment later was gone.

I shook my head. For nearly two years the call, the response was always the same after each victory. I thought about the phone conversation and TJ's wealthy computer mogul father and wondered if Anthony Benson knew what he was really missing. Sometimes, I wondered if maybe part of TJ's attitude was related to the lack of his father's attention.

With the truck loaded and the races over for the day, Les and Marty mounted the Semi with Tex and prepared for the drive home to Gainesville, Georgia, where they would leave the rig at my shop, retrieve their car and return to Birmingham, Alabama. I would remain until the morning, when I would catch a flight back to Atlanta.

Dotson and Mercury gave an open invitation to all the drivers to eat dinner at their trailer. I accepted as did Hanna who remained behind to fly home Sunday. Dotson continued to rave about Shannon's racing. Augie and Chappel also attended Dotson's dinner. I knew TJ would hate to learn he had flown out leaving Hanna behind with Shannon. After dinner I returned to the hotel.

On the drive to the hotel, I wondered how well Shannon would do during the season. His position in the race, realistically, was about as good as he could expect to finish in the old Crossle. In order for Shannon to advance, he still needed better equipment. If he had the equipment, could he beat the front runners? Everyone has a good race occasionally. Maybe this was what Shannon was having--that one good race.

At 9 p.m., the phone in my room rang. It was Jolit Torres who was in the hotel lobby.

"Hey, guy, I've got your information. Seems Shannon ran Go-carts but never really won anything. His father took him to the races and everyone I talked to says you couldn't have met two nicer people."

"I met Shannon and if the father is anything like his son, then they are good people."

"Great. Well, anyway, it seems he rented a Spec Ford from a place called Stevens Racing. They rent cars and run a racing school in Hallett, Oklahoma. Got a little road course there."

"Yeah, I've been to it but it was a long time ago. So?"

"Why don't I let Roland tell you the story. He works for Stevens Racing. Hold on while I call him and hookup on the three way," said Jolit as she temporarily put me on hold. A moment later she was back with Roland. She made the necessary introductions quickly.

"This kid you're talking about rented racers from us, Spec Ford three times and finished top ten twice."

"I thought those cars were equal?" I asked.

"They are," said Roland. "But see, we keep spares for occasional renters. They're back of the pack . . . you know, our weak cars, in case somebody really wants a car. It's better'n nothing, if you want to race real bad. In Shannon's case, it was all that usually remained. Shannon always got a dog . . . I felt really bad 'cause I could tell he was a better driver. And then, there was the third race."

"What was so special about it?"

"Shannon was stuck with the same old dog. Not a bad car, just not fast you know. He qualified like 15th on Saturday. The last qualifying was Sunday morning before the race. It rained all day, and of course Saturday's times were the fastest, so they used those times, but Sunday's rain qualification was something. See we got this guy, Tom, in the Midwest Division, who can fly in the rain. We call Tom 'The Rainman.' Nobody ever beat Tom in the rain."

"Boy, howdy, we got one like that here," I interjected. "Name is Ian Poirier and I don't think anybody ever beat him in the rain."

"Well, anyway, our guy Tom already had the outside of the first row for Sunday's race and was two seconds faster than anybody on Sunday . . ." For a moment Roland was silent as he reflected on the race and suddenly forgot to continue his story.

"Well, go on, what happened?" I urged.

"Oh yeah, well Tom was faster than anybody . . . except your friend, Shannon Kelly--he was two seconds faster than Tom! Never saw anybody drive in the rain like that. The race started and in five laps, Shannon moved from 15th to 2nd. Tom was about thirty seconds ahead, but each lap Shannon gained on Tom, and in fifteen laps, Shannon passed him. With two laps remaining, Shannon and Tom had lapped everybody. Shannon had the win clinched, then a spark plug wire came loose, and his car started missing badly with a lap remaining. He still finished second . . . it was the best race I ever saw!"

The awe in Roland's voice was evident as he recanted the seemingly unbelievable story.

"Thanks, Roland," said Jolit, breaking the silence.

Roland hung up and I expressed my gratitude, "Thanks, Jolit."

"Charlie . . . this is the hot one?" Jolit asked.

"I don't know," I said seriously. "The next few races should answer our questions . . . if their money holds out. What the kid needs is a win . . . and he won't get it in the Crossle."

MOSPORT PARK

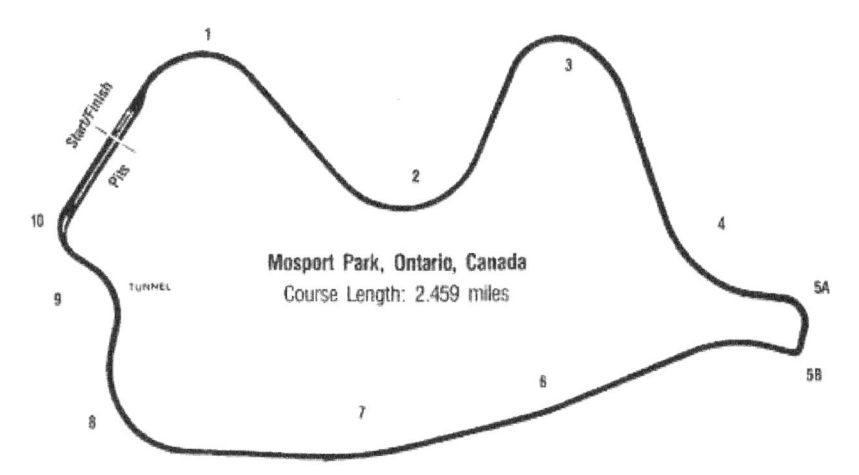

Mosport Park, Ontario, Canada
Course Length: 2.459 miles

    The second race, on the U.S. Formula Ford 2000 National Championship schedule, brought the small Indy-type, Formula Continental racers to Mosport Park. The race facility, located in Ontario, Canada, consisted of a challenging ten turn, 2.459 mile circuit.
    The Mosport road course was run in a clockwise direction and Turn 1 came immediately after the exit from the pits, the short straight to the pits and start/finish. Turn 1 was a fast, downhill right-hander many took flat out in fourth gear, hitting the apex at the end of the speed bumps and keeping the right tires on the curve for a distance until the racer pushed to the far left. Immediately the driver brought the racer back to the right for the downhill, left-handed Turn 2 still in fourth gear, which worked into a long, double apex turn. Turn 3, was a dangerous turn, with a decreasing radius and a slight off-camber change at the apex taken in second gear. To go in too fast at Turn 3, which would feel all right to the driver, would send him crashing into the concrete barricade on the other end of the turn. From Turn 3 the track went downhill, through the gears to fourth, and to the late apex left-hand Turn 4. Then came the uphill right of Turn 5a, where the driver flipped the throttle, dropped from fourth to third to second and would set the car for the slow, first gear Turn 5b with immediate hard acceleration to clip the left side of Turn 5c. Under full acceleration the

driver tried to make the kinks of Turn 6 and 7 straight, to maximize speed, as the Continental climbed through the gears to fourth. The Mosport Esses comprised Turns 8, 9, and 10. Turns 8, and Turn 9, taken in third gear, were late apexes setting up Turn 10, taken in second gear, bringing the driver back onto the main straight and finishing a lap at Mosport.

The race weekend was to be short, with the U.S. Formula Ford 2000 National Championship qualifying Saturday and a twenty-four-lap race Sunday.

With the cars ready, I took time to pass Shannon's new setup, and meet Shannon's father, Grant.

The familiar, yellow, Crossle, was next to an older but clean Winnebago parked to the side of Chappel. The trailer, which obviously housed Shannon's old Crossle, was as old as the Winnebago. The 25 foot trailer was fabricated from the same siding material as the Winnebago and not the new aluminum or fiberglass as were most racecar trailers. This only confirmed that Shannon and his father were "poor boying" their dream. I was impressed with the antiquated racers showroom new appearance.

When Shannon saw me, he called out to his father, then came to meet me. "Hey, Charlie," said Shannon, extending his hand in the familiar friendly handshake, "I want you to meet my Dad."

Shannon's father stepped away from the camper, holding a paperback novel of a Lamour western in one hand, his thumb still marking the place. Reading glasses hung from the bridge of his nose. He approached with the same smile and sparkle in his eyes, and extended a similarly warm hand. He had the same sharp, clean-cut features as Shannon. The same black hair but it was thin and greying, and his mid-section belied the comfort of his previous years.

"Dad, this is Charlie Pepper."

"Grant Kelly, Mr. Pepper."

"Nice to meet you and please, call me Charlie."

The smile was contagious and the handshake, strong and firm, like his son. The same eyes lit his dimpled smile. Shannon and Grant were a matched pair with only the years prominently showing on Grant.

"Shannon told me about the tires you gave him at Watkins Glen," said Grant. "I truly am grateful."

Suddenly, my face warmed, "It was nothing."

We moved to the white plastic fold out table with bench seats where I took a seat and Shannon offered me a cool drink. Shannon momentarily disappeared into the motorhome, and came back with the familiar peanut butter cookies. When I finished my drink, and a handful of cookies, I asked, "Shannon, why don't you show me your rig. I'd like to see it."

Shannon gave me a tour of the trailer, ingeniously rigged so the Crossle could be raised with a hand cranked winch, and locked in place. Doing this, enabled them to pull their small Suzuki Samurai Jeep type vehicle, in the trailer.

The real reason to see their trailer was to verify that they had no power tools or radios. As the weekend progressed, I would try to show them the things that were necessary to mount a racing campaign. If finances were critical, then radio's would be out. Still, they could manage a pit board for communications. They had no pyrometer for tire temps, and no stopwatch, so I told them to ask Carl Law at the Goodyear trailer to take temps and pressure. I also noticed no spare rims with which to season tires.

I tried to explain everything I could, without flooding them with too much information. A little later, I returned to the BRM trailer to prepare for qualifying.

* * *

The five-minute warning sounded and those drivers not already in their respective cars, went to them immediately. Shannon took a leisurely stroll to his outdated Crossle, followed closely by his father.

I already had TJ fastened in, while Les took care of Darrell, and Marty watched Augie. Cindy, the Grid Marshall, blew her whistle signaling the three-minute warning for all the drivers. At the three-minute warning, half the cars roared to life. Two grid workers walked down the line of Formula Continentals and held three fingers high, so all drivers would know three minutes remained.

Cindy blew her whistle for the one-minute warning and held up one finger. Poirier held up a clenched left fist letting her know he was ready.

I walked down the false grid to the fast pits with Les and Marty, where we would time the drivers we thought might be in contention for the race.

As I walked down the false grid, I stopped suddenly to watch a strange ceremony being exchanged between a father and his son.

Grant went through a short, quick ritual of shaking hands with Shannon. First they shook, let their hands rotate up and squeezed each others' thumb, they released, slid their hand back, curling their fingers about the others' fingers, then raised their thumb and pointed the index finger at each other, while the other three fingers still held tightly. They released the hold and Grant held a thumb up to his son, "Good luck, Shannon."

Grant picked up the battery starter and backed away from the Crossle.

I smiled at the closeness of the father/son duo and wondered if TJ's father would ever even attend one of his son's races. As Grant backed away, I moved to Shannon's side and held my thumb up. Shannon responded similarly and I could see him smiling, and much happier than the first race, and even more relaxed if that were possible. Shannon flipped the visor down, checked the clear plastic tearaways, and double checked his shoulder straps.

The Grid Marshall signaled the cars to leave.

As Grant walked along with me to the fast pits, he held his right hand over his heart.

"You okay?" I asked.

Grant laughed, "Yeah, but my heart gets up too about 150 beats a minute when Shannon gets out on the track. I get nervous as hell. It's been the same since he raced go-carts. Is that normal?"

Now I laughed, "Boy, howdy. Watching your own kid get out there, risking his neck, has got to be nerve racking. But don't worry, Shannon seems to have what it takes. Oh, he'll have his spills but these cars are pretty darn safe."

"Thanks, but I'm sure it won't slow my heart down," Grant sighed. "Sometimes it seems so bad, I have to jump up and down just to get my body up to my heart's speed."

Again, I chuckled, "You'll come around. Do you have a stop watch?"

"No," said Grant. "But to be honest I don't think I could do it as nervous as I am. I need to do something I can handle--like carry the Gatorade bottle . . . as long as it's plastic."

We both laughed. Now we stood at the concrete barricade separating the track from the fast pits. Les had the computer set on the stand, prepared to time the other cars. I took out my stopwatch, ready to time specific drivers.

I knew Grant had nothing with him, so I asked if Grant needed any help with the equipment and learned Grant had nothing in the pits, with which to help Shannon--not even a radio, should Shannon need to make a quick stop. Grant didn't even carry a pit board.

"You need tools, radio and if no radio, at least a pit board, to keep Shannon informed," I said. "At least, get a cart so you can keep the starter on it and you won't have to carry it around. Hell, you can strap the stuff to a cheap dolly."

"We hope to get the stuff later," Grant admitted, as he lay the starter on the ground. "The dolly does sound like a good idea."

It would be a long season for Shannon and Grant. I admired them for their determination, but knew they could not mount a challenge "poor-boying" as they apparently needed to do.

Qualifying was not good for our BRM team. Saturday, after qualifying, found me with no spare time at all. The May 14 race was less than twenty-four hours away, and all three cars confronted me with problems of some kind. A wreck for Augie, and a blown engine for Darrell. TJ had clipped the corner of his Van Diemen, but he refused to use the spare Van Diemen in the trailer. It was stupid not to use the spare since it was ready and fast--I knew it. But things were never meant to be easy for a mechanic so TJ's decision forced me to work furiously on TJ's favorite racer to have it ready in time for the race. TJ was fourth on the grid and unhappy about everything. He shoulda used the spare racer like I had said.

Really I wanted to spend time with Shannon and learn what he knew about race cars because I was afraid Shannon knew nothing about race preparation. Grant never used a pyrometer to check tire temperatures

FORMULA 2000, the Dream

during qualifying. Actually, Grant appeared too nervous during qualifying to be of any help for Shannon. Still, they needed help--and had to be told about the preparations they needed to make for each race.

* * *

Late in the afternoon, with an end to the work in sight, Les went to Timing and Scoring to retrieve an official Grid sheet showing the drivers qualifying position:

```
              SCCA/USAC
   U.S. Formula Ford 2000 National Championship
              Official Grid
                 May 14
                Mosport
             Ontario, Canada
              (2.459 miles)

    Car    Name              Model              Time       Time
    No.                                         1st        2nd

1.  (5)   Ian Poirier        Swift DB-8         1:24.98    1:24.25
2.  (7)   Ron Leclair        VanDiemen RF95     1:25.22    1:24.60
3.  (34)  Claude Marcoux     Swift DB-8         1:25.38    1:24.88
4.  (1)   TJ Benson          VanDiemen RF95     1:24.92    No Time
5.  (27)  Roberto Cruz       VanDiemen RF95     1:25.32    1:24.96
6.  (33)  Bob Dotson         Spirit             1:25.00    1:24.99
7.  (11)  Alan Reckert       Stohr              1:25 01    1:25.05
8.  (43)  Jude Dionne        Swift DB-8         1:25.30    1.25.10
9.  (71)  Gordon Chappel     VanDiemen RF95     1:25.20    1:25.22
10. (8)   Freddy Mercury     Reynard 95F        1:26.46    1:25.25
11. (69)  Phil Spratt        Reynard 95F        1:25.50    1:25.33
12. (47)  Darrell Pollard    VanDiemen RF95     1:26.60    1:25.35
13. (54)  Guido Pepin        Swift DB-8         1:26.20    1:25.48
14. (21)  Rick Henry         Swift DB-8         1:26.10    1:25.53
15. (22)  Augie Zuehl        VanDiemen RF95     1:26.44    1:25.63
16. (16)  Hanna Lee          Swift DB-8         1:26.33    1:25.69
17. (44)  Shannon Kelly      Crossle 71F        1:25.76    1:25.75
18. (30)  Bill Murfy         Swift DB-8         1:27.32    1:25.88
19. (27)  Ben Cifelli        Swift DB-3         1:28.45    1:26.10
20. (39)  Art Grindle        Swift SE-3         1:27.12    1:26.11
21. (88)  Barton Springs     VanDiemen RF91     1:26.74    1:26.22
22. (55)  Cliff Roe          VanDiemen RF94     1:26.25    1:28.47
23. (00)  Tom Craig          Swift DB-3         1:27.50    1:26.83
24. (74)  Mark McGrath       Swift DB-3         1:26.95    1:27.87
25. (60)  Rex VanHorn        Reynard SF91       1:28.66    1:27.23
26. (13)  Steve Smagala      VanDiemen RF89     1:29.50    1:27.80
27. (25)  Chase Wilder       Reynard SF90       1:27.85    1:30.47
28. (3)   Will Jones         Swift DB-8         1:28.45    1:28.33
```

With the blown engine Pollard had still managed to qualify 12th, with Augie 15th. TJ was still angry with his 4th position, and proceeded to tell everybody how he would have the pole, if they had only the first qualifying session. He said nothing about his off road excursion, which forced him in on a wrecker when he failed to complete the first timed lap of the second

49

qualifying session--and forced me to work my ass off just to have it ready.

I ran my finger down the sheet until I located Shannon in 17th position. I shook my head, knowing the kid had no chance in the Crossle. His lack of knowledge on racing setups and preparation, would continue to hinder his chances of making even a decent showing. Still my heart went out to the determination and enthusiasm Shannon and his father continued to show against overwhelming odds. One thing I did notice was Shannon's ability to learn the tracks. Even with the old Crossle, Shannon was competitive during the first session and usually unbeatable during the first three laps. Especially during early morning sessions when tires were cold longer and a mist clung to the track until the sun burned it away. Actually the track seemed to be covered with more of a goo until the sun dried it out. Hardly anyone could drive on it, but Shannon was usually the fastest in the morning session. For a moment, I thought about the telephone conversation with Jolit Torres and Roland after the Watkins Glen race, and wondered if the story were true.

Late in the afternoon with the help of Les and Marty, everything was under control.

As the sun started to set, TJ and Darrell went to the hotel while Augie went to visit his friend, Shannon Kelly. With the work on the race cars finished, Les and Marty covered them and went to the hotel. I wanted to learn more about Shannon's dream and the promise Grant had made so I strolled casually to the Kelly's camper.

The Crossle was covered and Shannon and Augie were gone. Inside the camper, Grant wore gold rim reading glasses and continued reading the same classic Western beneath the dim overhead light above the dining table. I knocked on the aluminum screen door and Grant graciously invited me in and put the book on the kitchen counter.

We chatted for a while, but before leaving I asked Grant, "Why are you and Shannon trying to race?" Grant smiled, "Because of a promise we made to each other." I'm sure I looked confused. Grant went to the refrigerator and held a beer toward me.

"Aw, hell, why not."

Grant snatched two beers, then returned to the table, and gave me one.

"This will take a minute if you have time," said Grant. I nodded and popped the tab on my beer as Grant continued. "It all started when Shannon flunked eighth grade. I'm not sure if it was a lack of interest, or maybe the fact his mother didn't see him much. Age 13 was really unlucky for Shannon. I still remember sitting on that brown sofa with the TV on but the volume off. I didn't know what to say. Shannon was such a pretty little boy with those deep grey-blue eyes, satin black shoulder length hair and that sweet face. Many times people pegged him for a girl."

I interrupted on that last statement, "Well, he sure looks like a man now."

"Yeah, and I'm proud as hell of him too," said Grant momentarily reflecting on his son and the past. Grant laughed, "Don't ever let him find out I told you or he'd kill me."

We both laughed, then Grant continued.

"I remember pacing in front of him, wondering what to say. I've raised him by myself since he was four. Not a bit of trouble either. I'd play softball and football and everywhere I went Shannon went with me. When he played football and did swim team, I was with him. "We went camping in Colorado, Arizona, Wyoming, and Montana, sleeping in the back of a truck. Teased a moose, chased some antelope across a prairie, and played in the snow in the middle of summer. We scuba-dived in Cozumel.

"Hell--we were always together. Raising Shannon has just about been the most fun I ever had."

Suddenly Grant realized he had gone off on a tangent and continued with the real story, "Sorry about that, Charlie. Anyway, my problem was how to instill in Shannon the interest in school he so desperately needed. I didn't want the desire for an education to come too late, but I didn't want to lecture him on the necessity of an education, and the importance of a college degree. At the time, I was more concerned about Shannon surviving the eighth grade.

"I still remember sitting beside Shannon on that old couch and laying the report card on the table in front of him. Shannon just sat there and stared at the floor.

"I told him his friends would be a grade ahead of him next year and Shannon shook his head in agreement.

"I told him he had to have an education to make it in the world. That he had to finish school . . . so he could be an engineer, dentist, or a doctor."

"Shannon looked at me and said, "I don't want to be any of those."

"I told him everybody has a dream and wants to be something. Then I asked, "What's your dream?"

"I'll never forget the sparkle in Shannon's eyes and the smile on his face. He looked me straight in the eyes and said, "Dad, I'm gonna be a professional race car driver and run the Indy 500 one day!"

"I was stunned. My son wanted to be a race car driver! We had gone to races together; but then, we did everything together. Until then, I never knew of Shannon's ambitious dream.

"We talked about racing for a while and when I knew he was serious, I promised to help him with his dream as long as he promised me something. As long as he passed, I would help with his racing. No pass--no race.

"We both made promises neither have regretted. The next year, he was on the honor roll and has made great grades ever since. But it's become more than a promise. Shannon has a dream, and I want to see him live it."

I was stunned, "Whew! That's a tall order. This racing is not easy and it's expensive. Are you ready for that?"

Grant smiled, his eyes were firm and steady, his voice unwavering, "I'd give everything I have, to see Shannon live his dream!"

I wanted to tell Grant all the negatives of such a grand undertaking, but I didn't have the heart to explain the grief and the massive expenses of such a venture. Shannon and his father lived in a dream world that for now was almost perfect, so I refused to interfere. Besides, I liked Grant and was beginning to enjoy Shannon's raw talent. Not to mention the peanut butter cookies.

Later, I arrived at the hotel. How could I tell this father and son duo the truth, when the dream and the promise meant so much to both?

* * *

Sunday morning while Les, Marty, and I worked without pause on the three race cars, Shannon took time to bring me biscuits and gravy. The biscuits were even better when they were freshly made. Grant was some kind of cook.

The morning was clear and cool and most drivers were prepared for the Sunday afternoon race.

With everything ready for the race, I took time at lunch to visit Shannon and Grant. Before leaving the BRM trailer, I took a few blank charts used for race setups, folded them, and put them in my pocket.

As usual, Grant and Shannon offered me a drink and a sandwich.

With a drink in one hand, and the sandwich in the other, I casually asked Shannon if he and his father took tire temperatures and pressures. They did take tire pressures, but they had no pyrometer for the temperatures. I explained how BRM used charts and graphs, and kept records of each race for future use and reference. The driver could guess at the proper setup decided by current weather conditions. When I finished explaining and showing Shannon what BRM used, I pulled the charts from my pocket and slipped Shannon a blank copy of sheets they used each race. I told Shannon to copy them and use them. One sheet was for each practice session showing tire temperatures and pressures before and after each practice and qualifying session including area for dates and weather conditions. The second sheet was a list of racing checks done to each car, before each practice and qualifying session.

I explained how we calculated the fuel by pumping the fuel cell dry with a small battery operated pump. We would then measure a specific amount of fuel for practice, marking number of laps run and after the session pump the fuel cell dry again. Thus, we could calculate fuel used, miles driven and formulate miles per gallon, which could be used to calculate amount of fuel needed since the race distance was known. With the information we could use minimal fuel for the qualifying session to keep the racer at minimum weight in an effort to lower lap times.

Shannon's eyes opened wide in wonderment and enthusiasm as he thanked me and promised to use the sheets for future races.

* * *

The skies were clear and the sun warm with temperatures in the mid 80's. A constant breeze prevented the heat from being intolerable making the day quite pleasant. The warmth was a sign of the heat that would continually increase with each coming race during the season. The hot days of summer tormented the drivers making races for some drivers unbearable. A midday setting for the race was perfect and the excitement in the air evident as the Formula Continentals proceeded to the grid. One by one, they drove down the grid, found their position, then backed in at a 45 degree angle and waited for the five-minute warning.

The drivers formed in clusters, with each of their teams. Many drivers clustered around drivers like Chappel, Dotson, Mercury, and Pepin, whose stories before race time were relaxing and funny.

Shannon was quickly accepted and a strong friendship had been firmly established between Augie and him.

The mechanics, for the most part, kept to themselves, except O'Brien and me. I kinda enjoyed hanging around guys like Mercury and Dotson, and telling my stories. Besides, with Tex almost permanently perched on my shoulder, I was more of a legend, with stories wilder and more unbelievable than Dotson's, only my stories were true. All I did was make winners.

Drivers like TJ, could be pleasant and enjoyable to be around--as long as they were winning. His arrogant attitude was belied by his ability to win. Some wondered if he could win without me. Even without me, TJ had the ability to race and win. I worked on the cars, but it was TJ who brought the Van Diemen around for the checkered flag. TJ was always quick to remind people of his racing ability. When TJ raced, he wanted the lead immediately and he usually kept it.

Poirier was another natural racer proving he could also win, but where TJ could run away with a race and have competitors cling to his tail without faltering, Poirier could not. He could not lead races for long periods, as he tended to make mistakes when competitors continued to follow closely on his tail. After two or three laps under heavy pressure, Poirier usually made a slight mistake letting a competitor pass. It was not a shortcoming, as Poirier recognized this, and used it to his advantage. Most of his races were won in the last few laps as he lay back in wait, the perfect predator waiting for his quarry to make a mistake. Then Poirier would pounce, many times taking the lead and victory.

Marcoux was unusual, neither a loner nor a mingler. He didn't seem to fit in and yet his racing ability could not be denied.

All the drivers were different and they all believed the same thing. They all felt they could win.

Cindy blew her whistle, sounding the five-minute warning. A few drivers scurried to their race cars nervously anticipating the start of the race. Most were eager and ready, others strolled calmly to their race cars, like Shannon and Augie.

Drivers lined the grid, like gladiators ready to do battle; the armor was the race car and the weapon their skill. Their decorative suits and helmets, and the colorful cars they raced easily recognized most drivers.

The three-minute warning sounded and almost in unison the drivers started the small Ford driven racers to warm the engines. Some flipped the throttle and soon the engines reached a deafening pitch. Mechanics and helpers yelled last minute instructions to the drivers, while some used the radios.

Poirier was first on the grid, with his lime green and white number 5 Swift, followed by Leclair in the bright orange Van Diemen, trimmed in black with black numbers. Leclair's running mate, Reckert, in seventh, bore the same color scheme. Then came Marcoux, another PACE team member, in a lime green Van Diemen. TJ was in fourth, with his number 1, red, white, and blue Van Diemen, with white stars filling the blue wing area. Next to him, and showing well was Cruz, for Spratt Racing, in his dark brown Van Diemen, with grey trim. Dotson was next with a dark blue Spirit, and dark blue number 33, set in a perfect white circle on both sides and the nose. A total reverse in colors was done on his teammate, Mercury, in tenth. Every color imaginable followed down the grid. Augie had his stripped in red, white, and blue using a different scheme but the same colors as his BRM team members. Hanna opted for a light sky blue, with black number 16. Shannon's number 44 was one of the easiest to spot with the bright yellow car trimmed in bright red and a blue wing.

The one-minute warning sounded and Grant went through the quick hand shake ritual with Shannon. Slowly the cars moved from the grid with Poirier taking the inside right for his pole position. Appropriately on his wing, for the following drivers to see, were the words, "God Hates a Coward."

In two perfect rows, Poirier led the 28 cars down the start/finish straight. The green flag waved and Poirier led them into Turn 1. Marcoux moved to second, followed by Leclair and TJ. The others followed closely, two and sometimes three, abreast without incident.

For the next five laps the drivers would pass, then be passed without much change in the racing order, except for Cliff Roe. In his white and black Swift DB-6 for GO Racing, Roe moved from 24th to 19th. On lap six, Poirier moved out at Turn 5 to block Leclair, and TJ moved to the inside keeping his position. This maneuver kept Poirier to the outside but the inside of the exit at Turn 5b, and in first gear TJ, carrying greater exit speed passed the closely knit group of Poirier, Marcoux and Leclair. As TJ came out of Turn 5c, in second gear, he was punched in the rear by Marcoux forcing TJ's right side into the dirt. TJ never lifted keeping his foot full into the throttle, continued through the gears, never losing momentum or his new position--first!

Another five laps, and TJ had pulled away from Poirier, as Poirier had from Marcoux and Leclair. Of the top six, all were Canadians, except the leader TJ.

By lap fifteen, TJ had what seemed an insurmountable lead and Poirier rested comfortably in second, as Marcoux did in third. Roe continued to move up and now held the 15th position. Shannon had moved from 17th to 13th and was directly behind Hanna.

On lap eighteen, with six laps remaining, a full course yellow came out when Steve Smagala and Roberto Cruz came together in Turn 5B, blocking the track through Turn 5.

TJ Benson was livid with anger as corner workers waved the yellow before Turn 5 and workers stood on the edge of the track to force the cars to a slower pace. The six-second lead over Poirier on his home track dwindled to nothing. The next three laps enabled the whole group to gather up again where Poirier poked his nose under TJ's tail. All positions would be up for grabs with the obvious mad dash in the last three laps.

TJ clicked the button on his steering wheel to engage the radio. "Damn it, I had it won." TJ's thoughts were on the start of the race when Poirier led the first four laps. "I had it sewed up. They can't do this to me."

"Listen, you still have it won," I said with a calm voice. "You know what Ian did on the start, use it to your advantage. He will be behind you. When you come out of Turn 10, watch for the flag but be accelerating all the way. You can win it."

"Yeah, yeah, okay," TJ answered in a much calmer voice.

Once more the racers sped single file past the cleared wreckage. The next time around would bring out the green, complete lap twenty-one and leave a three-lap dash to the end. TJ was in command of the race, it was his--to win or lose!

Behind TJ and Poirier followed in order; Leclair, Chappel, Marcoux, Spratt, Reckert, Dionne, Mercury, Dotson, Zuehl, Lee, and Kelly in 13th position. The race was the best showing for Augie, Hanna, and Shannon. A top ten finish for one or more of the three rookies was likely since the other aggressive rookie, Cruz, was out because of the wreck. Behind them, and with the same opportunity to improve their positions, were Pepin, Roe and Pollard.

TJ crept around Turn 10 in his red, white and blue number 1 Van

Diemen, in first gear, keeping his eyes on his rearview mirrors and Poirier. That was his undoing as halfway through the final turn, leading to the main straight, Poirier suddenly pulled out and started to pass TJ.

So intense was TJ watching Poirier, he failed to see the early green from the flag stand, for they were only halfway through the final turn and not even on the straight. TJ was caught watching his mirrors and not the flag stand, while Poirier watched the race and the flag.

All the Canadian boys saw the green as Leclair and Marcoux jumped Chappel, like Poirier did TJ. For a moment, Leclair and Marcoux even passed TJ and led him into Turn 1. Behind the first four followed Chappel, Reckert, Dionne, Dotson ,and Mercury, as they passed Spratt, who was also caught napping. Spratt found himself dueling with Hanna and Shannon both of whom passed Augie on the restart.

Before they reached Turn 1, Augie was in a duel with Pepin, Roe and Pollard.

For the next two laps, they separated into three groups changing as many as four positions many times each lap.

The last lap started with Poirier in a commanding lead of two seconds but TJ had broken away and was catching Poirier. Marcoux pulled ahead of Leclair and close behind were Reckert and Dionne, both having passed Chappel down the long straight on the previous lap. Dotson was closing fast with Chappel and Mercury close behind him.

At Turn 5 Spratt tried to hold off Shannon and Hanna and succeeded through the first two parts of the wicked three part Turn 5. On the left hander coming out of Turn 5b, the rear of Spratt's car broke loose when he shifted into second and over compensated, just as Shannon dove ahead of Hanna and below Spratt. Suddenly, Spratt's tires caught and he shot toward Shannon, who tried to avoid contact, and inadvertently hit Hanna with his left front tire, spinning her out. Spratt made contact with Shannon, spinning both in two complete circles, and to the outside and off the racing area just as Pepin, Roe, Augie, and Pollard charged through, barely missing the wreck themselves.

Poirier took the checkered with TJ second, while Marcoux finished third followed by Reckert, who passed Leclair by only inches at the finish line. Not far behind came Dionne who managed to hold back an aggressive Dotson, and Chappel held off Mercury for 8th. Four abreast down the straight came Augie, Pollard, Pepin, and Roe. Pollard took 10th and less than a car length separated the next three; Pepin, Roe and Zuehl. Augie's poor positioning out of the last turn relegated him to 13th, two positions behind his teammate Pollard.

The Pit Marshals directed the first three to the Winner's Circle for pictures and awards, while 4th, 5th, and 6th proceeded to Impound. After the impromptu awards ceremony, the other three went directly to Impound.

Once in Impound, TJ pulled his Van Diemen to the scales and shut off the engine. Les handed TJ a bottle of Gatorade while he and Marty pushed the victorious car along the wooden ramps, and upon the 3 inch high electronic scales. When the car was in position, Les and Marty stepped away, while TJ stepped into the seat of the racer and handed the bottle of Gatorade back to Les. TJ picked up his helmet and held it in one hand and waited for the weight to be documented. If the weight was above the minimum of 1175 pounds, including driver, he would be waved on. The tech workers read the weight and signaled TJ along.

TJ climbed from his racer angry enough to kill, knowing he deserved the win. Les and Marty pushed the Van Diemen off the scales and brought it to a stop where it would be checked and remain for the mandatory 30 minutes.

Poirier came to shake hands and TJ belatedly congratulated him for his victory. I was already beside the car, and congratulating TJ, as was LaForche for Ian.

"You did good, TJ," I said, with a big grin.

"Awk," screamed Tex.

"Damn it, Charlie," said TJ, slamming his right fist into his left palm. "They waved the flag too early. They shouldn't have waved it until we got on the straight."

I shrugged my shoulders, "You have to watch at all times, because you never really know when it will wave. At least Marcoux and Leclair didn't take you, which means you and Ian are in a tie after two races."

"Still, I should have won," snapped TJ, angry with the flagman and conveniently forgetting his momentary lapse on the track.

I could not tell whether TJ was mad because he should have won, which slightly irritated me or what I hoped but doubted--TJ understood his mistake and was angry with himself.

The Chief Scrutineer came around and ordered the top six to remove the rear fiberglass cover and pull the spark plugs so they could check the stroke of the 2-liter engine.

Les and Marty went to work on TJ's Van Diemen while I watched.

As the drivers milled around in Impound, watching their mechanics perform the task and have the Chief Scrutineer check the stroke, wreckers brought in Shannon and Spratt and took them to their respective pits. Hanna's car was towed in last and deposited next to Impound with Hanna. When I saw Shannon's car, I told Les and Marty to watch TJ's car and walked briskly to Shannon's pits hoping to prevent what I assumed would be an irate father. I knew the cost of the wreck would be a small financial setback. I had seen many angry fathers who got mad at their sons for wrecking a race car. I hoped to be the peacemaker, knowing even if Shannon were at fault, it was more than likely just a racing incident that could not be prevented.

Far behind me, Hanna watched Mercury and Dotson check the suspension damage with their mechanic O'Brien. TJ saw Hanna's car and asked his closest competitor, Dionne, what happened.

Dionne shrugged his shoulders, "Someone hit Shannon and he knocked her off the track."

"Shannon hit Hanna?" TJ shouted angrily.

"Yes."

TJ shook his head, walked away and mumbled, "Rookies are dangerous . . . they need to watch Shannon before he hurts someone."

Cruz and Pollard already dressed in shorts and shirts, walked toward TJ, who waited impatiently for Impound to end.

Cruz asked, "We heard Shannon hit Hanna."

TJ nodded, "That's right. Shannon just knocked her off."

Some drivers and spectators were talking and pointing to Hanna's car. Two more drivers asked TJ about the incident and he confirmed Shannon's negligence. A few minutes later, TJ walked over to Hanna to look at the car.

Rusty Thomas, the mechanic for GO Racing, shook his head, "Looks like Shannon creamed ya good but it's just a few suspension pieces."

Clenching both fists and holding her arms straight down at her sides, Hanna could not refrain from a groan of frustration touched with a little anger.

TJ touched Hanna on the shoulder, "I saw it in my mirrors--Shannon pulled into you for no reason."

"No!" Hanna said, disbelieving Shannon would do that.

"Yes," said TJ with a shake of his head. "Shannon drives dangerously and should be protested."

"Not Shannon," said Hanna.

"Yes," TJ said again. "If he hit you, protest his driving so it doesn't happen again. He should be warned, put on probation or given an official reprimand. Then when it happens again, he's gone."

"Shannon wouldn't do it on purpose?" asked Hanna, now unsure.

"It might not have been on purpose but he's a dangerous driver and I'll be a witness."

"Really?" Hanna asked. Now the anger evident in her voice, "You think so?"

"Well whatever, "TJ shrugged. Then he added, "But you better hurry, because you only have thirty minutes after the race to lodge a racing protest."

Hanna looked at her Swift one more time, and was convinced, "Where do I go?"

"The Chief Steward of the race," said TJ. "Come with me and I'll show you."

The two walked away from Impound, in search of the Chief Steward Andy Cobb. When they found Cobb, Hanna took a protest form, filled it out, and returned it, with the $100 protest fee. TJ was asked to fill out a witness form and did so promptly.

One Assistant Steward immediately clicked his radio and called the corner workers at Turn 5, and asked them to come in and fill out a report. Another Steward went to ask Hanna's mechanic what he saw. Two other Assistant Stewards went in search of drivers who might have witnessed the incident, and still another Steward went to find Shannon to inform him of the protest, and hear his side.

Within thirty minutes, everyone in the pits knew about Hanna's protest against Shannon for knocking her off. The only people who didn't know were Shannon, his father, and me.

* * *

I had no way of knowing what was transpiring behind me in Impound as I half walked and half jogged, making Tex spread his wings to maintain balance. Tex made the sound of screeching tires and a crash, his signal to stop. When I arrived at Shannon's trailer, the yellow Crossle was lowered from the wrecker and Grant stepped from the camper and moved toward Shannon, who stood looking at the left front of his Crossle, shaking his head. I didn't know what to expect. I had seen the same look in TJ's eyes after a wreck early in his first season. The first and last race I ever saw TJ's father attend. Mr. Benson had yelled unmercifully at TJ and ironically complained about the money it would cost to fix the wreck when he had enough reserve cash in his pocket to buy all the cars entered in the race. Grant was a very nice man but what would he do when he saw the wrecked Crossle? After all, Shannon and Grant were on a budget--a tight budget. They could not afford to buy another car like it was just a pair of pants. Mr. Benson could, but not Grant. I arrived as Grant confronted Shannon. Neither seemed to notice me.

Grant put his arm around Shannon's large shoulders and smiled, "Kinda looks ugly, huh?"

Tears filled Shannon's eyes but he managed a laugh. "Dad I sure screwed it up this time. It was my fault, I tried to miss Spratt and I hit Hanna. You can't keep doing this. We need to go back home where we belong."

"It's not your fault and we're not going back to Dallas. I made you a promise and if it was your fault you can still count on me being there. You did the best you could and I'm proud of you."

"School's out Dad."

"We'll fix it. If we don't have the parts, we'll get them. No matter what it takes, I'll be there for you. Do you understand?" said Grant. He looked up and saw me.

"Yes," said Shannon, still with his head down and his shoulders drooping.

I nodded my head in agreement, and found my throat was a little tight, "Your Dad is right, I think I saw enough spare parts in your trailer to fix it."

"Thanks," said Shannon, wiping his eyes on the sleeve of his racing suit.

Grant slapped Shannon on the shoulder, "Now you go in the motorhome and change, while me and Charlie look at the damage."

"Yes, sir," said Shannon, turning to the motorhome.

Looking at Grant, I said, "You amaze me Grant. Most fathers come unglued when their sons have a wreck. And on your budget . . . I was sure--"

"What? That I'd yell and scream?" Grant finished. "No. I did once when he first started racing. Made me feel terrible. Took me two weeks of trying to make up and I still felt like an asshole. It was then I realized how dangerous the sport is. Shannon coming back in one piece is more important than any old race car. I also realized he was trying his heart out, running that fine line of making it, or not making it, on every turn of every lap. Then I understood he needed somebody backing him up not somebody to chew him out. No matter what he does, I will always be there for him--I swear it!" His emotions seemed to build up and his voice broke on the last words.

"It shouldn't cost too much to fix the old Crossle," I said. "None of my business but can you afford to do this?"

Grant stood to his full height, and threw his shoulders back, "You don't understand Charlie. I'd give everything I have, I'd live in the gutter if it would help Shannon live his dream!"

Again, I nodded my head, "Well, I sure as hell admire you for that."

"Squirt," screamed Tex. If it wasn't TJ, then it usually meant trouble, which Tex had an uncanny ability to predict.

The approaching Assistant Steward, stepped up to Grant, "Is Shannon here?"

"He's changing," said Grant.

"Bring him to Impound. He's been protested by Hanna Lee for reckless driving."

"What?" said Grant.

"That's all I know," said the Steward.

Quickly I stepped in, "We'll bring Shannon when he finishes changing."

"All right." The steward turned, and went back to Impound.

* * *

A few minutes later, I walked back with Grant and Shannon. Shannon seemed stunned, hurt, and embarrassed. Again Grant surprised me with his composure, control, and positive attitude with Shannon. I offered encouragement and when Shannon arrived at the Stewards' trailer, he was emotionally prepared with the knowledge both his father and I were on his side. The Stewards gave Shannon an incident report form, like the others. Only Spratt had not filled out an accident report, and he arrived shortly after Shannon. Already Augie, Pepin, and Pollard had filled out reports and were waiting nearby.

Spratt walked over to Shannon and extended his hand, "Sorry about that little incident. I know it was my fault, seems like it got kinda carried away. Sorry you hit Hanna on my account."

"Thanks," said Shannon, with a shrug of his shoulders.

Hanna walked past, tried to avoid eye contact with Shannon, and went into the room to tell her side of the incident. A moment later, she walked out and moved to the side of the trailer away from us. Next was TJ, who looked at Shannon and frowned. Spratt finished the form, and gave it back to the Stewards, and waited with Shannon, Augie, Guido, and Darrell. When TJ finished, the Stewards talked to Spratt while TJ waited with Hanna.

Guido smiled at Shannon, "Hey, somebody just screwed up. We saw it. You couldn't avoid the wreck."

"Yeah," chimed Augie and Darrell.

"What a bummer!" Augie added.

The Stewards talked to three corner workers and when they finished, Andy Cobb walked out with the corner workers. The corner workers walked away to report to their corners as Cobb ordered.

Cobb stood in front of Guido, Augie and Darrell, "I've read your report you can leave." "You haven't heard their story," said TJ.

Cobb looked at TJ and said, "Don't need to!" He looked at Spratt and Shannon, "You two can go back to your pits, the protest has been thrown out. The accident was a racing incident with nobody at fault."

"All right!" said Shannon as he clenched both fists and gave them a shake, instantly relieved at the decision.

With that over and done with Spratt, Shannon and Grant went to their respective paddock area. I walked to the side where I wouldn't be noticed and kinda hung around. I wanted to hear what the Stewards had to say.

Cobb looked at Hanna, "Our findings indicated that Shannon was forced into you by Spratt. I'm sorry you sustained damage but the accident was unavoidable. You had sufficient grounds for the protest and I don't believe it was malicious, so we're returning your money."

"Yes, sir," whispered Hanna, rather embarrassed and hanging her head down, as she took the money Cobb handed her.

"You can leave," said Cobb.

TJ put his arm around Hanna, as she started to walk away, and was about to console her when Cobb spoke.

"Not you Benson. I need to talk with you," said Cobb.

The shock in TJ's face was apparent as he stopped and turned around to face Cobb. Hanna hesitated but continued to the Dotson trailer.

"What do you need me for?" asked TJ. "I didn't have the wreck."

"Let me tell you this. I don't know what you saw in your rearview mirrors, but it was not Shannon. He was too far behind and there were too many cars between you and him. You couldn't have seen that portion of the track and your report doesn't jive with the others. Only Hanna's story is different from the others but it's what would be expected from her point of view. I want you to know if the hundred dollars had been yours, I would have kept it."

Cobb spun around and walked back in the room without even giving TJ a chance to reply. For TJ and the others, the race weekend was over. Now me, I just tiptoed away before TJ saw me.

* * *

TJ disappeared after he dressed, leaving the chores of loading the trailer to Les, Marty, and me. For the first time it seemed he was embarrassed and said very little, although we could all tell he was angry with having lost the race to Ian. When they got back to Birmingham, Les and Marty were sure they would hear more about the race. Pollard was gone and Augie was over helping Shannon and Grant load the wrecked Crossle. After the BRM trailer was loaded, I said goodbye, then Les and Marty climbed into the semi-cab ready to drive to Atlanta where they would leave the rig for me to do the setup on all three race cars for the next race. They would also return Tex, since the parrot could not return on the airlines with me. From Atlanta, Les, and Marty would get their car, and return to Birmingham, Alabama.

When the truck pulled away, I loaded the rental car and drove it to the hospitality booth where I picked up a copy of the final results:

Ironically ,TJ took the new track record although he lost the race.

With the results in hand, I continued to Shannon's pit area. The trailer was loaded and hooked to the old Winnebago. I walked over to Shannon and Grant offering help if they needed any but they graciously declined. Shannon asked about the next race track, Indianapolis Raceway Park, so I tried to tell him what I knew about it. I sketched a map, showing the tracks location and the easiest way to drive there from Texas. As we discussed the best route, Hanna approached . . . with her head down. She wore white tennis shoes, a shirt commemorating the weekend race at Mosport and the brown fedora with her hair tucked beneath. In her right hand, she squeezed a shirt identical to the one she wore. Only the one she held was extra-large.

```
                    SCCA/USAC
          U.S. Formula Ford 2000 National Championship
                  Official Race Results
                         May 14
                        Mosport
                    Ontario, Canada
                     (2.459 miles)

     Car No.   Name              Car              Time       Laps

  1.   (5)     Ian Poirier       Swift DB-8       1:24.11     24
  2.   (1)     TJ Benson         VanDiemen RF95   1:23.72*    24
  3.  (34)     Claude Marcoux    Swift DB-8       1:24.21     24
  4.  (11)     Alan Reckert      Stohr            1:24.31     24
  5.   (7)     Ron Leclair       VanDiemen RF95   1:24.23     24
  6.  (43)     Jude Dionne       Swift DB-8       1:24.33     24
  7.  (33)     Bob Dotson        Spirit           1:24.03     24
  8.  (71)     Gordon Chappel    VanDiemen RF95   1:24.44     24
  9.   (8)     Freddy Mercury    Reynard 95F      1:24.32     24
 10.  (47)     Darrell Pollard   VanDiemen RF95   1:24.53     24
 11.  (54)     Guido Pepin       Swift DB-8       1:24.61     24
 12.  (55)     Cliff Roe         VanDiemen RF94   1:24.53     24
 13.  (22)     Augie Zuehl       VanDiemen RF95   1:24.60     24
 14.  (30)     Bill Murfy        Swift DB-8       1:25.24     24
 15.  (21)     Rick Henry        Swift DB-8       1:24.75     24
 16.  (00)     Tom Craig         Swift DB-3       1:25.83     21
 17.  (27)     Ben Cifelli       Swift DB-3       1:25.65     24
 18.  (25)     Chase Wilder      Reynard SF90     1:24.95     24
 19.  (39)     Art Grindle       Swift SE-3       1:25.75     24
 20.  (69)     Phil Spratt       Reynard 95F      1:24.40     23  NR
 21.  (44)     Shannon Kelly     Crossle 71F      1:25.20     23  NR
 22.  (16)     Hanna Lee         Swift DB-8       1:24.68     23  NR
 23.  (74)     Mark McGrath      Swift DB-3       1:25.63     22
 24.  (88)     Barton Springs    VanDiemen RF91   1:25.45     22
 25.  (60)     Rex VanHorn       Reynard SF91     1:25.50     21
 DNF  (27)     Roberto Cruz      VanDiemen RF95   1:24.64     17  NR
 DNF  (13)     Steve Smagala     VanDiemen RF89   1:25.73     17  NR
 DNF   (3)     Will Jones        Swift DB-8       1:26.20     14  NR

      FASTEST LAP
       Car      Time            Speed
        1      1:23.72*        105.73 mph
      *Track Record
```

She looked up, then back at the ground, then looked at Shannon, "I want to apologize for protesting you. I know you couldn't help what happened and even if you could, I know you wouldn't have intentionally hit me. I'm sorry."

"I'm really sorry I hit you." The light that shown in Shannon's eyes was as apparent as the relief in his voice, "Say, maybe we can go do something when I see you at Indianapolis?"

Knowing Shannon held no animosity, she smiled and stood up straight, "I'd really like that Shannon."

Still holding the shirt, she pushed her right hand toward Shannon, "This is for you."

Shannon unrolled the shirt, "Oh, wow! Thanks."

As they looked at each other Grant said, "Shannon, why don't you walk Hanna back while I visit with Charlie."

"Sure, Dad," said Shannon.

We all said our goodbyes and promised to get together at the next race, which would be in Indianapolis at Indianapolis Raceway Park, the night before the Indianapolis 500.

INDIANAPOLIS RACEWAY PARK

Indianapolis Raceway Park

.686-Mile
Paved Oval Track

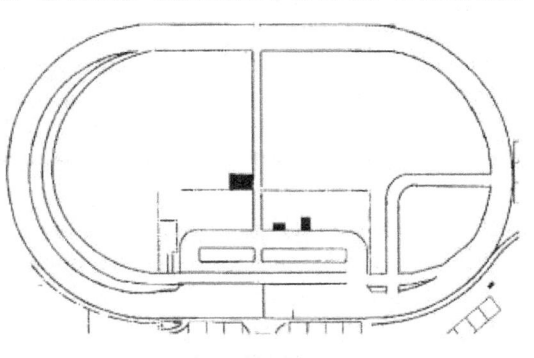

Specifications

Width: 60 feet in turns, 70 feet on backstretch, 80 feet on front straightaway.
Length of Turns: 1112 feet each, measured in fast groove (approx. 8-10 from outside wall).
Length of Straightaways: 699 feet each.
Degree of Banking: Varying at top of each turn. Declining to zero at inside.
Turn 1 - 6 deg. Turn 2 - 8 deg. Turn 3 - 7 deg. Turn 4 - 7 deg.
Front straightaway - 3 deg. Backstretch - 2 deg.
Turn Radius: 300 feet to inside of pavement, 340-345 feet to inside of fast groove.
Elevation: 1,000 feet above sea level.

Indianapolis Raceway Park, or IRP as most drivers called the racing facility, comprised a 2.5 mile road course, surrounding a five-eighths mile oval. Freshly paved, IRP was prepared for the May 27, U.S. Formula Ford 2000 National Championship race televised nationally the night before the INDY 500. Most racers seemed intimidated or in awe of the spectacle the city of Indianapolis had become for the world famous event occurring the day after their race. Like the Indy 500, the Formula Ford race was run on an oval. Like the Indy 500 the small Formula Continentals would run the course counterclockwise with their speed reaching less than half their Indy counterparts. Where the Indy cars would reach an average speed in excess of 225 miles per hour on the banked 2.5 mile oval, the little Formula 2000 racers would only average 100 miles per hour on the small, flat IRP oval.

IRP was the only race of the ten to be run on an oval. Seeing potential problems for drivers accustomed to road courses and ample runoff space, track officials made practice available to all participants both Thursday and Friday. Only Spratt had any oval experience and it was dirt tracking. Still Spratt was at the track to set his car for an extremely different type of racing. Only a few were allowed on the track at any time and for only a dozen laps at a time. A field of forty were ready for the race of which only 22 would qualify for the small oval race. Saturday morning's ten fastest qualifiers were assured of starting positions, while the other twelve would be determined by fifteen lap heat races.

All were confident, and Thursday's practice was going as
expected when Spratt and TJ came hot out of the box followed closely by the Canadians.

Shannon was one of the last to have his first session. He started out taking an excellent line and out of curiosity I held a stopwatch ready. When Shannon passed start\finish, I pushed the button and for a moment thought Shannon appeared very fast. Turn 1 was smooth, Turn 2 fast and Turn 3 excellent, but before Shannon reached Turn 4, a huge plume of blue smoke belched from the rear of the outdated Crossle. The engine had blown.

Back in the infield, Shannon received condolences and some helpful advice from Dotson. Dotson offered his spare engine but told him one cylinder was down.

"I'd give it to you but I think you'd be better off getting a new engine," said Dotson.

"He's right," I said. "Someone around here might have a spare engine if you check around."

Dotson shook his head, "Reminds me, I better start keeping a spare."
"Us too," I confirmed.

Practice continued for the others uninterrupted, while Shannon and Grant asked around for engines. They found four but all were slightly used and the drivers wanted the full price for them. TJ refused to sell the engine out of his spare Van Diemen unless given a premium price above the going rate. Grant barely had enough for an engine much less more than an engine was worth. Shannon called Quicksilver, Elite, Atwell, and Farley but none had any available, although all promised to have one by the following weekend.

Lunch found the disappointed duo in their motorhome discussing their alternatives. That's how I found the father and son when I intentionally wandered past them at lunch. I had an idea. "Look, there's a guy in Portland, Oregon, who makes an excellent engine and may have one. But it won't get in here today." I wrote down a number and handed it to Shannon, "Call Jay Ivey. Tell him I told you to call and tell him to give you a deal on an Ivey engine."

Grant and Shannon both were pleased and seemed like all their problems had disappeared with that one phone number. I went back to the BRM trailer.

As the sun disappeared to the west, I was making final suspension adjustments to all three cars when Shannon walked up. The broad smile told me everything.

"Thanks Charlie," said Shannon, handing him a covered Tupperware bowl. "Ivey was great. When he found out it was you who sent us, he asked for $2000 up front, and said we could pay the rest next month."

"Good," I said, taking a break and wiping my hands with a red rag and taking the bowl. "What's this?" I asked, already expecting or more like hoping it was peanut butter cookies.

"Peanut butter cookies," said Shannon with a wink and a smile.

I walked over to the ice chest next to the steps on the BRM trailer and took out a Fresca, popped the tab, and took the lid off the bowl.

"When's the engine going to arrive?" I asked before I bit off half a cookie.

Shannon shrugged his shoulder, "Tomorrow afternoon."

I felt sorry for Shannon. He needed the time on the track. "Doesn't look like you're gonna get any practice."

"At least I'll get to qualify and race," said Shannon with a smile.

With a full mouth I nodded and mumbled, "I'll give you the settings after the engine is in. See what I can learn with TJ's Van Diemen tomorrow. That oughta help a bit."

Shannon beamed, "That would be great!"

* * *

With Friday's final practice finished a confident smile flashed across TJ's face. Les and Marty took tire temperatures and pressures, then handed the sheet to TJ for his confirmation. Already finished with Darrell and Augie, and having sent them back to the BRM trailer, I waited for TJ's input.

TJ handed the clipboard back to Les. "Add a pound of air to the right side and stiffen the swaybar on the right front."

As Les marked the instructions down on the sheet, TJ sped back to the trailer, while I looked over Les' shoulder and nodded approval at TJ's demands. TJ was reading the car better and better--which could not be denied.

"After you print out the times, get the computer module out of TJ's Van Diemen and lets check the gearing to make sure we're right," I said, referring to the Van Diemen's expensive, on board, computer system.

Les nodded and we went to the trailer where the drivers were changing from the racing suits to street clothes.

With Tex on my shoulder, I stood beside Les in the BRM trailer waiting for a printout of the times from the small Dell laptop computer. The compact Epson printer ground out the times on the perforated sheets while the two waited. Les tore away the sheet and pulled each side off, then handed it to me, while the printer rolled out another copy of the preliminary times. TJ climbed the steps on the BRM trailer and waited impatiently for the second printout.

TJ was followed, not surprisingly, by Phil Spratt a former dirt tracker. Spratt was only a hundredth of a second behind and allowing for the error they might have, it was feasible Spratt could have the pole. After those two, the times were too close to call, with Reckert, Marcoux, Leclair, Dionne, Dotson, Poirier, Chappel, Mercury, and shockingly, Pepin.

If the times held true for Saturday night then Wilder, Grindle, McGrath, VanHorn, Smagala, Turtle, and old Will Jones, would only make the qualifying race and not the final event.

The list seemed to confirm the Canadians could run anything. All were at the top of the list, like they had been at Mosport. To beat the Canadians would be tough for everybody.

"Charlie, if I had bet you on Shannon this time, I would have gotten my money back," TJ gloated. I shook my head, "He blew an engine."

"Damn it Charlie, why do you always defend him? Mark my words he'll be a spectator like Jones Saturday night. We all know Jones won't qualify Saturday night and neither will Shannon. That's where Shannon belongs, not with the real racers like me!"

"Listen TJ, I'm not defending him but he can't do much with a blown engine. He'll do fine if he gets an engine"

TJ sneered, "Shannon was lucky in the first race and if Mosport hadn't been yellow flagged, he wouldn't have been close at the end. Just watch Spratt and Hanna Saturday night. You can bet they will be in the field for the final."

"I know," I said. "But both Hanna and Spratt have good teams. Shannon is just a kid trying to sort out a racer he's not familiar with."

"Well, maybe he should get out and come back when he knows what he's doing," snapped TJ.

I ground my teeth together, pulled two lemon drops from my coveralls pocket, and popped them both in my mouth. As I did so, Tex pulled on my right ear lobe, so I reached into my chest pocket, and gave Tex a sunflower seed.

* * *

With Friday's practice completed most drivers were trying to find some form of entertainment on the final night before qualifying, and the three elimination races early Saturday evening before the evening final. For Saturday's race, 43 cars were entered bringing many "wanna be's" from around the country. The IRP race was televised nationally on ESPN's Saturday Night Thunder, with the USAC Midgets, even though the race was run in conjunction with SCCA. The race was an opportunity for drivers to be seen and hopefully find sponsorships. For many it would be a night for rest while others prepared to explore the city. They knew they would be able to recuperate by sleeping late, since their timed session for the first two qualifiers was after lunch.

Shannon was one who was ready to party. The Ivey engine had arrived before lunch and he had it in and the suspension changed before dark. Even without practice he was ready to qualify.

The area around Dotson Racing was filled with the party racers. Dotson and Mercury, with their mechanic O'Brien's help, put together a catered meal from a local barbecue restaurant, and many were feeling free enough to drink beer. At the back, and a little behind Dotson's eighteen wheeler, steam rose from the bubbling hot tub. Occasionally someone would escape long enough to grab a drink or two and quickly scamper back to the warm water. Many team drivers and independents attended the party. It was usually free from antagonistic drivers since the party occurred before any qualifying sessions. Even Poirier and Dionne attended the event with only the French speaking Marcoux failing to appear.

After finishing with the hot tub, Cruz, Hanna, Augie and Shannon changed clothes, returned to the party and congregated around Mercury and Dotson who told stories about past racing exploits. Cruz, Spratt, Pollard, Chappel, Roe, Pepin, Henry, Leclair, Reckert, TJ, Murfy, Craig and Jones were listening to the stories intently.

Two small groups listened and chatted among themselves. With Tex perched on my shoulders, I discussed auto techniques with O'Brien and Thomas while Grant listened. I pulled an open bag of lemon drops from the deep pocket in my clean blue overalls and offered the others some. Grant and Wesley readily accepted the familiar yellow nuggets while Rusty declined. I popped two into my mouth and shoved them over to my cheek with my tongue. Tex pulled gently on my right ear lobe, the familiar sign Tex wanted something. This time I reached into my coveralls top pocket and pulled out two unsalted sunflower seeds and gave them to Tex. Tex grabbed one with his beak and the other with his claw.

Shannon and Hanna tried desperately to convince Augie that the young woman who worked grid, Cindy, liked him. TJ and Ian nursed their drinks and listened.

Hanna said, "I tell you when I went out today I was at the end and Cindy waved at you Augie. She didn't wave at anyone else."

"Aw, c'mon?"

"I saw it too," Shannon confirmed. "In fact when she walked down the grid, I saw her smile at you."

"She wouldn't go out with me," said Augie.

"Ask her," said Hanna, shoving Augie playfully. "The corner workers are having a party and I saw her when I changed earlier," said Shannon.

Trying to be funny TJ added, "Yeah, go ask her and then you can find another place to lose besides the track."

Hanna glared at TJ, while Ian chuckled and Augie actually seemed to get angry.

"I think I will ask her," said Augie and without even looking back he started to walk toward the corner workers' party.

With Augie gone, Hanna, Shannon, Ian, and TJ joined in Dotson's story. Soon Patches, Smurf, Turtle, and Moses added some of their stories. Seventy-one year old Moses told stories about races he entered before most of the driver competing in racing were ever born. A few heated arguments developed about who were the best drivers--past and present.

Ian and TJ were in the process of tossing challenges back and forth when Augie came back with Cindy. Augie seemed to put his arm halfway around her as though he was guiding her in the proper direction. He continued to pull back as though he should not touch.

Cindy no longer wore the baggy white corner worker clothes, baseball cap, and dark sunglasses. Instead she wore a pair of tight jeans, a tight fitting, low-cut blouse and a sky blue wind breaker revealing previously well hidden curves. Long shiny blond hair hung below her shoulders. Augie walked straight to TJ, and said, "I don't plan on losing on the track any more either."

Shannon and Hanna laughed, and Ian again chuckled, but Cindy looked puzzled.

Augie interrupted the party, "Hey, guys, this is Cindy, she works the grid."

Some nodded while others said "Hi" in unison.

"Get a drink and join in," said Mercury.

Dotson opened the cooler as Cindy approached, "Hey, Little Darlin,' you don't know how much we racers appreciate you protecting our asses out there."

"Thanks, but I just work the grid. It's the corner workers who save your asses when you get in trouble," Cindy smiled, emphasizing "asses."

"Uh, Cindy has a bunch of free Malibu Grand Prix tickets if any of you want to go," said Augie, obviously nervous from all the attention and the fact Cindy was with him. "The track is in town and we're going now. They have video games and other things."

"Yeah, we'll have a Malibu championship tonight!" said Dotson who stared straight at Ian and TJ. "Now you two won't have to argue any more, and we can determine a pre-race winner tonight."

Most of them agreed and even I thought it would be great fun. I caught a father and a son as they looked at each other. Shannon and Grant gave the same thumbs up hand signal I saw each time Shannon would leave the grid. Then I heard them whisper "Yeah" as they smiled at each other.

I never played much poker but the look in Grant's eyes was like those of a man holding four aces.

Everyone grouped together to decide who would drive. Only Reckert, Craig, Jones, and Henry retired from the party while the rest decided to make the trip to Indianapolis's Malibu Grand Prix Fun Center. Pepin offered his van and was going more to see which of the young ones could pull it off and to see if he could beat Moses. Moses, Spratt, Dotson, Mercury, and Smurf rode with Pepin. Leclair and Dionne rode with Ian in his truck. Augie took Cindy, Hanna and Shannon in his car. TJ squeezed Roe, Cruz, and Pollard in his rent car, while I dropped Tex at the BRM trailer, and took Grant and O'Brien with me. Pepin's mechanic, Rusty, declined the racing invitation and went back to his hotel room.

The trip over to the Malibu Grand Prix, in our caravan of rental cars, was a slightly competitive run between TJ, Ian, and Augie. Pepin and I took our time arriving a little after the others.

Everybody exchanged their coupons for five race laps and most bought five more to practice. A few crews from the Indianapolis 500 were running laps when they got in line.

Mercury managed to find two young women and lure them away from their group. He convinced them racing Formula 2000, as he called the Continentals, was much more dangerous and competitive than the Indianapolis 500.

"Let me tell you," said Mercury with flair, "those Indy cars have to go so fast just to keep from sliding down the steep banking."

"Really?" asked the slim, tall, brunette on his left.

"That's a fact," added Dotson, who moved slowly on the blond, hanging attentively on Mercury's right arm.

After convincing the women of his superior racing ability, Mercury added, "Plus the Indy teams have big bucks behind them--like Penske and Newman-Haas. All our drivers are equal."

"Wow," said the blond, who now had an arm around Dotson's left arm. "Can we watch you race tomorrow?"

"I can arrange that," said Dotson. He pulled out a business card and a pen and quickly scribbled something on the back. "Take this to registration and you can come in on our crew."

"Really?" asked the brunette again.

"Really!" mimicked Dotson.

As the two men and their new conquests neared the others Mercury said, "You know racing is the ultimate high."

"Yep," confirmed Dotson. He smiled as though he knew what was coming.

"Yes," said Mercury as he wrinkled his forehead. His momentary pause grabbed the attention of half dozen of their competitors, including Hanna, Shannon, Cindy, and Augie. "Yes, the ultimate high . . . even better than sex."

"No! Not better than sex?" asked the dumbfounded brunette.

"Well . . . " said Mercury rubbing his chin in deep thought. "Yes--but I am willing to let you prove me wrong."

Mercury squeezed the brunette around her shoulders and her face turned a deep red. Her blond friend laughed as did Hanna, Shannon, Augie, and Cindy. A few of the other drivers including me, who had heard the challenge from Mercury before, shook our heads and smiled.

All tossed friendly challenges back and forth. Poirier and TJ were the first in line and taunting the others.

"Watch and I'll show you guys how to run these little go-carts," said TJ.

With the heavy French accent Poirier added, "Yes, and watch while I teach TJ a thing or two."

"Really? Well, put your money where your mouth is," Dotson challenged, waving a ten-dollar bill in the air.

Immediately Poirier and TJ stepped from the line, to accept the challenge.

"In a hurry to lose your money?" asked TJ.

Dotson was busy counting heads with his right hand, "There are nineteen of us. I think Charlie, Wesley, Grant, and Cindy should be allowed to race without putting money up. If the others put up ten, that's a hundred and fifty. Seventy-five for first, fifty for second and twenty-five for third."

All the drivers chorused in and handed Dotson their money.

TJ laughed when he gave his money, "Why don't we give the twenty-five to best of the non-racers. Then you can give me and Ian the rest of the money."

"Good luck, because you two can't beat me and Bob. In fact, I bet old

FORMULA 2000, the Dream

Moses can beat you," said Mercury, joining in with his own challenge.

"We'll see," said TJ, continuing the challenge. "I've run these before."

Usually quiet and restrained, Grant smiled, "I'm sure we've all played with these at one time or another. I say we quit talking, and run."

All agreed $25 should go to the non-racer.

Cindy found a score card and a pencil, wrote down the names of those racing, and tried to make straight lines for the columns to separate the individual laps. Then they started running as the cars became available. Smurf, Pepin, and Leclair went first.

TJ stood in the middle of the group, as they watched times, and said, "Fifty-five is good for those who don't race. Everybody whose raced before should get in the fifty-fours. If you're good, then the fifty-threes and great is the high fifty-two's. I can get a low fifty-two."

Ian nodded his head and Hanna rolled her eyes, while Augie frowned and Shannon smiled.

Smurf managed a low fifty-five and Pepin beat Leclair by a tenth of a second with a 53.9 on his fifth run.

O'Brien, Roe, Pollard and me ran the next series of laps. Roe and O'Brien were unable to beat Pepin's best time. On his third run, Pollard managed a 53.1 and the last two also beat Pepin, but he was unable to beat his own third run. My last run was a 53.2, which brought a cheer from all the racers when I stepped from the Malibu racer. I bowed and smiled.

"Well, Charlie Pepper, it looks like you got the twenty-five," laughed Dotson.

"You beat 'em, Charlie," said TJ slapping me on the shoulder.

"I don't think so," I said, looking straight at Grant.

"No one can beat you with that time," said TJ.

In all seriousness of one who knew, Grant offered his hand to me, "Good run, Charlie."

I pulled Grant near and whispered, "You can beat my time."

Grant shrugged his shoulders, "I don't know until I run."

Suddenly, TJ took his helmet and bolted for an empty car, "That's the one I want."

While TJ settled in, Augie, Cindy, Hanna, and Dionne picked out cars. In three laps, Augie and Hanna were both in the 52's and Dionne had a 53 flat. TJ did as he predicted running a low 53 and the next four in the 52's and the next to last run in 52.35.

Surprisingly Augie and Hanna were next with a 52.41 and 52.46, respectively. Times that apparently surprised TJ, much to Augie's satisfaction as he and Hanna congratulated each otheNext were Mercury, Dotson, Poirier, and Chappel. It was wild to watch those four as they all ran a low 53 on their first run, followed with 52's on the second run. The third run brought their times near TJ's time. On the fourth run, Mercury and Ian ran identical times of 52.28, both faster than TJ, while Chappel and Dotson ran, 52.39 and 52.41, respectively. On the last run Ian ran a high 52 but Chappel came in with a 52.15 and Dotson a 52.26. Mercury flashed across with a 51.99. Mercury was the fastest, followed by Chappel, Dotson, Ian, and finally TJ.

Those standing on the other side of the fence, separating the cars from the spectators, went wild, screaming enthusiasm, jumping up and down or shaking their fists in the air. All except TJ, who was quiet. When they stepped from the cars, everyone congratulated them.

TJ and Poirier offered restrained congratulations. Of course Dotson gave belated condolences to TJ followed with a roar of his own laughter.

TJ looked at Mercury, "Well, I guess you and Chappel got the money."

Mercury laughed, "I hope so, but we still have four more to run. And after all, you said we couldn't beat you--remember!"

Immediately, Mercury and Dotson walked over to razz Shannon.

"Good luck," said Dotson. "Watch Turn 1, and that last turn at the back of the track. It's kinda tough."

Mercury shook hands with Shannon, "Good luck and I hope you don't beat me."

Shannon smiled, "fifty-one will be hard to beat."

"No one will beat Mercury's 51," snapped TJ.

Chappel walked up as did Augie and Hanna. Shannon and his dad exchanged their familiar racing hand shake.

As Shannon walked to his Malibu racer Dotson yelled, "We'll be watching you."

Shannon stopped and looked over his shoulder. "Don't watch me--watch my Dad!" he yelled.

Everyone heard. Dotson had a surprised look on his face.

TJ said, "What?"

And I mumbled, "I was afraid of that."

Cruz and Spratt started followed by Grant and Shannon. On the first run Cruz and Spratt turned high 53's. They were out of contention. Grant's first run was a 53.05 beating my best and on line to compete with Mercury, Dotson, and Chappel. Shannon came across with a 52.72. The only one to run a 52 on the first pass.

Half the group watching let out gasps, and oohhhs.

The second run found the father catching up to his son with a 52.65, which brought a cheer from the racing group. Shannon followed with a 52.33, his second run beating TJ's best.

Dotson looked at Mercury, "I think we're in trouble."

"You are, I'm not . . . yet," said Mercury.

I heard and laughed.

Grant followed with a 52.41 bringing another, "Ooohhh" from the racers. Shannon ran a 52 flat.

Dotson smiled at Mercury, "I think you're in trouble now."

Mercury laughed, "Well, you better watch the kid's father because the old man is about to beat you."

"They're both gonna beat you," cheered Hanna.

Augie was jumping up and down, cheering father and son on.

Mercury looked at Dotson and pointed to Hanna, "Is this girl on your team?"

"I don't think so," said Dotson, shrugging his shoulders.

The teasing brought a laugh from Hanna, Chappel, and me.

Everyone except two cheered the father and son on.

The fourth run found the two still chasing each other and getting better. Grant clocked a 52.29--better than TJ. Everyone waited to see Shannon's time--51.83. Shannon had the fastest time. Would he get better? Could Grant beat Dotson and Chappel on his last run?

All watched as Grant and Shannon wound around the track, on their last run. Grant came past on his fifth run. The timer flashed the numbers, 52.19--better than all but Mercury, Chappel, and Shannon. Then they waited . . . Shannon crossed--51.69.

All congregated around Shannon and Grant, asking how they did it. Both shrugged their shoulders and passed it off to luck.

Mercury walked over and smiled, "I grudgingly give you this money."

Dotson poked Mercury in the ribs. "--And thank your lucky stars this kid doesn't have a competitive car."

All three laughed.

Abruptly, TJ interrupted the celebration. "I had a bad car."

"Come on TJ," snapped Dotson.

While TJ complained, Mercury pulled Shannon aside and asked, "Can you run as good in all those cars?"

Shannon looked at the cars, then looked at Mercury and said, "Yes."

Mercury smiled and spoke up, "The fifty dollars I won says Shannon can beat TJ's time in the car TJ ran."

Suddenly, TJ was on the spot and his face reddened. "He can't beat my time in that car."

Dotson smiled, "Put your money where your mouth is."

Angered at the challenge, TJ accepted with one new condition. "Shannon has to beat my time on his first run."

Mercury hesitated and looked at Shannon with doubt in his eyes. Shannon looked at the car TJ had run, turned to Mercury, and nodded his head affirmatively.

The nod for Mercury was enough, "Done."

All seventeen gathered around while Grant walked Shannon to the car. After Shannon was strapped in, he gave him the same combination hand shake. As Shannon started the lap, Grant walked over to where I stood.

Even I had my doubts, "Can Shannon do it?"

Grant smiled at me, "He'll do it."

Shannon floated around the Malibu Grand Prix circuit as though he were on rails, hugging but never touching the concrete berms. When he crossed the finish line all heads twisted around to see the time--51.95! Shannon's time beat everyone but his own! Hanna and Augie's exuberance was like few of the others. Mercury shouted above the others, knowing he had just won another fifty dollars and the money would come from TJ's pockets.

Grant shook both fists and whispered, "Yes, yes."

"Ooohhh wwweee!" I yelled.

TJ turned away, as Mercury approached, held out his hand and said, "Fifty bucks."

"The race track will be different," said TJ, grudgingly, as he paid Mercury.

Mercury smiled, "It doesn't matter. I always enjoy taking your money."

While many congratulated Shannon, TJ immediately took those who rode with him and went back to the hotel. Augie and Shannon elected to stay and play video games then get something to eat. The rest of us departed the Malibu Grand Prix Fun Center, and either went back to our hotels or motor homes at the track.

On the ride back, I asked Grant, "You're pretty darn good. You two have done this before?"

"Well, thanks, Charlie." Grant laughed, stretched back in the seat, rubbed his stiff arm and yawned. "When Shannon was tall enough to get in one of those things we would always go and run when we got a chance. I remember when he finally beat me, he was fifteen and he thought I let him win on purpose. Not me, he earned it. I've never been able to beat him since."

"Looks like you could have been a driver yourself."

"Oh, I might have thought about it but I never did anything about it. Watching Shannon is fun. I guess if I could do anything in racing, it would be to run an endurance race with Shannon as my teammate."

* * *

TJ was the twentieth to qualify and was completing his fourth lap. The first three were smooth and fast. I clicked my stopwatch.

"24.62! You're the fastest so far!" I yelled over the radio. "Only Spratt and Reckert are in the twenty-four's."

The fifth qualifying lap was only hundredths of a second slower; but for the moment, TJ had the pole. Obviously, TJ felt the same as he shook his fists in the air when he completed the last lap. He moved to the infield pits where I waited with Les and Marty.

Immediately, the next qualifier was out on the five-eighths mile oval.

"Yes, yes!" yelled TJ confidently, still shaking a fist when he removed his helmet.

"Looks like ya got the pole TJ," said Les.

TJ laughed, "What do you mean looks like? The only two who can beat me are Sprat and Reckert and I'm ahead of them."

I interrupted, "You looked good."

"No kidding," laughed TJ.

Everyone waited, including TJ, as Augie went out on the track for his five laps. A few minutes later, he was in with a time that put him out of the top ten and forced him into one of the heat races. Two drivers later Pollard barely missed making the top ten.

I was making checks on Pollard's car when Shannon prepared to take to the track.

The announcer's voice blasted across the track, "So far it looks like TJ still has the pole with a 24.62."

"No kidding," sneered TJ, like who else would be on the pole. I could only shake my head at the cocky comment.

The announcer continued, "Only two other drivers are in the twenty-fours; Phil Spratt and Alan Reckert. The next qualifier will be Shannon Kelly. Talk about hard luck, this kid blew his engine and was unable to practice Thursday or Friday. Looks like he might need a little luck."

Again TJ sneered, "Give me a break, he'll need more than luck."

Augie, Les, and Marty stopped work on Augie's car and ran to the pit wall to watch Shannon's five laps.

I looked at TJ who was also watching. I crossed my fingers and kissed them and whispered, "Just for luck."

Shannon came around for the green and started his first lap. Shannon was doing what he did at every track the first three laps--attacking! Only five laps! If Shannon could continue to do like he usually did on tracks, I felt he would do well--very well!

Shannon completed the first lap and the announcer said, "Kelly's first lap is . . . my God--he just ran a 24.9. Shannon Kelly is fourth fastest and only the fourth in the twenty-fours."

On the second lap, the announcer said, "Shannon Kelly is third fastest." The end of the third lap, the announcer said, "Ladies and Gentlemen, Kelly is now your second fastest qualifier."

"Bull!" snapped TJ.

"Yes!" yelled Augie oblivious to TJ.

Crossing my fingers again for what I knew would be a useless effort, I glanced at TJ and whispered, "For TJ and humility."

The fourth lap completed, the announcer excitedly said, "Shannon Kelly is your new pole-sitter!" When Shannon completed his last lap, the announcer added, "Looks like no fluke. The last lap was not as fast, but it was also good enough for the pole!"

There was hell in the paddock back at the BRM trailer. I was only thankful there was no damage to any of my three cars and pleasantly enough, TJ had disappeared.

For the rest of the day and early into the evening, I worked on the last two cars to get Augie and Pollard qualified for the main event, which I did. Shannon came to help Augie. TJ never showed himself.

With the final qualifying heat completed and Augie in the show, Shannon invited all of us to eat before the race.

When we reached the BRM trailer, we found Mercury beaming and looking for TJ, "Where's TJ? He bet me Shannon wouldn't make the final event. Boy, was that easy money."

"Oh, no," groaned Les and Marty.

With a shake of my head I said, "Haven' seen him since Shannon took the pole."

This time, Mercury shook his head, "The pole. I never thought Shannon could do that. I was sure he would qualify--but not that well! Didn't he get a new engine?"

"Yep," I said. "An Ivey."

"An Ivey . . . I think I'll tell Dotson before he orders new engines." Mercury laughed, "Tell TJ I'm looking for him."

I nodded and Mercury returned to the Dotson trailer.

With the final checks complete, I walked from the BRM trailer to Timing and Scoring, took two copies of the official Grid sheet, and proceeded to Shannon's camper and a quick dinner, before the race.

Outside the camper, Shannon put together a fruit salad and made sandwiches.

Grant saw me and promptly stepped from the motorhome with an extra Fresca in his hand, giving it to me.

I nodded to Grant, handed him the grid sheet, then popped the tab on the drink, "Looks like you kicked ass."

"Couldn't have done it without your help," said Shannon, as he peered over his father's shoulders at the grid sheet. "Besides, these ovals are a blast. I like qualifying in five laps."

I laughed, "Don't tell TJ."

Shannon and Grant continued to peer at the grid sheet:

```
              SCCA/USAC
    U.S. Formula Ford 2000 National Championship
                Official Grid
                   May 28
            Indianapolis Raceway Park
              Indianapolis, Indiana
                (5/8 mile oval)


    Car      Name            Model            Time
    No.                                       1st

 1.(44)   Shannon Kelly    Crossle 71F        0:24.55
 2.(1)    TJ Benson        VanDiemen RF95     0:24.62
 3.(69)   Phil Spratt      Reynard 95F        0:24.70
 4.(11)   Alan Reckert     Stohr              0:24 85
 5.(34)   Claude Marcoux   Swift DB-8         0:25.10
 6. (7)   Ron Leclair      VanDiemen RF95     0:25.12
 7.(43)   Jude Dionne      Swift DB-8         0:25.20
 8.(33)   Bob Dotson       Spirit             0:25.22
 9.(5)    Ian Poirier      Swift DB-8         0:25.28
10.(71)   Gordon Chappel   VanDiemen RF95     0:25.31
11.(8)    Freddy Mercury   Reynard 95F        0:25.36
12.(54)   Guido Pepin      Swift DB-8         0:25.49
13.(47)   Darrell Pollard  VanDiemen RF95     0:25.50
14.(27)   Roberto Cruz     VanDiemen RF95     0:25.68
15.(21)   Rick Henry       Swift DB-8         0:25.80
16.(55)   Cliff Roe        VanDiemen RF94     0:26.15
17.(00)   Tom Craig        Swift DB-3         0:26.19
18.(22)   Augie Zuehl      VanDiemen RF95     0:26.22
19.(16)   Hanna Lee        Swift DB-8         0:26.23
20.(30)   Bill Murfy       Swift DB-8         0:26.32
21.(88)   Barton Springs   VanDiemen RF91     0:26.74
22.(27)   Ben Cifelli      Swift DB-3         0:27.75
```

I folded the grid sheet, and stuffed it in one of the oversized pockets in my overalls. Tex pulled on my ear and I responded mechanically, with another sunflower seed. Then from habit, I reached in my pocket and pulled out the lemon drops.

"Say, Dad baked some peanut butter cookies. Want some before we eat?" Shannon asked.

Just as quickly I smiled and placed the lemon drops back in the bag, "Yeah, I would."

I walked to the plate of cookies. The second cookie was aimed toward my mouth, while still chewing on the first, then grabbed a cookie for each hand. I told Shannon to stiffen the right side of his Crossle, since the race would be run counterclockwise, on the small, five-eighths mile oval. Also I told Shannon to cut the tire camber in half on the left and make them more vertical.

With everything finished on the old Crossle, and darkness fast approaching, the race was only an hour away.

* * *

The Indianapolis Raceway Park stands were filled to capacity, and the stadium lights made the night into day on the five-eighths mile oval. Drivers stood on the grid, in the oval infield, watching in awe as the huge crowds assembled just before the start of the 75 lap race. The roar from the crowd was thunderous when the National Anthem stopped. The fans were ready for racing.

The five-minute warning sounded.

Shannon, who was standing near the front of the grid with Augie and Hanna, took a moment to congratulate TJ. "Hey, dude, good luck."

"Thanks," said TJ, who was already sitting in his red, white and blue number 1 Van Diemen.

I stood beside the car ready to help TJ should he need it, as Shannon stepped to his Crossle--on the pole!

"Good luck, my ass," sneered TJ. "As if he has a chance. I'm gonna win this race. His time was a fluke. I'll lap him before the end of the race."

I knew otherwise, "I don't think you can lap him." I then handed TJ his helmet.

"What?" asked TJ stunned. "You wanna bet."

"Boy, howdy!" With a shrug of my shoulders, I added, "Are you sure you wanna lose more money?"

The three-minute warning sounded and TJ slipped the helmet over his head sock, attached the arm restraints, fastened the seat belt, and slipped his gloves on. Cindy blew the whistle alerting the drivers to the one-minute warning. Next to Benson, Grant finished his ritual with Shannon and held his thumb up, as Shannon held his clenched left fist as high as the wrist straps would allow which let the grid workers know he was ready.

Slowly, the Formula Continentals moved from the grid and pulled behind the red Corvette pace car to begin the third race, in the U.S. Formula Ford 2000 National Championship series. After two parade laps, the pace car would pull in then a pace lap and the start to the race.

Shannon shifted from first to second. The race would start in second gear at the high end of the torque curve. Something I told him to do. They would increase speed, going into fourth gear where they would stay during most of the race except coming up on slower traffic and during yellow lap cautions.

The corvette pulled into the pits. Shannon slowed and bunched the field of 22 drivers. He came around the fourth turn and started down the 670 foot straightaway in front of the crowd and the start/finish line.

The starter waved the green flag and in twos, they attacked Turn 1, and by twos, they came out of Turn 2. Entering Turn 3 Shannon pulled away, showing his control and dominance on cold tires, while TJ held a slight advantage over Spratt. Dotson dropped to 8th behind Poirier. Third through seventh were locked down by the Canadians; Reckert, Marcoux Leclair, Dionne, and Poirier.

In ten laps, Shannon was passing slower traffic taking Cifelli first, then Murfy and extending his lead to nearly half a lap. TJ expected to catch Shannon easily but the bright yellow racer continued to pull away. By lap twenty, only ten cars remained on the same lap.

The race continued without incident until lap twenty-five, when Dionne touched Ben Cifelli's Swift DB-3 going into Turn 1. Dionne hit the wall straight on, while Cifelli popped into the air. The rear end came around and slammed into the wall. For three laps the field ran at pace lap speeds and slower while wreckers and crew cleared the wreckage away and spread the white powder "Quick Dry" over the spilled fuel and radiator coolant.

On lap twenty-eight, Shannon brought the field around for the green flag and again pulled away on the cold tires. To TJ's surprise, Spratt charged and took second. Poirier moved to sixth just behind teammates Leclair and Reckert while Dotson clung tenaciously to Poirier's tail.

Ten laps later, TJ resumed second while Poirier dropped to ninth behind Chappel and Mercury.

With forty laps gone, only seven cars remained on the same lap with Shannon

Lap forty-nine brought out another full course yellow when Rick Henry tangled with Cruz, leaving Cruz against the unforgiving, main straight wall. On the restart, Shannon again pulled away but in five laps, TJ appeared to close in as did Spratt.

With fifteen laps remaining, Dotson had moved into fourth behind Spratt, TJ, and Kelly. Behind Dotson was Poirier, charging quickly to the front. Seven cars remained on the lead lap. Shannon was putting on a show and in control, even though TJ and Sprat had caught up.

The last yellow came out on lap sixty-five when Tom "Patches" Craig and Barton Springs came together in Turn 3, both glancing against the wall. The nose on Patches Swift was missing when he entered the pits. Spring's Van Diemen drifted down to the inside edge of the track against the concrete barricade. A lap later he was pulled into the pits.

Again, Shannon brought the compact group around for the start. Going into Turn 3, Poirier charged below Dotson and both cars made contact. They recovered, but not before they had dropped back to 5th and 6th. Both cars started to slow slightly with obvious suspension damage, but both were determined to complete the race. Spratt took 2nd from TJ.

With five laps remaining, Poirier and Dotson lost another position making Dotson the last car on the lead lap with all the others having been lapped. Shannon now had Spratt and TJ on his tail separated by only inches.

Just before Shannon completed lap seventy-three, he passed Dotson leaving only six on the same lap and all the others at least one lap behind the leaders. With Spratt on his tail, Shannon suddenly slowed on the main straight forcing Spratt to brake and drop down while TJ took the high side and the lead at Turn 1. Shannon made a quick turn to the infield, where I along with Les and Marty rushed to his side, only to find the ignition system dead. Shannon's spectacular race was over.

One lap remained and TJ held a car length lead over Spratt. Behind them came Marcoux, Reckert, Leclair, and Poirier. A lap down were Dotson, then Chappel and Mercury closing in quickly. Poirier and Dotson managed to hold their positions to the finish.

The tenth position was up for grabs until TJ passed Pollard, to the outside of Turn 3 and ending his race at lap seventy-three. He had been lapped three times, thus giving 10th position to Shannon who was in the pits and no longer running.

TJ beat Spratt to the checkered flag. The crowd stood and roared its approval.

While everyone exited the track and went to their respective pit areas, the top six, except TJ, Spratt and Marcoux went directly to Impound. TJ stopped directly in front of start/finish, took the checkered flag and completed a victory lap while Spratt and Marcoux went to the podium.

With the victory lap complete, TJ went directly to the podium in the infield directly across from the fans at start/finish. All three of them received trophies and a kiss by the beautiful Indianapolis Raceway Park Queen. They also showered each other with oversized bottles of champagne, and ESPN quickly followed this with interviews.

The top three continued to the Impound area for weigh in and inspection. TJ found Les, Marty, and I waiting. To his dismay, again, the talk was about the race Shannon had completed and not about his victory.

When I walked up and congratulated TJ, he snapped, "Everybody is talking about Shannon!"

I tried to smile, "I know but you put on an excellent racing show."

"Then why is everybody talking about Shannon?" TJ growled.

"You were expected to win--even you said that. No one expected Shannon to do well, much less finish tenth, the way he did. He ran with you, he just broke."

"This is just a stupid oval, anyone can run an oval."

I could only shake my head, "Don't tell that to AJ Foyt. Remember, if you want to run Indy, you have to be able to run ovals."

"Shannon was just lucky. You see who won and if he hadn't been blocking me, I would have passed him."

Frowning I said, "Shannon didn't block."

"I was about to catch him. If he hadn't broken down, do you think he could have won?" TJ asked.

For a moment I hesitated, but it was enough to anger TJ and he stormed off without his answer.

"Yes," I mumbled, so low no one could have heard me.

During impound TJ cooled down after receiving many congratulations, including two women his age, who asked for his autograph. They invited him to a party and a little while later, he was packed and gone, again, leaving the chores of loading the race cars to Les, Marty, and myself.

While we were loading the trailer, Pollard packed and left the track to fly back home. Augie returned to the BRM trailer with Shannon and copies of the race results, gloating over Shannon's time, which was fifth best, even though he was not running at the end of the race. Augie pointed to the time, "Awesome."

Shannon seemed embarrassed. We all took time to look at the final results:

```
              SCCA/USAC
   U.S. Formula Ford 2000 National Championship
              Official Race Results
                  May 27
           Indianapolis Raceway Park
             Indianapolis, Indiana
                (5/8 mile oval)


      Car    Name              Model            Time        Laps
      No.

  1.  (1)    TJ Benson         VanDiemen RF95   0:23.69**   75
  2.  (69)   Phil Spratt       Reynard 95F      0:23.72*    75
  3.  (34)   Claude Marcoux    Swift DB-8       0:23.75*    75
  4.  (11)   Alan Reckert      Stohr            0:23.81*    75
  5.  (7)    Ron Leclair       Swift DB-8       0:24.03     75
  6.  (5)    Ian Poirier       Swift DB-8       0:23.95     75
  7.  (33)   Bob Dotson        Spirit           0:23.99     74
  8.  (71)   Gordon Chappel    VanDiemen RF95   0:24.05     74
  9.  (8)    Freddy Mercury    Reynard 95F      0:24.02     74
 10.  (44)   Shannon Kelly     Crossle 71F      0:23.73*    73  NR
 11.  (47)   Darrell Pollard   VanDiemen RF95   0:24.23     73
 12.  (55)   Cliff Roe         VanDiemen RF94   0:24.53     72
 13.  (22)   Augie Zuehl       VanDiemen RF95   0:24.60     72
 14.  (16)   Hanna Lee         Swift DB-8       0:24.68     72
 15.  (54)   Guido Pepin       Swift DB-8       0:24.61     72
 16.  (30)   Bill Murfy        Swift DB-8       0:25.24     72
 17.  (88)   Barton Springs    VanDiemen RF91   0:25.45     63  NR
 18.  (00)   Tom Craig         Swift DB-3       0:25.83     61  NR
 19.  (21)   Rick Henry        Swift DB-8       0:24.75     49  NR
 20.  (27)   Roberto Cruz      VanDiemen RF95   0:24.64     49  NR
 DNF  (43)   Jude Dionne       VanDiemen RF95   0:24.33     25
 DNF  (27)   Ben Cifelli       Swift DB-3       0:25.65     24

  FASTEST LAP
  Car      Time            Speed
   1      1:23.72**       105.73 mph
  **New Track Record
   * Broke Track Record
```

A few minutes later, Augie announced that he had tickets for the Indy 500 and offered them to me, Les, and Marty. I accepted, while Les and Marty reluctantly declined, pointing out they had a long drive home and did not want to get caught in the Indy 500 crowd leaving Sunday.

Augie and Shannon caught up with Hanna and talked her into staying another night and seeing the Indy 500 with them, Grant, and me.

The next day, we spent a relaxing and enjoyable day at the Indianapolis 500, where I introduced them to three drivers: Lyn St. James, Al Unser Jr., and Danny Sullivan. I managed to find Penske's main helper and Shannon's idol--Rick Mears. Graciously, Rick Mears spent nearly half an hour of his time talking about racing with Shannon. I stayed alongside Shannon with a smile on my face and listened to the legend talk to the kid with the dream.

On that Sunday dreams proved reality for Hanna, Augie and Shannon as their dreams and fantasies were near fulfillment.

DALLAS GRAND PRIX

The Dallas Grand Prix circuit was located in the heart of downtown Dallas, off I-35, at Reunion Arena. The turning twisting street course used part of I-35 feeders, streets circling Reunion Arena, and bordering the Hyatt Regency Hotel. The 1.3 mile, ten- turn, clockwise course provided challenging elevation changes along with risky high speed turns. Friday and Saturday were set for the multi pro-race qualifying. Saturday and Sunday, June 12-13, would be filled with the actual race events.

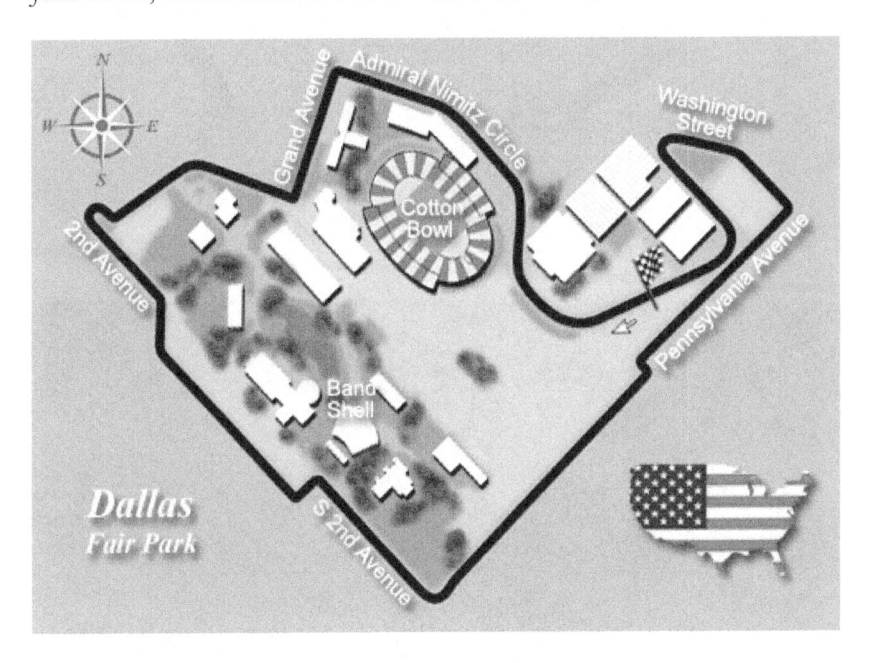

Registration was held at Union Station where a tunnel connected Race headquarters to the Hyatt Regency Hotel. Most drivers opted for the comfort of the Hyatt while others stayed in motorhomes in the parking areas around Union Arena. The Celebrity and Trans-Am paddock area was located near Turn 1, and just behind the fast pits. The grid was next to this area, located on Memorial drive. The Arena sky chalets overlooked this whole area all the way to Turn 6, including most of the main straight. The rest of the Reunion Arena parking area along I-35 was where the World Challenge, Olds Pro, Dodge Shelby, Formula 2000 and Kart paddock were located. This was also the location of the fastest straight, created from the frontage road to I-35.

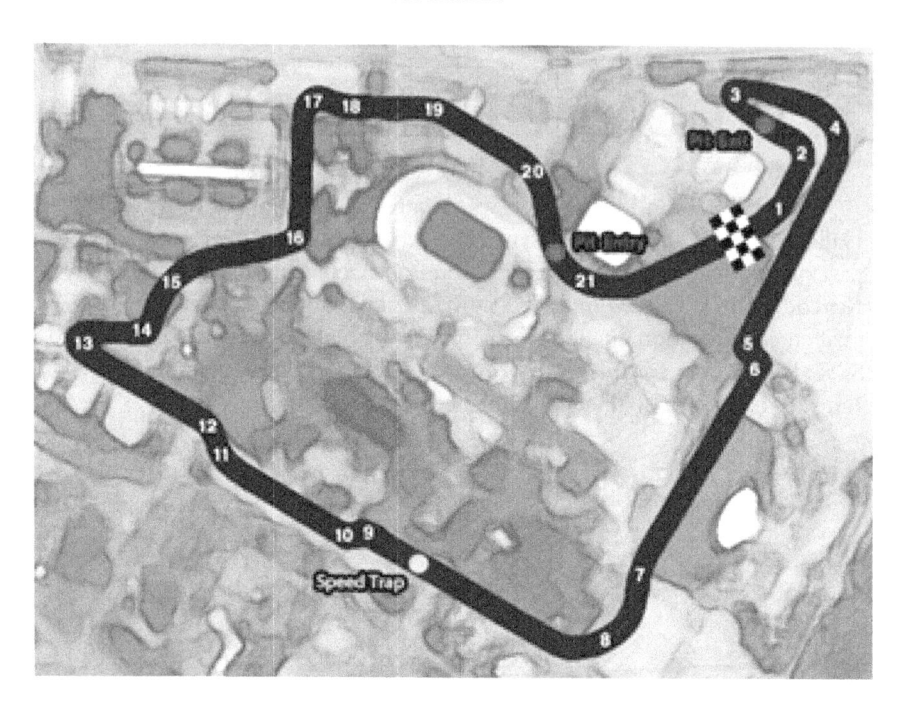

Three pedestrian bridges provided access for spectators in, out, and around the track. One bridge along the main straight gave access to the high Pit Lane Suites, located across the main straight from the pits. Another bridge crossed between Turn 4 and Turn 5 giving spectators access to the grandstands between these turns and with a view of Turn 3 thru Turn 6. The third bridge gave access to race headquarters at the Hyatt Regency near Turn 9 which was part of Reunion West Drive and Hotel Street now part of the main straight.

The grandstands were filled. People mulled around the vendor-filled, grassy knoll area between the Hyatt Regency and the Reunion Arena. The first practice session for the U.S. Formula Ford 2000 National Championship was underway.

TJ roared into view down the main straight, past the entrance to the pits, at over 125 miles per hour across the fastest portion of the track. I clicked the stopwatch. TJ had the fastest times of the first session. That pleased me.

TJ neared Turn 1, a very tricky area, where he swung wide to the left, broke hard, using the transaxle as he downshifted to third. As the car became loose, he tried to get control as he continued to go down through the gears to first, where he made a late, sharp, right-handed 120 degree turn, coming close against the wall near the apex. During the race, Turn 1 would be an excellent point to pass competitors to the right by braking late, because it was a late turn corner. Turning in early would throw the car out and possibly against the tire barricade.

Coming out of Turn 1, TJ shifted to 2nd and attacked the slowest part of the track from Turn 2 thru Turn 7. He swung wide of the right-hander at Turn 2, going wide to the left to set up properly for Turn 3, a 90 degree right turn. TJ broke early and apexed very, very, late, downshifted to 1st and set up for Turn 4, the immediate 90 degree lefthander. To lift in Turn 4 is to do the turn improperly. TJ stayed full in the throttle, the Van Diemen wiggled, coming near the concrete and wire fence barricade, then he shifted to second. Keeping close to the concrete on the right, TJ broke late, downshifted to 1st and, again, apexed extremely late at Turn 5, a lefthander. Staying left for the immediate 90 degree right of Turn 6, TJ, again, kept full throttle. Only inches away from the wall at the exit of Turn 6, he grabbed second gear and a moment later was in fourth gear. He passed two competitors before Turn 7, a long flat-out 45 degree right turn. The turn was relatively easy, unless the driver turned in too early. From Turn 6 to Turn 8, the Van Diemen bounced along the Freeway access road sending a spectacular spray of sparks from the titanium skid pads with each dip.

Pressing the button, installed on the removable steering wheel, TJ asked, "Time?"

"Third fastest of the session," I responded.

TJ continued his attack on the course. Turn 8 widened to the left and TJ moved left to take full advantage of the space. He came down hard on the brakes, dropped to second gear, then took Turn 8, a dramatically off camber, right-handed, wide sweeping turn, apexing the curb where it ended. TJ cruised through the dangerous turn easily. If done improperly, many drivers would be thrown down and against the wall. The short straight to Turn 9 kinked slightly to the left. Turn 9 made a sharp 90 degree turn to the right, but TJ stayed on the throttle and remained in second gear. The speed threw him out to the left and within six inches of a near vertical concrete wall, which was part of Hotel Street. The street went uphill very quickly at the apex. With a spray of sparks, he set his car for the roller coaster, spark filled, ride down the main straight. The main straight went up and down hills, bent left and then right, then darted into a blind dark tunnel. By the time TJ's eyes adjusted, he shot out of the tunnel, passed pit entry and had another dangerous hump, under high speed, where Memorial drive crossed the front straightaway, again, taking a toll on all three protective titanium skid pads. He passed the start/finish line and was ready for another lap.

On the next lap, I verified TJ as one of the four fastest. The checkered flag waved, and TJ took a cool-off lap before he entered the pits, where Les and Marty took tire temperatures and pressures for teammates, Zuehl and Pollard.

Friday's practice and first qualifying went without incident. Saturday would have another qualifying session, which was good since the Kelly's had tow vehicle problems, arriving an hour before the qualifying session, but too late to get teched and get on the track. Shannon would only have Saturday's qualifying which would be followed at day's end with the race.

Two hours later most were preparing for the Hyatt Regency's drivers' party. The initial qualifying had Poirier with the fastest time followed by Chappel, Mercury, TJ, Cruz, Dotson, Spratt and Marcoux. The majority were not concerned with their positions since there was still another qualifying session. I would have TJ's Van Diemen ready.

As I ate dinner with the Kelly's it was still hard to believe how friendly and welcome Shannon had become in the series. Shannon had become a friend and a favorite to all the drivers and workers and he didn't even know what was happening. And Shannon talked to all the drivers, making it a point to mingle with those who segregated from the other drivers. Soon some of the more timid drivers came out and began to socialize.

I finished dinner with Shannon and Grant, and prepared to return to the BRM trailer and make last minute adjustments on the three race cars for the following day's final qualifying and race. Shannon was dressed and ready for the drivers' party

"Here's a little spending money," said Grant giving Shannon some money from his billfold. Shannon took the money and looked a little embarrassed, "Thanks, Dad." "You taking Hanna?"

The question appeared to startle Shannon, "Uuuhhh, yeah. . . I'm taking

Hanna. Say, Dad can I use the Suzuki for a while?"

"Wouldn't it be easier to use the spectator bridge to get to the Hyatt?"

Shannon looked down and shuffled his feet, "Well, yeah, but I need to get something. Yeah, something for Hanna."

Grant shrugged his shoulders, "Sure, go ahead."

Together Shannon and I walked from the motorhome. Shannon offered me a ride in the Suzuki. On the way to the BRM trailer, Shannon made a request.

"Are you gonna be around tonight?" Shannon asked.

"Yeah, till about ten; then, I'm going back to the hotel. Why?"

"My Dad will be by himself. Would you mind keeping him company tonight? And when he goes back to the motorhome, would you please go with him?"

"Sure, but what makes you think he'll come see me?"

Shannon smiled, "Oh, he will."

I didn't understand the request, but visiting with Grant would not be a problem, since work on the three BRM cars was near completion. I just wanted to make preparations for the cars in the future and do an inventory check.

When Shannon drove away, I resumed working. A little while later, TJ arrived at the trailer. Tex spread his wings and hurled a few insults TJ failed to hear. After TJ picked up some things for the party, he was off again.

As the sun dropped low in the sky, I continued uninterrupted work with Marty and Les. About an hour after TJ had gone, Hanna appeared and came directly to me. Les and Marty momentarily stopped to stare at Hanna. She looked stunning in the long simple blue dress. Her radiant long red hair bounced below her shoulders.

"Hey, pretty lady, aren't you supposed to be at the party with Shannon?" I asked, half teasing.

Hanna appeared sad and surprised, "I wanted to go with Shannon, but he asked me if I would do something else with him and not go to the party. I told him I wanted to go with the other drivers and asked him to go with me, but he said he had something more important to do first and couldn't go. Charlie, do you know what's happening?"

I remembered Shannon had told his father he was going with Hanna. It made no sense to me whatsoever but for some reason I was involved. Where was Shannon? Why wasn't he with Hanna? There wasn't a driver at the race that wouldn't want to be with her. What the hell was Shannon doing? More important--what was I going to say?

"I'm sure Shannon had a good reason for missing the party," I said, trying to console Hanna.

As I talked to Hanna, O'Brien walked over and saw Hanna, "Aren't you supposed to be at the party?"

Hanna frowned at O'Brien.

"What do you need, Wesley?" I asked.

"Nothing. Shannon said if I had time to come by cause you and Grant would be around," said O'Brien.

"What?" I chimed in with Hanna, but before we could say anything more, Grant appeared.

Immediately, Grant noticed Hanna. He smiled and asked, "Where's Shannon?"

Hanna looked around and started to stumble over her words, "Uuuhhh, well, I, he, uuuhhh . . . I was running late. Yes, I was running late and told Shannon I would meet him at the party." Hanna's feelings were hurt; but even more so she didn't want to hurt Grant.

Again, Grant smiled, "You sure look pretty. Can't believe Shannon wouldn't wait for you."

All of us shrugged our shoulders and looked at each other dumbfounded. With their curiosity piqued, Les and Marty wiped their hands clean and moved closer to listen.

"Listen, Shannon said you might be hungry. Why don't you come to my trailer? I have some dinner ready and you can join me." Grant looked to Les and Marty, "You two come on with us." Then, he looked at Hanna, "Why don't you eat before you go to the party?"

"I . . . well, okay," said Hanna, dropping her head.

As they walked back to Grant's motorhome, we chatted about the next day's race and the series. Hanna and I were careful to avoid talk about the drivers party, while Les, Marty, and Wesley were more curious than ever about what happened to Shannon--as was I.

When we got to the motorhome, Grant opened the door and let the others in ahead of him. Hanna was first, followed by me, who heard her gasp. I looked up to see streamers hanging from the ceiling, a chocolate cake on the kitchen table with a box next to it, and a banner hanging across the bed above the driver's chair with the colorful words, "Happy Birthday Dad."

"Oh, wow, it's a surprise birthday party," said Les. He looked at Marty and both understood what the confusion was over.

Grant tried to talk, but choked up, and wiped a tear from his eye, "I thought you were at the party?"

"It's your birthday, Dad," said Shannon, lifting the present from the table and handing it to his father. "Here, open it."

Grant tore open the wrappers and glanced at the cake; then at the five of us, who were also victims of the surprise party, "Chocolate cake and icing--my favorite."

From the box, Grant pulled out a beautiful, blue Oxford shirt. Grant held it up so the others could see, "What a great color. If it wasn't for

Shannon I don't think I'd have any nice shirts."

Grant was having trouble finding the right words to express his feelings, as he slipped the shirt over his t-shirt.

Hanna's eyes were misty, and I tried to blink away a tear. It's a good thing I didn't have to talk.

"C'mon, Dad, let's have a piece of cake and eat," said Shannon.

"Yeah, everybody stay and eat with us," Grant invited.

We all gathered around with O'Brien and Marty cramming into the Winnebago's driver and passenger seat. Les, Hanna, and I sat on the couch across from the table where Grant and Shannon sat, cutting the cake and passing out the drinks. We all laughed and talked about the surprise party. Grant confessed that Shannon managed to succeed every year in surprising him on his birthday. Shannon talked about some of his father's surprises, like when he sold the house, bought the race car, and had it waiting at home for Shannon on his last birthday.

After they ate, O'Brien, Les, and Marty departed for their hotels. With Grant's approval, Hanna convinced Shannon to change and see if they could make it to the drivers' party.

Outside the motorhome, Hanna grabbed Shannon and planted a big kiss on his lips. "That was one of the sweetest things I ever saw a guy do." Her eyes were tear-filled, "I love the person you are, Shannon Kelly."

Again, they kissed. For a long moment, they clung to each other. Then they continued to the bridge at Turn 9, which led to the Hyatt Regency and the party.

Inside the motorhome, I still sat across the table from Grant. I said, "You have a heckva boy, there."

Grant smiled, leaned on his chair, and took a deep breath, "I know."

"I like the two of you, a hellva lot. But this racing is tough without sponsors."

"I tried to contact sponsors," said Grant, reflecting on his past efforts. "Seems they don't want to help unless you've proven yourself, but you can't prove yourself unless you have the money to do it. You see, when I promised Shannon I would help him with his dream, I knew that the only way for him to make it was for me to sell my house and do what I've done."

"You don't want to lose all you have . . . even for a promise," I said.

Grant laughed, "I've lost nothing. I have Shannon and I have my memories." Grant leaned over the table and looked me in the eyes, "It's not just a promise--I will give up everything I have to see Shannon have the opportunity to live his dream!"

* * *

The morning qualification went without a hitch as far as I was concerned. Not the same could be said for Shannon who seemed hesitant at best and was obviously the worst qualifier--even behind Turtle.

At the BRM trailer, I had Les check the computer once more. I decided to use a fourth gear with two less teeth so we could get more RPM's from the 2-liter Ford engine. The computer showed clearly that TJ was not within the desired torque curve for the main straight, although our preliminary times showed TJ had the pole. The gear change would knock at least a tenth of a second off his time.

I had promised to eat lunch with Shannon and Grant as had Hanna and Augie. Just before lunch, I was almost finished with the gear change when Marty came running up with the Official grid and the latest points standings.

Les, Marty, and I scanned the sheets:

```
                       SCCA/USAC
         U.S. Formula Ford 2000 National Championship
                  Official Points Standing
                         (3 Races)

         Car     Name              Car              Team           Points
         No.

   1.   (1)     TJ Benson         VanDiemen RF95   BRM              86
   2.   (5)     Ian Poirier       Swift DB-8       PACE             72
   3.   (34)    Claude Marcoux    Swift DB-8       PACE             66
   4.   (7)     Ron Leclair       VanDiemen RF95   TART             59
   5.   (11)    Alan Reckert      Stohr            TART             58
   6.   (71)    Gordon Chappel    VanDiemen RF95   MOSES            40
   7.   (69)    Phil Spratt       Reynard 95F      Spratt Racing    39
   8.   (8)     Freddy Mercury    Reynard 95F      Dotson Racing    37
   9.   (43)    Jude Dionne       Swift DB-8       PACE             32
  10.   (33)    Bob Dotson        Spirit           Dotson Racing    32
  11.   (47)    Darrell Pollard   VanDiemen RF95   BRM              29
  12.   (54)    Guido Pepin       Swift DB-8       GO Racing        26
  13.   (55)    Cliff Roe         VanDiemen RF94   GO Racing        25
  14.   (44)    Shannon Kelly     Crossle 71F                       21
  15.   (22)    Augie Zuehl       VanDiemen RF95   BRM              21
  16.   (21)    Rick Henry        Swift DB-8                        19
  17.   (16)    Hanna Lee         Swift DB-8       Dotson Racing    11
  18.   (30)    Bill Murfy        Swift DB-8       Smurf Racing     14
  19.   (00)    Tom Craig         Swift DB-3       TC Racing         9
  20.   (27)    Roberto Cruz      VanDiemen RF95   Spratt Racing     8
  21.   (88)    Barton Springs    VanDiemen RF91                     6
  22.   (27)    Ben Cifelli       Swift DB-3                         5
  23.   (25)    Chase Wilder      Reynard SF90                       4
  24.   (39)    Art Grindle       Swift SE-3                         3
  25.   (74)    Mark McGrath      Swift DB-3       M & M Racing      2
  26.   (60)    Rex VanHorn       Reynard SF91                       2
  27.   (3)     Will Jones        Swift DB-8                         2
  28.   (13)    Steve Smagala     VanDiemen RF89                     2
```

```
                    SCCA/USAC
         U.S. Formula Ford 2000 National Championship
                    Official Grid
                      June 12
                  Dallas Grand Prix
                    Dallas, Texas
                     (1.3 miles)

     Car        Name              Model              Time
     No.                                              1st

    1.(1)    TJ Benson         VanDiemen RF95       0:57.17*
    2.(69)   Phil Spratt       Reynard 95F          0:57.71
    3.(71)   Gordon Chappel    VanDiemen RF95       0:57.97
    4.(8)    Freddy Mercury    Reynard 95F          0:57.99
    5.(11)   Alan Reckert      Stohr                0:58.19
    6.(27)   Roberto Cruz      VanDiemen RF95       0:58.24
    7.(34)   Claude Marcoux    Swift DB-8           0:58.43
    8.(5)    Ian Poirier       Swift DB-8           0:58.51
    9.(33)   Bob Dotson        Spirit               0:58.57
   10.(7)    Ron Leclair       VanDiemen RF95       0:58.62
   11.(47)   Darrell Pollard   VanDiemen RF95       0:58.71
   12.(43)   Jude Dionne       Swift DB-8           0:59.24
   13.(54)   Guido Pepin       Swift DB-8           0:59.26
   14.(55)   Cliff Roe         VanDiemen RF94       0:59.30
   15.(60)   Rex VanHorn       Reynard SF91         0:59.31
   16.(22)   Augie Zuehl       VanDiemen RF95       0:59.59
   17.(16)   Hanna Lee         Swift DB-8           0:59.98
   18.(30)   Bill Murfy        Swift DB-8           1:00.04
   19.(21)   Rick Henry        Swift DB-8           1:00.23
   20.(88)   Barton Springs    VanDiemen RF91       1:00.42
   21.(13)   Steve Smagala     VanDiemen RF89       1:00.46
   22.(00)   Tom Craig         Swift DB-3           1:01.43
   23.(74)   Mark McGrath      Swift DB-3           1:01.60
   24.(27)   Ben Cifelli       Swift DB-3           1:01.85
   25.(39)   Art Grindle       Swift SE-3           1:02.62
   26.(25)   Chase Wilder      Reynard SF90         1:02.85
   27.(3)    Will Jones        Swift DB-8           1:03.10
   28.(44)   Shannon Kelly     Crossle 71F          1:03.40
   *Under Track Record
```

    TJ had the expected pole position and Shannon the unusual position of last on the short street course. Shannon had looked bad on the Dallas Grand Prix course. I had been sure Shannon would prove himself on the short courses where the Formula Continentals aerodynamics and straight line speed were not as great a help like on the road courses with long straights. Unlike the natural racer Shannon had appeared at IRP, he now made a poor showing. And for the second race in a row, Poirier was having a poor outing for himself as he gridded 8th.

    The street courses were another animal all together. A street course had no allowances for mistakes, because a mistake would take the driver into concrete barricades. The only chance a driver had on a street course was the safety run off area just before a turn from a major straight. The Dallas

Grand Prix provided runoff areas at Turn 1, 8, and 9.

With Tex on my shoulder, I reveled in the wonderful summer weather but still wondered about Shannon. The day was clear, without a cloud anywhere, and only a slight breeze gave any kind of relief to the heat. Still it was a beautiful day--a wonderful day to race. I was excited. The cars felt good. TJ was ready and the cars were ready. Even TJ was in a friendly mood and seemed to hold no animosity or anger toward anyone during the whole weekend.

Outside the camper, Shannon put out a bowl of fruit and a plate with a few sandwiches.

Hanna, Augie, and Shannon were rather dejected at their own positions. Both Hanna and Augie had expected to do better, but only managed to grid 16th and 17th, respectively.

Grant saw me and promptly stepped out of his motorhome with an extra Fresca in his hand and handed it to me.

I nodded to Grant, handed him a grid sheet, then popped the tab on his drink, "Looks like you had some problems."

"My brakes," said Shannon, as he peered over his father's shoulders at the grid sheet. "Want some peanut butter cookies before we eat?" Grant asked.

I was thinking lemon drops until he said that, "Boy, howdy." I put one in my mouth, then grabbed a handful. "Shannon, if your dad will finish the sandwiches, why don't you show me the problems you're having with the brakes."

"Great," said Shannon, instantly handing the knife and fork to Grant. Both Augie and Hanna helped Grant prepare the sandwiches.

Carefully, I inspected the car by first getting in the Crossle's tight cockpit and testing the pedal with my foot. The expected hardness was missing, replaced instead with an uncomfortable softness that slowly continued to fall until it reached bottom. Instantly, I knew air was in the lines.

"Did you bleed the brakes?" I asked.

"Yes."

"All four?"

"Yes. We still seemed to bleed foam and went through three pints of brake fluid."

"You aren't using silicon or some strange fluid?"

"No. I use Dot 4 and a good brand."

Slowly, I tried to pull myself from the racer, but in the end I needed Shannon to help. "Well, I'll never make it as a racer. I'm amazed you can drive with as little room as you have," I laughed. "Now, let's check the brake calipers."

"Sure is scary without brakes," said Shannon.

"Boy, howdy! I'm surprised you even stayed out there." When I looked at the calipers, I instantly recognized the problem. "The calipers are the problems. Anybody been working on the brakes."

Shannon looked down, "I rebuilt them after IRP. Did I screw 'em up?"

"Not really. I'm sure you did a fine job just like you've done on the rest of the car," I said, with a comforting tone that relieved Shannon.

"Then what did I do?" Shannon asked.

"Where's the bleeder on the calipers?" I asked.

Shannon ran his hand along the caliper touching the bleeder at the bottom of the caliper. "Here," Shannon asked more than stated. Now he was unsure of everything.

"Yes." I laughed, "This racing is not as difficult as many people think. Most is common sense. You need gas for the car to run, a spark to burn the gas . . . and gravity. Up is up and down is down. What does air do in oil?"

Shannon shrugged his shoulders, "It doesn't mix."

Again, I laughed. I laughed so hard I had to wipe the tears from his eyes. "Oh, God. I'm sorry, Shannon. I didn't mean to laugh. When you scuba-dive, which way do your bubbles go?"

"Up?"

"They do the same thing in brake fluid . . . only slower. Now, look at those calipers."

Shannon stared hard at the calipers and the bleeder near the bottom of the calipers. Then his face lit up and he spun about to face me, "The calipers are upside down!"

I winked and pointed my finger at Shannon, "Bingo. You switch sides with those calipers, put the bleeder at the top so the air can escape, and you'll have brakes again. Why don't you do it now. I'll help you bleed them after we eat. Then you'll be ready for tonight's race."

Shannon yelled, "Hey, Augie, get a load of this--my calipers are upside down."

Before Grant finished making the sandwiches, Shannon with Augie's help had completed switching sides with the calipers. After we ate, I helped Shannon bleed the brakes. At the same time giving him insight to racing and techniques. With everything finished on the old Crossle, the race was little more than an hour away.

* * *

Reunion Arena overflowed with enthusiastic spectators and the grandstands for the Dallas Grand Prix were filled. Everyone waited for the thunder of the engines to come to life and the start to the Formula 2000 race. Twenty-eight Formula Continentals were aligned on the false grid waiting for the five-minute warning and the beginning of the forty lap race.

TJ waited patiently for the race to start and to extend his points lead in what might become a runaway. Poirier hoped to win and stop TJ's onslaught on the points record. While Mercury, Dotson, Reckert, and Leclair hoped to take a win from the two leaders. Word had spread around the pits as to what Shannon's real problem had been. And many waited to see if this young gun, Shannon Kelly, would again assert himself.

The whistle blew alerting the drivers to the five-minute warning. TJ and Poirier were near their racers. While Shannon took his normal leisurely stroll to the waiting yellow Crossle--at the back of the bus. The three-minute warning sounded as I pulled at TJ's harness. Engines screamed to life with a thunderous roar.

"You ready?" I yelled, at the side of TJ's helmet.

TJ's eyes radiated confidence, as he yelled through the full face helmet, "I've got it made, Charlie. The race is mine."

The confidence was what I expected, but I thought I detected a bit of arrogance. Something I hoped would fade away, but seemed present even more in TJ's attitude lately. I wondered if it could be the points lead or the two victories in three races.

At the one-minute warning, the drivers raised their clenched left fists in the air.

Like the others, TJ checked the clear tearaways covering the shield on his helmet. When the Grid Marshall, again Cindy, signaled TJ out on the track, he flipped the plastic cover down, revved the engine and went to her right side. Poirier moved to the left. The field of racecars followed, alternating left and right, until all 28 drivers were on the track.

Slowly, TJ pulled the field around. Anxiously anticipating the start, Poirier pulled out, but his racer was not the only one as they came down the straight, three and sometimes four wide.

The Starter held up his hand with one finger pointing up signaling a wave off and another pace lap. Immediately, the lead drivers raised clenched fists, a signal warning the following drivers of the wave off. The lap counted, leaving 39 of the 40 laps when they came around and gave TJ credit for leading the first lap.

Next time around was a clean start as TJ crossed the hump at Memorial Drive. At Turn 1, Dotson was closed in when Marcoux, also on the inside, slammed on his brakes forcing Dotson to come down hard on his brakes, since Cruz and Poirier were on the outside cutting Dotson off. The move enabled Poirier to pass Reckert and Marcoux, but it also forced those behind Dotson to pile up since there was no evasive course of action; either close in behind each other or kiss the concrete barricade. Pollard and Roe bumped each other and the nose on Kelly's Crossle buckled when he tagged Ben Cifelli's Swift.

When Shannon was again racing with the others, he found himself quickly passing Cifelli, Grindle, and Smagala. Far ahead, Hanna and Augie avoided the pileup and now had Roe on their tail.

In Turn 3 Reckert bumped Spratt; and instantly, old Moses pulled into 2nd followed closely by Cruz. The three formed a train through Turn 6 and were quickly away from the others, with Cruz and Chappel in their best start of the season.

Behind them, Spratt, Mercury, Poirier, and Marcoux fought for position. Close behind them came Dotson, Leclair, Reckert, and Pollard managing to recover quickly from their start. The third group also formed a train, refusing to fight for position, instead concentrating on catching Mercury, Poirier, and Marcoux.

In the first five laps, Shannon passed Craig, Jones, VanHorn, McGrath, and Murfy and continued his onslaught on the rest of the field.

On lap ten, Shannon hit Turn 9 perfectly coming out under maximum acceleration, nearly grazing the concrete wall on his left as he charged the hill. While Augie and Pepin fought the same turn and each other. Shannon passed both down the straight with all but Shannon's car making a virtual fireworks display with sparks from their skid pads. Shannon did leave his own trail of sparks from the much cheaper and worn steel skid pads.

Augie and Pepin managed to overtake Shannon before Turn 1. Shannon swung to the right of both as they setup to the left for Turn 1. Shannon broke extremely late and managed to pass Pepin and Augie, then flew through the next five turns.

In each of the next two laps Shannon took Springs first, then Wilder in Turn 1. On the next lap he made a dynamic pass on Henry in Turn 5, cutting him off at Turn 6 and moving into 15th. On the same lap, he passed Roe at Turn 8 and on the following lap, Dionne at Turn 8. He passed Reckert in Turn 1 to move into 12th.

For half the race, the two groups chased the leaders until they became a group of eight dicing for positions and changing position each lap between the third and eleventh positions.

With thirty laps gone, TJ was clearly in the lead and Chappel had a comfortable lead over Cruz as Cruz did over the group fading behind. On lap thirty-one Poirier broke away from the group stretching two seconds over 5th position. Behind Poirier, Spratt and Reckert touched in Turn 1 and instantly dropped to 8th and 9th. Slowly Reckert started to fade with slight damage to the wing on his nose. His teammate Leclair, for some unseen reason, started to drop back. With three laps remaining, Shannon had moved into 10th, passing Hanna and Leclair who were slowly fading. Shannon was closing quickly on Dotson, Pollard, Mercury, Spratt, and Marcoux.

Unless a mechanical breakdown occurred, first through fourth were locked in; TJ, Chappel, Cruz, and Poirier.

The battle was in the next group of five with no clear leader and

Shannon was catching up to them.

It was too little, too late, as Shannon managed to catch the group going into Turn 9 on the last lap but their speed and power over Shannon were evident as they pulled away down the straight. The group crossed the finish line with Dotson taking 5th and right behind them Pollard, Mercury, Marcoux, and Spratt. Spratt had to block Shannon at Turn 9 to retain his position and give 10th to Shannon.

They came into the pit area and the Pit Marshall pointed the top six to Impound. The first three were temporarily detained at the winner's podium located near the flag stand at start/finish. There they received awards and TJ sprayed Chappel and Cruz with champagne. After a short interview for ESPN, they too continued to Impound for weigh in and inspection.

Excitement filled the Impound area as Cruz made the most impressive finish for a rookie over the first four races.

Hanna, Augie, and Shannon were quick to return to Impound and congratulate the man from Mexico who also had aspirations of becoming an Indy car driver.

Again, talk in the pits revolved around Shannon's impressive climb during the race. Dotson enjoyed talking about Shannon's show when he saw how angry it made TJ.

Dotson looked at TJ and added, "In fact if there had been two more laps I think Shannon would have passed me and finished fifth."

When TJ stormed away, Dotson and his mechanic O'Brien along with Mercury, laughed and slapped each other with a high five.

I was just as impressed because I had also seen the whole race, but I was a bit quieter about my feelings, making sure to congratulate TJ and Pollard, for their finishes.

When TJ walked away I interrupted Dotson, "You know what you've done is going to make the rest of my weekend miserable."

"I know," laughed Dotson. "Isn't it wonderful?"

I only shook my head and continued with the mandatory checks required by the stewards.

When Impound ended Les and Marty and I returned to the BRM trailer where we found TJ dressed and ready to leave in his rental car. Once again we loaded the truck alone.

An hour later, Shannon, with the trailer and the motorhome loaded, stopped by to say goodbye, giving us a copy of the final results, and leaving me a bag of homemade peanut butter cookies.

As they drove away, Shannon was excited when he yelled out, "See you in Sebring. I can't wait to race down there."

I shook my head and bit into a peanut butter cookie. Tex pulled on my ear and quickly received a sunflower seed.

Then I took time to view the final results:

FORMULA 2000, the Dream

```
                    SCCA/USAC
         U.S. Formula Ford 2000 National Championship
                 Official Race Results
                       June 12
                   Dallas Grand Prix
                    Dallas, Texas
                     (1.3 miles)

     Car No.    Name              Model           Time        Laps

 1.   (1)    TJ Benson         VanDiemen RF95    0:57.17*      40
 2.   (71)   Gordon Chappel    VanDiemen RF95    0:58.67       40
 3.   (27)   Roberto Cruz      VanDiemen RF95    0:58.39       40
 4.   (5)    Ian Poirier       Swift DB-8        0:57.87       40
 5.   (33)   Bob Dotson        Spirit            0:58.93       40
 6.   (47)   Darrell Pollard   VanDiemen RF95    0:59.46       40
 7.   (8)    Freddy Mercury    Reynard 95F       0:59.09       40
 8.   (34)   Claude Marcoux    Swift DB-8        0:58.75       40
 9.   (69)   Phil Spratt       Reynard 95F       0:58.90       40
10.   (44)   Shannon Kelly     Crossle 71F       0:58.50       40
11.   (7)    Ron Leclair       VanDiemen RF95    0:58.23       40
12.   (16)   Hanna Lee         Swift DB-8        0:59.68       40
13.   (11)   Alan Reckert      Stohr             0:58.13       39
14.   (43)   Jude Dionne       Swift DB-8        0:58.52       39
15.   (55)   Cliff Roe         VanDiemen RF94    0:58.73       39
16.   (21)   Rick Henry        Swift DB-8        0:59.12       39
17.   (25)   Chase Wilder      Reynard SF90      0:59.17       39
18.   (88)   Barton Springs    VanDiemen RF91    0:59.91       39
19.   (22)   Augie Zuehl       VanDiemen RF95    0:59.60       39
20.   (54)   Guido Pepin       Swift DB-8        0:58.44       39
21.   (30)   Bill Murfy        Swift DB-8        1:00.24       39
22.   (74)   Mark McGrath      Swift DB-3        1:00.63       39NR
23.   (60)   Rex VanHorn       Reynard SF91      1:00.50       37
24.   (13)   Steve Smagala     VanDiemen RF89    1:01.73       36NR
25.   (3)    Will Jones        Swift DB-8        1:03.20       35
26.   (00)   Tom Craig         Swift DB-3        1:01.83       36NR
27.   (27)   Ben Cifelli       Swift DB-3        1:01.65       22NR
DNF   (39)   Art Grindle       Swift SE-3        1:03.75       15

    FASTEST LAP
    Car    Time          Speed
     1    0:57.17*       81.86 mph
   *Track Record
```

Again, TJ had a pole, a victory, and a record.

In my heart, I knew Shannon had what it took to be a good driver. Shannon had already shown his ability the previous two races. Although no one seemed to notice, Shannon was the second fastest on the Dallas street course. The lack of money would hurt and the Crossle would not be competitive at Sebring where the long course dictated only the fastest of racers would be winners.

Even in my wildest dreams, I never thought Shannon would have been able to do what he had done the two previous races at the IRP oval and the Dallas Grand Prix street course. Still, I knew the race in Sebring would be a disappointing weekend for Grant and Shannon because the only thing that could make Shannon a winner at Sebring was a fast competitive racecar--or an act of God!

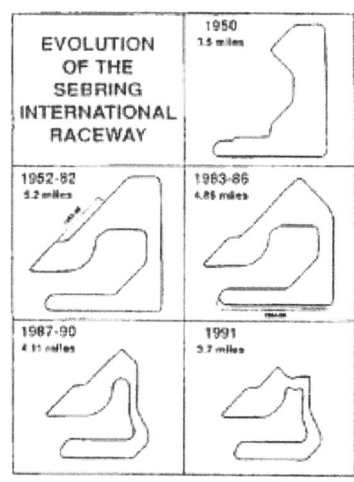

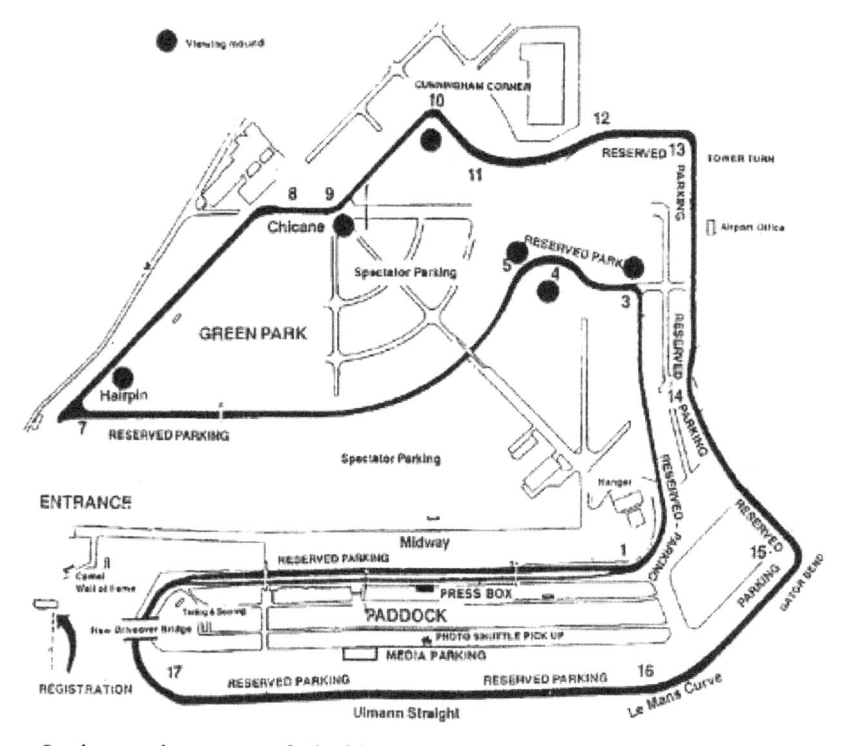

SEBRING INTERNATIONAL RACEWAY

EVOLUTION OF THE SEBRING INTERNATIONAL RACEWAY

1950	1952-62	1963-86
1.5 miles	5.2 miles	4.86 miles

1987-90	1991
4.11 miles	3.7 miles

17 turns
2.3 miles asphalt/1.4 miles concrete

In the southern part of Florida, just north of Lake Okeechobee, Sebring beckoned to the racing world. Sebring Airport worked closely with race organizations for decades to put on such races as the yearly "12 Hours of Sebring." Drivers brought exotic race cars like the 1965 Ford GT-40 together for a 12 hour marathon race on one of the longest race courses in the world. A course nearly five miles in length. Men like AJ Foyt, Dan Gurney, Parnelli Jones, and Mario Andretti had competed in races of legendary proportions. Simultaneously, Sebring Airport remained an operational airport with one runway converted into a permanent race facility, where they constructed two-story racing pits.During the 1991 racing season, the original 4.8 mile road race configuration changed again to create a new seventeen turn, 3.7 mile race course to be permanently in service and no longer interrupt air traffic as was originally done the previous years. The Sebring road race course, run clockwise, became a permanent entity working together with the Sebring Airport.

Presently, the legendary Sebring was the sight for a Sunday six-hour Showroom stock race and a Saturday U.S. Formula Ford 2000 National Championship race. Sebring was the fifth race for the U.S. Formula Ford 2000 National Championship race series. Most entrants had spent Thursday testing out the Sebring course for the Saturday, June 26, race. Friday morning's qualifying sessions were already completed, with only the afternoon session, and one Saturday morning session remaining before the Saturday afternoon race.

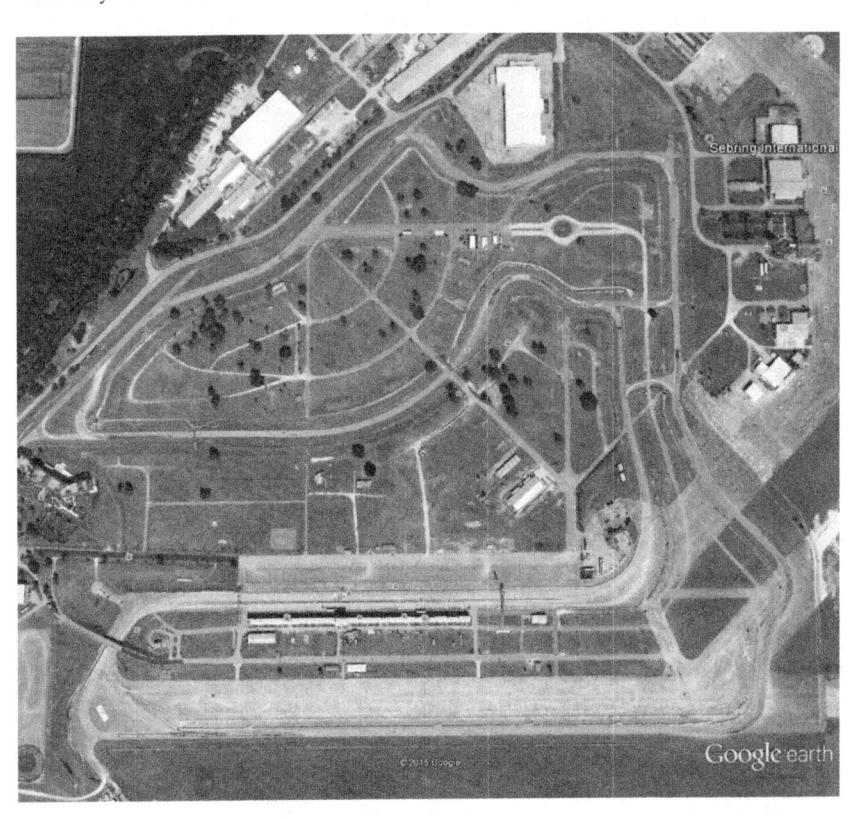

I retrieved a few sheets from registration listing the points leaders, then went back to the BRM trailer. As I walked through the pits, I scanned the printout of the current U.S. Formula Ford 2000 National Championship standings:

```
                       SCCA/USAC
              U.S. Formula Ford 2000 National Championship
                     Official Points Standing
                           (4 Races)

         Car     Name                  Car              Team
Points   No.

  1.  (1)    TJ Benson         VanDiemen RF95    BRM              116
  2.  (5)    Ian Poirier       Swift DB-8        PACE              92
  3.  (34)   Claude Marcoux    Swift DB-8        PACE              79
  4.  (7)    Ron Leclair       VanDiemen RF95    TART              69
  5.  (71)   Gordon Chappel    VanDiemen RF95    MOSES             66
  6.  (11)   Alan Reckert      Stohr             TART              66
  7.  (69)   Phil Spratt       Reynard 95F       Spratt Racing     51
  8.  (8)    Freddy Mercury    Reynard 95F       Dotson Racing     51
  9.  (33)   Bob Dotson        Spirit            Dotson Racing     50
 10.  (47)   Darrell Pollard   VanDiemen RF95    BRM               45
 11.  (43)   Jude Dionne       Swift DB-8        PACE              39
 12.  (44)   Shannon Kelly     Crossle 71F                         32
 13.  (27)   Roberto Cruz      VanDiemen RF95    Spratt Racing     31
 14.  (55)   Cliff Roe         VanDiemen RF94    GO Racing         31
 15.  (54)   Guido Pepin       Swift DB-8        GO Racing         27
 16.  (21)   Rick Henry        Swift DB-8                          24
 17.  (22)   Augie Zuehl       VanDiemen RF95    BRM               23
 18.  (16)   Hanna Lee         Swift DB-8        Dotson Racing     20
 19.  (30)   Bill Murfy        Swift DB-8        Smurf Racing      15
 20.  (00)   Tom Craig         Swift DB-3        TC Racing         10
 21.  (88)   Barton Springs    VanDiemen RF91                       9
 22.  (25)   Chase Wilder      Reynard SF90                         8
 23.  (27)   Ben Cifelli       Swift DB-3                           6
 24.  (74)   Mark McGrath      Swift DB-3        M & M Racing       3
 25.  (60)   Rex VanHorn       Reynard SF91                         3
 26.  (3)    Will Jones        Swift DB-8                           3
 27.  (39)   Art Grindle       Swift SE-3                           3
 28.  (13)   Steve Smagala     VanDiemen RF89                       3
```

The noon heat was stifling and my shirt clung to me like a wet rag. Beads of sweat rolled down the middle of my back, finally clinging to my already perspiration soaked underwear. Still, I managed time to relax before the one hour lunch break prior to Friday's final afternoon qualifying run. The U.S. Formula Ford 2000 National Championship cars would qualify next to last, late in the afternoon. The last session would be the showroom stock cars, practicing in the dark of night, to test their lighting systems. Casually, I walked back to the pits where Les and Marty were making final checks on TJ Benson's, Darrell Pollard's and Augie Zuehl's Van Diemen's.

Still loaded in the 40 foot trailer sat TJ's new unused spare Van Diemen. When I arrived at the BRM trailer, Les and Marty stood on the steps leading into the white trailer trimmed in red and dark blue. I took them a copy of the standings.

TJ stood near the ropes enclosing the racecars and preventing spectators from walking into the area and touching the racecars. He was talking to a spectator and still clenching sheets with times and standings in one hand. I walked over to congratulate him.

"Nice run this morning," said the spectator, holding a small bag which he opened and offered to TJ, "Want some jelly beans?"

"No thanks," said TJ.

"My name is Pat and I was wondering if I could sit in one of those cars?"

"Sorry, the racers are not toys. If I let you sit in it, then everybody would want to do the same thing."

"Sure," said Pat. "I can understand that."

When I walked up, Pat offered me some jelly beans so I reached into the bag and took a couple of pieces. Pat looked at the racecars then walked slowly down the rope in front of the cars, leaving TJ and me alone.

"Everyone wants to sit in the racecars," complained TJ with a sneer as he unfolded the current standings and studied them carefully.

"Congratulations, TJ, looks like another pole position," I said.

"Yeah," said TJ not looking up. "Ian's a half second behind and the others are more than a second off the pace. After the race tomorrow, I'll have over a hundred and forty points."

I looked at the sheet, "If you win."

TJ laughed and dropped his hand with the sheets clenched tightly and looked at me, "Who could beat me?"

"Well, Ian for one. Don't count out, Mercury, Dotson, Leclair and Marcoux. Even Shannon might one day," I added with a shrug.

"Get real, Charlie. Shannon can't win in that Crossle. It's a piece of crap."

"You were the one who said he couldn't finish higher than fifteenth in that piece of crap. In four races, Shannon has managed to finish tenth twice."

"Just luck," TJ sneered. "Even if the ones you mentioned could beat me, I'd finish with more than 270 points and break the previous record of 230."

Again, I made quick calculations, "That would be a second in the rest of the races."

"You think I can't do it?"

"Oh, you can," I said. "Being realistic, I doubt it, but I guess it would take a miracle to beat you." "Well, you'll see."

"I'm going over to Grant's and have lunch," I said, then started to walk away.

"You spend too much time with Shannon and his father. I suppose Hanna will be there?"

I stopped and spun around, "Listen, Squirt, I'll eat where I want and do what I want with my time. As long as your car is ready, I don't want to hear a thing. As far as Hanna is concerned, why don't you ask her?"

Knowing Hanna was a sore subject with TJ, I walked away. Hanna was one of the few races TJ had ever lost, either in a car or with another woman. Yet Shannon seemed to have won Hanna's attention over TJ's.

When I arrived at the Winnebago, the overhead car cover was rolled out over the old Crossle, protecting it from the intense summer heat, waiting for the day's final session of qualification. I received the customary greeting from Grant, who stopped cooking on the barbecue pit and opened the old Styrofoam cooler and quickly offered me a cola. Inside the camper, Shannon and Hanna were preparing a salad and baked potatoes. "Hey, Shannon," I yelled. "What happened to you in qualifying today? I think you're about 20th."

"Yeah," frowned Shannon. "My throttle wasn't completely engaged so I didn't have full power but it's fixed now. Hopefully, I can move up in this afternoon's practice."

"What a shame," I said.

Grant flipped the top on the small barrel-sized barbecue pit back and slowly picked the sizzling sausage and steak from the charcoal fire and placed the meat on a plastic plate. The hickory smoke mixed with the sumptuous smells of sausage and steak made my mouth water. I was ready to eat.

"Boy, you can really cook," I said as I stepped into the trailer. I asked Shannon, "Hey, where's your old Suzuki?"

"Rear-end trouble. Dad left it in Avon Park. Suppose to pick it up Saturday so we can roll out of here Sunday," said Shannon.

"Avon Park is kinda far away. You shoulda let me see it," I interjected.

"You've done enough for us," said Grant. He climbed into the camper with the plate of meat in one hand.

"Aw, hell, I haven't done anything I didn't want to do," I said. "You better get it early Saturday, so you'll be back here for the race tomorrow."

Grant smiled, "I wouldn't miss Shannon's race for anything in this world."

"Got a car?" I asked.

Hanna spoke up, "Grant is going to use my rent car. It has a hitch and can pull the Samurai back."

Everyone sat inside at the fold out table. Shannon, dressed in shorts and a T-shirt, switched on the radio, and they began to eat.

"Congratulations on TJ's times," said Shannon. "He looks awesome."

He held an empty glass of ice tea, occasionally taking a piece of ice out and sucking on it.

"Yeah, it would take an act of God to beat TJ," I said.

As though in answer to my statement, the wind suddenly picked up and the temperature dropped. I twisted my head and glanced out the side window in the camper. In the distance, ominous dark clouds rolled lazily toward the race track.

"I thought the front wasn't supposed to roll in until Sunday?" said Grant. He stood and quickly tuned in the weather band.

The radio disc jockey on the air warned of a front moving across southern Florida earlier than first thought due to two hot air masses colliding . He warned the front would be followed with moderate to severe thunderstorms, which would end quickly and be through before sunrise Saturday.

In the distance, lightning flashed and a dozen seconds passed before thunder rumbled across Sebring. Tiny droplets of rain stirred dust from the asphalt and the winds stopped. Before we finished eating, a steady rain started to fall. Shannon and Grant cranked the storm side windows half closed. When the meal was finished, Grant and I stepped from the camper to watch the rain. Grant offered me a yellow raincoat which I readily accepted and hurriedly slipped on.

"Better prepare for a wet qualifying," I yelled to Shannon who was still in the camper with Hanna.

Shannon smiled, nodded to me and waved. "Good luck."

As I sloshed through the rain, I could hardly repress a smile. "I'll need more than luck," I thought, because I knew of TJ's intense hatred of rain. Only twice in the last two years had TJ driven in the rain. Both times, Ian Poirier, the "Rainman," had been the victor, almost lapping the entire field in both races. Always, I had wanted to know if TJ's hatred--no, his intense fear of racing in the rain was justified. In both rain races, TJ had failed to complete even the first lap coming away with two DNF's. The first time, TJ went off the track and got stuck. The second time, he was involved in a mishap on the fourth turn of the first lap.

To be a good racer, a driver must face the elements and the unknown. Rain was part of racing, so inevitably races would undoubtedly be run in the rain. If not the race, at least the qualification would offer to test TJ's fear in rain.

When I arrived, I found TJ pacing nervously beneath the huge cover, attached to the long racing trailer. Already, TJ had forced Les and Marty to put his Van Diemen on jack stands, with rain tires in position and the locking lugs loose. Dry slicks lay beneath each rain tire, should the rains abate or completely stop. Now it was a waiting game, to see which would be used should the rain stop. If the rain stopped, would there still be enough rain on the track to warrant rain tires? Surely at best only a judgmental call but if the rains continued, there would be only one choice--grooved racing rain tires.

Les and Marty made no effort to change Zuehl's or Pollard's tires, as both men sat calmly beneath the protective cover waiting. TJ paced nervously about. Augie read a book and Darrell watched the rain while he sipped on a coke and ate an apple.

"Well, what do you boys want?" I asked.

"Looks like rains," said Pollard.

"They said it would be like this all day," said Augie. "Better give me rains too. TJ, can I follow you in the rain?" Poor Augie he had no way of knowing it would be easier for TJ to follow him.

"I don't have time. Find somebody else to take care of you Augie. I have a series to win and I don't have time for this BS," TJ hissed.

"Do you want rains?" I asked TJ.

"It doesn't matter," snapped TJ. "I've already got the pole. Besides, it will stop in the morning."

"Maybe, but you need time in the rain, and I want to see what effect the rain will have on the Van Diemen."

TJ stormed up the steps and into the dressing area which was at the far front of the tractor trailer to change into his race suit.

"Touchy, touchy," I whispered.

Tex spread his wings in a defensive maneuver and squawked, "Squirt!"

I wanted to see all right. I wanted to see how TJ handled the rain--but more than watching TJ, I wanted to see Shannon in the rain. I wanted confirmation on Jolit Torres's story about Shannon Kelly in the rain! I glanced at my watch. In another hour, I would have the answer. Even if there were problems, TJ still had the backup car, with still another qualifying round Saturday morning.

TJ was so rattled and nervous, I sent Les and Marty ahead with Augie and Darrell. When I arrived at the grid, the cars were rolling out on the track for qualifying. I was angry but didn't show it. I wanted to see Shannon--to look him in the eyes and see his reaction to the current situation. All I saw in TJ were the eyes of a frightened child. TJ was so nervous he forgot to put his gloves on. When he fastened the five point harness, he forgot the shoulder straps. Calmly, I handed TJ the gloves. As TJ slid the gloves on, I fastened the shoulder belts.

Les and Marty waited for me, and together we walked to the pits where we had the timing set up on the second floor. From our vantage point, we could see the back straight, the turn leading onto the main straight, and across to where the hairpin turned and led into the esses. On race day, the vision of the track would be obscured with more than 100,000 spectators. It would turn Sebring not only into a race but make it a "happening."

The morning qualifying was run in the 2:07's to 2:09's, but the wet track would slow the afternoon times into the high 2:20's and 2:30's. Marty sat behind the laptop, where each car was programmed into a timer. And at the sessions end, he would print them out. I took a hand held timer for my personal use and timed, Ian, TJ, Dotson, Mercury, and Shannon.

Without completing the first lap, Ben Cifelli came in with no time. After the first lap, Rick Henry, Cliff Roe, and Chase Wilder were off the track and stuck in the mud. Excitedly, I checked my stopwatch and found TJ was running 2:36's and appeared to be one of the slowest. Like I guessed Ian, Dotson, and Mercury dropped down to 2:29, then 2:28, but no one else dropped below 2:30. I was disappointed when Shannon could only manage a 2:31 and appeared to struggle with the old Crossle. Ian continued to cut seconds off his time finally reaching 2:26. A far cry from the 2:07's during the dry session but nearly two seconds faster than anyone else in the rain--and almost six seconds faster than Shannon. TJ was the slowest excluding the four drivers with no time.

At session's end, I made Marty wait and print the times. I checked the times and they were close to mine. The computer printed out the fast lap in the rain and listed their positions. It was Ian followed closely by Mercury and Dotson. Shannon was in 12th position followed by Augie and Hanna. For this session TJ was--"at the back of the bus." But qualifying was based on the fastest time--which was Saturday morning's dry time in the 2:07's and 2:09's.

As Les, Marty, and I walked down to the arriving cars in the hot pits, Pollard and Zuehl were waiting. Shannon and many other drivers had already passed and returned to their paddock area.

While we made the routine checks, three wreckers passed either pulling or carrying Henry, Roe, and Wilder's cars. All three cars lacked the all-important treaded rain tires, an obvious reason for their inability to complete a single lap.

TJ hurried to the trailer while I took time to talk to Pollard and Zuehl.

Augie was the last I talked to. Augie's eyes were bright, like a kid with a new toy as he waved his hands in the air, "You shoulda seen it, Charlie, cars were going everywhere. Man, the car felt great. You shoulda seen Shannon. He could barely keep his car on the track. He waved me to follow him and

Hanna. I didn't realize it was so different in the rain. But my car handled a hell of a lot better than Shannon's." Augie smiled, "I can go even faster in the rain--I know it."

"Whoa, Augie. There'll be another day in the rain." Then I asked, "Why do you think Shannon was having problems?"

Augie was still excited from his ride but he took a moment to reflect, "I don't know." Again, Augie smiled as he started his car, "I hope it rains tomorrow."

For me it didn't matter. If it rained, TJ would be hell to be around, and Ian would most probably win. False visions had filled my mind, but I found an ache in my throat I refused to acknowledge. Visions of the natural driver I expected to see flash through the rain failed to appear--where was the racer I had anticipated? At best, Shannon was just average in the rain. What had happened to Shannon Kelly?

At the BRM trailer, I was happy to find no damage and quickly set the racers for the next morning, leaving the rain tires in place. A change that would be made easier when the rains stopped in the morning.

Inside the trailer, I could hear TJ yelling obscenities at Les and berating Augie and Darrell as they changed. "It will be different tomorrow when the rain stops--you'll see!" snapped TJ.

Immediately, TJ stormed from the trailer, leaving the others behind, found his rental car and quickly departed to the motel for a hot shower and dinner. Les and Marty walked from the trailer and did some final checks on the cars.

"He's an asshole," Les said to Marty.

Marty laughed, "TJ's the only guy I know with PMS."

I laughed inwardly, and continued to listen to the two boys release the anger out of their system. Someone called my name, and I looked over my shoulder to see Shannon.

"Hey, Charlie, you wanna come over and have some popcorn and marshmallows and watch the rain?" Shannon asked.

"No gourmet meals?" I asked.

"Well, no," said Shannon, almost dejectedly.

"Just kidding Shannon, I wouldn't miss it for the world. 'Sides I need to bring back your raincoat."

Augie stepped from the trailer.

"Hey, Dude, what's happening?" asked Shannon as he greeted Augie with a smile and a high five. He then extended the same friendly invitation, which Augie accepted. Augie retrieved his rain coat, and as he started to leave he looked at me and sighed. "Man, TJ and Shannon are different as night and day."

"Boy, howdy," I said, scratching my neck.

A few minutes later, I put on my raincoat. With Shannon's raincoat tucked under my arm, I aimed myself for the impromptu party. When I arrived, the festivities were in full swing. Guido Pepin, Mercury, Augie, Darrell, and Hanna were already there along with Moses, Turtle, and Patches who were talking to Grant. The old Crossle was covered, and pushed to the side of the trailer, with dry racing tires already mounted for the following day.

Grant popped the tab on a beer and gave it to me, "He did very good today, don't you think?"

"Yep," I said, trying to hide my disappointment. "Driving in the rain is pretty tough."

Somehow, Freddy Mercury managed to find a couple of young women, and when Shannon tuned his radio to a local station, many were soon dancing beneath the cover that was used for the racer.

Dotson walked over to me and Grant. "Did you see a spectator today who was giving jelly beans away? Seems like he went past a lot of our pits. Nice guy. Wanted to sit in our car."

I nodded, "Yep, but TJ ran him off."

"His name is Pat," said Grant. "Shannon let him sit in his car."

"We let him in, too," said Dotson. "Seemed harmless. Besides, if a fan is persistent, you gotta remember they back the series. Besides, I like jelly beans . . . except for those black ones."

We laughed about the incident and talked about the next day's race.

A few hours later with everyone gone, Shannon walked Hanna to her car, so she could return to her hotel. Grant turned the radio's volume down, and he and I made ourselves comfortable beneath the camper's roll-out cover. The relatively light rains continued without any sign of abating.

Shannon came back a little later and walked beneath the cover where Grant and I sat enjoying cold beers. A weather bulletin blared across the radio: "The front has stalled over Florida and will continue until late Sunday. Expect the same continuous rains until then. Watch for flooding in low lying areas, which could hamper travel on local highways."

I jumped to my feet, "Wheweee--gonna be one really pissed- off rich kid in the morning." Pointing to the old Crossle, I laughed, "Hey, Shannon, you better put your rains back on."

Shannon looked confused and shook his head, "They are on."

"No, no, no," I said, while rubbing my head with my right hand. "The tires you used today."

Grant had the same confused look as Shannon, "Those are the tires we used today."

I couldn't believe what I was hearing and gasped, "You couldn't have run on those!"

Shannon and Grant nodded as though embarrassed.

It was like someone had hit me hard in the gut, and I staggered back.

"Where are your rains?"

"We don't have any," said Grant.

Suddenly, my mind started to spin when I realized what Shannon had accomplished in the rain using slicks. "We got to get Shannon some rains!" I yelled, thinking about grooved racing tires.

Grant looked down, "I don't have any money with me."

"Never mind," I said, with an ever confident take charge attitude. "We'll hang in there Grant. We'll do something. I'll be back in a minute."

Without so much as a glance back, I raced to the Goodyear truck, but it was closed. I returned to Grant and Shannon who were busily cleaning party remnants. I took Shannon to the side and into the trailer. Inside, I found a set of four steel rims. Then, I ordered Shannon to take the steel rims to the Goodyear trailer first thing in the morning and have rain tires mounted, quickly explaining I had just gotten it okayed with Goodyear, since Goodyear didn't want any competitor in a dangerous situation just because of financial problems. Of course Shannon asked why the steel rims and not the lightweight magnesium rims, and I explained the steel rims were as much as ten pounds heavier, and the added weight would help give traction in the rain. With Shannon satisfied, I said goodbye, and went to my hotel.

I was so excited, I could hardly sleep. I called Les and Marty telling them not to get me in the morning because I would return to the track early. Finally, I forced myself to sleep.

* * *

My internal alarm sounded thirty minutes before the call from the desk. I danced a little jig when I opened the curtains and saw the rain still coming down. When I went to the front desk and asked the manager about the weather, she apologized for the fact that it would not stop until Sunday. They looked at me rather strange when I slapped the counter with my hand and yelled out, "Great!"

* * *

When Carl Law arrived at the Goodyear trailer, he found me patiently waiting, sipping coffee from a Styrofoam cup, while rain rolled from the bright yellow raincoat.

"Kinda in a hurry, aren't ya?" Carl asked.

I almost pushed Carl inside, "What's it worth to you to see the best race you've ever seen."

"Are you crazy, Charlie?"

"No, I need four rain tires."

"I'll put 'em on the bill."

"They're not for me. They're for Shannon Kelly."

"Hey, Shannon's a nice kid, but I can't extend credit."

"You give a set to the winner?"

"You're crazy, Charlie."

"Look, I don't have any money with me, and I don't want it billed to BRM," I said. "Tell you what, if he doesn't win . . . I'll pay you double. But no one knows about our deal."

Carl smiled, "The kid is going against "The Rainman." I've seen a lot of drivers try, and none can come close to Poirier in the rain. Are you sure, Charlie?"

"Dead sure!" I said, the confidence in my words evident.

"Durn you, Charlie," said Carl shaking his head. "Oh, all right. Tell you what, if Kelly can give Poirier a run for his money, I'll chunk in another set of race tires."

Suddenly, I was reaching across and kissing Carl, "You're a sweetheart."

"Charlie, if you do that again, I'm gonna start charging you double for tires," said Carl wiping his face with a wet sleeve. "Now, get outa here you crazy old fool."

Things weren't finished yet. I raced to the media room to find sports writer Jolit Torres. Quickly, I told her the story and said if she wanted a personal interest story--watch the race. On the way back to the BRM trailer, I passed Shannon rolling back two rain tires.

"Any trouble?" I asked.

"No," said Shannon with a smile as tears filled his eyes. "I don't know how you did it . . . but thanks, Charlie, . . . I wish I could tell you what it means to me and my Dad."

"Aw, shut-up," I said, with a smile, suddenly wiping my eyes. For a moment, I managed to control himself. "Oh, go full soft on your shocks and let out the sway bars . . . and kick some ass for your old man today."

The sparkle returned to Shannon's eyes, "No problem."

"Good luck," I said. "Gotta go take care of TJ now."

Before I reached BRM's trailer, I could hear Tex yelling "Squirt." Squirt was dishing out more hell than any woman I had ever heard of on PMS.

"Shut that damn bird up, before I do," snapped TJ when he saw me approaching.

"I'll get rid of Tex now, if you want . . . only I go with Tex," I said.

That seemed to calm down TJ. "I want my car ready," TJ ordered.

"It is," I said. "The rain tires are on."

"Get me when it's time for qualifying." TJ spun around and disappeared into the dry, temperature-controlled comfort at the front of the BRM trailer.

A half hour later, I was busily making final checks on TJ's Van Diemen. I had given explicit instructions to Les and Marty to stay away from TJ's racer. Neither one wanted anything to do with the race car so the request was a blessing for them. I wanted to make sure TJ vented all his rage only on me, should anything happen.

While working on the Van Diemen, I found I missed the buttermilk biscuits I had grown so fond of, and as though answering my thoughts, Shannon appeared tapping me on the shoulder.

Shannon held out a small sealed, plastic, food container toward me, and smiled, "You forgot these."

The container was warm, but before I could pull the lid off, Shannon had disappeared and headed back to his camper. Inside the container were two fluffy buttermilk biscuits smothered with butter and honey.

"Hey, thanks," I yelled.

Shannon never slowed, only turning with a smile and a wave.

I walked toward the trailer's steps, sat on the third step, and quickly ate the biscuits. Just before I finished, Tex yelled, "Squirt to port."

Since Tex was facing the door, port was to the bird's left, which meant TJ was coming from the heated room. Never looking back, I asked, "Whatcha need TJ?"

"How'd you know it was me?" asked TJ.

"Same way I make your car a winner. I just know," I said, rather amused.

"Is the car ready?"

"Almost."

TJ went to the heated room, to change to his race suit. A few minutes later, Augie, Darrell, and TJ emerged, dressed in their fireproofed racing suits. Each driver had a head sock, gloves and arm restraints, stuffed into their helmets.

Soon, they were on the grid, earlier than most, and ready for their thirty minute session. Ian Poirier was in front ready to impress the others with his speed in the rain. He was intent on lapping and humiliating as many drivers as he could--especially TJ Benson. Following Poirier were Mercury, Dotson, Chappel, Cruz, Leclair, and Reckert ready to challenge Poirier and test his mettle. Ben Cifelli was not on the grid, refusing to practice in the rain.

Darrell, Cruz, Augie, Hanna, Guido, Les, Marty, and Shannon were standing in a cluster in front of Augie's racer. Shannon seemed to radiate an ease that also helped the others relax. In the past, Shannon and Augie had relaxed by kicking a hacky sack until the five-minute warning, but today it was too wet. Still, the relaxed atmosphere was evident. I listened as they talked.

"Can I follow you?" asked Augie.

"Sure," said Shannon, good naturedly. "I'll pick up speed for four laps and see how it goes."

"Me, too," begged Hanna.

I smiled to myself, realizing that even if Shannon could not do what I hoped Shannon was capable of, the effort would be worth it anyway. If only TJ Benson had the soft kindness in his personality like Shannon. I looked at TJ, who sat rigid and terrified in his Van Diemen, already strapped in, waiting impatiently like a child at the dentist who wants his visit to be over.

The whistle blew for the five-minute warning and everyone hurried to their respective racers, all except Shannon who waved to the participants and gave a thumbs up. As Shannon walked down the line, I followed to personally wish Shannon luck.

Shannon went directly to Poirier's racer and extended his hand. Ian seemed stunned and looked around like the hand was a trap.

They shook hands, "Hey, Dude, nice run yesterday, good luck on this session."

"I don't need luck. No one can beat me in the rain," said Poirier confidently.

I heard, and thought how amusing it would be if Poirier and TJ could be on the same team. God, forbid.

Shannon shrugged his shoulders and smiled. "Good luck, anyway."

Shannon walked down the grid and climbed into his Crossle, while I walked to the right side across from Grant who nervously handed his son the head sock. When the three-minute whistle blew, Grant jumped. I found watching Shannon, who seemed so relaxed, tended to make even me nervous. Slowly, Shannon put on one glove at a time and as he secured the last glove, the one-minute warning sounded. Each driver raised their left-hand signaling they were ready.

I watched Grant repeat the quick short ritual of shaking hands. They released the hold and Grant held a thumb up to his son, "Good luck, Shannon."

Shannon smiled, and lowered the visor on his helmet. He made a quick check of the thin plastic tearaway covers over his visor, making sure as each one became hard to see through, he could tear it away to another clear layer of plastic beneath.

Grant and I backed away from the Crossle.

"That's some ritual you and Shannon have," I said with a smile.

"Something I've done before every race since he ran go-carts," Grant smiled. "I tell you what, it sure makes me nervous. Just seems like he oughta get ready sooner. Is that normal?"

I laughed, "No, it's not normal. Most drivers are nervous enough to be ready -- especially when there are bad conditions like today. But if I had a choice, I'd much rather my driver be relaxed like Shannon."

"Well that makes me feel a lot better," said Grant. "Oh, and thanks for all you've done."

I shook my head, "My pleasure. Now come on, let's see how their times are."

The cars started moving from the pits. The crew for each driver quickly sought their respective spot on the second floor of the fast pits. Qualifying was about to begin. The first lap was run under full course yellow, so no passing was allowed. This gave the drivers the luxury of one non race lap to get accustomed to the wet conditions of the track. As they came around for the second time, the green flag was waved.

Even with the wet conditions on the first lap, Ian Poirier started to pull away with Mercury and Dotson in hot pursuit and not too far behind came old Moses. The others fell behind. When they came past for the first timed lap, Poirier was down to 2:27. Mercury and Dotson: 2:29 and Chappel 2:31. It surprised me to see Shannon, Augie, and Hanna seemingly fly past the others. Their time: 2:31.

The next lap, Poirier dropped his time a second as did Mercury, Dotson, Chappel, Shannon, Augie and Hanna. The next lap brought a drop in time of another second. None of the other drivers were below the 2:30 mark.

On lap five, Poirier was down to the 2:24's. Mercury and Dotson were in the 2:26 range, while Chappel pegged a time at 2:27.60. Down the straightaway came Shannon, Augie, and Hanna on each other's tail with a time of 2:27.30. As they passed, Shannon waved to Augie and Hanna. They waved back. As they entered Turn 1, it seemed as though Shannon suddenly pulled away in his old Crossle. TJ managed a high 2:31. Drivers continued pulling the clear plastic tearaways from their face shields, to gain better visibility, while tossing them away and have them flutter through the air until they reached the ground.

The next time around, the first four ran similar times as the previous lap. I kept my eyes on the stopwatch, keeping mental count of the intervals between the cars in my mind as they passed, knowing within a few seconds Shannon would reappear. But as those thoughts entered my mind--Shannon appeared. Disbelieving, I stared at the stopwatch and waited for Shannon to cross the imaginary line in front of me.

Shannon flew past, raising a tall rooster tail of water behind. The stopwatch read 2:24.50--faster than Poirier's best time yet in the rain.

"Boy, howdy! Go Shannon, go!" I yelled.

With my excitement out of control, I showed Grant the time and explained my enthusiasm. Stunned at Shannon's time, I forgot to reset the stopwatch, but when Shannon passed, I was sure the time was even quicker, since Shannon had passed Moses, and was only three seconds behind Mercury and Dotson. If Shannon could run another 2:24, he would be on Mercury and Dotson's tail the next time around.

I held my breath. Grant held his breath. Les and Marty watched in stunned amazement as did a woman reporter and a man who worked for Goodyear.

Any moment now, the three would be coming around the turn onto the straightaway. Suddenly, the unmistakable yellow and blue Crossle slid to the straightaway ahead of Mercury and Dotson. The bright yellow racer, shooting a high rooster tail of water behind, brought cheers from all the drenched diehard spectators and those who lined the pits. Even without stopwatches, it was easy to see what was taking place.

"All right!" screamed Les and Marty, simultaneously.

Grant yelled and jumped up and down like a yo-yo, all the while shaking his fists in the air.

"Go, kid, go," I whispered, with my stopwatch poised.

When Shannon splashed past, I touched the button and could scarcely believe my eyes. The time was 2:22.70--two seconds faster than Ian Poirier.

"Shannon's in the Zone," I said in amazement.

"What?" Grant asked.

"The Zone," I repeated. "I've seldom seen it, but when it's there they can't be beat. It's kinda like watching Michael Jordan two points down and throwing a three-pointer at the buzzer or Joe Montana with the football and down by a touchdown, with less than a minute to go. Neither one of them can be beat--neither can Shannon!"

For the next seven laps, Shannon steadily closed the gap on Poirier, and even though it was only qualifying, the spectators broke into a frenzy of cheers. While the rains continued to fall Poirier maintained his high 2:24's, while Shannon scorched the rain filled track with consistent 2:22's and leaving a water plume rooster tail in his wake.

Shannon was less than a second behind Poirier, "The Rainman," when the checkered flag was waved, signaling the end to qualifying. A chorus of boos followed as the crowd wanted one more lap so they could see Shannon pass Poirier. The lap was not to be, but the race was only hours away in the early afternoon and would soon fulfill the crowds' desire and demand for more thrills and excitement.

Grant and I stood near the wall in the fast pits when Shannon entered. We waved two thumbs up to the boy. Shannon flipped the visor on his helmet and flashed a wide grin at me and his father.

The fire was in Shannon's eyes! Poirier would have a race in the rain!

While Grant fairly ran from the fast pits to the camper and Shannon, I waited patiently for an irate TJ Benson. Standing alongside the cars of Augie and Darrell, TJ did not even give me a courtesy wave as he drove past and on to the BRM trailer. Les and Marty showed their obvious excitement, slapping Augie on the back and praising his ability in the rain.

I congratulated Augie, then Augie pulled on my arm, "Awesome Dude, like awesome! Did you see, Shannon? He was the fastest--he had to be. I've never seen anything like it."

I smiled, "He was the fastest."

"Look, I'm gonna change out of my suit. You can find me at Shannon's camper. I have no desire to stay around TJ," said Augie.

"Save me a place," I laughed. "They never said my job would be easy."

The job was definitely not easy. When I arrived, TJ was throwing things in the trailer, and Tex was screaming "Squirt." Tex was also mimicking a car screeching to a halt, then a crashing sound, each time TJ threw something. This was Tex's way of saying "stop."

I tried to calm TJ, but all of my efforts proved unsuccessful. TJ was on a mad tirade.

"Look at the times Marty gave me. I'm almost dead last in the rain!"

"You still have the pole," I said calmly. "If you work the race car, you can still finish pretty high. The rain will take its toll."

TJ Benson spun around to face me, with a wild look in his eyes, "I'm supposed to win this race, dammit!"

The words stunned me and took me over the edge, "You arrogant sonofabitch! No one is supposed to win the race, much less someone as undeserving of victory as you."

"You can't talk to me--"

"Listen, Squirt, I can talk to you like I darn well please. You race for the challenge. If you were supposed to win, no one would race against you. It's you against them--and each one of them has the dream of winning and with that dream a chance to win. And a lot of those drivers have the desire and ability to beat you at any given time."

"Oh, yeah! You'll see. I'm going to the Stewards to protest the race and have it postponed."

"Stupid rich kid! Go ahead."

"You'll see, Charlie, you'll see who's stupid," said TJ defensively. He charged from the trailer to talk to the Stewards. "You'll be sorry you talked to me like that."

TJ was out of ear shot when I said, "I'm only sorry I work for you."

Even Tex had his own parting words, "Squirt." Then Tex mimicked the sound of brakes and a crash, again.

A few minutes after TJ departed, Marty arrived with an official qualifying sheet. I scanned it carefully: Looking at the times with only one dry practice did not give a true reflection of the drivers and the times they were capable of attaining. I had expected Shannon to qualify as high as tenth, but with the problems and no other dry time, he would start in 22nd position. Shannon was number one in the rain, but even his dry times were quicker than his wet times. And for this race, the rules were clear: The fastest time for either Friday or Saturday took the pole position for the race

The opposite was true of TJ. He had the pole, but was the slowest in the rain. TJ's fear and slow speed would be a hazard to the other drivers at the start of the race. Sebring would be Poirier's race to win. Leclair who was only slightly faster than TJ would start on the outside behind TJ. I was sure

Poirier would use Marcoux to block and delay Dotson and Mercury, who were the next fastest, followed by Chappel. Augie and Hanna followed Chappel. Although they showed speed and ability in the rain, they would be hindered by their starting position of 17th and 18th.

```
                    SCCA/USAC
       U.S. Formula Ford 2000 National Championship
                   Official Grid
                     June 26
                     Sebring
                 Sebring, Florida
                   (3.7 miles)

       Car      Name              Model           Time        Time
       No.                                        1st         2nd

 1.    (1)    TJ Benson          VanDiemen RF95   2:07.45*    2:30.21
 2.    (5)    Ian Poirier        Swift DB-8       2:07.85*    2:24.60
 3.    (7)    Ron Leclair        VanDiemen RF95   2:08.25     2:29.60
 4.    (34)   Claude Marcoux     Swift DB-8       2:08.27     2:28.44
 5.    (27)   Roberto Cruz       VanDiemen RF95   2:08.32     2:29.00
 6.    (33)   Bob Dotson         Spirit           2:08.35     2:26.81
 7.    (11)   Alan Reckert       Stohr            2:08 40     2:28.65
 8.    (43)   Jude Dionne        Swift DB-8       2:08.43     2:28.50
 9.    (71)   Gordon Chappel     VanDiemen RF95   2:08.44     2:27.15
10.    (8)    Freddy Mercury     Reynard 95F      2:08.46     2:26.75
11.    (69)   Phil Spratt        Reynard 95F      2:08.50     2:28.50
12.    (39)   Art Grindle        Swift SE-3       2:08.60     2:30.85
13     (50)   Don Reese          VanDiemen RF95   2:08.70     2:28.92
14     (99)   Peter Hurst        Swift DB-8       2:08.75     2:30.00
15.    (54)   Guido Pepin        Swift DB-8       2:08.83     2:28.40
16.    (21)   Rick Henry         Swift DB-8       2:08.92     2:29.23
17.    (22)   Augie Zuehl        VanDiemen RF95   2:09.15     2:27.23
18.    (16)   Hanna Lee          Swift DB-8       2:09.23     2:27.01
19.    (47)   Darrell Pollard    VanDiemen RF95   2:09.25     2:30.44
20.    (30)   Bill Murfy         Swift DB-8       2:09.45     2:31.88
21.    (27)   Ben Cifelli        Swift DB-3       2:09.45     No Time
22.    (44)   Shannon Kelly      Crossle 71F      2:10.62     2:22.53
23.    (88)   Barton Springs     VanDiemen RF91   2:10.74     2:31.53
24.    (55)   Cliff Roe          VanDiemen RF94   2:11.51     2:32.47
25.    (00)   Tom Craig          Swift DB-3       2:12.50     2:30.83
26.    (74)   Mark McGrath       Swift DB-3       2:13.95     2:32.99
27.    (60)   Rex VanHorn        Reynard SF91     2:15.97     2:30.88
28.    (13)   Steve Smagala      VanDiemen RF89   2:16.50     2:29.80
29.    (25)   Chase Wilder       Reynard SF90     2:06.45     2:30.47
30.    (3)    Will Jones         Swift DB-8       2:18.45     2:29.33

       *Below Track Record
```

An hour later, TJ was back and refused to talk to anyone. Evidently the Chief Steward, Jerry Dieter, and Andy Cobb refused to listen to his protest and said the race would be run in the rain. TJ clung to the radio, praying to hear the rain would stop.

Just before noon, I made my way to Grant and Shannon's camper. As I passed the Goodyear trailer, Carl Law stopped mounting a tire and ran to me.

"Those tires were worth it. I've never seen anything like it," said Carl in utter amazement. "You can bet I'll be watching the race. Looks like we got a new Rainman."

I smiled, "I told you so."

Before I reached the camper, Jolit Torres caught me, "Hey, guy, I went to the announcer's stand and gave them a bio on your prodigy."

"I just know the kid, that's all," I said sheepishly.

"Uh, huh--I talked to the Goodyear man . . . would you like to explain?" Jolit asked.

"Hey, he's just a deserving kid whose father has just about given up everything he has for his son and doesn't even know it."

Jolit smiled, "I know, I just talked to Shannon. He's a great kid, and I guarantee if he wins, I'll have something written about it. You know everyone in the broadcast booth is calling Shannon the "Rainman" after he caught Ian. Oh, and thanks for the scoop, Charlie."

I nodded and continued to the camper where I found Shannon refueling his car and checking the tires.

"Where's Grant?" I asked.

"Went to get the Suzuki. Should be back in an hour or so," said Shannon.

I frowned, "He better hurry, the race is at three."

* * *

The concern on the grid was obvious in most of the drivers faces, since the rumor had the rain diminishing and stopping soon. The Eastern skies seemed to lighten, so a few came to the grid with slicks, while others kept a spare set near their racer, should they change their minds at the last moment.

The familiar smile was gone from Shannon's face, but for a different reason, as he strained his eyes past the fast pits, with still no sign of his father. Three friends stood near to offer comfort and support, Hanna, Augie and me. Moses, Patches, and Turtle were close to us. Dotson was already alerted to the problem by his team mate, Hanna.

Dotson slapped Shannon on the back, "Perk up, Shannon. Grant probably just ran into some delay or bad traffic. He'll be okay. You have to concentrate on this race for him."

Those words seemed to ease Shannon's worries, as the five-minute warning neared.

I added, "Dotson's right. Concentrate on this race for your Dad. You know he'd want you to think only of the race."

Shannon nodded his head, and smiled, but continued to stare from the pits. "Other than Watkins Glen, this is the first race my Dad ever missed."

Augie looked at me and pointed to the tires. "Which ones? And why isn't Ian out on the grid?"

I know my confident, smile and nod, gave no doubt, "Rains! It might look dry on the straight, but you can count on some bad puddles on the rest of the course and in the corners. Rain tires are just as fast as the slicks down the straight--but you need the rain tires for the turns today. And forget about Ian, he's a master of mind games. Listen, there's always gonna be some mental head banging to psych your opponent--that's why Ian isn't on the grid. Just look at the other drivers wondering what Ian will pick. Let me tell you, Ian will also be on rains or he's a fool."

Augie, Shannon, and Hanna accepted my statement.

Hanna walked over, grabbed Shannon around the neck, and planted a kiss on his lips. She pulled away and smiled, "Just for luck."

Shannon smiled and looked at Hanna, "If I win you gotta promise to keep doing that."

Suddenly I spied the terrified child as TJ waved frantically to me, even though Les and Marty stood ready to change tires, should TJ demand it. I moved quickly to learn the problem.

"Where the hell is Ian?" TJ demanded rather than asked, already psyched out by Ian's failure to show.

"Playing with your head, TJ," I said. "Look, a couple of cars have slicks--I want dries, too, the rain is gonna stop and Ian knows it--I want slicks, too!" TJ ordered.

"No!" I said.

Ron Leclair had his car on two quick jacks, waiting for a sign, and hopefully to see Ian's choice. For now, he had rains mounted, but slicks quickly available, with one tire laying near each corner. Leclair's mechanic, Jay Defee, was ready with another helper to change all four. Two other drivers seemed just as nervous as Leclair. Peter Hurst and Cliff Roe waited in the same position, with the only difference being they each had only one helper.

While most of them were amazed at Shannon Kelly's accomplishment in the rain, they knew full well, from years of experience, what Ian Poirier could do in the rain and his uncanny ability to choose just the right tire to use when the weather was near a transition point. After all, Poirier was the "Rainman." Shannon had no such experience as he relied only on an old mechanic's guess. My guess!

The five-minute warning sounded. TJ was already strapped snugly in his red, white, and blue number 1 Van Diemen nervously waiting for the race to start, as he appeared to wring the life out of his steering wheel with a death grip.

Still, no Poirier on the grid.

Peter Hurst and Cliff Roe made their final decisions, with Hurst opting for rain tires, while Roe's mechanic quickly changed to slicks. Leclair signaled Defee to remove the two rear tires, so when the decision was reached as to which tires to use, only two would need changing.

Ready to race, Marcoux looked down the line of competitors, scoping each competitor . . . but his eyes kept returning to Shannon Kelly. Marcoux's hands squeezed the steering wheel on the green and blue number 34, much like a hunter who takes careful aim and waits patiently for the deer to step into the clearing and into his line of fire!

I made a quick check of Augie and Darrell, then returned to TJ.

The three-minute warning--and still no Poirier!

As they started one by one, the roar of the engines became deafening.

Leclair signaled Defee, who started putting on the rain tires. Good or bad everyone was now set for the race.

"Slicks, Charlie, slicks!" yelled TJ.

"No! Besides it's too late now," I noted. I looked at Les and Marty who had already started Augie and Pollard's engines, "Make sure TJ is okay."

Quickly, I jogged down to Augie and checked on him. Satisfied, I moved around Hanna to Pollard, waving at Hanna in the process. Pollard was strapped in and ready, and gave a thumbs up.

Content with my three drivers, I went directly to Shannon's Crossle, where I found Shannon fumbling with his gloves. The car was already running. Thanks to Dotson's orders to one of his helpers for assistance. I knelt beside the shiny yellow and blue Crossle, took the gloves from Shannon and handed him one. Shannon looked up and smiled. The look-- the fire--was in Shannon's eyes!

"I wish my Dad was here," Shannon managed, undaunted by the weather conditions, or the mind games Ian Poirier was using. Shannon was set and confident.

"I know," I said, then handed Shannon the other glove.

Just before the one-minute warning, Poirier raced his Swift down the grid for his number two position, slowing down in front of Shannon, as the one-minute warning sounded--Ian was on rains!

Ian paused to view Shannon's tires, as Shannon and I both glanced up in time to see Poirier slam his fist into his steering wheel when he saw the rains on Shannon's racer. Ian Poirier was worried about Shannon Kelly!

Shannon calmly attached the last glove's Velcro strap around his wrist. Mechanically, he pulled the shoulder harness tight, and started to check the tearaways on his visor. I pulled the lap belt snug. When Shannon raised his left-hand, I reached for Shannon's right hand and shook it with mine.

But I didn't stop there. My hand slid back and we squeezed each other's thumb, released then curled our fingers about the each other's fingers, raised our thumb and pointed the index finger at each other, while the other three fingers continued to hold tightly. I released the hold and held my right thumb up, "Good luck, Shannon."

Shannon smiled, "Thanks, Charlie--I won't let you down." Then he lowered the helmet visor and made a quick check of the face shields protective clear plastic tearaways.

I backed away and waited. With a roar the cars rolled from the pits and entered the race track. Quickly, I walked to the second floor of the fast pits where Les and Marty busily prepared for the start.

When I arrived, Les had bad news. "Boy, is TJ pissed at you for hanging around Shannon."

"What's new. Gimme the stopwatch, I have a race to watch," I said . Before I turned my attention to the race at hand, I looked long and hard through the pits for Grant but saw no sign of him or the small Samurai.

The announcer's voice echoed around the track as he called out each driver, and occasionally gave a brief biography where possible. He made a special note for the spectators to watch the yellow, blue and red number 44 and the driver Shannon Kelly, the youngest in the field, who had the best time in the rain and would surely be moving up fast. He also noted Augie Zuehl and Hanna Lee, two more who would be moving through the pack.

I continued to watch until the cars came around the last turn and accelerated toward the starter stand. The green flag waved! The race was underway, and immediately dozens of rooster tails rose in the warm, damp air, as the cars spread five wide coming down the straight toward the sweeping lefthander of Turn 1 and Turn 2.

Poirier immediately shot in front of TJ, while Leclair was forced to TJ's left by Marcoux, who then went to TJ's right in an effort to hold back Dotson. TJ appeared to straddle the middle of the track. After the sweeping lefthander, they charged the wide 90 degree left of Turn 3, taking it in second gear. Then, the narrow short chute where three cars might fit side by side for a short distance, to the right, then left of Turn 4, and left of Turn 5, where they dropped into first gear, followed with a curving right straight, they went through the gears leading to the tricky and dangerous, first gear, 180 degree hairpin of Turn 7.

Marcoux kept side by side with TJ, who seemed to be holding the other drivers back in the short chute. Leclair assumed second, then TJ and Marcoux, chased closely by Cruz and Dotson. Chappel passed Reckert and Dionne to close on Dotson as did Mercury. Augie and Hanna moved from 17th and 18th, respectively to 13th and 14th position. Already Shannon was in 16th but separated by a wide margin due to the hesitation of the slower drivers in front of him.

At the chicane, the sharp right and left of Turn 8 and Turn 9, Marcoux shifted down to second and suddenly shot ahead of Leclair and TJ, pinching the aggressive Dotson and Mercury behind and leaving a clearing for him to the first gear 90 degree right at Turn 10.

Poirier was two seconds ahead of the pack with teammate Marcoux quickly pulling away. Mercury, Dotson, and Chappel were closed in until after Turn 10, but through the sweeping left of Turn 11, Dotson passed Leclair and TJ. Mercury passed the same two cars at the slight right kink of Turn 12, but Chappel was held back. Coming out of the second gear, right-hand Turn 13, leading to the back straightaway, Chappel passed TJ.

Poirier opened up a four second lead over Marcoux, while Marcoux was three seconds ahead of Dotson and Mercury, who were closing on him fast. Two seconds behind them, Chappel finally passed Leclair at the left kink of Turn 14. Leclair was just ahead of TJ, now nothing more than a moving obstacle.

As TJ tried to negotiate Gator Bend, the wide, sharp 90 degree right-hander of Turn 15, Reckert, Cruz, Spratt and Dionne passed. Down the long back straightaway, closing behind TJ, were Augie and Hanna moving into 12th and 13th position.

Dionne pulled away from TJ and Leclair, at the sweeping right; of the high speed Turn 16, called the LeMans Curve. TJ managed to stay on Leclair's tail down the long back straightaway until he neared what in reality was a combination of two sweeping rights of Turn 17, bringing them back to the main straight. Hanna dove in on Augie, to take him in the combination turns with both passing TJ and Leclair for 10th and 11th. Neither Hanna nor Augie were prepared for the gutsy move by Shannon, who seemed to streak past through the turns on the very dangerous, inside portion of the track and complete the turns fifty feet ahead. Both waved to Shannon as he moved from 22nd to 10th in less than a lap.

As Shannon streaked past the pits raising a large rooster tail, Les and Marty started to cheer.

I mumbled, "The Zone."

One lap down with sixteen to go. Shannon was in tenth place but already Poirier was twenty seconds ahead of Shannon. Just chasing down Poirier would be difficult without having to pass the likes of Dotson, Mercury, and Chappel.

The next time around, Poirier stretched his lead to eight seconds over Mercury and Dotson, who had passed Marcoux. They were set in single file to catch Poirier, waiting to duel each other until the final few laps. Racing in such fashion, they established a comfortable six second gap over Chappel who also passed Marcoux.

Shannon came around the final turn of the second lap in 8th, having passed Dionne and Spratt. Still, he was twenty seconds behind.

Two laps later, Poirier had a ten second lead. Shannon moved into 6th, passing Reckert and Cruz with ease, and now eighteen seconds behind Poirier. Hanna and Augie continued to move well taking 8th and 9th from

Dionne and Spratt.

Down the curving straight to the hairpin, Shannon caught Marcoux and moved right to the inside but Marcoux moved over almost forcing Shannon off the track. Shannon dropped two tires from the wet asphalt, slid sideways but managed to catch the Crossle before the hairpin. Marcoux tiptoed through the Turn 7 hairpin but Shannon attacked the turn aggressively coming out and catching Marcoux before the quick right and left or Turn 8 and Turn 9. Again, Marcoux tried to force Shannon but Shannon pulled even and refused to give ground. Their tires touched and Marcoux lifted slightly giving the turns to Shannon. Shannon simply flew past Marcoux and continued his pursuit of the others. Shannon was now in 5th with only four more ahead: Chappel, Mercury, Dotson and Poirier.

The encounter with Marcoux proved costly for Shannon more than twenty seconds behind Poirier when he came past start/finish with five laps completed and only twelve remaining. Catching Poirier seemed impossible for Shannon with the added task of passing Chappel, Mercury, and Dotson. Mercury and Dotson would be no easy feat.

Two laps later, Shannon took Chappel with ease down the start/finish straight. Ten laps remained and Poirier held only an eighteen-second lead. Six seconds ahead were Dotson and Mercury, who had fallen twelve seconds behind Poirier.

Already out of the race, stuck in mud or damaged from contact with various concrete barricades were: Cliff Roe, Darrell Pollard and Art Grindle who took a hard shot into the wall through the chicane. White flags waved to warn the drivers of a slow-moving vehicle on the race track, meaning an ambulance or wrecker. In this situation, a wrecker was sent out to remove Grindle from his hazardous position on the track and potential danger to the other drivers. Grindle's race was finished while Roe and Pollard were pushed clear of the track by the ever present and vigilant, white suited corner workers.

Two laps later, Grindle was removed from the track. Shannon was only two seconds behind Mercury and Dotson. They remained in single file racing together, hoping to prevent Shannon from catching them and in a cooperative effort to catch the fleeing Poirier. Poirier maintained his lead over Mercury and Dotson but lost four more seconds to Shannon.

Another lap brought cheers from the crowd as Shannon brought the bright yellow number 44 down the main straight only a hundred yards behind Mercury and Dotson--and closing quickly.

Like the human wave at a football game, I could easily see where Shannon was on the track. The spectators screamed and cheered their approval when Shannon passed before them. I could hear the wet, excited crowd roar their approval, even over the thunder of the race cars. Shannon was, again, in "The Zone!"

To add insult to injury, TJ was lapped and passed on both sides by Mercury and Dotson down the curving straight leading to the slippery hairpin. On their tail clung Shannon.

All three noticed the yellow, waving flag. A warning of trouble in the hairpin. Cars were on both sides of the hairpin. Dionne's lime green Swift to the inside and across from him, Spratt's silver, black and red number 69. Both drivers had taken each other out.

The rules were clear: no passing under the yellow. Cautiously but still under racing conditions, Dotson reached the hairpin first with Mercury close behind. Both drivers swung wide, while Shannon started the turn wide came in close and held the inside. All three of them were separated with less than a racecar length. Virtually side by side, with none having passed the other. Instantly, all three strained their eyes for the next corner, Turn 8, leading to the chicane, they all spied the corner workers; there were no waving yellow flags!

For Mercury, Dotson, and Shannon, it was a drag race to the chicane. The power of Mercury's white and blue Swift was obvious as he pulled teammate Dotson. Only slightly did they pull Shannon, who at first pulled them with his greater exit speed from the hairpin. Still, near the end of the straight, Mercury held two lengths over Shannon who pulled even with Dotson.

Mercury waited till the last possible moment, waited a little more, then pumped the brakes to prevent them from locking up and going into a slide. Before he turned to the right, he was stunned to catch Shannon out of the corner of his eye pull even, drop two tires over the rumble strip and go side by side with Mercury through the dangerous chicane, barricaded on both sides with immovable protective concrete barriers. The crowd roared with delight.

Immediately after the right came a quick left turn. Only inches separated Shannon from the concrete on his right and the number 8 Reynard of Mercury on the left. Again, Shannon carried a greater exit speed and pulled away from Mercury. He down shifted to first and took the sharp right at Turn 10, clearly ahead of Mercury and pulling away.

Splashing past the start/finish line, Shannon had two seconds on Freddy Mercury. Seven laps remained but if Shannon continued his torrid pace in the rain; then mathematically, Poirier clung to a precarious twelve-second lead.

Electrified, the crowd sensed what was about to occur and they screamed their approval in eager anticipation of a repeat and conclusion to the mornings qualifying. Each lap Shannon continued to cut Poirier's lead two seconds or more. The crowds chanted, counting off the seconds each time Poirier passed until Shannon streaked past. The lead steadily dropped: ten seconds, eight seconds, six seconds, four seconds . . .

The lime green and white number 5 Swift slid onto the main straight and approached the start/finish. Shannon slid around Turn 17 in his bright yellow, outdated Crossle closer than the lap before, bringing an earth shaking cheer from the crowd that instantly became silent as Poirier crossed the start/finish with only two laps remaining. The spectators, as they had done the four previous laps, began to count, "One, two." When they reached "two" Shannon crossed the finish line signaling a lead now of only two seconds.

"We have a race, ladies and gentlemen!" came the announcer's excited voice, which was nearly drowned out by the crescendo of the crowd.

The announcer needed to say nothing--the crowd knew!

Les and Marty and I jumped up and down for joy like little kids.

Nearly as impressive as Shannon's run for the lead was Augie and Hanna's race, having moved from 17th and 18th, respectively to 6th and 7th and now only a few car lengths from overtaking Moses Chappel. Likewise, the crowd recognized this and cheered them on.

I watched the stopwatch closely. My heart pounded madly in my chest and I crossed my fingers. Any moment now, Poirier would come around Turn 17 for the last lap.

Poirier and Shannon slid around Turn 17, side by side. The spectators went crazy! Poirier held the advantage and pulled away with his straightaway speed but through the left-hand turn Shannon closed again. Poirier moved to block at the sharp left turn and again the curved straight leading to the hairpin.

Shannon stayed glued to Poirier's tail then jerked to the right at the final moment in preparation for the right-handed hairpin. Poirier anticipated and moved right to block. Just as quickly Shannon moved left, anticipating the block and forcing Poirier into an overly tight turn and putting Shannon wide of the hairpin. This gave Shannon a wider turning radius. He completed the turn quickly and was on full power before Poirier could complete his turn. Although Poirier was more than three car lengths ahead, Shannon came out carrying far greater speed and simply motored away from the superior Swift before Poirier could recover. Shannon's raw skill in the rain was evident when he took the chicane with ease and stretched his lead to a second over Poirier.

Only the long one mile back straight remained where Poirier and his much faster Swift could easily close the gap. Again, Shannon carried a much greater exit speed out of Turn 15 onto the straightaway and maintained his lead. But Poirier refused to let go, running faster than he had any time before in the rain. Pushing to the limit, he managed to close the gap down the long back straightaway pulling alongside Shannon.

Meeting the pressure of the challenge, Shannon went in deeper to the combination two right-handers of Turn 17 than Poirier was capable of doing. Poirier's Swift broke loose and instantly he eased the throttle back, caught the racer and was back on the throttle.

Shannon came around the final turn two lengths ahead of Poirier. He pulled away from Poirier all the way to the checkered flag, as the crowds cheered their approval.

Mercury finished 3rd, followed by his teammate Dotson. Augie and Hanna's strong performance propelled them into a fine 5th and 6th finishing position. TJ Benson finished a dismal 13th, and if thirteen was ever bad luck, then the race was an extreme disappointment for TJ.

Les, Marty, and I were both excited and leery. Excited for having seen one of the best races in our lives but leery of returning to the BRM trailer and the wrath of TJ Benson, because we were in a mood for celebration. If there was any other place we could have gone, we would. The one place we started for was Impound, where the top six finishers would be for the first thirty minutes after the race for inspections of their racers. We all wanted to congratulate Shannon, Augie, and Hanna, since they were all in Impound for the first time.

On the way to Impound, the Goodyear man, Carl Law, stopped me. Les and Marty continued, leaving me behind.

"Well, it sure looks like you knew what you were talking about," said Carl Law. "About the best damn race I can remember."

I nodded and shook hands with Carl, "Thanks, and don't forget the other tires."

Carl winked and continued to the Goodyear truck, while I continued to Impound, only to be stopped by Grant, who seemed extremely concerned.

"Charlie, I just got back. The traffic was terrible. A wreck had the road blocked for almost an hour. They said the race is over and Shannon isn't back at the motorhome. Is Shannon all right?" Grant asked, worry and fear evident in his eyes.

I laughed, "Grab hold Grant." Then I squeezed Grant's shoulders, "Shannon just kicked ass. He's in the Winner's Circle."

"What?"

"Shannon won! Best race I think I've ever seen."

"He won?"

"Yep."

Tears came to Grant's eyes and rolled down his cheeks and his voice wavered when he spoke, "I knew he could do it . . . and I missed his race."

"Your boy did great. Now come with me and let's go congratulate the kid. He was worried sick about you. I know he'll be glad to see you're okay."

As we hurried to the Winner's Circle, Grant wiped his eyes and mumbled, "He won."

We arrived in time to see Shannon mount the podium between Poirier and Mercury. Shannon saw his father, waved, and flashed a wide grin, then shook his tall trophy in the air so Grant could see it. Grant raised both fists and waved back.

A few pictures later, Shannon's turn came to spray his fellow competitors with champagne.

When they stepped from the podium, five reporters stuck microphones in Shannon's face, and ESPN trained a camera on the tall, good-looking boy.

"What do you think of your first win?" Jolit Torres managed to ask before the others.

"Awesome . . . ," said Shannon. He pointed to Grant, "I couldn't have done it without my Dad."

Grant's lips quivered and a tear rolled down his cheek.

Jolit Torres asked a few final questions, and had Shannon speak into her hand held recorder. The rain stopped, and the sun broke through the clouds to shine down on Shannon's victory. Some drivers made the short walk to Impound to offer their congratulations. Among them were Murf the Smurf, Tom Craig, Will Jones, and Guido Pepin along with Moses Chappel.

At the first opportunity, Grant was at Shannon's side. Shannon and Grant embraced.

"I won, Dad," Shannon whispered in his father's ear.

"I know," said Grant as tears rolled down his cheeks. "I knew you could do it."

"I couldn't have done it without you."

They clung to each other for a few moments, then pushed away allowing Grant time to wipe his eyes, then laugh.

A few minutes later, the top three were in Impound with the others. In Impound, four of the top six finishers stood around Shannon still congratulating him. Only Poirier stood away from the rest, having already reluctantly offered his congratulations.

Bob Dotson walked up to Grant and extended his hand, "Your son put on a hellva racing display today, let me tell you. You know I've got a video camera mounted in my race car and if you'd like, I'll make a copy for you."

Grant shook hands, "I'd like that very much."

I took time to slap Shannon on the back and shake his hand, "You did an unbelievable job, Shannon."

Shannon smiled, "Thanks, Charlie."

Jolit Torres drew me to the side, as a stranger walked up behind Shannon, and waited patiently to talk.

"Thanks for the scoop, Charlie," said Jolit. "Keep an eye out in Autoweek and SportsCar for the story."

"They won't print anything about this."

"Wrong," smiled Jolit. "It's a special interest story and don't forget this is an SCCA series, so each time a member of SCCA makes it big, it makes for good reading--like Al Unser Jr. Something like 'Young Gun Beats Sebring' what do you think?"

"I'm sure whatever you can do, won't hurt."

As Jolit walked away, the waiting stranger tapped Shannon from behind, "Excuse me, my name is Jimmy Smith. I'm a member of SCCA and I was wondering if you'd like to sell your car. I just saw the race and I'd like to take it auto-crossing."

The Sports Car Club of America was an organization spread across the United States with regional clubs putting on events where courses were laid out and single cars would run the course for time, much like a Malibu Grand Prix event, only individuals used their own cars, and could enter a variety of classes, one of which would accommodate the outdated Crossle.

"Thanks," said Shannon, shaking his head. "I've got $15,000 tied up in it, but it's all I have."

"Sure, I understand." Smith handed Shannon a business card. "Call me, if you change your mind."

Then Smith walked away, while Shannon slid the business card in a pocket on his soaked racing suit.

I shook my head and wished for a way to sell the Crossle, and find a more competitive racer. I knew when the races were dry, Shannon would be hard pressed to finish in the top ten with the old Crossle.

I took time to congratulate Hanna and Augie for a race both drivers ran extremely well.

The top three had the engine heads removed to check cylinder size. When "Tech" had finished the inspection, the sun was out warming the spirits of most present. Dotson offered an open invitation to all who wanted to bring a little food, drinks, and their swimsuits to party at his trailer and relax in the hot tub, an offer most readily accepted.

When Les, Marty, Augie, and I arrived at the BRM trailer, we discovered not all spirits warmed to the changing weather, as we found it still stormy inside the trailer. From a distance we could hear clanging and banging, and Tex mimicking the sounds of brakes then a crash. Above this commotion came the sounds of things being thrown around in the trailer.

As we stepped inside, we found Pollard gone and TJ throwing a fit.

TJ twisted his head and glowered at Les and Marty, "Where have you been?"

Marty said, "The rules require the mechanics to be present."

"It doesn't take three of you," TJ snapped.

"Excuse me," said Augie. Quickly, he darted into the front of the trailer to grab his bag of clothes. Before the arguments started, he was out with a bag in hand. "I'll just go change at Shannon's and see you guys at Dotson's trailer."

Augie was down the steps and gone none too soon.

"Shannon, Shannon! That's all I ever hear any more!" snapped TJ. He pointed to Les and Marty, "You two need to load the trailer."

They were down the steps, and gone from view, quicker than Augie departed. Only I remained.

"You spend too much time with Shannon and I don't want you to hang out in their area anymore," TJ ordered.

"Squirt," screamed Tex.

"Listen, I take care of your car, but you don't tell me who I can talk to-- its none of your business."

"I'm making it my business. I don't want you with them or offering them help anymore. If you concentrated on your job, maybe I could have won."

"Hey, Butt Breath!" I snapped.

"Hey, Butt Breath," mimicked Tex in a voice that sounded disgustingly like mine.

I continued, "Look you ungrateful little turd, you couldn't have won the race today if your life depended on it, because as a driver, you're worthless in the rain."

"I don't need you. Everyone was right. You're lucky I gave you a second chance. After that guy died at Indy, you were washed up."

Anger overwhelmed me and I charged TJ, throwing him against the trailer wall and pinning his neck with my left forearm while I held him with my right hand.

"You sonofabitch, Marcelo was ten times the man you ever will be! You aren't worthy of changing the oil in his race car--and there are a half dozen racers here better than you! I've just given you the edge!" I snapped. Slowly, I released my hold, then pushed TJ away.

TJ dusted himself off and sneered at me, "Really? Then go work for them--while I continue to win without you!"

"Fine with me, Squirt! In fact, Shannon's better than you and with an equal car--he will kick your ass!"

TJ raised his nose in the air, "Not in your wildest dreams will Shannon ever beat me."

I laughed, "You need to pay more attention to current events, Pusshead. Shannon just beat you today! Plus, Shannon's got two things you never will have--he's got heart and fire in his eyes no one here has!"

TJ pointed to the door, "Then get the hell out."

"Good! You can take this whole durn mess and shove it up your butt. I quit."

"Fine. I can find somebody else. Get out and take that damn bird with you."

"Squirt," squealed Tex.

TJ spun about and stormed to the front of the trailer and slammed the door with a loud bang.

I took a deep breath, tried to count to ten, exhaled. I pushed a straight finger under the yellow belly until Tex hopped on. I moved my hand around to my shoulder where Tex stepped off near my neck. With the perch in one hand and the cage in the other, I walked down the steep steps leading from the trailer. I paused and looked at Les and Marty who had stopped what they were doing.

"Sorry, boys," I said shaking my head. Les and Marty nodded their heads.

The walk to Shannon's trailer took me past Art Grindle's trailer. Grindle was loaded and ready for the trip home.

"Charlie," yelled Grindle. "Know anybody interested in buying a car?"

"You're not getting out, are you?" I asked.

"Yeah, I promised myself if I had a wreck that would be it for the year. Besides the rain today told me I need to sit out for a while."

"Hey, the rain is tough on a lot of the drivers. Look what happened to TJ."

While I talked, I also inspected the damage to the Swift SE-3. The front right corner was ruined and the rear suspension bent. Only the new Van Diemen and Swift DB-8 were the winners for the class. But the Swift SE-3 could be modified to almost equal the Swift DB-8. In the right hands, it could be a winner. My thoughts returned to the man who wanted to buy the Crossle. Grindle's SE-3 could be fixed for as little as $2000 and the modifications done for less than $1000.

"Looks like a lot of damage . . . how much?" I asked.

"Aw, hell, I'll sell it to you with all the spares for . . . how's $19,000 sound?"

"With the engine and spares?"

"Yes."

"Sounds okay," I said. "I'll give you a call when you get home."

We talked for a few minutes while I inspected the spares. A few minutes later I was at the Kelly's trailer. I asked Shannon for the business card of the man who wanted to autocross the Crossle. Shannon went to the race trailer where he had hung his race suit and fished out the card.

When Shannon returned, I told him and Grant about the deal with the Swift SE-3. Grant hesitated explaining they had no money.

I reminded them the victory was worth $4500 in prize money. I also detailed the modifications cost and soon I had Shannon and Grant excited.

"But we need a mechanic," Grant added.

"Well, it just so happens I'm available. I quit working for Benson as of today."

"Wow, that's great," popped Shannon.

FORMULA 2000, the Dream

Grant was more serious, "I'm sorry."

I smiled, "Don't be. Like Shannon said, it's great!"

"What do they pay a mechanic?" Grant asked.

TJ paid me a thousand a day plus extra for major damage and engine work. I thought for a moment and then looked into Shannon's eager eyes.

"Well, they pay helpers a hundred a day. A good mechanic can get five hundred a day," I said.

Grant said, "Well we want you. I just don't know if we'll have enough after fixin' that Swift SE . . . whatever."

"SE-3 Dad."

I smiled, "Look, I think what you won will cover the difference in racecar price, cover the repairs, and pay me for a couple of races. Tell you what, if it gets tight, I'll just wait until Shannon wins some more money-- because I can make Shannon a winner."

"I don't know what to say," said Grant surprised at the changing events.

"Say yes, Dad."

Grant shrugged his shoulders, "Well, what do I do?"

I extended my hand, "Just shake and it's a done deal."

Grant, Shannon and I all shook hands. The deal was done. I had a new team and Shannon and Grant had a new mechanic.

"Now, I'm your mechanic."

"Hey, let's go to the party and tell everybody," Shannon suggested.

Grant and I agreed, and after I set up the perch, and deposited Tex on my shoulder, the four of us were on our way.

More than twenty people were already at the party. The wild and waving gestures Les and Marty made with their hands indicated they were obviously talking to Guido, Dotson, and Wesley about my departure from BRM. As they talked, they would point and gesture to sheets they held which I surmised to be the official final standings for the Sebring race. The three of us moved to where the conversation was in full force. Hanna waved to Shannon, who quickly joined her and Augie in the hot tub. All three had cause to celebrate for a race well done.

When Grant and I walked up, Dotson handed us a copy of the current standings. Guido congratulated Grant on Shannon's victory.

Bob Dotson pulled me aside and expressed his sorrow over TJ's actions.

"Look, Charlie, just because Benson got rid of you, there's no reason for you to stay away from the series. I'd like you to work for my team and I'm willing to pay you the thousand a day TJ did, plus an additional two hundred a day. You will also be paid extra for major work or engines. Plus, all your expenses," said Dotson.

"Thanks, Bob, but I've already accepted another job."

"Shannon?" Dotson asked.

I confirmed with a nod of my head.

Dotson smiled, "Well, if I can't have you, I can't think of a better person to get you. If it weren't for the Crossle, I'm sure you'd get him in the Winner's Circle. I sure don't know how he got you on his budget, but I guess he knows a good thing when he sees it."

"Well, thanks, but if I can help it, this is the last race for the Crossle," I assured Dotson.

Dotson went back to the party while I took a few minutes to scan the final race results and an updated sheet of the current standings:

```
                        SCCA/USAC
           U.S. Formula Ford 2000 National Championship
                    Official Points Standing
                         (5 Races)

         Car    Name              Model          Team
Points
         No.

 1.  (1)    TJ Benson         VanDiemen RF95    BRM             124
 2.  (5)    Ian Poirier       Swift DB-8        PACE            118
 3.  (34)   Claude Marcoux    Swift DB-98       PACE             90
 4.  (71)   Gordon Chappel    VanDiemen RF95    MOSES            80
 5.  (11)   Alan Reckert      Stohr             TART             78
 6.  (8)    Freddy Mercury    Reynard 95F       Dotson Racing    74
 7.  (7)    Ron Leclair       VanDiemen RF95    TART             73
 8.  (33)   Bob Dotson        Spirit            Dotson Racing    70
 9.  (44)   Shannon Kelly     Crossle 71F                        62
10.  (69)   Phil Spratt       Reynard 95F       Spratt Racing    51
11.  (47)   Darrell Pollard   VanDiemen RF95    BRM              45
12.  (27)   Roberto Cruz      VanDiemen RF95    Spratt Racing    44
13.  (22)   Augie Zuehl       VanDiemen RF95    BRM              41
14.  (43)   Jude Dionne       Swift DB-8        PACE             39
15.  (54)   Guido Pepin       Swift DB-8        GO Racing        36
16.  (16)   Hanna Lee         Swift DB-8        Dotson Racing    36
17.  (55)   Cliff Roe         VanDiemen RF94    GO Racing        31
18.  (21)   Rick Henry        Swift DB-8                         30
19.   50)   Don Reese         VanDiemen RF95                     10
20.  (30)   Bill Murfy        Swift DB-8        Smurf Racing     18
21.  (00)   Tom Craig         Swift DB-3        TC Racing        11
22.  (88)   Barton Springs    VanDiemen RF91                     11
23.  (25)   Chase Wilder      Reynard SF90                        9
24.  (3)    Will Jones        Swift DB-8                          8
25.  (99)   Peter Hurst       Swift DB-8                          7
26.  (27)   Ben Cifelli       Swift DB-3                          6
27.  (74)   Mark McGrath      Swift DB-3        M & M Racing      4
28.  (60)   Rex VanHorn       Reynard SF91                        4
29.  (39)   Art Grindle       Swift SE-3                          3
30.  (13)   Steve Smagala     VanDiemen RF89                      3
```

```
                        SCCA/USAC
            U.S. Formula Ford 2000 National Championship
                        Official Race Results
                             June 26
                             Sebring
                         Sebring, Florida
                          (3.7 miles)
        Car      Name              Model          Time      Speed
Laps    No.
```

Laps	Car No.	Name	Model	Time	Speed	
1.	(44)	Shannon Kelly	Crossle 71F	2:21.60	94.02	17
2.	(5)	Ian Poirier	Swift DB-8	2:23.85	92.31	17
3.	(8)	Freddy Mercury	Reynard 95F	2:26.63	90.83	17
4.	(33)	Bob Dotson	Spirit	2:26.65	90.85	17
5.	(22)	Augie Zuehl	VanDiemen RF95	2:26.45	90.98	17
6.	(16)	Hanna Lee	Swift DB-8	2:26.35	91.05	17
7.	(71)	Gordon Chappel	VanDiemen RF95	2:26.95	90.57	17
8.	(27)	Roberto Cruz	VanDiemen RF95	2:28.37	89.80	16
9.	(11)	Alan Reckert	Stohr	2:28.54	89.65	16
10.	(34)	Claude Marcoux	Swift DB-8	2:28.73	89.54	16
11.	(50)	Don Reese	VanDiemen RF95	2:28.13	89.93	16
12.	(54)	Guido Pepin	Swift DB-8	2:29.75	88.95	16
13.	(1)	TJ Benson	VanDiemen RF95	2:30.40	88.55	16
14.	(99)	Peter Hurst	Swift DB-8	2:30.00	88.80	16
15.	(21)	Rick Henry	Swift DB-8	2:29.22	89.27	16
16.	(3)	Will Jones	VanDiemen RF95	2:29.45	88.01	16
17.	(7)	Ron Leclair	Swift DB-8	2:29.25	89.24	16
18.	(30)	Bill Murfy	Swift DB-8	2:30.88	88.33	15
19.	(88)	Barton Springs	VanDiemen RF91	2:31.32	88.01	15
20.	(25)	Chase Wilder	Reynard SF90	2:31.16	88.11	15
21.	(00)	Tom Craig	Swift DB-3	2:31.22	88.14	15
22.	(74)	Mark McGrath	Swift DB-3	2:33.45	86.75	14
23.	(60)	Rex VanHorn	Reynard SF91	2:33.27	88.60	14
DNF	(13)	Steve Smagala	VanDiemen RF89	2:45.45	80.35	7
DNF	(43)	Jude Dionne	Swift DB-8	2:28.44	89.85	7
DNF	(69)	Phil Spratt	Reynard 95F	2:28.64	88.60	7
DNF	(39)	Art Grindle	Swift SE-3	2:30.57	88.65	6
DNF	(47)	Darrell Pollard	VanDiemen RF95	2:30.22	88.35	6
DNF	(55)	Cliff Roe	VanDiemen RF94	2:29.15	88.24	6
DNS	(27)	Ben Cifelli	Swift DB-3	No Time		0

```
FASTEST LAP
Car      Time            Speed
```

The party became a stomping ground for TJ where he became the brunt of jokes when it became common knowledge I no longer worked for BRM. Soon the conversation moved to the race at Sebring, and the awesome display of racing put on by Shannon--the new "Rainman."

Two hours after we arrived, Grant and I, with a beer in hand, went to Grant's camper. We left Shannon behind to basque in the glory with his friends, Augie and Hanna.

Inside the motorhome, Tex jumped from my shoulder and to his perch, where I deposited a handful of sunflower seeds in a small dish attached to the perch. Then I popped two lemon drops in my mouth and took a sip of beer.

Emotionally exhausted and loosened with the drink, Grant sat at the small dining room table and cried.

"I can't believe I missed the race and Shannon won," moaned Grant. "Tell me about it."

So I sat back and recanted the race in great detail and enthusiasm, even describing, again, "The Zone."

Grant would nod his head and occasionally mumble, "Uh, huh." A few times, his eyes opened wide and he would say, "Really?"

Grant stopped me so he could use the bathroom. He retrieved two more beers from the refrigerator and gave me one, which I eagerly accepted.

When I finished reciting the race, I said, "I want to see Shannon have the chance he deserves. I've seen it before. Shannon's like a wild stallion with speed and power, but it's outta control. Like breaking a stallion, someone needs to harness Shannon's skills, polish them, then turn them in the right direction. What happened today was a good example. The other experienced thoroughbreds were forced to run the wild stallion's race."

"Really?"

I nodded, "Boy, howdy. Give me some more time with that wild stallion and we'll have a few more wins."

All I could think about was the Swift SE-3 and the opportunity to give Shannon a chance.

"Hey, Charlie," said Grant, slurring his words as he spoke. "Tell me about Shannon's race again."

"Well," I said, "Shannon started in 22nd place."

"Uh, huh."

Again, with the help of the beer and a few more colorful words and properly placed metaphors, I described the event but this time going into even greater detail. About the race, the victory . . . and the "Rainman!"

PEPPER AUTOMOTIVE

The Road Atlanta road racing course lay nestled in the red clay hills of Georgia only two miles from the small town of Brasleton. It was famous for a conglomerate headed by the actress Kim Bassinger, who purchased the town. Still months away, Road Atlanta would be the sight for the final race in the American Continental Championship series. Eight miles from Road Atlanta lay another small town, Gainesville. On the outskirts of Gainesville to the Brasleton side rested my car repair shop. The white concrete block building, situated atop a bluff, looked down on the road. Bold blue letters on the front called out the name--Pepper's Automotive. A large fenced in area behind my shop contained cars being repaired. Others were stored for customers, and those I hoped to rebuild in the future. This included the '49 Ford pickup I had almost fully restored except for the body work and paint.

With five races remaining, I worked at a feverish pace just to repair and set the Swift SE-3 once belonging to Art Grindle.

With the Mid-Ohio race only two weeks after Sebring, I had misjudged the time element. When I returned to Atlanta, Grant and Shannon had remained behind for three days to close the deal on the Crossle with Jimmy Smith. With the transaction completed, Grant and Shannon drove to Atlanta where they reunited with me at my shop in Gainesville. The following Saturday, they received a commitment from Grindle. While Grant remained behind, Shannon drove to St. Louis, picked up the Swift SE-3 and promptly returned to Pepper Automotive, arriving late Sunday night.

Grant and Shannon were to leave Thursday morning for Mid-Ohio. I had only three days to repair the Swift. Shannon ran wild with the shop portion containing the body repair and paint booth. Quickly, Shannon repaired the fiberglass and painted the car with the familiar yellow, blue, and red colors and the now familiar dark blue number "44." The airbrush design on the mid-section blended all three colors. The mid-section was yellow and the rear wing the familiar blue with bright yellow number "44." One-inch strips of blue and red followed the contours on the Swift SE-3 from the mid-section to the tail.

The body work impressed me and I said to Shannon, "Hey, maybe I can hire you permanently to do my work. I got an old '49 Ford pickup I've been wantin' to do for ten years."

We both laughed about it but I was really rather serious.

Even with time limited, I forced Shannon to set the suspension. I made the initial call on settings, then taught Shannon the intricacies of suspension setup, the differences, and the results from the variety of settings.

When I first learned Shannon had no practical knowledge of suspension techniques at the Dallas Grand Prix, I wanted to help desperately but was unable due to my commitment to Benson. Since I no longer worked for Benson, I was determined to put Shannon on a quick, forced-learning curve. Where most new drivers might experiment and learn over a few years, I expected Shannon to learn within the next few races. Teaching TJ had taken me a whole year before I saw any results.

Slowly and with great patience, I showed Shannon the settings. Setting a race car was not like going down to a garage and having a car aligned. The main settings were the caster, camber, toe-in and bump steer. The caster was the tire position in front or behind the axle. The camber, or vertical angle of the tire, was always set with a negative angle, where the top of the tire tilted in toward the racecar; likewise, positive camber was when the bottom of the tire tilted in. The toe-in was the tire's horizontal forward angle, where the tire pointed in or out, to the center of the racecar. This was usually set to zero. Occasionally on a loose suspension, a driver would set the tires to point slightly in, then under full acceleration the tires would pull out and point straight ahead. Bump steer also changed the geometry of a racer under compression, cornering, or braking. Under loads to springs, sway bars, and shocks, the tires moved in a vertical plane making tires point in or out. The bump steer adjustment eliminated the angle change and maintained a near forward parallel direction as loads increased or decreased on a tire.

The adjustment amazed Shannon. The settings on the rear of Grindle's old car pointed to the left on both tires. Some drivers would count this as an added advantage on a course with mostly left turns, but as I pointed out, Sebring was mostly right turns, which would also explain the tremendous problems Grindle encountered. As he turned right, the rear of the Swift SE-3 wanted to turn left.

Next, I taught Shannon about the shock and sway bar settings. Why had I told Shannon to set the shocks and sway bar softer at Sebring? Because a hard firm ride would break loose, where a loose soft suspension would always stay in contact with the ground in the rain. A firm suspension would keep a race car from pitching and rolling on a dry course. Some drivers preferred a stiffer suspension, while others liked slightly softer. Again, a drivers preference. The swaybar settings would affect the front end "plowing or oversteer" or the reared kicking out or "understeer." A simple sway bar adjustment could eliminate or create either problem. The shocks were set soft, firm, or extra firm. Again, depending on the driver and his preference.

Shannon and I pushed the Swift SE-3 up two-inch high wooden ramps and onto electric scales. Once on the scales, I checked the meter, reading the weights of each corner. After the wreck, the weights were off with the left front more than the right front and just the opposite true on the back tires.

Again I explained the choices. Some drivers liked to preload a side, for a track with a majority of turns to the opposite side. Some drivers chose the reverse setup. The third choice was to balance the car so the feel was the same no matter which way the turns. Shannon chose the third as I hoped. After what I had seen through the first half of the season, I felt Shannon could jump into any setting and adapt within a few laps and still be competitive. I was sure he had never had a car setup properly which only excited me more at the thought of what he would be like when we found the proper combination and setup for him.

Shannon watched as I tightened the spring on the right front. The meter showed an increase in weight on the right front, a decrease in weight on the left front, and a slight increase on the left rear. Enthusiastically Shannon asked to fix the rear. He watched as the weights changed and finally balanced. The front was slightly off, so he changed it again until the fronts and the rears matched.

Being a tutor was easy. Shannon was a quick learner and his tremendous desire pushed him faster. When I quit at night, Shannon remained behind, still working on the suspension settings. In the morning when I arrived at the garage, Shannon was already working on the Swift.

I had just enough time to repair the damage from Sebring and set the suspension for the Mid-Ohio road course. I took time to make Shannon set the suspension and watched. While Shannon worked, I pulled an old set of Uniden FM radios from a box in the back of his shop. Occasionally, I advised Shannon on the suspension. After checking out the radios, I ordered new batteries, set up my mobile unit, and wired Shannon's helmet. I put a microphone in the front bar of the helmet protecting Shannon's chin, and two speakers near where Shannon's ears would be in the helmet. Then, I attached a plug to the bottom left of the helmet. In the Swift SE-3 cockpit, I riveted a case on the interior left panel to hold the radio, then ran a wire up the steering column where I attached a button to the removable steering wheel. The button allowed the driver to speak over his two-way radio, and the cord had a plug for easy removal from the driver's helmet. After the radio batteries arrived and were installed, Shannon situated himself in the Swift, plugged the helmet radio in, pulled the helmet over his head, and switched the radio on, while I walked outside the garage.

I slipped the earphones over my ears, adjusted the squelch, and pushed the button, "Radio check. Do you read me, Shannon?"

Inside Shannon pushed the button on the steering wheel, "Loud and clear. But it sure seems loud."

I pushed the button, "No problem, there's a volume knob on the radio you can adjust, but I'm sure when you start the race, it won't seem loud."

Before we stopped, I walked down the hill and checked the radio again. After a few more checks, I was content with the Uniden's performance. The radio's had a distance of two miles, and would function at most tracks, except those with hills where portions of the track would make the radio dead. Still, I was extremely satisfied with the test.

While we worked on the cars, Grant felt helpless, so he continued his search for an apartment and applied for substitute teaching at the local high school.

The day before we were to leave for Mid-Ohio, Grant came running into the garage, yelling at Shannon and me and waving a current Autoweek. When Grant reached us, he hurriedly opened the magazine and pointed to an article about the race in Sebring. Above the article was a photo of Shannon leading Poirier to the checkered flag in the rain. Jolit Torres had written the article, more about the father and son team than about the race itself:

Young Gun Splashes to Victory

Rookie sensation Shannon Kelly won the fifth race of the American Continental Championship series in a rain-filled event at Sebring. Ian Poirier, previously unbeaten in the rain, had the title "Rainman" taken away by the new kid on the block. Shannon's father . . .

The article went on to tell about Grant and Shannon--and the last two sentences told about them joining with me. Her last words were: *With Charlie Pepper, this team will win again* before the year is over.

"Can you believe?" said Grant impressed and amazed.

"Boy, howdy!"

"Awesome!"

* * *

Suddenly the time was gone, and it became necessary to load for the trip to Mid-Ohio. When the sleek Swift SE-3 was loaded, the paint was still wet. I didn't even have enough time to make my usual double check. Those checks would need to be made at Mid-Ohio, on Friday, after we arrived.

Usually, I would fly in on Friday mornings in time for practice. This time I opted for the drive with Grant and Shannon, as the three of us, including Tex, would start the trip on Thursday.

MID-OHIO

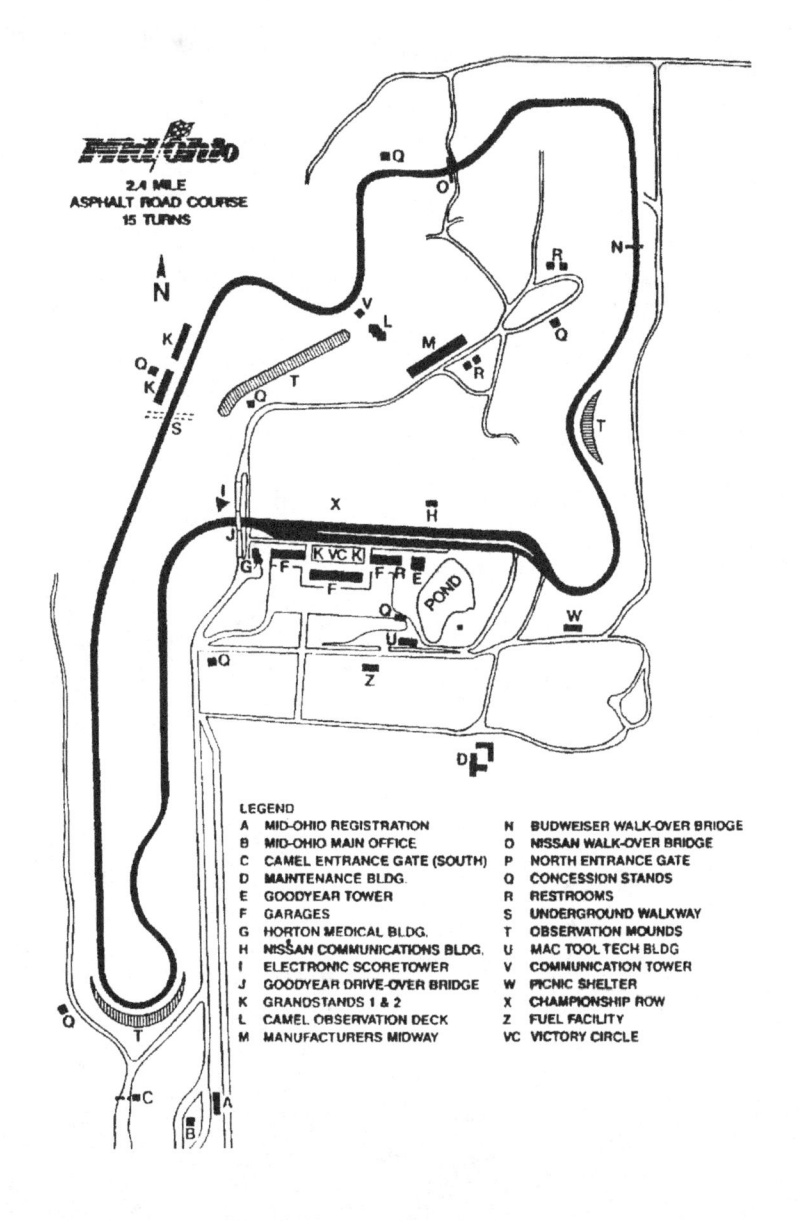

Mid-Ohio
2.4 MILE
ASPHALT ROAD COURSE
15 TURNS

LEGEND
A MID-OHIO REGISTRATION
B MID-OHIO MAIN OFFICE
C CAMEL ENTRANCE GATE (SOUTH)
D MAINTENANCE BLDG.
E GOODYEAR TOWER
F GARAGES
G HORTON MEDICAL BLDG.
H NISSAN COMMUNICATIONS BLDG.
I ELECTRONIC SCORETOWER
J GOODYEAR DRIVE-OVER BRIDGE
K GRANDSTANDS 1 & 2
L CAMEL OBSERVATION DECK
M MANUFACTURERS MIDWAY
N BUDWEISER WALK-OVER BRIDGE
O NISSAN WALK-OVER BRIDGE
P NORTH ENTRANCE GATE
Q CONCESSION STANDS
R RESTROOMS
S UNDERGROUND WALKWAY
T OBSERVATION MOUNDS
U MAC TOOL TECH BLDG
V COMMUNICATION TOWER
W PICNIC SHELTER
X CHAMPIONSHIP ROW
Z FUEL FACILITY
VC VICTORY CIRCLE

Mid-Ohio Sports Car Course

FORMULA 2000, the Dream

The Mid-Ohio Sports Car Course lay outside the small town of Lexington, Ohio. The challenging course was the sixth stop on the U.S. Formula Ford 2000 National Championship series for the Formula 2000 racers set for Sunday, July 9. Friday found most entrants present and taking advantage of an open day of practice. Qualifying was set for Saturday with the race at noon on Sunday followed by the SCCA Trans-Am race.

The track appeared to be carved from a forest of beautiful elm, ash, and giant oaks. The course wound down, around, and over the hilly green terrain. In places, the track was cleared to allow plenty of runoff room for stricken cars or accidents that might occur. The straightaways were lined with Armco steel barriers. The infield provided a higher point for spectators to safely observe the race with access provided by pedestrian bridges across the track. The drivers' paddock area was located on the outside of the track behind the pit area.

The Friday afternoon practice was hot with more July heat predicted for the weekend.

Since this was my first race weekend with Shannon and Grant, I tried to avoid contact with TJ, but found TJ more than ready to avoid me. When TJ found Shannon already in the fast pits preparing for the practice session, he moved to the opposite end. Pitted to one side of Shannon was Guido and his GO Racing team. While on the other side was Dotson racing, and Hanna Lee.

With the second session of Friday's practice underway, I continued to spot racers with my hand held stopwatch since we no longer had access to the expensive computers like those of BRM. Still, the times I took were remarkably accurate. I had my new driver in the top five.

The start/finish area was flat and presented a clear view of the final three turns before the main straight. A portion of the long straight leading to Turn 6 could also be viewed from the start/finish. Shannon streaked past the pit area passing Chase Wilder before he reached the medium speed Turn 1 where under braking he passed Van Horn. The passes showed the excellent passing opportunities Turn 1 provided. Shannon was careful coming out of Turn 1, where adverse camber exiting the turn, created an understeer situation, yet high exit speed was essential to low track times. He managed a high speed exit, carrying him into the critical right-left-left at Turn 2 and 3. Shannon carried maximum speed into Turn 2, and held tight to the apex on the double left of Turn 3, to setup for the keyhole at Turn 4.

The keyhole was one of the most important corners at Mid-Ohio. The turn was slow. The drivers who followed a slow line and came out of the turn with full power, usually came away winners because the exit brought the racer onto the longest and fastest straightaway on the track. Shannon went in and came out the Keyhole fast, aiming for Turn 6, at the end of the long straightaway. Turn 5 was only a slight bend in the straight taken under full power with the only problem that of overtaking and passing slower traffic. The slightly banked right-handed Turn 6 provided higher speeds than first estimated and was another premier braking/passing corner at Mid-Ohio as Shannon was learning when he passed Phil Spratt. After the pass, he was quick to pull back right, holding tight to the right for the uphill left-handed Turn 7. He took the downhill, late apex, forcing the car into a drift he controlled expertly where many drivers failed to recover. He pulled to the left, setting up for hard braking before the right at Turn 8. Smooth power out set Shannon up for the next series of turns. Slightly uphill, suddenly the track dropped downhill at Turn 9. He stayed in tight to the left at the crest of the hill and Turn 9 so he could set up for the right at Turn 10. After Turn 10 came hard braking for Turn 11 carrying maximum speed from the turn and uphill until the jump. Pulling tight to the right for Turn 12 took Shannon into the off camber left-hand Turn 13. Apexing early and applying constant power, Shannon setup for the Carousel or Turn 14. It was a misleading horseshoe type turn where most drivers wanted to accelerate. This would throw them out into the pit entry and away from Turn 15, the lefthander, leading onto the start/finish straight. Shannon held back and took Turn 15 perfectly streaking past start/finish. I clicked the stopwatch one more time.

 A few minutes later, the session ended and all cars pulled into the fast pits while some went directly to their paddock area. Shannon and Augie pulled down pit row, letting the respective crews check their tire settings. Hanna pulled just ahead of Shannon where Mercury and Dotson deciphered what O'Brien had written down. Both gave input to settings they preferred.

 I concentrated on the setup for the Swift SE-3, while Shannon visited for a moment with Hanna and Augie, who had walked down the pits from where TJ set his team. The practice enabled me to learn more about Shannon Kelly and his racing ability. Now I knew for sure Shannon had the potential to be a great driver. The previous five races proved Shannon had the ability, especially in the rain, as he had proved at Sebring. The problem I found was Shannon could drive the car in any setting, but I needed feedback from Shannon, which I was not getting. After each session, I changed the suspension settings on the car hoping to obtain a response from Shannon, only to have him give me the same answer, with a shrug of his shoulders and the words, "It's okay" or "fine."

 Angered at Shannon's inability to know what he wanted or needed, I loosened the rear sway bar radically. Doing this to the Swift would make the rear end sway to extremes through the corners and kick the reared out creating oversteer. At first I hesitated, knowing the dangerous situation it created--but if Shannon was to be a good racecar driver he would need to feel the problem and learn the solution. I just hoped Shannon could bring the car back and prayed Shannon's natural ability would keep him from wrecking the new racer. With the incorrect setting, I estimated Shannon would take an additional ten seconds--if he completed the first lap at all.

With fingers crossed, I sent Shannon back onto the road course, watched as the yellow racer took the left at Turn 1 and disappeared, building speed for the next series of turns.

I adjusted the headset and stepped over the wall to where Grant waited. I clicked in the radio, "How's it feel?"

"Fine," was Shannon's response.

"We'll see," I said, smiling to myself.

Although I could not see Shannon, I sensed Shannon would be moving through the esses up to the Turn 2 right-hander, then the combination left of Turn 3. Those turns would be followed by Turn 4, a slow, slow turn where he would come back the opposite direction and up the long straight and through the kink at Turn 5. Momentarily he would pop into view, then disappear toward Turn 6.

As Shannon streaked down the long straightaway, he pushed the button attached to the steering wheel with his left thumb, "Hey, Charlie, the car feels funny."

I smiled, "Be careful. If there's a problem, bring it in."

Shannon was not one to use the radios and seldom asked anything unless he needed something or to acknowledge me when I spoke to him. A moment later, Shannon clicked the button again, "Charlie, I almost lost it."

"What's wrong?" I asked.

"The reared is kicking out."

"What do you think?"

"Don't know. Maybe the tires are cold."

The answer made me frown, but I knew I could not expect Shannon to guess the problem so quickly, when he knew nothing about the suspension settings. When Shannon passed, I started the stopwatch.

Shannon complained about the car one more time, but when he passed the pits, I clocked him at only five seconds off his original pace. I was stunned, knowing Shannon was lucky to even finish the lap. The next time past, Shannon cut a half second from his time. Two laps later the time dropped another half second. I was as amazed at Shannon's ability to adapt to the impossible setting, as I was angry at Shannon's inability to identify the problem and come up with a solution.

Two laps later, I called Shannon in and asked him what the problem was, since he was four seconds slower.

Shannon explained how the SE-3 was trying to spin out on him, and the rear would kick out, so he would turn early, crank the front wheels to keep the back from spinning around, and with that technique, he would scrub speed when the rear would catch before he went off the track, and he would continue.

"What should we do?" I asked.

"I don't know," said Shannon with the all too familiar shrugging shoulders. "I'm sorry, Charlie."

I could only sigh at the response, angry Shannon could not pinpoint the problem, and still shocked at Shannon's on track solution to the problem. "Sounds to me like it's the swaybar. Let's stiffen it a little." I worked steadily on the Swift and was soaked from the July heat. Even the red rag, hanging from the back pocket of my coveralls, was soaked. I replaced it with another dry rag and wiped the perspiration from my brow with a forearm. I watched Shannon as he sat in the shade in his racing suit that was also soaked and told him to undo the front and drink liquids. A half hour later, I completed the change, refueled the car, and Shannon was on his way again. I would have to tell Shannon about the "Red Mist."

Two laps later, Shannon ran his fastest lap of the day. "How's it feel," I asked, but my lips made the answer to the all too familiar response, "fine."

"Fine."

As Shannon flashed past the pits and pushed out of Turn 1, I thought I noticed a puff of smoke from the engine. The engine was smoking, bringing another item of concern for me, and something I didn't want to share with Shannon or Grant. I crossed my fingers and shook my head, "Please God . . . not this weekend." Now, I regretted not switching engines and keeping the Ivey engine which was only three races old.

* * *

The drivers stood around the false grid waiting for Saturday's second and last qualifying session to begin. The summer sun beat down on the drivers unmercifully. Most tried to find shade. Crew members held umbrellas over the driver's heads preventing as much heat from reaching them as they could.

Guido Pepin was one well shielded from the sun. In the past the heat had bothered him to such an extent, he installed a bottle of ice water in his racer with a clear plastic tube running beneath his helmet and into his mouth, where he sucked the refreshing fluids during the race as he desired. Mercury and Dotson kept cold wraps around their neck. The cold wrap fabricated from material like a bath towel was, in reality, a long slender tube, more like a sock, the drivers could fill with ice, then wrap around their neck and snap the end together with velcro. They did this to prevent the dangerous "Red Mist" from occurring during the race.

"Red Mist?" asked Shannon.

"Boy, howdy," I said, as I made final checks on the engine. "And don't eat anything at least an hour before you race."

"Don't eat?"

"Yep," I answered. "When it gets hot like this your system has to work extra on food, and when you sweat and dehydrate in the heat, your brain seems to send delayed signals to your body. Kinda like your body's electrical system has a short circuit, so drink a whole bunch of fluids before the race and not those darn Cokes because the carbonation will affect you. Drink all the Gatorade you want, we got plenty. I've seen guys crawl out of their cars and puke for half an hour. Sometimes, they even have to take a driver to a hospital. So make sure you drink fluids."

I checked the oil and noticed it was low. The engine was definitely burning the oil. Now, if the rings would just hold through the race, I thought. I put more oil in the engine, screwed the oil cap down, and replaced the engine cover.

The whistle blew giving the drivers five minutes before the start of the last qualifying.

As usual, Shannon was relaxed and it carried over to his closest friends Augie and Hanna. For me, the weekend had been peaceful. No TJ to argue with and the tension gone. Racing was fun once more.

A few minutes later, the colorful array of racers entered the track, set on doing the best they could to snag a high position on the grid for Sunday's race. Some expecting the pole, some hoping for the pole and all dreaming of the pole.

I had said nothing and Timing and Scoring did not issue a qualifying sheet after the first session but rumor and my numbers had Shannon third on the grid. Marty and Les had verified the numbers with me, and they also let me know TJ was very angry, and taking his anger and frustration out on them and Augie.

I knew Shannon was a quick learner. Often going out and being competitive in the first few laps where it took most drivers a few sessions to dial in their cars. Only two questions remained; could Shannon better his time and remain in the hunt--and would the engine hold together?

Thirty minutes later the session ended and I was relieved to see Shannon running just as fast as in the first session.

In the pits, I tried to get feedback from Shannon but continued to get the same response, "fine." I made Shannon check all the suspension settings himself while I tended to the engine and drive train. A few hours later, with the adjustments finished and all the checks complete to my satisfaction, the two of us along with Grant attended a drivers' party at the Dotson trailer. The sun had disappeared, making temperatures tolerable, and a slight breeze brought relief to everyone at the party. The extreme heat made the hot tub out of the question. Not only were we attending another of Dotson and Mercury's parties, Shannon was fulfilling a promise to Hanna.

The day before, Shannon had shown Hanna some of his art work and she was amazed at his ability to draw and paint caricatures. She begged him to do one for her. Shannon smiled and told her that since the day he met her, he had an idea.

So with a few drivers congregated around, Shannon worked on the side of Hanna's racer with his air brushes. While Shannon sketched lightly with a felt pen, Augie came running up with copies of the grid in his hand. Quickly, he passed the copies out and everyone took time to check their position:

```
                         SCCA/USAC
              U.S. Formula Ford 2000 National Championship
                      Official Points Standing
                       (After 6 of 10 events)


         Car       Name            Model           Team              Points
         No.

         1.(1)     TJ Benson       VanDiemen RF95  BRM                 147
         2.(5)     Ian Poirier     Swift DB-8      PACE                119
         3.(33)    Bob Dotson      Spirit          Dotson Racing       100
         4.(8)     Freddy Mercury  Reynard 95F     Dotson Racing       100
         5.(71)    Gordon Chappel  VanDiemen RF95  MOSES                98
         6.(34)    Claude Marcoux  Swift DB-8      PACE                 91
         7.(11)    Alan Reckert    Stohr           TART                 79
         8.(7)     Ron Leclair     VanDiemen RF95  TART                 74
         9.(69)    Phil Spratt     Reynard 95F     Spratt Racing        67
        10.(47)    Darrell Pollard VanDiemen RF95  BRM                  65
        11.(44)    Shannon Kelly   Swift SE-3                           65
        12.(27)    Roberto Cruz    VanDiemen RF95  Spratt Racing        51
        13.(16)    Hanna Lee       Swift DB-8      Dotson Racing        48
        14.(22)    Augie Zuehl     VanDiemen RF95  PHAR Motorsports     49
        15.(55)    Cliff Roe       VanDiemen RF94  GO Racing            40
        16.(43)    Jude Dionne     Swift DB-8      PACE                 40
        17.(54)    Guido Pepin     Swift DB-8      GO Racing            37
        18.(21)    Rick Henry      Swift DB-8                           35
        19.(19)    Maxwell Jordan  Swift DB-8                           26
        20.(50)    Don Reese       VanDiemen RF95                       23
        21.(30)    Bill Murfy      Swift DB-8      Smurf Racing         22
        22.(88)    Barton Springs  VanDiemen RF91                       21
        23.(99)    Peter Hurst     Swift DB-8                           18
        24.(25)    Chase Wilder    Reynard SF90                         15
        25.(00)    Tom Craig       Swift DB-3      TC Racing            14
        26.(3)     Will Jones      Swift DB-8                           10
        27.(27)    Ben Cifelli     Swift DB-3                            7
        28.(74)    Mark McGrath    Swift DB-3      M & M Racing          4
        29.(13)    Steve Smagala   VanDiemen RF89                        3
        30.(39)    Art Grindle     Swift SE-3                            3
```

"Awesome! Look where Shannon is," yelled Augie.

Augie spread out the grid sheet and pointed to Shannon's name in the sixth position. Grant and Hanna hovered over Shannon's shoulder and pointed to Shannon's name. I smiled, content with what we had accomplished.

On the other side of the room where drivers were partying Dotson yelled, "Hey, Pepper, it looks like your boy is ready to play."

I waved a finger at Dotson, "It sure looks like you and your Spirit have become competitive."

```
                         SCCA/USAC
            U.S. Formula Ford 2000 National Championship
                        Official Grid
                            July 9
                   Mid-Ohio Sports Car Course
                       Lexington, Ohio
                         (2.4 miles)

        Car    Name              Model            Time
        No.

    1.  (1)    TJ Benson         VanDiemen RF95   1:28.11*
    2.  (33)   Bob Dotson        Spirit           1:28.19*
    3.  (8)    Freddy Mercury    Reynard 95F      1:28.25
    4.  (5)    Ian Poirier       Swift DB-8       1:28.38
    5.  (34)   Claude Marcoux    Swift DB-8       1:28.59
    6.  (44)   Shannon Kelly     Swift SE-3        1:28.67
    7.  (7)    Ron Leclair       VanDiemen RF95   1:28.73
    8.  (27)   Roberto Cruz      VanDiemen RF95   1:29.01
    9.  (47)   Darrell Pollard   VanDiemen RF95   1:28.95
   10.  (71)   Gordon Chappel    VanDiemen RF95   1:28.88
   11.  (69)   Phil Spratt       Reynard 95F      1:28.92
   12.  (16)   Hanna Lee         Swift DB-8       1:29.43
   13   (50)   Don Reese         VanDiemen RF95   1:28.99
   14.  (11)   Alan Reckert      Stohr            1:28.78
   15.  (43)   Jude Dionne       Swift DB-8       1:28.80
   16.  (22)   Augie Zuehl       VanDiemen RF95   1:29.15
   17.  (55)   Cliff Roe         VanDiemen RF94   1:29.25
   18.  (99)   Peter Hurst       Swift DB-8       1:29.75
   19.  (54)   Guido Pepin       Swift DB-8       1:29.83
   20.  (21)   Rick Henry        Swift DB-8       1:29.92
   21.  (30)   Bill Murfy        Swift DB-8       1:30.45
   22.  (27)   Ben Cifelli       Swift DB-3       1:31.22
   23.  (88)   Barton Springs    VanDiemen RF91   1:31.74
   24.  (00)   Tom Craig         Swift DB-3       1:31.80
   25.  (74)   Mark McGrath      Swift DB-3       1:31.95
   26.  (60)   Rex VanHorn       Reynard SF91     1:31.97
   27.  (13)   Steve Smagala     VanDiemen RF89   1:32.50
   28.  (25)   Chase Wilder      Reynard SF90     1:32.55
   29.  (3)    Will Jones        Swift DB-8       1:32.98

        *Below Track Record
```

Dotson shrugged his shoulders and tried to give an innocent appearance. "After watching Shannon at IRP and Dallas, I got a new engine from Jay Ivey. Got another engine for Freddy too. Must be the Ivey engine."

I laughed, then walked over to Shannon, "You've done good. Just keep the car together tomorrow and you'll do just fine."

The party continued, while Shannon tried to finish his artistic work on Hanna's light blue number "16" DB-6 Swift. Augie refilled their drinks and returned to watch Shannon work. Hanna sat on the other side of the racer, since Shannon refused to let her see the work until he finished. Augie only made the wait worse as he gawked over the art work.

After obviously having had too much to drink, Les approached me, "You need help, Charlie?"

"Why?"

"Since you quit, TJ has been nothing but an asshole. I'm miserable working for him. I think Marty is too, but he won't say," said Les.

I wrapped my arm around Les' shoulder, "Look, you're more than welcome to come work for me. I always thought you should come to Atlanta anyway."

"Thanks, Charlie. I might just be coming to Atlanta after this race," Les smiled and took a chug from his drink. "Well, I better get back."

As Les walked away, I moved over to Hanna's car to see Shannon's handy work. I could only wonder at what Les and Marty were going through with TJ, and yet TJ still had the pole. Even without me, TJ was a good driver, maybe even great, and could still win.

Shannon was wiping his hands clean when I arrived. Shannon smiled at Hanna and waved her around the car.

For the first time, Hanna saw what Shannon had painted on the side of her car. The picture was a castle high atop a hill, with a road winding down the hill, guarded by a happy green dragon with the letters "Puff" over him. Beneath the scene in calligraphy was a single word "Hanna Lee." Immediately, Hanna recognized the scene from the song, "Puff the Magic Dragon."

"Oh, how cute," said Hanna, as she squeezed Shannon's arm. She grabbed him and kissed him on the lips.

Hanna yelled to Dotson and Mercury to come and see the work Shannon had done. While she pranced in front of the art work, Augie pulled Shannon to the side.

"I think I'm gonna quit after this race," said Augie.

"What?"

"Yeah. It's impossible being around TJ, and he's made racing lose its interest. It used to be fun," said Augie obviously upset at the prospect of racing coming to an end. "I don't need to put up with an attitude like TJ's. I don't act that way around the people who work for me, and I sure don't intend to put up with it when I'm supposed to be doing something I like. Being around TJ is a real intense bummer."

Shannon's eyes lit up, "Then join our team."

"I can't," said Augie shrugging his shoulders.

They discussed the idea a little more until Hanna interrupted them. She needed to go to the hotel and asked Shannon to drive her back. Soon everyone dispersed to their hotels or motorhomes.

* * *

The five-minute warning sounded and again the drivers repeated their individual rituals before the start of the race. Shannon and Augie quit playing with the hacky sack. Shannon tossed the small leather pouch to Grant while he walked Hanna toward her car. Halfway to her blue number 16, he squeezed her hand then went to his Swift SE-3.

The heat was bad and they had all made provisions for it. At the three-minute warning, Guido Pepin poured ice down his back and down the front of his racing suit, then stuffed the clear plastic tube, carrying ice water, in his mouth. Dotson did the same with ice in the front of his suit, then wrapped an ice filled tube around his neck, connecting the velcro strips. Shannon chugged the Gatorade before slipping the helmet over his head.

The whistle warned of three minutes to the race. One by one the Formula Continentals coughed to life, and the small Ford engines revved higher and higher as the drivers flipped the throttles, checking the oil pressure and warming the engines.

Again the whistle--only one minute remained. Grant pushed near and again he and Shannon conducted the all too familiar handshake that meant so much. Les and Marty appeared tense. Pollard was high on the grid in 9th. Augie had struggled and was down in 16th. TJ appeared nervous as he barked orders to Marty while Les tried to accommodate both Augie and Pollard. Dotson in 2nd and Mercury in 3rd were ready. All held a fist high.

The Grid Marshall signaled the drivers.

Slowly the cars moved from the grid. TJ moved left for the pole position, Dotson right, Mercury left. They alternated until all were gone from the grid and proceeding along the race track. Coming out of Turn 4, they weaved back and forth warming the tires.

I adjusted the Uniden and another radio I had pulled from the mothballs at the back of my shop--a scanner. The scanner would enable me to listen to the chatter between corner workers and the Stewards of the race. I squeezed the button on the Uniden radio, "Do you hear me, Shannon?"

"Yes."

"Good. Now forget about me and concentrate on the race. I'll let you know if there are any problems on the track, and tell you when there are five laps remaining."

"Okay."

The train of race cars pulled slowly through the carousel and onto the straight leading to start/finish. Dotson, on the outside front row, kept popping his car forward, which seemed to rattle TJ who came down hard on the throttle when they entered the straight. In doing so, TJ left the others behind. Instantly, the flagman shook his head and held his finger high signaling a wave off and one more lap before the start of the race. Only twenty-four laps remained in the race since the second pace lap counted as the first race lap.

The next time, TJ brought the group of 29 drivers around more slowly . . . so slowly that when the pack took the green, Dotson jumped ahead of TJ as did Ian who followed closely behind Dotson. Shannon squeezed in close behind Poirier and managed to swing in behind TJ and take 4th, passing Mercury and Marcoux.

Pollard and Chappel caught Spratt and Leclair, passed them and managed to cling to the lead six. By the second lap, the first eight broke away. Spratt and Leclair led the next pack of seven with Barton Springs, Cruz, Hanna, and the two new drivers, Don Reese and Peter Hurst, whose only previous race was rain plagued Sebring. Suddenly, Hanna passed Springs and Cruz in the back at Turn 11. Immediately, Reese and Hurst followed past Cruz and Springs and started dicing through the turns with Chappel, Spratt, and Hanna. This enabled the top eight, who remained in single file, to slowly pull away over the next five laps. The second group's fight for position let the others close in from behind.

For the first time in five races, the Canadians were having a bad day as Reckert and Dionne made a slow charge to the rear, losing a position each lap. After five laps, they were in 19th and 20th, respectively, with chances of a top ten finish vanishing with each turn in the track.

On lap seven, Smagala and McGrath came together at Turn 13, spinning off the track through the carousel of Turn 14. Both reentered the track and hobbled to the nearby pit entry with suspension damage and finished for the day.

As lap eleven started, Dotson continued to lead and through the Turn 2 and 3 chicane, Shannon and Mercury moved past TJ and Poirier, taking 2nd and 3rd. Marcoux was close behind in 6th.

The Mid-Ohio Sports Car Course took a toll on the Canadians. Pushing to catch TJ out of Turn 4, Poirier dropped his two right tires off on the inside of the turn. The Swift broke loose and Poirier jerked left, then right before he regained control, but too late as his teammate, Marcoux, tagged him in the rear, crumpling Poirier's exhaust. The contact shoved Marcoux's wing up and back making it nonfunctional and his camber was slightly out. Both continued but at Turn 6 and 7 the next group caught them. Chappel passed them at Turn 8 and Spratt took them at Turn 10. Hanna, Reese, and Hurst passed Marcoux and Poirier before they made it back around to start/finish. On the next lap, Cruz, Springs and Augie passed them.

On the twelfth lap, the Canadians last hope faltered as Leclair dropped back. The heat affected his ability to operate his racecar. The heat had the same effect on Guido who pulled in on lap thirteen, knowing he received one point for finishing half the race.

Still, Poirier nursed his car around the track and continued to fall farther back. Marcoux pulled in on lap sixteen as did Dionne. Leclair retired on lap seventeen with Cifelli.

With two laps remaining, Shannon continued a strong 2nd and actually caught Dotson, but as he pulled out of Turn 4, he called in, "The car's missing. It sounds bad, Charlie."

My heart sank. The engine was letting go.

"Should I come in?" Shannon asked, the anxiety obvious in his voice.

"No!" I screamed. "You're too durn close to the end. Stick it out even if that sonofabitch blows."

Mercury passed Shannon before they reached Turn 6, but Shannon managed to hold TJ off through the turns and actually pulled away. On the straight, in front of start/finish, and with lap twenty-four ending, TJ passed Shannon. Smoke started to come from the back of Shannon's Swift.

One lap remained.

I prayed the engine would hold together but the next group was closing in on Shannon. Between Turn 4 and 5, Pollard and Chappel passed Shannon. Old Moses waved to Shannon as he passed. Spratt closed in but Shannon held him off until he came out of Turn 11 and started uphill. Spratt also waved at Shannon when he passed, instantly recognizing the engine problem. Shannon had dropped from 2nd to 7th--and the others were closing fast.

Reese passed Hanna and closed quickly on Shannon in Turn 14 and the carousel.

Hanna was not far behind and close to her was Hurst, Springs, and Roe who took 12th from Cruz and Augie.

Shannon fought Reese and pulled away from him coming out of Turn 15. Reese closed on Shannon down the straight, but Shannon reached the finish line first and retained his 7th place. As he crossed the finish line, the car belched smoke. Shannon cut the power and immediately pulled off the track before Turn 1. The engine was gone.

The next six positions remained the same except Augie passed Cruz at the flag.

Again, the top six reported to Impound with the first three making a quick stop in the winner's circle for awards, pictures, and champagne.

Grant and I waited for Shannon to be pulled into the pits, so we could congratulate him. I felt like I had cheated Shannon, because the engine went bad and I knew about it, but there was no disappointment in Shannon's eyes when they met with mine.

Shannon pulled his helmet off and yelled at me, "I can do it. If the engine hadn't gone, I think I could have taken Dotson."

"I'm sorry, Shannon," I said. "I was afraid the engine would go . . . and it did."

"Charlie, it's not your fault," said Shannon who put his arm around me and startled Tex.

"Squirt!"

Grant added, "There wasn't enough time to do any more than you did."

The excited look in Grant's face caught me off guard. I tried to hold back the tightness from my throat. "Humph, I'm so used to TJ, this is hard to take. But I guarantee the car will be ready for the next race."

Back at the motorhome, the mood was festive and excited as though we had won.

We went to Impound where we congratulated Mercury and Dotson. TJ intentionally avoided us. Even Hanna had done well and finished in the top ten.

A few hours later, Shannon, Grant, and I were reviewing the race results:

FORMULA 2000, the Dream

```
                    SCCA/USAC
       U.S. Formula Ford 2000 National Championship
                 Official Race Results
                       July 9
              Mid-Ohio Sports Car Course
                    Lexington, Ohio
                     (2.4 miles)
```

	Car No.	Name	Model	Time	Laps	
1.	(33)	Bob Dotson	Spirit	1:27.80**	25	
2.	(8)	Freddy Mercury	Reynard 95F	1:27.93*	25	
3.	(1)	TJ Benson	VanDiemen RF95	1:28.20	25	
4.	(47)	Darrell Pollard	VanDiemen RF95	1:28.22	25	
5.	(71)	Gordon Chappel	VanDiemen RF95	1:28.25	25	
6.	(69)	Phil Spratt	Reynard 95F	1:28.34	25	
7.	(44)	Shannon Kelly	Crossle 71F	1:27.85*	25	
8.	(50)	Don Reese	VanDiemen RF95	1:28.23	25	
9.	(16)	Hanna Lee	Swift DB-8	1:28.35	25	
10.	(99)	Peter Hurst	Swift DB-8	1:28.50	25	
11.	(88)	Barton Springs	VanDiemen RF91	1:28.32	25	
12.	(55)	Cliff Roe	VanDiemen RF94	1:28.65	25	
13.	(22)	Augie Zuehl	VanDiemen RF95	1:28.55	25	
14.	(27)	Roberto Cruz	VanDiemen RF95	1:28.37	25	
15.	(25)	Chase Wilder	Reynard SF90	1:28.66	25	
16.	(21)	Rick Henry	Swift DB-8	1:29.22	25	
17.	(30)	Bill Murfy	Swift DB-8	1:29.88	25	
18.	(00)	Tom Craig	Swift DB-3	1:29.22	25	
19.	(3)	Will Jones	Swift DB-8	1:29.45	24	
20.	(11)	Alan Reckert	Stohr	1:29.54	24	
21.	(60)	Rex VanHorn	Reynard SF91	1:30.27	24	
22.	(5)	Ian Poirier	Swift DB-8	1:30.85	24	
23.	(27)	Ben Cifelli	Swift DB-3	No Time	17	NR
24.	(7)	Ron Leclair	VanDiemen RF95	1:28.65	17	NR
25.	(34)	Claude Marcoux	Swift DB-8	1:28.43	16	NR
26.	(43)	Jude Dionne	Swift DB-8	1:28.44	16	NR
27.	(54)	Guido Pepin	Swift DB-8	1:29.75	13	NR
DNF	(74)	Mark McGrath	Swift DB-3	1:30.45	7	
DNF	(13)	Steve Smagala	VanDiemen RF89	1:30.45	7	

FASTEST LAP

A few minutes later, we put away the results and were loading the trailer when Augie approached, obviously upset.

Augie congratulated Shannon then started to talk, "This is my last race. I'm quitting!"

"You can't do that," said Shannon.

"You're doing too good to quit," I said.

"I'm tired of TJ. He makes racing miserable," said Augie.

Shannon's eyes lit up and begged permission as he looked at me. I knew and smiled, then nodded my head.

Instantly, Shannon spun about to face Augie, "Augie, join our team."

Augie shook his head, "I can't impose on Charlie."

Then I interrupted, "Yes, you can, and I'd like you to be a part of our team."

We discussed the plan and decided to get Augie's car immediately. When we went to the BRM trailer, the task of retrieving the car was made easier when we discovered TJ was already gone, having hurried to the airport to catch his flight back to Birmingham. Les volunteered to drive past Atlanta on the drive back to Birmingham and drop off Augie's car.

With the plans complete and everything set, Shannon, Grant, and I returned to the motorhome. As we walked away, Les called out to me. I stopped and let the others go ahead. Les ran over and pulled me to the side.

"Listen, Charlie," said Les, stumbling with his words and kicking at the dirt with his tennis shoes. "I'm quitting TJ. I don't want to work with him. When I drop the rig in Birmingham, I'm finished. You know?"

When I realized Les was asking for a job, I almost laughed.

"That's too bad, Les. Say, I was looking for help on my team and with my garage. Do you know where I could find some help?" I asked with a smile.

"Well, yeah--me!" Les blurted.

"That's a great idea," I said. "Can you move to Atlanta?"

"Hell, yeah!"

"When?"

"How about I show up, Tuesday?"

"You're hired."

We shook hands. Now I had another team. My team. All I needed was a team name.

PHAR MOTORSPORTS

Upon arriving at Gainesville, Shannon and I struck an agreement. I would rebuild the engine for the Swift SE-3 and Shannon would do his artistic work on my old '49 Ford pick-up. Shannon asked if it was all right to paint a cartoon on the tailgate, and when I remembered the cartoon Shannon painted on the side of Hanna's car, I gave permission for Shannon to do whatever he wanted.

Although the engine gave up at Mid-Ohio, our spirits were high. Shannon proved he could be competitive and with a strong engine, a win was more than possible. My job was made easier with the addition of Les to the crew. Les prepared Augie's Van Diemen and Shannon's Swift while I demanded Shannon set the suspension on his Swift. Only with hands on experience would Shannon learn the suspension; and hopefully, recognize the adjustments he needed.

The trailer was modified slightly to hold both racers and the two four wheelers with ease. Cabinets were built into the front of the trailer, and shelves were added for the tires, tools, and equipment kept permanently in the trailer, which included a small compressor and welder.

Les took time to find an apartment. So did Grant, who had fallen in love with the Georgia countryside. A week after Les arrived, Marty suddenly appeared asking me if I needed any help. I peered at Les and frowned, looked at Marty and smiled. The next morning, Marty reported for work full time at Pepper Automotive. Les let Marty stay with him until they could find a two-bedroom apartment. The old team was back together and the only difference was we had switched TJ for Shannon. The atmosphere was more than perfect, and I was more than willing to listen to TJ complain. I had a complete team with what appeared to be two competitive drivers.

While Grant looked for a place to live, he and Shannon stayed in the motorhome, in the fenced in area, behind Pepper's Automotive. One afternoon, Grant and Shannon looked at a rent house between Braselton and the track Road Atlanta. On the way, they saw a house for sale near Chestnut Mountain, only a few miles from the track. The sign in front read, "Open House." They stopped to tour the house partly out of desire, and partly because it was so appealing from the highway.

The light green house, with brown composition shingles, was a hundred yards from Highway 53, and only thirty feet off the crushed stone road that wound up and around Chestnut Mountain. Oaks and pine surrounded the Victorian style wood frame house. A porch hung from the front of the house, looking down the lot and toward the highway. The sloping hill was covered with thick runaway kudzu and in some places, it had climbed completely up a few of the trees. To the back of the half acre lot was a two-car garage with an attached paved area wide enough for cars, boats, or motorhomes. In the back yard was an octagon shaped gazebo with built-in seats. Built on the stone path between the garage and the porch at the back of the house was a stone barbecue pit.

Shannon and Grant parked the car and walked to the front of the house. Wooden steps led up to a porch, protected with a heavy pine railing and posts. At the other end of the front porch was an old, well kept, wooden slat swing, suspended by two large steel eyehooks and chain leading to the front and rear of each armrest. Inside the small two bedroom, one bath house, were a large combination living and dining, with old polished oak floors. The small but adequate kitchen was covered with vinyl, and a back door that led to the utility room and the back porch. The bedrooms were small; one with new carpet and the other with the same oak floors.

Immediately Grant knew Gainesville, Georgia was where he wanted to live.

Grant pulled Shannon to the side, "I don't know if we can pull this off, but I've decided this would be a nice place to live. What I'm saying is I don't want to live in Texas anymore. What do you say Shannon?"

The sparkle in Shannon's eyes told Grant everything. "Dad this is the best place. I just didn't know if you wanted to stay. I wanna stay here in Georgia."

"We'll see about the house, and I'll start looking for a teaching job."

Grant talked to the real estate agent, and made the agent work up a price, but his heart felt heavy when the agent announced the down payment would be $10,000. Grant did not need to look at his account to know he had less than the required down payment. The money he had, he would need for Shannon to complete the season. A moment later, Grant declined and said he would be in touch with the agent later. Shannon was ready to quit racing to see his father get the house he wanted. Neither brought the subject of the house up again, although both thought about it often.

A few days later, Grant found a two-bedroom apartment in Gainesville; and soon, the father and son were settled in.

Two weeks after the Mid-Ohio race, Shannon and I completed our respective jobs. I completed the engine, and Shannon completed the '49 Ford pickup.

With Les, Marty, and Grant present, Shannon made me close my eyes, and led me into the garage, where Shannon had completed the body work and painting. Once inside, I opened my eyes.

Not only did I see the truck, but behind it was the racing trailer also painted to match the pickup. The truck was painted in blues and greys that blended together, and on the tailgate of the '49 Ford, was a caricature of the truck with a donkey sitting in the bed and the large letters "PHAR" beside the cartoon. The trailer had the same cartoon only after "PHAR" was "Motorsports."

Slowly, I moved around the truck with my mouth open, "It's beautiful. I don't know what to say."

After circling the truck, I stopped at the tailgate to admire the cartoon of my truck and the donkey. I stood up and looked at the trailer and then at Shannon and asked, "Okay, I give up. What does PHAR mean?"

Shannon smiled and Grant laughed, while Les and Marty blurted out, "Pepper's Haul Ass Racing. PHAR Motorsports. It's your team, Charlie."

Tears came to my eyes, and I choked on my words, "Boys, I…this is a hellva surprise. But I've got one for you, Shannon."

The four looked at me inquisitively.

I smiled and wiped my eyes, "I've got permission to use Road Atlanta and let you test your car before the race at Charlotte this weekend. We test day after tomorrow." I looked at Les and Marty, "Boys, we've got an engine that needs to go in a race car."

* * *

Road Atlanta was just outside Braselton off Highway 53. Coming from Braselton, Grant turned slightly to the right and went into a wide paved area, parallel to Highway 53 for two hundred yards. The gates were open and they drove through. A road turned directly to the right, went down the hill, and back up to an elevation slightly higher than where they were. At the top of the hill, the road went to the left, where a bridge crossed the Road Atlanta road course over Turn 11. Turn 11 went into a short, steep, downhill straight to Turn 12 or the exit on the driver's left for the pit entry. Grant and the others viewed all of this from the motorhome.

"Awesome!" mumbled Shannon.

"Cool, isn't it?" said Marty more as an answer than a question.

A few teams were testing their cars when Shannon, Grant, Les, and Marty pulled the motorhome and trailer through the gates of Road Atlanta. Grant went to the main building to check in. When he was finished, they moved through another gate and down a hill. To the right was a garage area used during the races. It was also used to house the cars for the Road Atlanta racing schools. Directly behind the garage and down a steep hill was the four story Timing and Scoring Tower. They followed the hill slightly down hill, where it opened to a large flat paved area. This paddock area served as parking for the different race teams during race weekends and provided an excellent skid pad used to teach drivers the art of driving in wet conditions.

To the right were two paved roads leading to the fast pit area. Grant stopped on the flat, paved paddock area. Les and Marty unloaded the racer, while Shannon changed to his racing suit. I explained our objective to Shannon; shakedown the car, set the suspension, and check the lap times.

What I failed to tell Shannon was my determination this day to have Shannon give input for the setup of the Swift SE-3.

The longer I worked with Shannon, the more frustrated I became. Shannon had the racing ability, but he still couldn't give input for setup or settings he needed.

The new engine was operating fine. In a few laps Shannon managed to bring his speed near the record time of 1:21.81, with laps hovering around the high 1:22's and low 1:23's.

An hour past noon, Les and Marty returned to the shop while Shannon and I remained behind. We took some chips, sandwiches, and soft drinks from the ice chest and walked to the small, heavily wooded fenced in park area behind the four-story Timing and Scoring Tower and below the garages and offices. We sat at a wooden bench near a stone monument atop which was a bronze bust of a former racecar driver.

"What is that monument?" Shannon asked.

I stood up and with a sandwich in one hand and a drink in the other said, "C'mon, I'll show you."

The granite stand had a brass plaque engraved with the name, "Jim Fitzgerald."

"Who was he?" Shannon asked.

"Jim used to be an instructor for Road Atlanta. He raced here a lot. Raced for Bob Sharp with Paul Newman."

"You mean like Newman and Haas of Indy racing?"

"Yes," I said, still thinking of Paul Newman as "Cool Hand Luke" and "Hombre" fame. "Jim Fitzgerald raced with Paul Newman here at this track many times. He was killed in a Trans Am race a few years back." For a moment, I looked at the stone monument dedicated to the former driver and shook my head, "Jim once said about racing, 'When you do it, and you do it right--it's the best turn on in the world.'" "Man, that's right," said Shannon. "So, he was an instructor here?"

"Along with others, like Doc Bundy and Beaux Barfield. Both had racing aspirations like you, and they pursued their dreams successfully." "I'd like to be an instructor," said Shannon.

Tex squawked, and I smiled, "You'd make a good instructor. Why don't you run up the hill to the office and get an application for instructor while I go fill the Swift with fuel."

Excited, Shannon immediately darted up the embedded railroad ties used as steps jumping over the asphalt curb, while I returned to the fast pits and the race car.

Late in the afternoon, Shannon came in from a practice session complaining the left front tire was low on air, because the Swift was understeering. I checked the tire and smiled when I found Shannon was correct in his guess. Shannon asked to stiffen the suspension, and he was away again. With Shannon's suggestions, his lap times dropped. But I knew, however slight they might be, the times were dropping because of the input dialed in by Shannon!

At one of the breaks, Grant arrived excited with some kind of news.

"I got it, I got it," said Grant, excitedly and grabbing Shannon by the shoulders, all the while jumping up and down.

"The job?" asked Shannon.

"Yes," said Grant. "I start teaching at Chestnut Mountain Elementary next week." The initial excitement subsided, "If we could get that house, it would be perfect."

"Yeah," said Shannon, hoping his father would be able to get the house.

Just before day's end, Shannon posted a time of 1:21.91. A tenth of a second off the track record. Les and Marty cheered, and I did everything to quiet the two down. I forced Les and Marty into silence about Shannon's times.

Shannon's learning curve was moving along quickly. PHAR Motorsports was ready. Nothing could stop us at Charlotte.

CHARLOTTE MOTOR SPEEDWAY

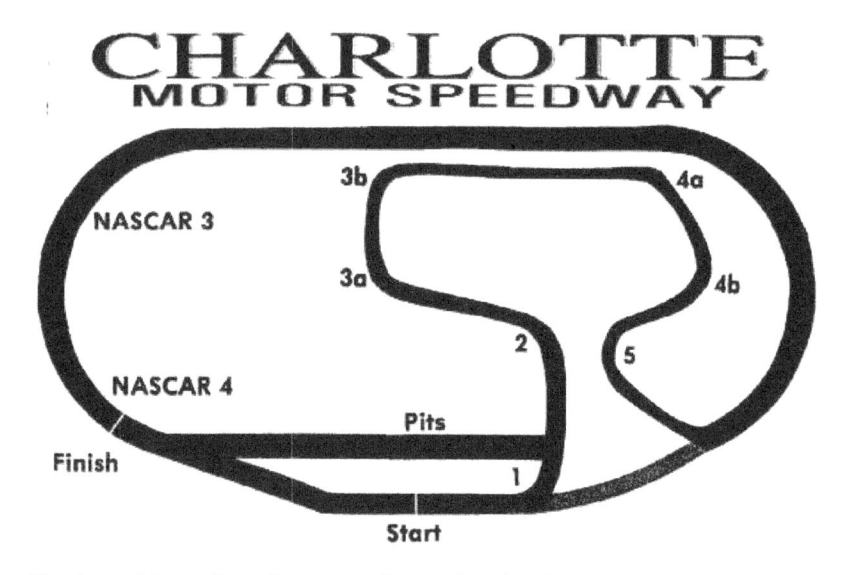

Charlotte Motor Speedway was the setting for the seventh race on the U.S. Formula Ford 2000 National Championship schedule. Preparations were being made for the Saturday morning practice, followed by a qualifying session late in the morning and the afternoon. The race would be the following day, Sunday, July 23.

The paddock area for the drivers was in the infield of Charlotte. Access to the infield was through a long tunnel beneath NASCAR Turn 4. Most teams setup close to the fast pit area.

Charlotte was best known for the 2.0 mile oval, where drivers from NASCAR raced regularly each year. It also had a unique road course, winding through the infield, then back onto the oval for a challenging and fast, counter clockwise, 2.3 mile road course.

PHAR Motorsports was buzzing since our driver, Shannon Kelly, was the fastest among all drivers during the Friday open practice session. Shannon was developing fast and this pleased me. Things were coming around quickly. The excitement was contagious. Hanna and Augie had followed Shannon all day Friday, and their times were in the top five. Surprisingly, Poirier and TJ were having problems of their own. Poirier's car broke and TJ's time put him in 10th place. Dotson and Mercury were right behind Shannon with their times.

FORMULA 2000, the Dream

    The morning's thirty minute practice session began and in two laps Shannon was below Friday's times.
    On lap three, Shannon approached Turn 1 from the 5 degree banked superspeedway straight, under full speed. He came down

on the brakes hard and dove down the banking to the left, where he made three pavement transitions: from the super speedway, the pits, and then the road course. The turn took the Swift SE-3 between three-foot high concrete walls protecting the pits, and guarded heavily, with double rows of tires should drivers stray off course. Shannon turned left, apexing Turn 2 late, and staying to the left down the short chute for the combination right-hand Turn 3a and 3b. Many times, Turn 2 could be apexed early to catch the leader as passing was excellent through Turns 3a and 3b. The only problem for the Turn 3 combination was the dip and then the rise in elevation through the braking area of Turn 3a. He took the dip and came out of Turn 3b on the infield straight, for the flat right-hand Turn 4a. He climbed a short hill to the crest, then the decreasing radius, right-hander of Turn 4b. The bumps on the apex of Turn 4b made it the slowest turn on the track as he down shifted to first. This combination turn was another daring passing area, which Shannon proved when he passed Rick Henry.

Shannon accelerated out of Turn 4, moved down a short straight and turned left. Immediately the track rose into the last turn on the infield. He took Turn 5, an off camber, decreasing radius turn, where the track flattened before it turned left onto the oval. Making adjustments, and under full power, he drifted onto the track, turned slightly left, and came roughly onto the banked NASCAR turn. He passed another racer as he followed the 1.3 mile superspeedway straight. The 24 degree banking of NASCAR 3 and 4 required no special technique except for the driver to be alert in a passing or being passed mode since the car might become light and hard to control. Shannon passed another and prepared for another.

I clicked the stopwatch. The fastest lap of any driver.

On the beginning of lap four, Shannon approached Turn 1 in excess of 145 mph. He downshifted into third gear and dove in, pulling slightly to the left, in order to pass the slower car in front of him. As he dove in, Rex VanHorn, who was directly in front, had just made the surface transition from the banked straight to the heavily barricaded concrete barrier that formed a portion of the pits. Just as Shannon started to pass, VanHorn momentarily lost control, and his Reynard lurched to the left. Not much, but just enough, so Shannon was unable to avoid tagging VanHorn in the left rear, with the right front of the Swift. The contact tore Shannon's front tire away.

The Swift's left side caught the tire barrier, turning the front tire around 180 degrees, where it rested against the side of the cockpit. The Swift made the next transition to the infield road course sideways and sliding to the left and off the track. Jagged remains of the right front suspension embedded in the soft dirt infield, flipped the car over, where it continued a series of rolls before coming to a stop upside down and away from the track to the left. Immediately yellow flags waved at Turn 1 and the corner workers rushed to the stricken driver.

From the pits Grant and I had seen the wreck. The scanner squawked as the corner workers confirmed the wreck over the two-way radio.

"This is Turn 1. Car 44 has contacted car 74. Car seven-four has proceeded on. Car 44 is heavily damaged and upside down. Please send an ambulance."

I tensed, and tried to see if Shannon would crawl out. Grant started on a run, in the direction of the accident and his son. I yelled for Grant to wait, but futilely. Being just as anxious as Grant, I understood.

VanHorn managed to continue on around and back into the pits.

The ambulance started through the infield toward the accident.

Grant arrived in time to see Shannon pulled from the wreck. Although, he tried to move through the fence, corner workers restrained him. Shannon, with the help of two corner workers, was assisted to the waiting ambulance. The Doctor had stepped from the ambulance and opened the back doors, where he waited for Shannon.

When Shannon arrived, the Doctor helped him inside the ambulance.

"Is he hurt?" Grant asked a corner worker standing near.

"I don't think so. Not if he could move under his own power," said one of the white suited corner workers, restraining Grant.

The ambulance proceeded to the infield hospital as did Grant. Grant arrived before the ambulance. The ambulance stopped and the doctor stepped from the ambulance with Shannon.

Shannon pointed to Grant, "This is my Dad."

The Doctor turned to Grant, "You need to take him into town and have his neck X-rayed."

"What's wrong?" Grant asked.

The Doctor smiled, "Probably nothing. His eyes look fine and everything else checks out. Shannon says his neck hurts, so the X-rays are just precautionary."

Grant nodded and escorted Shannon back to the motorhome. On the way, I intercepted them and Grant explained where they were going. Shannon continued to ask about the Swift, and I promised to check it out before he returned from the hospital. I was relieved, knowing when a driver is more concerned about the race car than himself, then the driver was all right.

When Grant drove away, I returned to the pits and told Les to wait for Augie, while Marty and I went to the paddock to wait for the Swift to be carried back.

The practice session ended and soon after the session a wrecker brought the mangled Swift hanging in midair from the wreckers hook. Before going to Shannon's paddock area, the wrecker stopped at Tech where the Chief of Tech slapped a sticker on the damaged racecar. The sticker indicated the car was to be re-teched before entering the race track again. A formality, but necessary none the less, to protect not only the driver involved in the incident, but also his competitors. The Chief of Tech called Timing and Scoring on his radio, and said the car was not to be driven on the race track until he cleared it through Tech again.

A few minutes later the Swift was deposited in our paddock area and pushed beneath the canopy attached to the PHAR Motorsports trailer. Quickly, I surveyed the damage which revealed all four corners bent, the engine mounts busted from the welded brackets, one rim ruined, both front brake lines and calipers ruined, and the rollbar mangled. My heart almost stopped. It would take me two days to complete the work. There was no way Shannon would make either qualifying sessions. It would be a minor miracle to even make the next day's race. Without a qualifying session, Shannon would also require a waiver from the Chief Steward just to start at the back of the pack, and that was "if" the Swift was ready for the Sunday noon race!

I told Les and Marty to dismantle the four corners, while I attended to Augie. But Augie was more concerned about Shannon as was Hanna, who came from her pit area almost immediately after the practice session. Hanna was intent on going to the hospital to be with Shannon, but I convinced her Shannon was fine, and the hospital stay was just routine. I was sure Shannon would want both her and Augie to make the qualifying session.

Hanna promised to stay at the track as long as I promised to let her know when Shannon returned. I promised and continued working on Augie's Van Diemen.

Two hours after lunch, the final qualifying session ended. Still Shannon had not returned from the hospital. I made final checks on Augie's car and satisfied with the setup, directed my full attention to Shannon's Swift.

The work was slow and tedious, but Les and I continued hoping by some chance, we might get the racer ready.

A little after four, Grant and Shannon arrived back from the hospital. Shannon went immediately for the race car, and his shoulders sagged when he saw the damage for the first time.

"You can't fix it, Charlie," Shannon almost whispered. "Can you?"

"Boy howdy. Old Charlie Pepper can fix it," I lied. Still, I was determined to try.

A spectator walked up and held out a bag of jelly beans.

"Tough break," said Pat, but this time he had no takers and the long faces told him the story. "You sure were doing well before the wreck."

"Thanks," said Shannon, who folded his legs and sat on the ground beside his Swift.

"Good luck," said Pat, then he walked away.

No one had to find Hanna. Because when she saw Shannon coming into the paddock area, she was promptly at the trailer offering her help.

Shannon and Grant, along with Augie and Hanna, pitched in to help. Shannon started to complain of headaches and a stiff neck. I ordered him to the motorhome with instructions to take some aspirin and put a heating pad on his neck to relax the stretched muscles. Of course Hanna followed with a promise to rub his neck.

Grant seemed overly concerned, so I tried to calm him down. Suddenly Grant stood up, and said he had something to take care of but would return soon.

I wiped my hands and threw the dirty red rag at the car. "The four corners are bent. We only have enough parts to fix two corners, and that's if we take what we need from Augie's reserve parts."

"Go ahead," said Augie enthusiastically. "Let's do what it takes to get Shannon on the track."

Tex pulled on my ear, and mechanically I searched for a sunflower seed in the top pocket of my dirty overalls. Tex took the seed, and momentarily played with it, before he broke the shell with his beak.

I took the open plastic bag from my pocket and carefully picked two lemon drops with my greasy fingers. After a quick inspection for grease, I was satisfied, popped them in my mouth, and shoved them into my cheek with my tongue. I pointed to the broken race car with my finger and started to complain.

"We need this and this," I said, touching the trailing arm and sway bar with my finger. I continued to touch parts we didn't have. Shoving both hands deep in my front pockets I finished with, "And a Mig welder. Well, boys, we're up the creek without a paddle."

"What a bummer," Augie sighed. "Hey, I'll be back in a few minutes. Do you need me?"

I waved my hand, "No, go ahead, what we need is a miracle."

A few minutes after Augie walked away, Rex VanHorn walked up carrying an extra copy of the grid sheet and gave it to me. VanHorn apologized in earnest, and I quickly called it an unfortunate racing incident. When VanHorn went to the motorhome, I took time to study the grid sheet:

```
                    SCCA/USAC
       U.S. Formula Ford 2000 National Championship
                    Official Grid
                      July 23
               Charlotte Motor Speedway
                Charlotte, South Carolina
                     (2.3 miles)

      Car      Name              Model              Time
      No.
  1. (33)  Bob Dotson         Spirit            1:15.87*
  2. (8)   Freddy Mercury     Reynard 95F       1:15.88*
  3. (5)   Ian Poirier        Swift DB-8        1:15.91*
  4. (19)  Maxwell Jordan     Swift DB-8        1:15.95*
  5. (1)   TJ Benson          VanDiemen RF95    1:16.11
  6. (34)  Claude Marcoux     Swift DB-8        1:16.19
  7. (7)   Ron Leclair        VanDiemen RF95    1:16.23
  8. (22)  Augie Zuehl        VanDiemen RF95    1:16.25
  9. (16)  Hanna Lee          Swift DB-8        1:16.33
 10. (71)  Gordon Chappel     VanDiemen RF95    1:16.38
 11. (69)  Phil Spratt        Reynard 95F       1:16.42
 12. (27)  Roberto Cruz       VanDiemen RF95    1:16.51
 13. (47)  Darrell Pollard    VanDiemen RF95    1:16.55
 14. (50)  Don Reese          VanDiemen RF95    1:16.69
 15. (11)  Alan Reckert       Stohr             1:16.78
 16. (43)  Jude Dionne        Swift DB-8        1:16.80
 17. (55)  Cliff Roe          VanDiemen RF94    1:16.85
 18. (99)  Peter Hurst        Swift DB-8        1:16.89
 19. (54)  Guido Pepin        Swift DB-8        1:16.93
 20. (21)  Rick Henry         Swift DB-8        1:16.98
 21. (30)  Bill Murfy         Swift DB-8        1:17.15
 22. (27)  Ben Cifelli        Swift DB-3        1:17.22
 23. (25)  Chase Wilder       Reynard SF90      1:17.25
 24. (88)  Barton Springs     VanDiemen RF91    1:17.34
 25. (00)  Tom Craig          Swift DB-3        1:17.40
 26. (74)  Mark McGrath       Swift DB-3        1:17.95
 27. (60)  Rex VanHorn        Reynard SF91      1:18.17
 28. (13)  Steve Smagala      VanDiemen RF89    1:18.50
 29. (3)   Will Jones         Swift DB-8        1:18.96
     (44)  Shannon Kelly      Swift SE-3        No Time +
    *Below Track record
    +Driver must see Stewards before start of race
```

Mercury and Dotson were less than a hundredth of a second apart. And only a second separated the first 20 drivers! The race would be fast and tight. Also, the local racer Maxwell Jordan, who was rumored to have a Formula Atlantic ride for the next year depending on his showing at Charlotte, was fourth on the grid and also below the current track record. With a decent showing, he would have his sponsorship. Most important, TJ was not on the pole. Not counting Sebring, TJ was unable to get his Van Diemen under the lap record for the first time in eight races, dating back to the last two races of the previous year.

I took the grid sheet and placed it in a drawer inside the PHAR

Motorsports trailer.

Once outside the trailer, I saw Grant walking toward the trailer with a new racing collar in his hand. The collar was thick foam, encased with heat resistant cloth, and attached with a velcro strap just below the chin. A driver would wrap the collar around their neck to prevent injury during a wreck. The neck collar limited movement and also helped the neck through the force of high G's in cornering.

Grant waved the collar in the air, "I've always thought about it. Now I know it's something Shannon has to have."

I nodded approval, "Can't be too cautious about safety. I should have thought about it myself. In fact, if we get this thing running again, I'm gonna make a double check of his harness."

When Grant went to the motorhome to give the collar to Shannon, I looked at the Swift dejectedly, then at Les and Marty.

"Well, boys . . . I don't think we can have this one ready," I said.

Neither Les nor Marty said anything.

While we stood in silence starring at the bent and broken Swift, Moses Chappel pulled up and stopped his dually crew cab. As Moses stepped from the truck, Augie jumped from the bed and lowered the tailgate.

Moses said, "I heard you needed parts for the Swift. I have some spares I can lend you. You can replace them at the next race."

I thought about the Mig welder he would need to fix the rollbar and the mounting brackets for the engine, not to mention the suspension parts he still needed.

"Thanks, but I need . . . ," I paused as Dotson and Mercury pulled alongside Chappel.

In the back of Dotson's rent car were the other parts we needed for the Swift. Surplus parts they carried and Swift parts they had borrowed from other drivers. O'Brien was with us. I was about to say thanks when Dotson spoke.

"I don't want that kid to beat me, and the only way I can stop him is to get him on the track," said Dotson as though he were doing himself a favor.

"Goes double for me," said Mercury. "Besides, our cars are ready for the race, and Wesley said he could do whatever you needed."

O'Brien nodded to me, "Charlie, Charlotte is that TBA race. Remember? C'mon, Charlie, let's get Shannon in the race."

I started to choke and couldn't speak. I wiped my eyes and wished for the Mig welder.

Just then, Guido Pepin rumbled up in a borrowed truck and stopped in front of the group. Guido waddled to where the others stood, his face flush and sweating profusely. Along with him was his mechanic Rusty Thomas.

"Augie, said you needed a Mig welder. Well, it's hot and I'm tired but the welder is in the back of the truck. I'm really sorry but I have to get out of the heat; besides, I can't help with the car. Rusty wants to help if you need him," Guido said.

My face lit up, "Yes, we can do it now!" I looked at Augie, "You did this."

Augie nodded his head enthusiastically.

A moment later, Wesley, Rusty, and I discussed the point of attack on the car as each of us took a corner. Marty, Augie, Dotson, and Mercury unloaded the trucks. Les brought lights from the trailer and ran power cables near the car; then, started the generator and the air compressor for the air tools.

Darkness fell as the three of us worked furiously while Tex perched on top of the damaged rollbar squawked encouragement. Les and Marty tended to our every demand also keeping us supplied with iced down drinks as we continued to sweat even in the darkness. The heat still clung to the race track.

I had munched down a whole bag of lemon drops, tossing the empty bag to the side. Tex hopped from the rollbar and wriggled his tiny body within the bag looking for discarded sunflower seeds. When Tex found none, he flapped his wings and landed on my shoulder, where he promptly pulled on my ear. Tex soon had his sunflower seeds.

Shannon and Hanna stepped down from the trailer. Shannon looked better, even though he continued to move his head side to side, in an effort to stretch the muscles and ease the soreness. He asked to help, but I told him there was nothing for him to do but rest.

We were hungry, so Grant offered to go into town to get everyone something to eat. We all decided on a large bucket of chicken with mashed potatoes, gravy, and biscuits. Wesley, Rusty, and I continued to work on the car, making obvious progress.

Around nine o'clock, we all took a break when Grant, Shannon, and Hanna arrived. Shannon, carrying a grocery bag stocked with necessities, walked over to me and pulled a bag of Lemon drops from the brown paper bag.

"I thought you were low," said Shannon.

"Well, thanks, Shannon," I said, obviously surprised. "I was out."

The bucket of Chicken and other items were spread out on a table beneath the trailer cover, along with plastic forks, spoons and paper towels.

We started laughing and telling stories about the race. Shannon told about his wild ride, even managing a laugh about the whole thing and promising me to move through the pack quickly if we finished the car. Grant confided how nervous he would get when the races started and added his heart never beat as fast as it did when he saw Shannon flip the car.

When we finished eating, I ordered Shannon to bed. Hanna followed

Shannon into the motor home where she rubbed his neck again, and when Shannon fell asleep she went back to her hotel.

In awe, Augie watched our activity on the race car until midnight. Then Augie, at my order, retired to his hotel.

I cut the old rollbar away and installed the new rollbar with the assistance of Les and Marty.

At two in the morning, Les and Marty retired to the race trailer and quickly fell asleep. A half hour later the work was complete. While Rusty and I bled the brakes and the radiator, Wesley went to the Dotson trailer to get the electronic scales, ramps and leveling equipment.

For another hour and a half we aligned the Swift, and balanced the corner weights. A little after 4 a.m., we completed the work. I thanked them immensely, but both men shrugged it off, content with the impossible job completed. Both Wesley and Rusty opted to go to their respective race trailers and catch as much sleep as they could, before the drivers arrived in the next few hours.

When they were gone, I took a spare nose and wing from the trailer and mounted them on the Swift.

Satisfied with the work I glanced at my watch and saw the time was 5 a.m. I groaned and crawled into the trailer near Les and Marty, laid a blanket on the steel plated floor, arranged a bag of red rags for a pillow, and fell asleep as soon as my head touched the rags.

* * *

It seemed like I had just laid my head down on the rags, when the sounds of engines aroused me. I rubbed my face and eyes, and my body ached and felt hot. The trailer wall clock showed 9 o'clock. I stood and stretched the weariness from my body, and stepped from the trailer.

Les and Marty were gone as was the Swift. I could smell biscuits.

"Hey, Charlie, come and get it," yelled Grant.

I followed my nose to the motorhome and the welcomed breakfast I had come to expect. Inside the trailer, I sat at the table and looked around for Shannon while Grant prepared a plate.

"Where's Shannon and the boys?" I asked.

Grant laid the full plate, with a hot cup of coffee, in front of me, "Shannon's talking to the Steward to get permission to race. Les and Marty have taken the car to Tech."

"Good," I said, the tenseness in my shoulders quickly disappearing. I sipped the coffee and felt good about what Wesley, Rusty, and I had accomplished.

"You did a wonderful job, Charlie," said Grant.

"Couldn't have done it without the others," I said. "Now all we have to do is wait for the race."

* * *

The July heat was almost unbearable on the Charlotte racetrack, and the bowl shaped track kept wind from blowing across the track. Drivers used cool wraps around their necks and body. Some waited with ice to fill the fireproofed race suits before the race started. A few like Guido used a container of ice water with a tube running from the container to their mouth so they could suck the water during the race.

The five-minute warning sounded. It found many in unfamiliar positions. Dotson was on the pole with a chance to take his second consecutive race. TJ was in 5th position, Augie was in 8th and Shannon had the distinction of starting last. Although not a current model Swift, Shannon and I had proven we had a car that could compete with the others, since his time was the fastest during practice. Of all the races, Charlotte would carry one of the highest lap average for speed since the race would use more than three-quarters of the banked NASCAR track. All were prepared for the 2.3 mile high speed course and the twenty-seven laps to the checkered flag.

Shannon congratulated Mercury and Dotson, and proceeded to the last car lined up along the fast pits--his own! The Chief Steward had granted Shannon permission to start the race, even without a qualification time. The only stipulation was that Shannon start last. Les and Marty took care of Augie, while Grant and I helped Shannon.

Engines sputtered, chocked and popped to life in all but one of the Formula 2000's.

The one-minute warning sounded, and the drivers lifted their left fist. Shannon and Grant went through their ritual, and down the line, TJ's new mechanic stood ready beside him.

Les checked the radio with Augie, and I clicked the radio to check Shannon.

Shannon pushed the button on the steering wheel, "Thanks, Charlie."

I came back with, "Just kick some ass."

Cindy, who was at her hometown track this time, was satisfied, and signaled the drivers out. Dotson went to the left, Mercury to the right, with the others alternating positions as they moved from the grid. At the end of Pit Row, the drivers made the sharp 90 degree turn toward Turn 2 and the infield.

Only one car failed to leave the pits. Ironically, it was Rex VanHorn, the driver who started the incident putting Shannon at the back of the pack. Shannon had moved up one notch and the race had not even started. For a moment I hesitated when I saw the inexperienced mechanic in a quandary because of the car's failure to start, Les, Marty, and I hurried to the drivers aid.

Van Horn's mechanic had already removed the engine cover and was looking for the problem. The smell of gas was prevalent indicating the engine was flooded.

"What happened?" I asked.

"It started fine, then stalled when we started out of the pits."

"Well, it's flooded for sure," I said. Already I was removing the air filter to the carburetor. I placed my hand over the carburetor to suck the fuel out. "Crank it," I yelled to VanHorn.

The small two-liter, inline four cranked at the order but failed to start. Now, was a time of trial and error and there was not much time. The smell of gas proved the fuel was flowing, so spark would be the next immediate problem to check.

The two-row racing procession was leaving NASCAR 2 and moving slowly down Charlotte Motor Speedway's long back straight led by the Ford Mustang pace car.

Cindy stood in front of Van Horn's Reynard SF-91 and monitored the race.

My hand moved for a sparkplug wire when I saw the problem. The coil wire had somehow jarred loose and dangled freely making no connection. Immediately, I shoved the wire back into the coil until I felt it fit snugly in the bottom.

"Try it now," I yelled.

The engine cranked over twice sputtered, spewed out the raw gas, then roared to life. The mechanic rushed to fasten the engine cover while the Pit Marshall ordered them to stay in the pits.

Cindy yelled to VanHorn and his mechanic, "Wait till they come around and you can start at the back."

"We'll be a lap down," yelled VanHorn, squirming around in the cockpit of his racecar.

"The pace lap doesn't count. You will not be a lap down. If you go out now, you'll never catch up," said Cindy.

Both the mechanic and VanHorn nodded their understanding.

"Go to the pit exit and wait," Cindy ordered with a wave of her hand.

VanHorn proceeded to the end of the pits where he was stopped by a Pit Marshall to wait until every car passed.

The mechanic for VanHorn thanked me. Then Les, Marty, and I hurried to our position behind the pit wall where Grant waited.

Dotson led the drivers onto the Charlotte banking of NASCAR Turn 3 and the others closed in forming two tight rows.

"Shannon," I said over the radio. "I'll tell you when the green comes out. You won't see it so accelerate hard when I tell you."

"Okay."

Dotson slowed and kept them bunched through NASCAR Turn 3. The pace car pulled into the pits well ahead of the Formula Continentals. Coming out of NASCAR Turn 4, Dotson and Mercury accelerated anticipating the start. They were correct in their guess as the green flag came out. Those at the back of the pack had not begun to accelerate.

"Green! Go, go!" I yelled over the radio.

From their vantage point in the pits, Grant and I could see Shannon drop down and pass Smagala and Jones. On the straightaway, he passed McGrath's yellow Swift, Craig's green and yellow Swift, then Springs' purple and green Van Diemen.

Far ahead Jordan took Poirier in Turn 3b.

Under full throttle, in an untested car, Shannon charged the turn where he had crashed the day before. He showed no sign of hesitation as he pulled down and dove to the inside of Wilder's gold and brown number 25. At the same point where he wrecked the previous day, he swung left and blasted past Cifelli's Swift.

Going into Turn 2, Shannon had already moved into the 22nd slot, just behind Smurf's blue and white. Shannon set him up and took Murf to the inside right of Turn 3b. When the last car passed, VanHorn charged from the pits and out onto the track in last place, but in the race.

Already coming out on the banking, Dotson, Mercury, Jordan, and Poirier pulled away from the rest leaving the second group of TJ, Marcoux, and Leclair behind. Not far behind them came Chappel, Hanna, Spratt, Augie, and Cruz.

Dotson held the lead until lap ten when Jordan made a daring dive for position at Turn 1, passing Mercury and Dotson.

Poirier closed in, and Mercury passed Dotson at Turn 2.

Shannon had moved to 15th behind Reckert.

On lap fifteen, McGrath took Turn 1 too wide and caught the right front at the barrier crossing the fast pits. The impact sheared the right tire off. McGrath managed to move ahead, and pull safely off the course to the right and away from the driving area. The corner workers moved McGrath to safety and when assured there was no longer any danger they ceased waving the yellow.

Shannon took 12th.

The yellow allowed the separate clusters of drivers to bunch up. Chappel moved past TJ, while Leclair and Marcoux made minor off road excursions, dropping both behind Hanna, Augie, and Cruz.

On lap twenty, Poirier challenged Dotson through the Turn 4 series and going into Turn 5, tagged Dotson in the rear knocking him off the track. Poirier continued on but his front right tire had severe toe-out . . . about 45 degrees of toe-out. Chappel and TJ passed and close behind came Hanna, Augie and Cruz in 8th.

Dotson tried to re-enter the track but the corner workers held him back until the track cleared, letting Leclair and Marcoux pass. Dotson pulled out, shifted to second and as he climbed the banking of NASCAR Turn 3, Shannon streaked past into 11th.

Shannon pulled the Canadians on the long straight, passing Poirier who was limping back to the pits with a squealing tire audible even above the thundering exhaust. Shannon made a gutsy pass on Leclair in Turn 1, showing absolutely no fear through the turn where he had wrecked only the previous day. The same damaged Swift was performing excellently. At Turn 3, Shannon took Marcoux, and moved into 9th. Far ahead were his friends, Hanna and Augie and close on their tail was Cruz.

On lap twenty-three, Mercury took the lead from Jordan again for the final time. Both drivers were far ahead of their challengers, Chappel and TJ. Closing on them were Hanna, Augie, and Cruz and coming up fast was Shannon.

On lap twenty-four, Shannon again made a pass in Turn 1 leaving Cruz behind. Shannon took his teammate Augie in Turn 3a and Hanna through Turn 5. Shannon waved after he passed each and they returned the wave. Shannon had moved into 5th.

Two laps remained, but Chappel and TJ were too far ahead to catch. It didn't matter to the spectators. They let out a thunderous roar each time Shannon passed another Continental. Shannon literally gobbled up the real estate between him and the drivers in front.

On the last lap, Shannon closed down the long straight and would have passed them except the finish line was located in NASCAR 4 and different from the start on the main straight.

Mercury crossed the finish line with Jordan alongside of him. Shannon was passing TJ, as they crossed the finish line, but TJ came across only two feet in front of Shannon and a car length behind Chappel. Another 200 feet and Shannon would have passed TJ and Chappel.

The crowds went crazy!

As usual, the top six drivers reported to Impound. This time the top six was extremely different: Mercury, Jordan, Chappel, TJ, Shannon, and Hanna. Mercury, Jordan, and Chappel took their time to shine in the Winner's Circle and the ceremonies before going to Impound.

Shannon and Hanna hugged and kissed in celebration, which was rather unusual for competitors. Augie was quick in returning to Impound to congratulate them as was Dotson, who was also congratulating his teammate Mercury. TJ stood to the side, somber in his fourth place finish.

After Impound, several of the drivers, corner workers and Grid Marshalls came to the motorhome, at Grant's invitation, to continue the celebration.

I celebrated with the others for a while. As the sun set, Augie arrived at the trailer with a copy of the final results and the current standings:

```
              SCCA/USAC
    U.S. Formula Ford 2000 National Championship
              Official Race Results
                    July 23
             Charlotte Motor Speedway
             Charlotte, South Carolina
                   (2.3 miles)

     Car    Name              Model           Time         Laps
     No.

1.   (8)    Freddy Mercury    Reynard 95F     1:15.85*     27
2.   (19)   Maxwell Jordan    Swift DB-8      1:15.83*     27
3.   (71)   Gordon Chappel    VanDiemen RF95  1:16.05      27
4.   (1)    TJ Benson         VanDiemen RF95  1:16.00      27
5.   (44)   Shannon Kelly     Swift SE-3      1:15.67**    27
6.   (16)   Hanna Lee         Swift DB-8      1:16.10      27
7.   (22)   Augie Zuehl       VanDiemen RF95  1:16.13      27
8.   (27)   Roberto Cruz      VanDiemen RF95  1:16.37      27
9.   (7)    Ron Leclair       VanDiemen RF95  1:16.42      27
10.  (33)   Bob Dotson        Spirit          1:15.91*     27
11.  (47)   Darrell Pollard   VanDiemen RF95  1:16.45      27
12.  (34)   Claude Marcoux    Swift DB-8      1:16.53      27
13.  (11)   Alan Reckert      Stohr           1:16.54      27
14.  (50)   Don Reese         VanDiemen RF95  1:16.63      27
15.  (3)    Will Jones        Swift DB-8      1:16.75      27
16.  (21)   Rick Henry        Swift DB-8      1:16.22      27
17.  (69)   Phil Spratt       Reynard 95F     1:16.64      27
18.  (99)   Peter Hurst       Swift DB-8      1:16.94      27
19.  (55)   Cliff Roe         VanDiemen RF94  1:16.78      27
20.  (54)   Guido Pepin       Swift DB-8      1:17.10      27
21.  (25)   Chase Wilder      Reynard SF90    1:17.16      27
22.  (43)   Jude Dionne       Swift DB-8      1:16.44      27
23.  (88)   Barton Springs    VanDiemen RF91  1:17.32      27
24.  (30)   Bill Murfy        Swift DB-8      1:17.52      26
25.  (00)   Tom Craig         Swift DB-3      1:17.22      26
26.  (60)   Rex VanHorn       Reynard SF91    1:17.54      26
27.  (27)   Ben Cifelli       Swift DB-3      1:17.83      26
28.  (13)   Steve Smagala     VanDiemen RF89  1:17.45      25
29.  (5)    Ian Poirier       Swift DB-8      1:16.14      20  NR
DNF  (74)   Mark McGrath      Swift DB-3      1:17.49      15  NR

     FASTEST LAP
     Car    Time           Speed
     44     1:15.67**      109.69 mph
```

Shannon was 7th in the points standings but more important was Shannon's times during the race.

"Look!" screamed Hanna. "Shannon set a new track record!" She clapped her hands together, wrapped her arms around Shannon's neck, and gave him a long, lingering kiss.

Mercury held his drink high, "To Reynard's first victory in two years and Shannon's record."

"How about Hanna and Augie finishing in the top ten," said Shannon.

"And here's hoping we finish in the top ten in the last three races."

Augie yelled, "To the victory Shannon's gonna have before the season ends--no, make that victories!"

```
                        SCCA/USAC
         U.S. Formula Ford 2000 National Championship
                   Official Points Standing
                    (After 7 of 10 events)


         Car    Name              Model            Team               Points
         No.

   1.   (1)    TJ Benson         VanDiemen RF95   BRM                    167
   2.   (8)    Freddy Mercury    Reynard 95F      Dotson Racing          130
   3.   (71)   Gordon Chappel    VanDiemen RF95   MOSES                  120
   4.   (5)    Ian Poirier       Swift DB-8       PACE                   120
   5.   (33)   Bob Dotson        Spirit           Dotson Racing          111
   6.   (34)   Claude Marcoux    Swift DB-8       PACE                   100
   7.   (44)   Shannon Kelly     Swift SE-3       PHAR Motorsports        94
   8.   (11)   Alan Reckert      Stohr            TART                    87
   9.   (7)    Ron Leclair       VanDiemen RF95   TART                    86
  10.   (47)   Darrell Pollard   VanDiemen RF95   BRM                     75
  11.   (69)   Phil Spratt       Reynard 95F      Spratt Racing           71
  12.   (27)   Roberto Cruz      VanDiemen RF95   Spratt Racing           64
  13.   (16)   Hanna Lee         Swift DB-8       Dotson Racing           64
  14.   (22)   Augie Zuehl       VanDiemen RF95   PHAR Motorsports        63
  15.   (55)   Cliff Roe         VanDiemen RF94   GO Racing               42
  16.   (43)   Jude Dionne       Swift DB-8       PACE                    41
  17.   (21)   Rick Henry        Swift DB-8                               40
  18.   (54)   Guido Pepin       Swift DB-8       GO Racing               38
  19.   (50)   Don Reese         VanDiemen RF95                           30
  20.   (19)   Maxwell Jordan    Swift DB-8                               26
  21.   (30)   Bill Murfy        Swift DB-8       Smurf Racing            23
  22.   (88)   Barton Springs    VanDiemen RF91                           22
  23.   (99)   Peter Hurst       Swift DB-8                               21
  24.   (3)    Will Jones        Swift DB-8                               16
  25.   (25)   Chase Wilder      Reynard SF90                             16
  26.   (00)   Tom Craig         Swift DB-3       TC Racing               15
  27.   (27)   Ben Cifelli       Swift DB-3                                8
  28.   (74)   Mark McGrath      Swift DB-3       M & M Racing             5
  29.   (13)   Steve Smagala     VanDiemen RF89                            4
  30.   (39)   Art Grindle       Swift SE-3                                3
```

Shannon appeared embarrassed at Augie's toast, but he was quick to offer his own, "Here's to my Dad, Wesley, Rusty, and Charlie for fixin' my car."

We all toasted, and Shannon added another toast, "To Charlie . . . without him there would be no record."

RUAN GRAND PRIX

The Ruan Grand Prix, located in Des Moines, Iowa, had become a beacon to street racing. First established in 1988 and located in one of the fastest growing metropolitan areas in the country, the track was located off

I-235 near the Des Moines River. Working together with SCCA, a street circuit was laid out and designed for maximum competition and spectator comfort and viewing. The brain child of John Ruan, a devoted racing enthusiast and president of Ruan Transportation Management Systems. His interest spanned decades going back to when he bought the first Corvette delivered in Iowa--and that was in 1953.

The three-day event would include some of the finest pro-racing SCCA had to offer: Olds Pro Series, Trans-Am, Dodge/Shelby Pro Series, a Celebrity race, the SCCA/USAC U.S. Formula Ford 2000 National Championship and the World Challenge. The Formula 2000 race was scheduled for Saturday, August 12.

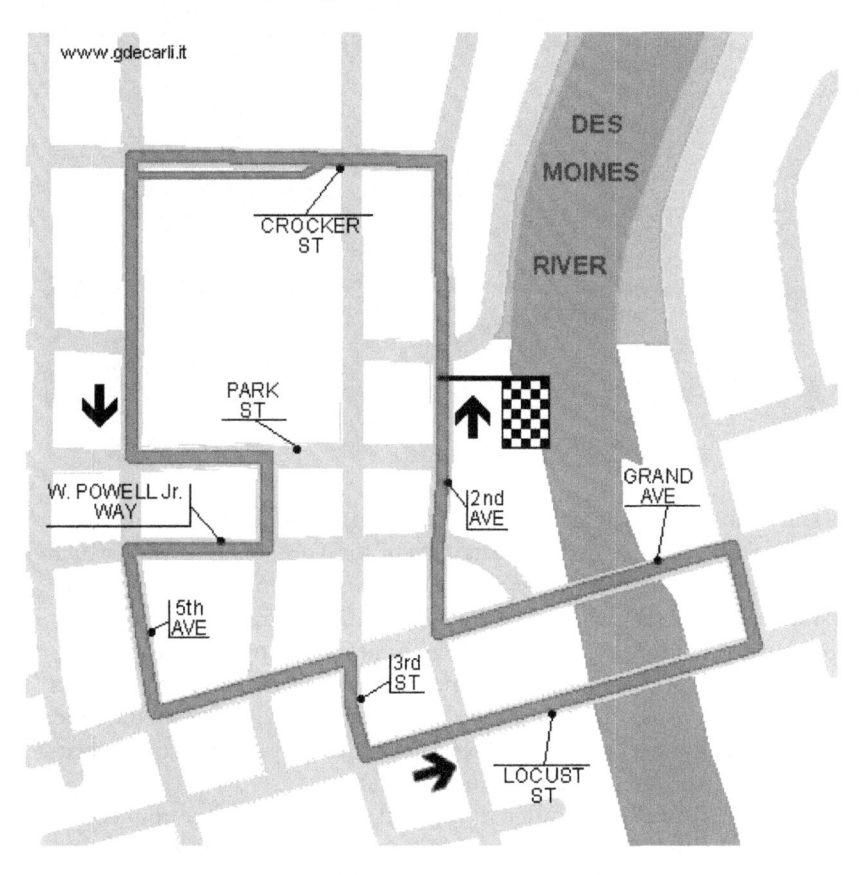

Inside the air-conditioned lounge area, attached to the three rows of open garages, I wiped the perspiration from my hands on the legs of my coveralls and collected the grid sheets for the race.

Instantly, I scanned the sheets to look for my drivers. Even though I knew their current position, I wanted to assure myself everything was as it should be. Tex sat on my shoulder and acted like he was also reading the sheet.

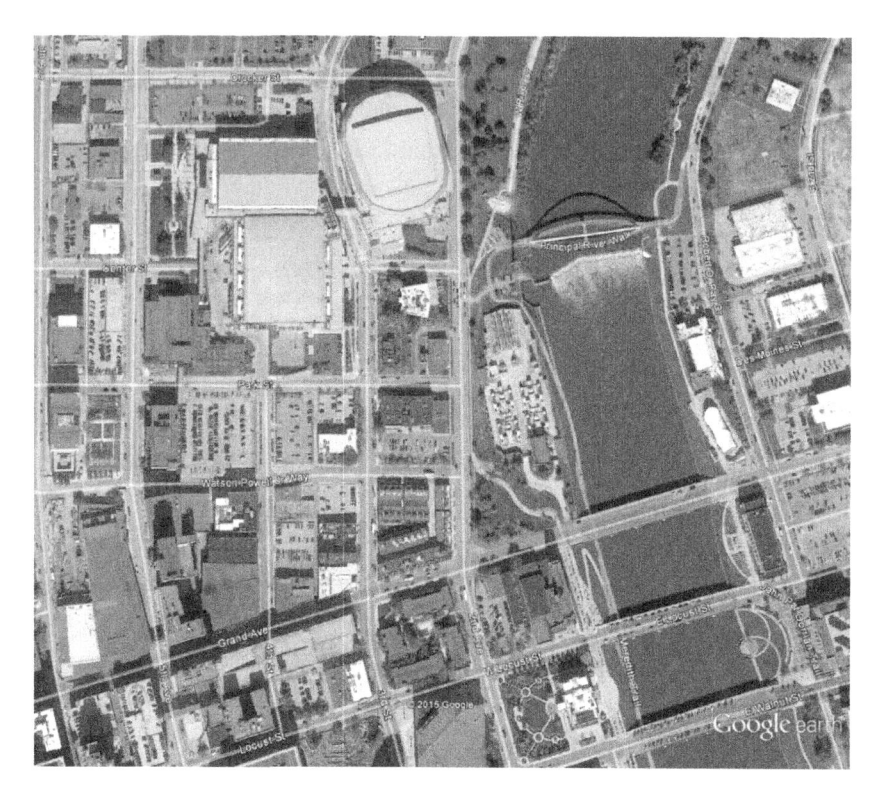

The course provided a challenging ten-turn, counter clockwise course. All turns were sharp 90 degree turns, except for Turn 4 and Turn 9, which were slightly sharper than 90 degrees. One unusual thing about the Ruan Grand Prix course was all turns were taken in first gear; whereas, all other courses provided turns taken in a variety of gears, but not so at the Des Moines course. This forced the drivers to shift approximately 35 times per lap. Another unusual thing about the Ruan Grand Prix, unlike all the other races, was the course crossed the Des Moines River twice. Once between Turn 6 and 7, and again between Turn 8 and 9.

On this hot, sweltering, August weekend, SCCA/USAC continued its highly touted Formula 2000 series with race number eight. The Formula 2000 race would be the third race after lunch Saturday and would follow the Dodge/Shelby Pro race.

All racers had spent a minimum of Friday practicing.

With Saturday's qualification near completion, the track thundered to the last qualifications of Trans-AM around the 1.8 mile Des Moines street course only an hour before the noon lunch break. Most of the Formula

2000 drivers made final adjustments or repairs as they waited for lunch, and later the beginning of their race. The intense summer heat kept most racers under cover or in the air conditioning of their motorhomes or trailers.

Under my guidance, Shannon had moved from 13th to 7th position, and would have been even higher, if not for the misfortune of the engine and the wreck. Even Augie Zuehl had improved, moving from 18th to 13th. From this point, the climb became even more difficult. I was pleased with Shannon's girlfriend, Hanna Lee, as she clung to the position just behind Augie. When I saw the insurmountable lead TJ had built in the points standings continue to dwindle, I smiled.

While I studied the grid sheets, Augie walked into the lounge looking for his own copy of the grid sheets, minus his traveling companion, Shannon.

"Where's Shannon?"

Augie rolled up two grid sheets, "He's over at Tom Craig's trailer. Old Patches sure looks bad. You know, what with the heat and all."

In their spare time, Augie and Shannon would hang around Patches, Turtle, Smurf, and Moses, offering help and listening attentively to their stories.

Patches was the name those close to Craig called him and although Craig didn't flaunt his wealth, he was another who used his wealth to enjoy the expensive hobby of racing. Patches was aggressive but managed to run only mid pack. His aggression resulted in a constant tendency to venture off well maintained road courses. This earned him the nickname of Patches, since he was constantly patching the nose on his yellow and green Swift DB-3. Seldom did the nose match the colors of the car after the first or second practice session. Shannon had come up with the idea for Patches' team, using the first letter of his first and last name, TC, and calling the team "Toadal Chaos," for Patches' off road excursions. Shannon even went as far as painting a cartoon on the side, with frogs jumping in all directions and the words, "Toadal Chaos" painted beneath the cartoon.

"What's wrong with Patches?" I asked.

Augie stopped at the door and walked back, "He was getting sick, so Shannon offered to repair the nose before the race. He told Patches to go in his motorhome and rest while he fixed the nose."

I frowned angrily at the thought of Shannon working in the heat, but admired him for helping Craig. "Tell Shannon not to get worn out himself," I said, while I scanned the grid sheet.

"Sure, Charlie," said Augie, turning to leave the lounge.

Something on the grid sheet made me think, "Hey, Augie."

Augie paused at the door, turned, around and raised his head to acknowledge me.

"How many RPM's were you turning down the long straight?"

"About sixty-five," said Augie.

Instantly, I knew Augie meant 6500 rpms. I needed to make a change. "Get Shannon and come back to the trailer."

Augie nodded and went to get Shannon. My thoughts returned to the current grid, and I scanned the qualifying sheet to check my drivers' positions on the grid. Shannon's name was in fourth, sandwiched between Poirier and Dionne with TJ again on the pole by only hundredths of a second:

```
                    SCCA/USAC
        U.S. Formula Ford 2000 National Championship
                   Official Grid
                    August 12
                   Ruan Grand Prix
                   Des Moines, Iowa
                    (1.8 miles)

      Car     Name            Model           Time        Time
      No.                                     1st         2nd
 1.   (1)    TJ Benson        VanDiemen RF95  1:29.453    1:28.212*
 2.   (34)   Claude Marcoux   Swift DB-8      1:29.270    1:28.214*
 3.   (5)    Ian Poirier      Swift DB-8      1:29.534    1:28.215*
 4.   (44)   Shannon Kelly    Swift SE-3      1:28.653    1:28.218*
 5.   (43)   Jude Dionne      Swift DB-8      1:29.430    1:28.300
 6.   (7)    Ron Leclair      VanDiemen RF95  1:30.252    1:28.333
 7.   (27)   Roberto Cruz     VanDiemen RF95  1:30.327    1:28.526
 8.   (33)   Bob Dotson       Spirit          1:29.000    1:28.613
 9.   (22)   Augie Zuehl      VanDiemen RF95  1:30.544    1:28.688
10.   (16)   Hanna Lee        Swift DB-8      1:30.423    1:28.783
11.   (47)   Darrell Pollard  VanDiemen RF95  1:29.258    1:28.876
12.   (11)   Alan Reckert     Stohr           1:29 486    1:29.059
13.   (71)   Gordon Chappel   VanDiemen RF95  1:30.447    1:29.458
14.   (69)   Phil Spratt      Reynard 95F     1:31.507    1:29.500
15.   (40)   Ernie Goolsby    Swift DB-8      1:31.754    1:29.523
16.   (55)   Cliff Roe        VanDiemen RF94  1:33.515    1:29.750
17.   (50)   Don Reese        VanDiemen RF95  1:31.223    1:30.005
18.   (99)   Peter Hurst      Swift DB-8      1:32.750    1:30.069
19.   (54)   Guido Pepin      Swift DB-8      1:30.980    1:30.234
20.   (21)   Rick Henry       Reynard 95F     1:32.925    1:30.355
21.   (8)    Freddy Mercury   Swift DB-8      1:30.223    1:33.222
22.   (30)   Bill Murfy       Swift DB-8      1:32.454    1:31.435
23.   (27)   Ben Cifelli      Swift DB-3      1:31.620    1:31.654
24.   (88)   Barton Springs   VanDiemen RF91  1:33.768    1:32.234
25.   (00)   Tom Craig        Swift DB-3      1:32.333    1:33.048
26.   (13)   Steve Smagala    VanDiemen RF89  1:35.500    1:32.800
27    (25)   Chase Wilder     Reynard SF90    1:32.900    1:34.230
28.   (3)    Will Jones       Swift DB-8      1:34.455    1:33.337

   * Below current Track Record
```

Less than two seconds separated the first 20 drivers. If they had only one qualifying session, Shannon would have the pole and Freddy Mercury would be in 9th, instead of in his current 20th position. Misfortune with the Reynard on the second qualifying session pushed Mercury back with a slower time overall. I was excited because Shannon was asserting himself and was now in the front of the competition with the updated Swift SE-3. How different, now that Shannon had a competitive racecar. What amazed me was Shannon's ability to dial a car in so quickly on new tracks regardless of conditions. On unfamiliar tracks, I found Shannon could usually be running competitively within three laps. With a few changes and special tweaks I felt were necessary, I believed Shannon would positively be the fastest.

Something troubled me about the gearing in both Augie's and Shannon's cars. I thought we had the right four gears; 17-34, 19-33, 21-30, and 23-26. I would need to change fourth gear. The other teams had made the changes and that was why they were faster.

When I arrived at the PHAR Motorsports trailer, Shannon, with Augie's help, had already set a table with fruits and drinks. With the severe heat, most drivers would eat light or nothing at all. Grant remained in the motorhome, with the generator providing enough electricity to run the air-conditioning.

I laid a copy of the grid and points standings on the table.

"Looks like you two and Hanna are in the top ten. You boys did real good. I'm proud of you. Now concentrate on the race and eat light, or the "Red Mist" will control your driving--and drink the Gatorade!"

Shannon and Augie put their drinks aside and rummaged through the cooler until they each found individual, drink-sized, Gatorade bottles. Both Augie and Shannon were dressed in tennis shoes, t-shirts, and shorts, still the perspiration from the high humidity had both boys' shirts wet as was my shirt, under the suspenders of my overalls.

"How's Patches?" I asked.

"He's fine," said Shannon.

"You should see the work Shannon did. He even managed to match the paint with the spray cans Patches had," beamed Augie.

Shannon shrugged his shoulders, "It was nothing."

"What did he pay you?" I asked rather curiously.

Shannon only shrugged his shoulders.

Augie spoke up, "Man, Patches pulled out a wad of money and tried to give it to Shannon. You know what Shannon took?" Augie paused to let it sink in. Shannon frowned at Augie and I looked at Shannon. "Shannon asked for a Coke! Can you believe it, a Coke! I mean, like that was a hell of a job, and all he took was a Coke."

"That's all I wanted; besides, Patches needed help," said Shannon rather defensively.

Amazing, I thought. Tex pulled on my ear and I mechanically reached into my top pocket and pulled out a sunflower seed, holding it out until Tex stretched out with his beak and took the small seed. Then I reached into my pocket, pulling out the open plastic bag, took two lemon drops out, popped them in my mouth.

I looked at Augie and Shannon. "Listen, I want to make a change on each of your cars that I think will make you go faster. I should have done it for this morning's last session, and I didn't. So, I'm gonna do it now--if you both agree."

"Sure," both boys said in unison.

"Shannon, how many RPMS were you turning before you reached Turn 7?" I asked.

"Sixty-seven."

"Boy Howdy," I muttered. "Wish we had those on board computers. Is the track breaking up at Turn 6?"

Augie and Shannon looked at each other; then at me, and simultaneously said, "Yeah."

I nodded my head, "Here's the deal. You two are coming out of Turn 6 slower than we were last year. The other teams figured it out and have changed the fourth gear from the 23-26 the two of you are using." Rubbing my chin in thought I said, "I think we need to go with a 23-28 for fourth."

"Sure," said Augie.

Shannon followed, "Fine with me."

"Time to get to work," I said, then looked at Les and Marty, "Well, boys get those two cars up and pop the back. We got gears to change and a short time to change them out."

Les and Marty were already rolling out the quick jacks before I had finished. I glanced at Augie and Shannon with a sly smile, "You two should pick up a half second or more with those gears."

"All right," said Shannon with a shake of both fists.

The roar of the Trans-Am racers dwindled and finally stopped, bringing the final qualifying session to an end and an hour break for lunch.

"Are you okay, Shannon?" I asked. "You seemed a little down when we first got here."

Shannon smiled, "I was just upset because the house my Dad wanted to buy was sold."

"I'm sorry."

"It's okay. I wanted to see him get it," said Shannon.

I said, "Try to relax before the race, and don't try to win it all at once. There's twenty-eight laps and let me tell you, those boys out there will start acting plenty crazy with their driving half way through this thing, so keep alert--and please kick some ass for old Charlie."

* * *

The five-minute warning sounded. As usual, Shannon and Augie were kicking the hacky sack between them to relax prior to the race. This time when the five-minute warning sounded, they didn't have far to walk. Both were gridded in the top ten along with Hanna.

The only familiar face, not in the top ten, was Freddy Mercury who would start in the 21st position after a poor qualifying in the second session. But having solved the electronic problem, Mercury was confident he would move quickly through the field.

TJ had the pole but the top ten were separated by only a half second. The race would be close and quick. For the first time in many races, I noticed TJ didn't have the cocky confidence he usually carried into the start of a race. Rumor around the pits had TJ angry with me for quitting and also unhappy with his new mechanic and help. From the original BRM team, only Pollard remained. When TJ would walk past our trailer Les and Marty would tease TJ to his immense displeasure, while I smiled inwardly, and Tex would always screech, "Squirt." I knew the boys were funning with TJ, and God knows he deserved it, yet somehow, from time to time, I felt sorry for TJ. I really liked the kid and I hated to see our relationship come to this.

Before the three-minute warning, TJ was already strapped in, while Shannon calmly put on his head sock, helmet, and gloves. The one-minute whistle found Grant and Shannon giving the familiar hand shake before Shannon raised his fist signaling he was ready.

Satisfied with the field, Cindy, again Grid Marshall, signaled the Formula Continentals out on the track for the start of the eighth race in the ten race SCCA/USAC series. TJ went to the left of the Grid Marshall for his familiar but delicate pole position. Marcoux moved to the right for the outside pole. TJ made a quick, 90 degree turn to the left and through the fast pit wall from the grid. One by one, they followed in single file, grouping in twos behind a new Mustang used as the pace car for the weekend. They swerved back and forth on the asphalt paving to warm the tires for the start of the race.

Slowly the cars followed the 1.8 mile course through Turn 10. The pace car pulled into the pits, and the field of racecars rolled onto the Ruan Grand Prix street course's main straight in front and below the Pit Row Suites off to the left. The anxious crowd of spectators waited enthusiastically.

TJ pulled the field slowly toward start/finish located near the center of the Fast Pits, on the right. He forced Marcoux to the right, near the outside 3 foot high concrete barrier wall, topped with 8 foot hurricane fencing to protect spectators from accidents and flying debris. Pushing out enabled TJ to have a wider area of track to the inside left and prepare for Turn 1 and the 90 degree left turn. Marcoux kept his engine revved, leaving it in first gear as did the others. TJ preferred the slow start and the drag race to the first turn where he excelled over the others. Marcoux kept pace with TJ as did Poirier and Shannon.

The green flag waved and the 28 drivers charged Turn 1. TJ shifted to second gear and just as quickly came down hard on the brakes while going down to first gear. Making a late diving entry to the wide 90 degree turn, the first four rows went through side by side in perfect pairs. On the outside of the track at the end of the straight, an electric sign listed the top five drivers.

The tall downtown buildings made their presence known to the drivers, as it seemed more like driving through a canyon, than a road course. TJ hit 2nd, 3rd, then came down hard on the brakes downshifting to first gear and accelerated into Turn 2.

Turn 2 was a deceiving, 90 degree left because the course became very narrow like turning off a main street to a back alley. Turn 2 did allow for excellent run-off should the driver misjudge his entry. Marcoux opted to fight TJ for the turn, which closed in the cars behind.

A quick spurt in second and immediately down to first gear for Turn 3, a 90 degree wide right hand turn where late braking and passing frequently occurred, Marcoux out broke TJ and took the lead with Shannon swinging in behind and Poirier only inches away from Shannon. Then came Dionne, Leclair, and Dotson who moved ahead of Cruz while Augie and Hanna clung to Cruz's tail. In quick succession came Pollard, Reckert, and Spratt who took Chappel in Turn 3. Mercury moved to 15th.

From Turn 3, the course went downhill directly toward a garage and a runoff going beneath the garage. The top was filled with suites and sky boxes providing a view of most of the track.

TJ hit 2nd and then 3rd. Then two quick shifts down to first, and into Turn 4, sharper than 90 degrees and ahead of Marcoux.

Still the group remained clustered close. Buildings lined the streets with spectators crowding behind barricades and literally hanging from the upper floors of the parking garage on Grand Ave.

Making a daring move, Shannon took Marcoux through Turn 4. Still, the top eight were separated by only inches. From Turn 4, TJ, who held only a slight advantage over Shannon, remained in first for the right of Turn 5 and left of Turn 6.

The exit to Turn 6 was critical, leading to Locust Street and the longest straight that also crossed the Des Moines River. Watching his mirrors, TJ straddled the middle of the course, preventing Shannon's rapid charge and keeping him from passing. Shannon swung wide right giving him excellent exit speed and a jump on TJ. Down the straight, Shannon moved past TJ bringing Marcoux, Dionne, and Poirier with him.

Shannon held the lead over the bridge, going through the gears to fourth and toward the roughest part of Locust Street and Turn 7. A thunderous roar followed the cars clustered together, leaving behind a spectacular array of sparks as all charged for the next turn.

Turn 7, a 90 degree left was one of the most exciting parts of the track where the car seemed to jump all over, seemingly out of control. Here the driver went down from fourth, to third, to second, to first, then took Turn 7 and stayed in first for another 90 degree left, at Turn 8, and onto Grand Avenue and back across the Des Moines River, pointing straight for the heart of downtown and all the high-rise buildings. The race headed for the sharp, wide right at Turn 9.

The track widened and it became a drag race with Poirier going to the left of Shannon while Dionne took to the right and Marcoux and TJ closed on Shannon's tail. As they neared Turn 9, Poirier dropped behind Shannon and in front of Marcoux.

Shannon failed to see Dionne, or Dionne pushed farther than he should, overly excited with his unusual position. Either way, as Shannon cut sharply right into Turn 9, he touched Dionne. Both cars twisted, crunched each other and spun, going safely into the runoff area at the end of Turn 9. Poirier narrowly missed the collision but managed to squeeze to the inside as did Marcoux. TJ took evasive action to the right, barely missing the wreck. Before TJ could recover, Leclair and Dotson passed him. Quickly, TJ dropped in behind.

"I'm off! I'm off!" yelled Shannon over his radio. "I hit Dionne!"

Immediately I clicked my radio, "Can you get back on?"

"I don't know. Man they're all passing me!" moaned Shannon, as the other Formula 2000's safely cleared the corner.

Poirier shifted smoothly through the gears as he sped down 2nd Avenue and the final turn of the first lap. He came back down through the gears to first and made the sharp, slightly uphill left at Turn 10 and crossed the start/finish, with the lead after the first lap. Close behind were Marcoux, Leclair, Dotson, and TJ.

All the cars passed Shannon and Dionne before the corner workers could separate them. Dionne took off first with his Swift obviously mishandling. The right front wing of Shannon's Swift was bent in a near vertical position, and the nose was shoved back, with a hole the size of a fist in the fiberglass.

Shannon smoked the tires when he re-entered the track and as he shifted to third he had already caught Dionne and passed him when he hit fourth. As he made Turn 10 and started slightly uphill, he could see no other Formula 2000's. Shannon was in 27th with only Dionne trailing.

"They're gone," said Shannon, immensely dismayed with his situation after the spectacular start.

"No," I countered. "They just made Turn 1. Go get 'em, Boy!"

Far ahead Marcoux worked as a buffer between the next group of Leclair, Dotson, TJ, Augie, Hanna, and Spratt.

From Turn 3 to Turn 9 Marcoux seemed to block Leclair and Dotson intentionally. So intentionally, it became evident to the corner workers who reported it.

On the next lap, I heard another report come in over my scanner, "Turn 5, car 34 moved in a blocking manner on car 7."

The report suggested Marcoux's 34 was blocking Leclair's number 7 Van Diemen.

A moment later, "Turn 8, car 34 moved down on car 33 forcing him off the track. Car 33 has continued on."

Again Marcoux moved to block. This time Dotson's blue and white number 33. Not far behind and closing in quickly were TJ, Hanna, and Spratt.

My scanner continued to squawk when the Chief Steward addressed the problem.

"This is the Chief Steward. I want Start/Finish to wave the furled black at car 34. Corner stations please report any more activities on car 34."

Poirier roared through Turn 9 as Marcoux, Leclair, and Dotson blasted across the Des Moines River. Marcoux's indecision about which driver to block enabled Leclair and Dotson to split Marcoux on both sides and pass at Turn 9. Once past Marcoux, they resumed their pursuit of Poirier, as did Marcoux of them.

TJ was closing in on Marcoux when start/finish waved the furled black flag at Marcoux. The furled black flag indicated a driver had done something wrong and to stop it. Most of the times, the drivers knew what the flag was being waved for. Marcoux knew the black flag was a warning to stop his blocking.

Poirier was ahead, but what he didn't count on was the determination and anger of the drivers Marcoux had intentionally blocked.

At Turn 3, Marcoux blocked TJ pushing him out on the right-hand turn. TJ broke hard and moved wide going into the run-off area at the end of Turn 3. As he aimed for Turn 4, Marcoux was far ahead and Cruz, Augie, Hanna and his teammate Pollard were all over him with Cruz actually shooting ahead. TJ had all he could do to keep Augie and Hanna from passing.

The corner workers came to life, "Turn 3, car 34 forced car one off the track."

"Turn 4, we confirm Turn three's report. Car one has re-entered the track."

"Start/Finish, this is the Chief Steward--black flag car 34. I want the Pit Marshall to hold car 34 and explain the reason. Tell him if he forces anybody else off during the race, his race today will be finished."

I continued to listen as the reports came in. "All right," I mumbled, shaking a clenched fist. I clicked the radio, "Go get 'em, Shannon."

Shannon popped to the left at the last moment and passed Pepin on the inside of Turn 4.

The open, black flag was waved at Marcoux as he approached the Start/Finish line. The open black flag meant the driver was to come directly into the pits. Marcoux continued under race speed with Cruz, TJ, Augie, Lee, Pollard and not far behind was Chappel, Reckert, Mercury, Spratt and Reese.

Shannon passed Craig easily at Turn 9, and Murfy moved wide giving Shannon Turn 10.

On the next lap, the open black flag again waved at Marcoux when he failed to enter the pits. Shannon passed Jones at Turn 5, then took Cifelli in the daring, sliding part of Turn 7 at the end of Locust Street.

Dionne succumbed to the damage sustained in the incident with Shannon, as he came slowly around Turn 10 and entered the pits. He went directly to his paddock area and the PACE trailer ending his race after only five laps.

The next time around, Marcoux raced into the pits to where his mechanic LaForche waved him down. A Steward walked over and spoke to Marcoux, who was obviously angry at the situation as his waving hands demonstrated, even though the French speaking Marcoux understood nothing the Steward said. When the Steward finished, he stepped back while a Pit Marshall stood in front of Marcoux's green and blue Swift with his arm pointing straight in Marcoux's direction and a flat palm facing him indicating Marcoux to wait.

The Pit Marshall waited patiently, occasionally nodding his head and speaking into the radio when he received instructions from the Chief Steward. Angrily Marcoux waited. At one point, he beat his fists against the steering wheel and bashed his helmet back into the headrest to show his anger and frustration.

The Pit Marshall suddenly stepped aside and waved Marcoux back onto the track. What seemed an eternity to Marcoux was in reality less than fifteen seconds, nearly enough to put him out of the race.

Marcoux lit up his tires, squealing and smoking through the pits down to where he entered the track at Turn 1. Far ahead the race continued.

Shannon passed Springs at Turn 9, and Shannon passed Henry to the inside of Turn 10. Marcoux exited the pits and roared into Turn 1.

On lap ten, Barton Springs wriggled slightly in Turn 2 and just barely kissed the concrete barricade with his right front tire but enough so the tire no longer touched the track. He pulled off and behind the protective barricade for the corner workers at Turn 5, finished for the day.

The drivers pushed for position. On lap eleven, Shannon had moved into 13th, having passed 14 cars on the tricky Des Moines street course. Just seconds ahead of Shannon was Marcoux's green and white Swift.

The anger and determination, even the adrenalin rush of the drivers following Poirier, could not deny the fact Poirier was an excellent driver and in control of the race at Des Moines. Poirier had run up front too many times to let pursuing drivers concern him. But on lap fifteen, Leclair and Dotson caught Poirier in Turn 1.

Moving into 9th with sixteen laps gone, Marcoux pushed to catch his teammate but each time he passed someone, so did Shannon. Now Shannon closed in on Marcoux and was only a few feet off his rear wing as they came through Turn 1. Marcoux moved back and forth in a blocking maneuver as both drivers charged for Turn 2, and the narrow exit it provided. Marcoux prepared to turn, suddenly slowed and forced Shannon to the outside concrete barricade.

Shannon reacted instinctively, tapping Marcoux, while avoiding a concrete termination of his race, then pursued Marcoux savagely toward Turn 3. The anger in his voice was evident as he spoke to me, "He intentionally slowed and blocked me!"

"Be careful of Marcoux," I said, taking one earphone off so I could hear the scanner and let Shannon know of any changes. "Don't let him sucker you in the wall by braking too late. Run your race Shannon. Not his!"

Coming out of Turn 3, Shannon pulled beside Marcoux, but Marcoux cut him off at Turn 4, then locked his brakes, smoking his rear tires at Turn 5, putting Shannon to the outside of Turn 6.

Shannon broke late and Marcoux broke later. Marcoux nearly locked the brakes on his Swift, almost forcing him off the track and beneath the parking garage. Shannon had to delay turning to keep from hitting Marcoux. From Turn 6, it was a drag race to Turn 7's unnerving turn. Nerve was something neither the young rookie Shannon, nor the old veteran Marcoux lacked. Both were determined to come away with the lead at Turn 7.

Shannon moved to the left. Marcoux moved left. To the right, Marcoux followed. Shannon pulled on Marcoux, started left and instinctively Marcoux moved in a defensive blocking manner. When Marcoux checked his mirrors, he found Shannon with his front tires to his right. Shannon was in the draft and pulling. Marcoux's right rear tire touched Shannon's left front, center to center, bouncing Marcoux away and pulling Shannon even. Side by side, the two Swifts were taken through the gears expertly.

Near his normal braking point Shannon hesitated, then came down hard on the brakes and flipped the throttle as he went to 3rd, 2nd, then 1st. All the time, the Swift jumped and wriggled all over the track nearly out of control.

Marcoux had waited and when he saw Shannon brake, he followed in the same procedure. Only, Marcoux carried too much speed into Turn 7. Still, he instinctively moved his steering wheel toward the apex. Marcoux broke loose and slid across in front of Shannon, who had anticipated the move and waited to turn in. Much slower than normal, Shannon made Turn 7. But he made the turn--something Marcoux failed to do.

Turn 7 proved to be Marcoux's undoing as he too went off course. Shannon swung in under him and charged Turn 8, while Marcoux kissed the three-foot concrete barricade with his right front, then right rear tire. Shannon took 9th and moved quickly across the bridge in pursuit of those ahead.

Marcoux continued, but he had a severe case of toe-in on the right front and 5 degrees negative camber on the rear. Ignoring the damage, he tried unsuccessfully to reach racing speeds as he took Turn 8, crossed the bridge across the Des Moines River, nearly hitting the concrete barricades on both sides, when he over corrected. At Turn 9 he slowed, went slowly toward Turn 10 and entered the pits, his day finished. Marcoux would have no bearing in the final outcome of the race.

Chappel and Hurst made contact. Slowly, Chappel dropped back.

On lap eighteen, Dotson bobbled and Leclair moved into second. Far behind, TJ fought with Augie, Hanna, and Pollard.

As though demon possessed, Shannon charged up Pollard's exhaust having moved from 28th to 8th in nineteen laps and running nearly two seconds faster than Poirier's 1:29's. He was gaining on the leaders!

Over the next four laps, Shannon passed four more. First Pollard then Hanna. Next he took Augie, who followed him past TJ when they came back across the Des Moines River and toward Turn 9. Augie made the pass over TJ stick and held 5th when he came across start/finish.

Shannon was in 4th, pulling away from Augie and quickly closing on Dotson and Leclair with Poirier barely ahead of them with five laps remaining.

Augie controlled his lead over TJ who struggled to maintain the torrid pace. Not too far behind, Hanna led the next cluster of drivers.

The heat showed no mercy as the lead drivers were careful in passing the slower cars, whose drivers were obviously affected by the severe heat and humidity.

Guido Pepin faltered, not making his apexes and finding it hard to stay on track. On lap twenty-four he slowed through Turn 2 and pulled safely from the track at the Turn 3 corner worker station. Already unstrapped, he fell from the car, and crawled on all fours for a few feet as the corner workers ran to his side. Guido pulled the helmet from his head letting it fall to the ground, jerked the head sock from his head, and while on all fours, puked on the Ruan Grand Prix's hot concrete surface.

The first corner worker to Guido's side waved to the other corner workers, signaling with a drinking motion. Instantly another corner worker, dressed in all white and a thermos in one hand, ran to Guido's side. A moment later Guido was in a sitting position, being helped with drink from the thermos, while one corner worker shielded Guido from the sun, another opened the front of the hot fireproof suit. Under the corner workers assistance, Guido staggered back to the covered corner workers station at Turn 3.

"This is Turn 3. The driver in car 54 is suffering from heat exhaustion. He appears to be okay. We'll keep you posted."

Shannon was obviously faster than Poirier and closing the gap. Far behind, Augie pulled out to a rather comfortable one second lead over Hanna who had passed TJ.

The passing was fast, furious, and multiple times each lap as the drivers gauged and set up their opponents for the final laps. They prepared to better the current positions in hopes of adding to their winnings and final points standings.

With two laps remaining, Shannon chased down Dotson at Turn 6 and passed to the inside. Another drag race to Turn 7 where Dotson and Shannon took Turn 7 and 8, side by side, with Shannon getting an advantage and a clear lead before Turn 9.

Shannon started the last lap making rapid gains on Leclair and Poirier. Dotson and Augie raced far behind and comfortable in their positions. TJ took 6th back from Hanna in Turn 3. Behind them came Cruz, Spratt, and Mercury, who dove in on Spratt in Turn 1, but failed. Reese, Pollard, Hurst, Goolsby and Reckert led the next group and were followed closely by Roe, Chappel, and Wilder.

With less than a lap remaining, Shannon over took Leclair at Turn 4. Leclair regained the lead at Turn 5, Shannon again took Leclair at Turn 7, where he had passed Marcoux laps earlier. Only this time Shannon took Leclair to the inside. Leclair slid underneath Shannon and regained the lead coming out of Turn 8. Then at Turn 9, where Shannon had been knocked off at the beginning of the race, he took Leclair, beat him to Turn 10, and took the outside as Leclair came underneath. Carrying speed out of Turn 10, he saw Poirier taking the checkered. Shannon held on for 2nd. Leclair took 3rd and Dotson was close behind.

The thousands of spectators rose to their feet screaming their approval of a race well run. Augie cruised past the checkered in 5th.

Hanna took TJ coming out of Turn 10 but was in an awkward position, so TJ beat her by inches. Spratt passed Cruz for 8th, with both pursued intensely by Mercury. Pollard managed to beat Reese to the finish line, and Reckert took 13th from Goolsby and Hurst.

On the cool-off lap, Turns 1, 2, and 3 waved the white flag showing a slower vehicle on the track, either a wrecker or ambulance. The corner worker with the radio at Turn 3 had called for an ambulance, reporting Guido having problems with the heat.

Before the top six reported to Impound, the ambulance loaded Guido and took him to The Quack Shack, as the trailer with the race doctor was humorously called.

This time when Shannon went to the podium at the winners circle, near start\finish, two things had changed since Sebring; Grant had seen the race, and I was the mechanic. Trophies, champagne, and more interviews.

Jolit Torres made a point to attend and promised me to mention my "Young Guns."

I hurried to Impound for the impromptu celebration. PHAR Motorsports had twice as much to celebrate as both team members were in the top six, with Augie finishing 5th.

In Impound, workers were quick to give drinks of Gatorade to all the drivers. Only Leclair seemed to exit his race vehicle with wobbly legs, but the drinks quickly revived him and brought the color back to his face. The crews arrived giving additional drinks to their drivers and putting ice-filled cold wraps around their necks.

For one of the few times in two years, TJ barely managed to finish in the top six. While the "Young Gun," Shannon Kelly, was on the move having taken 2nd. Poirier was victorious and TJ's insurmountable points lead continued to dwindle.

Poirier stood alone as did TJ. Both were at opposite ends of the top six and eyeing each other, while Leclair and Dotson gave hearty and sincere congratulations to Shannon and Augie. Only a few minutes passed before Chappel and others came to Impound to congratulate their fellow competitors. Hanna came to congratulate her favorite driver--Shannon.

All waited anxiously for word about Guido Pepin. The wait seemed long but in reality was short lived when they heard Guido suffered from heat exhaustion and would return to the track in a few hours.

As the sun set, Augie, Shannon, and I made preparations for the race at Elkhart Lake, Wisconsin in two weeks. Something that would help Shannon was the $3000 for second. Augie was thrilled with his highest finish since the rain soaked race at Sebring, buoying his confidence in the dry heat of Des Moines. His fifth place finish was worth $1200 and bolstered his confidence, not only in himself, but me as well.

We loaded the trailer and talked about the coming race at Road America. Marty went to the Hospitality room to retrieve copies of final results and current points standings.

When he arrived, we took time to study both:

```
              SCCA/USAC
 U.S. Formula Ford 2000 National Championship
            Official Race Results
                 August 12
              Ruan Grand Prix
              Des Moines, Iowa
                (1.8 miles)
```

	Car No.	Name	Model	Time	Laps
1.	(5)	Ian Poirier	Swift DB-8	1:29.05*	28
2.	(44)	Shannon Kelly	Swift SE-3	1:27.59**	28
3.	(7)	Ron Leclair	VanDiemen RF95	1:29.15	28
4.	(33)	Bob Dotson	Spirit	1:29.36	28
5.	(22)	Augie Zuehl	VanDiemen RF95	1:29.53	28
6.	(1)	TJ Benson	VanDiemen RF95	1:29.70	28
7.	(16)	Hanna Lee	Swift DB-8	1:29.72	28
8.	(69)	Phil Spratt	Reynard 95F	1:29.75	28
9.	(27)	Roberto Cruz	VanDiemen RF95	1:29.77	28
10.	(8)	Freddy Mercury	Reynard 95F	1:29.81	28
11.	(47)	Darrell Pollard	VanDiemen RF95	1:29.82	28
12.	(50)	Don Reese	VanDiemen RF95	1:29.93	28
13.	(11)	Alan Reckert	Stohr	1:30.54	28
14.	(40)	Ernie Goolsby	Swift DB-8	1:30.00	27
15.	(99)	Peter Hurst	Swift DB-8	1:30.99	27
16.	(55)	Cliff Roe	VanDiemen RF94	1:30.05	27
17.	(21)	Rick Henry	Swift DB-8	1:31.12	27
18.	(25)	Chase Wilder	Reynard SF90	1:31.71	26
NR 19.	(71)	Gordon Chappel	VanDiemen RF95	1:29.95	26
20.	(27)	Ben Cifelli	Swift DB-3	1:30.88	25
NR 21.	(3)	Will Jones	Swift DB-8	1:31.57	25
22.	(54)	Guido Pepin	Swift DB-8	1:30.08	24
NR 23.	(30)	Bill Murfy	Swift DB-8	1:31.88	24
24.	(00)	Tom Craig	Swift DB-3	1:31.22	22
DNF	(34)	Claude Marcoux	Swift DB-8	1:29.63	16
DNF	(88)	Barton Springs	VanDiemen RF91	1:31.40	10
DNF	(43)	Jude Dionne	Swift DB-8	1:31.44	5

Everyone was excited to see Shannon with the track record.

The points had changed somewhat as Poirier had vaulted back into second. Shannon continued moving up in the points standings. Augie had moved to 12th with the three positions in front of him in easy reach. TJ continued his backward slide, although he continued to hold a commanding lead. A miscue or unfinished race on TJ's part would put a half dozen drivers within striking distance. TJ could ill afford not finishing a race because to win the championship, he would need to finish the last two races.

```
                    SCCA/USAC
        U.S. Formula Ford 2000 National Championship
                Official Points Standing
                  (After 8 of 10 events)
```

	Car No.	Name	Model	Team	Points
1.	(1)	TJ Benson	VanDiemen RF95	BRM	183
2.	(5)	Ian Poirier	Swift DB-8	PACE	150
3.	(8)	Freddy Mercury	Reynard 95F	Dotson Racing	141
4.	(33)	Bob Dotson	Spirit	Dotson Racing	131
5.	(71)	Gordon Chappel	VanDiemen RF95	MOSES	123
6.	(44)	Shannon Kelly	Swift SE-3	PHAR Motorsports	120
7.	(34)	Claude Marcoux	Swift DB-8	PACE	101
8.	(7)	Ron Leclair	VanDiemen RF95	TART	109
9.	(11)	Alan Reckert	Stohr	TART	95
10.	(47)	Darrell Pollard	VanDiemen RF95	BRM	85
11.	(69)	Phil Spratt	Reynard 95F	Spratt Racing	84
12.	(22)	Augie Zuehl	VanDiemen RF95	PHAR Motorsports	81
13.	(16)	Hanna Lee	Swift DB-8	Dotson Racing	78
14.	(27)	Roberto Cruz	VanDiemen RF95	Spratt Racing	76
15.	(55)	Cliff Roe	VanDiemen RF94	GO Racing	47
16.	(21)	Rick Henry	Swift DB-8		44
17.	(43)	Jude Dionne	Swift DB-8	PACE	41
18.	(54)	Guido Pepin	Swift DB-8	GO Racing	39
19.	(50)	Don Reese	VanDiemen RF95		39
20.	(99)	Peter Hurst	Swift DB-8		27
21.	(19)	Maxwell Jordan	Swift DB-8		26
22.	(30)	Bill Murfy	Swift DB-8	Smurf Racing	24
23.	(88)	Barton Springs	VanDiemen RF91		22
24.	(25)	Chase Wilder	Reynard SF90		19
25.	(3)	Will Jones	Swift DB-8		17
26.	(00)	Tom Craig	Swift DB-3	TC Racing	16
27.	(27)	Ben Cifelli	Swift DB-3		7
28.	(40)	Ernie Goolsby	Swift DB-8		7
29.	(74)	Mark McGrath	Swift DB-3	M & M Racing	5
30.	(13)	Steve Smagala	VanDiemen RF89		4
31.	(39)	Art Grindle	Swift SE-3		3

The PHAR Motorsports trailer was loaded and ready for the drive home to Atlanta. The talk eventually went to the next race and preparations for Road America.

ROAD AMERICA

Road America, one of the longest road courses in North America, was located in Elkhart Lake, Wisconsin. The four mile, fourteen turn, clockwise course, wound around and over the heavily wooded, rolling hills of eastern Wisconsin.

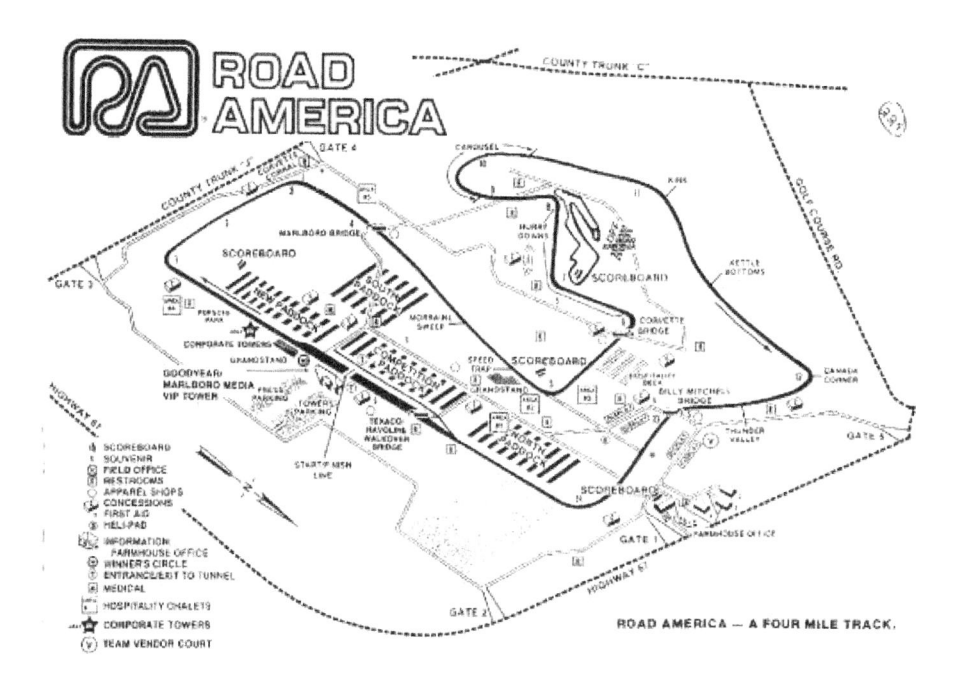

ROAD AMERICA — A FOUR MILE TRACK.

This would be the ninth race in the U.S. Formula Ford 2000 National Championship series, Formula Continental race cars. The event would be Sunday, August 27, after the Shelby Can-Am race at noon. Following the Formula 2000 race, would be the popular and well attended Formula Atlantic race televised over ESPN.

The four-mile course consisted of the main straight that rose slightly uphill, peaking in front of the start/finish line, then dropped to Turn 1, the fastest 90 degree turn on the course where a lot of passing took place. The short straight to Turn 3, had a slight kink to the left, dropped downhill and was marked as Turn 2. In reality, it was more a part of the straight from Turn 1 to Turn 3. Coming down on Turn 3, the driver would brake late and

FORMULA 2000, the Dream

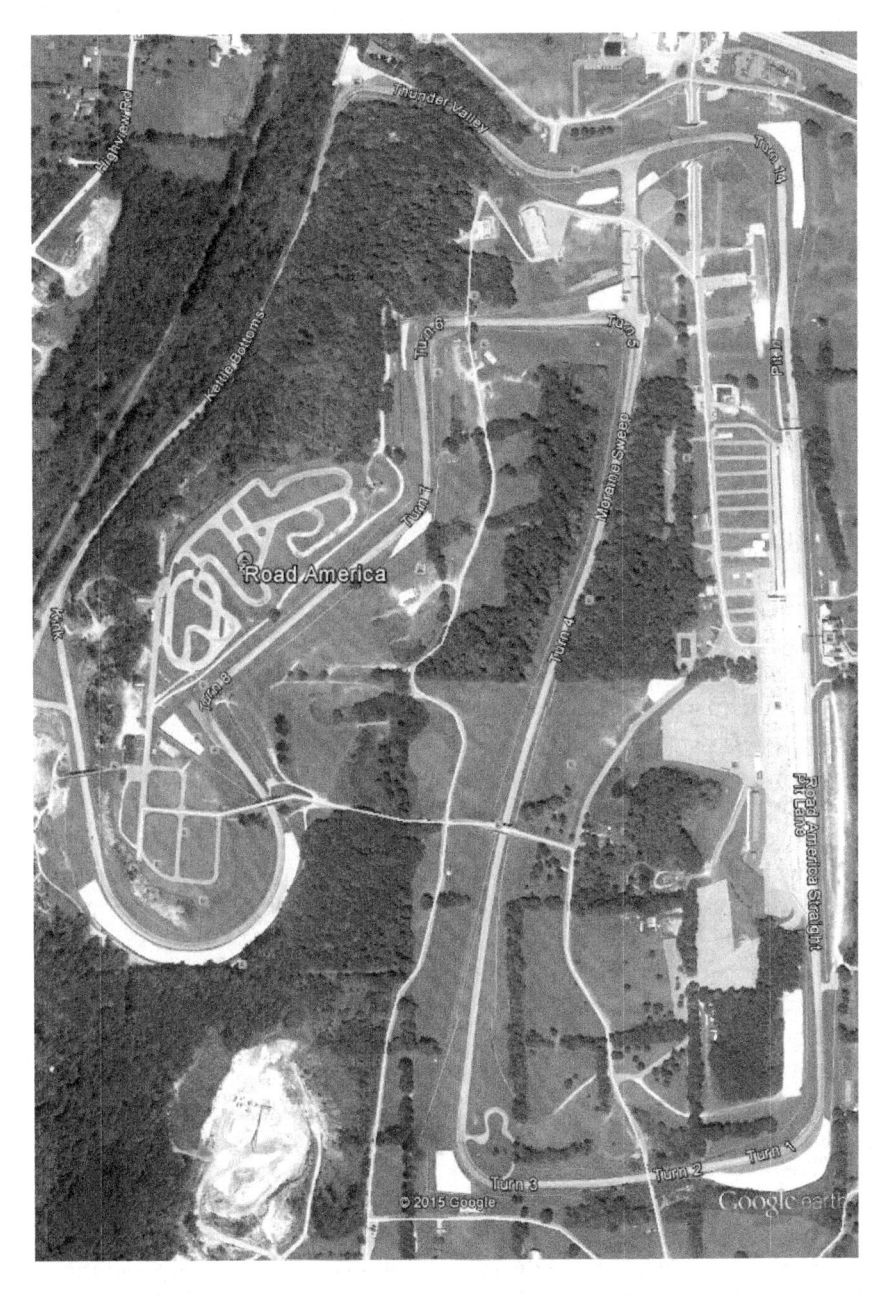

hard, then late apex the right hand turn, and start slightly uphill past the bridge, where the track kinked and started downhill (actually part of the straight but the transition was called Turn 4). The track dove into the left-hand Turn 5 before it flattened out, then made a steep climb from beneath a bridge to the slow, late apex at Turn 6, a lefthander, then a short straight

195

to Turn 7. Turn 7 was a quick, right-hand turn downhill to Turn 8, another 90 degree turn, to the left, another short straight, and then the Carousel. The Carousel consisted of Turn 9 and 10, a continuous right-handed 180 degree turn, where the driver applied power through the turns. The driver tried to stay in the middle, coming out of the Carousel under full throttle, and onto what sometimes was the fastest straight. The "fastest" straight was determined by the drivers ability to take the "Kink" with little or no braking. Those who took the right "Kink" the fastest came away with the best times. The "Kink" or Turn 11 was taken gently with a late apex. The straight continued to drop downhill to Turn 12, a sharp, uphill right turn with a very late apex. The track went sharply uphill to another bridge and Turn 13, a lefthander, taken under full acceleration using all the track. The driver would gradually pull back to the left and set up for the greater than 90 degree right-hand, Turn 14, and back on the uphill, main straight and Start/Finish.

Friday's practice was over, and Saturday morning's first of two practice sessions was underway with a qualifying session scheduled after lunch.

Input from Shannon was increasing, and I felt the feedback was reaching the point I wanted, but I still continued to get the same response when I asked how the car felt. Always, the car felt, "Fine."

With the first session over and the cars in the fast pits, Marty and I were taking pressures and temperatures on Shannon's car, while Les did the same on Augie's. As near as I could tell, Shannon's times were one of the fastest, if not the fastest.

I looked at the temperatures and pressures and noted adjustments to be made when we returned to the paddock area. For adjustments, I would add a half degree camber to the left rear tire, a pound of air to the right front, and stiffen the rear sway bar slightly.

Shannon interrupted my thoughts, "Can I see the temps and pressures?"

Curious about what input Shannon might have, I agreed, "Sure."

"Looks pretty good," said Shannon. "But how about if we add a pound of air to the right front, and would it be okay if we gave it a little more camber on the left rear?"

My eyes lit up and I asked enthusiastically, "Anything else?"

"Well . . . yeah. I'd like to stiffen the rear sway bar a little. You think that would be okay?"

I greeted Shannon's request enthusiastically, "Boy, howdy!"

Shannon and Augie drove the racers back to the paddock area and the PHAR trailer while Grant, Les, Marty, and I walked back.

"What are you so excited about?" asked Grant.

I smiled, "Because Shannon is beginning to know what he wants in a car. Oh, he can drive anything but when he finds what it is he needs--he'll be unbeatable. And I think that time has arrived."

The second session started and Shannon charged the track, his times dropping a full second. Four laps into the session, I asked over the radio, "How's it feel?"

"Great!" came Shannon's response.

"Boy, howdy!" I screamed, startling Grant, Les, and Marty, and ruffling Tex. "We've done it!"

Tex spread his wings and screamed, "Boy, Howdy!"

Shannon's times were the sessions fastest, followed by TJ, who appeared to be on a rebound. Marcoux and Poirier kept pace with close times of their own.

After the qualifying session, I had promised to take Augie, Shannon, Grant, Hanna, Les, and Marty to my favorite lake, only a few miles away, one of many lakes found throughout Wisconsin. I added the trip to the lake would be possible only if Shannon and Augie brought both cars back intact.

We ate a light lunch and waited for the qualifying session.

Shannon was out on the grid early as was Augie, Poirier, TJ and Marcoux. All of them hoping to break away, get clean air, and a fast qualifying session.

When the five-minute warning sounded, Shannon and Augie quit playing hacky sack and walked over to their race cars. At the one-minute warning, Shannon and Grant exchanged the all too familiar good luck exchange.

The drivers held up their hands and the session began.

Again, it appeared Shannon had the fastest time. Once again, I asked Shannon how the car felt and Shannon responded with the unfamiliar but pleasant word, "Great."

When the session ended, all the cars went to the paddock area. Shannon prepared to make the suspension changes when I walked up and told Shannon to get away.

"Why?" Shannon asked.

I smiled, "Today, you graduated. Now that you understand the suspension and what you need, I will do the settings and fix the car--you will drive."

Les, Marty and I made minor changes to the Swift and the Van Diemen, fueled them up and covered them, to await Sunday's race. Hanna arrived at the PHAR Motorsports trailer ready for the swim. All we waited for now was Marty to return from Timing and Scoring with the Official Grid for the race. Shortly after Hanna arrived, Marty arrived with copies of the grid. The excitement on his face was obvious as he pointed to the sheets.

We all took time to study the positions for the race:

```
                    SCCA/USAC
          U.S. Formula Ford 2000 National Championship
                    Official Grid
                     August 27
                    Road America
                  Elkhart, Wisconsin
                     (4 miles)

       Car       Name           Model              Time
       No.                                         1st

   1.  (44)  Shannon Kelly   Swift SE-3         2:17.611*
   2.  (1)   TJ Benson       VanDiemen RF95     2:17.753
   3.  (34)  Claude Marcoux  Swift DB-8         2:17.770
   4.  (5)   Ian Poirier     Swift DB-8         2:17.884
   5.  (69)  Phil Spratt     Reynard 95F        2:18.007
   6.  (33)  Bob Dotson      Spirit             2:18.100
   7.  (22)  Augie Zuehl     VanDiemen RF95     2:18.144
   8.  (16)  Hanna Lee       Swift DB-8         2:18.223
   9.  (8)   Freddy Mercury  Reynard 95F        2:18.243
  10.  (27)  Roberto Cruz    VanDiemen RF95     2:18.267
  11.  (71)  Gordon Chappel  VanDiemen RF95     2:18.287
  12.  (7)   Ron Leclair     VanDiemen RF95     2:18.292
  13.  (47)  Darrell Pollard VanDiemen RF95     2:18.308
  14.  (11)  Alan Reckert    Stohr              2:18 486
  15.  (43)  Jude Dionne     Swift DB-8         2:18.490
  16.  (00)  Tom Craig       Swift DB-3         2:18.533
  17.  (40)  Ernie Goolsby   Swift DB-8         2:18.554
  18.  (55)  Cliff Roe       VanDiemen RF94     2:18.615
  19.  (50)  Don Reese       VanDiemen RF95     2:18.723
  20.  (99)  Peter Hurst     Swift DB-8         2:18.850
  21.  (54)  Guido Pepin     Swift DB-8         2:19.080
  22.  (21)  Rick Henry      Swift DB-8         2:19.225
  23.  (30)  Bill Murfy      Swift DB-8         2:19.354
  24.  (27)  Ben Cifelli     Swift DB-3         2:19.620
  25.  (13)  Steve Smagala   VanDiemen RF89     2:20.200
  26   (25)  Chase Wilder    Reynard SF90       2:20.345
  27.  (3)   Will Jones      Swift DB-8         2:20.455

   * Below current Track Record
```

Shannon had the pole--his first pole position which was below the track record. And to make things better, both Hanna and Augie were in the top ten. With plenty of reason to celebrate, we all piled into Augie and Hanna's rental cars.

Following my directions, we found a quiet, crystal-clear lake lined with thick full green ash and elm, with their long leafy branches stretching out and over the water. Hanna brought out two buckets of chicken, mashed potatoes, and corn-on-the-cob. While Augie and Shannon charged the lake at running speed. Not far behind, Les and Marty tried desperately to keep up and reach the water first.

Less than 50 feet from shore was a floating platform, fifteen feet square and nearly flush with the water.

Grant helped Hanna with a blanket spreading it beneath the shade of the tall trees. She covered the food and then joined the others on the platform.

For three hours, they played in the lake, spending some of their time swimming to shore to retrieve drinks from the coolers, only to return to the floating, wooden island to basque in the sun. Grant and I lounged on the blanket beneath the trees, occasionally going into the water. Once we even ventured to the platform and watched the little minnows and small perch swimming near.

Late in the afternoon we ate, then laid around and waited for the beautiful, orange and blue sunset, before we returned to the track. The sky was clear and star filled.

Grant and I remained in the motorhome talking while Les, Marty and Augie went to the motel. Hand-in-hand, Shannon and Hanna disappeared to walk around the track. We all relaxed and enjoyed the pleasant surroundings. An hour later, Shannon walked quietly into the motorhome, folded down the bunk over the driver's seat, and slid beneath the sheets, while his father and I continued talking late into the evening. Near midnight, Grant convinced me to sleep on the motorhomes couch and avoid the drive back to the motel.

I had barely fallen asleep, when I detected a knock on the camper door. Before I could react, Shannon sat erect in the bunk-type bed as the camper door squeaked opened.

Wrapped in a blanket, Hanna, stepped up into the camper. Shannon put his finger to his lips and pointed to me, then jumped quietly to the floor, and quickly slid on his jeans. They thought I was asleep but I kept my eyes open just enough so I could watch.

Moving near Shannon, Hanna said, "You know, I think racing is just about the best high you can get."

"Really?" asked Shannon, with a smile.

"Yes, really," said Hanna, nodding her head. "In fact, I think racing is better than sex."

"No," whispered Shannon, as he slipped his shirt over his head.

"Yes, really." Hanna pulled her arm from beneath the blanket, extended her hand to Shannon, and let a giggle slip. "But I'm willing to let you prove me wrong."

Shannon smiled and took her hand. Together they walked quietly from the camper and disappeared.

I could hardly suppress a smile. I closed my eyes and a moment later was asleep.

The beautiful summer day ended with a beautiful cool romantic Wisconsin night. Some slept but all waited with anticipation for the following days race.
* * *

When the five-minute warning sounded, Hanna, Augie, Dotson, Mercury, and Shannon cut their conversation short and went to their cars as some yelled, "Good luck." Others gave thumbs-up salutes.

Shannon stepped to his Swift, hesitated, then moved to his right and TJ's red, white and blue Van Diemen. TJ sat nervously in his car, already strapped in, ready for the race, and preparing to slip his head sock on while his mechanic stood over him, shading him with an open umbrella.

Shannon bent over and extended his hand, "Good luck, TJ."

TJ looked shocked. Then he smiled, lowered his head sock and extended his hand, "Good luck to you, Shannon. You've done a heckva job."

"Charlie did it."

TJ squeezed his lips together in deep thought and a little sadness shown in the corner of his eyes. Then he nodded his head, "Yeah, I know. He's the best."

TJ resumed his work with the head sock while Shannon stepped into his Swift and started to fasten himself in.

The three-minute warning sounded and the drivers were already in their cars, adjusting the arm restraints and the five-point harness.

Shannon crossed the velcro strap to the neck brace his father had given him for the Charlotte race. Les and Marty tended to Augie. Les checked the radio with Augie, and I checked the radio with Shannon.

When the one-minute warning sounded, Grant exchanged the familiar hand shake with his son Shannon. As Grant walked away, I walked near and offered my hand--then I too went through the same ritual. Boy, howdy, this hand ritual was something!

Because of the roar of the engines around us, I clicked the radio, "Hell, if one is good two is better . . . good luck."

Shannon pushed the button on his steering wheel, "Thanks."

"Nervous?" I asked. I could see the eyes, and knew Shannon was smiling, even though I could not see Shannon's face.

"Maybe . . . a little," said Shannon, making a final check of the clear tearaways.

"Well, go get 'em for old Charlie Pepper."

Again the drivers held up their left hands. Satisfied they were ready, the Grid Marshall motioned Shannon out and to her left, putting Shannon on the inside right with the pole position.

TJ went to her right. The rest of the field followed alternating to each side of the Grid Marshall.

A brand new red Camaro led the procession around on the pace lap. Back in the pack, the drivers rocked the Indy-type Formula Continentals back and forth trying to warm the tires.

They rounded Turn 14 and started the hill toward the starter stand and Start/Finish. The Camaro pulled into the pits. Shannon controlled the start accelerating slowly up the hill.

The green flag waved as the two rows came up the hill in perfect order. Shannon gave it full throttle as did the others. Shannon pulled TJ by only a foot at the start. Poirier pulled to the outside of TJ and Marcoux to the inside of Shannon, yet neither gained. Four wide, they crested the hill and shot down to Turn 1. Shannon came down hard on his brakes at the last possible moment as did TJ and Poirier. Two wide they started into Turn 1. None seemed prepared for what happened next, except for Poirier. Marcoux didn't brake. Instead, he moved to the grassy part at the inside of Turn 1, sliding dangerously back on the track in front of Shannon. TJ lifted but still shot past Shannon who had to brake in order to avoid hitting Marcoux. TJ's hesitation was Poirier's opportunity as Poirier also shot past Shannon and managed to pull to the inside of TJ taking the lead into Turn 3. Marcoux was 3rd and closing in on TJ as Poirier seemed to be holding up TJ intentionally. Not far behind Marcoux, followed Shannon, angry and determined.

Poirier ran fast enough for the lead four drivers to pull away from the rest of the field. Marcoux continued to get dangerously close to TJ as though he were intentionally trying to hit him. When Shannon came too close, Marcoux tried unobtrusively to block him since all four cars were in such close proximity.

Shannon yelled over the radio before the first lap ended, "Oh, my God, Marcoux almost hit TJ!"

"Watch him," I warned. "Remember the last race." I checked to make sure my scanner was on.

As the second lap began, the corner workers finally noticed, "Turn 6, car 34 seemed to aim for car one intentionally."

Turn 12 and 13 mentioned the same two cars. The Chief Steward alerted the corners and asked to be told if it happened again.

Then it happened as the four completed lap two and neared Turn 1. TJ swung to the outside left to prepare for Turn 1. Marcoux also went to the outside but on a line just inside TJ's right side. Shannon moved to the inside. TJ touched his brakes, having reached maximum speed. Marcoux waited, pulling slightly on TJ. When he got his front tires past TJ's rear tires, he pulled over, letting his front left tire move between TJ's right front and rear tire. Marcoux came down hard on his brakes. The right rear tire of TJ's red, white, and blue number 1 Van Diemen hit Marcoux's left front tire, catapulting TJ's car almost vertically and forward with a speed in excess of 100 mph.

The Van Diemen carried through the air for a 150 feet before the back dropped. TJ locked the brakes but in a futile effort as the racer was still in midair. The corner workers scurried for safety and away from the uncontrolled, airborne missile.

The racer bounced on the ground less than 100 feet from the earth embankment and the two-row barrier of tires. The front hit with tremendous force, pushing the nose back two feet, and the momentum flipped the car upside down and on top of the embankment, near the same spot where AJ Foyt had broken his feet, only a few years before his retirement from Indy racing.

Just as quickly as they dispersed, the corner workers swarmed the crushed and battered racer.

Shannon pulled past Marcoux but took time to push the button on the steering wheel, "Charlie, he hit TJ."

"Don't worry about TJ. He'll be okay, just don't let Marcoux catch you," I warned.

"He took TJ out!" screamed Shannon.

The scanner came to life.

"This is Turn 1. Car 34 has knocked car one off the track and continued on."

"This is the Chief Steward, black flag 34. I want him in the pits. I want the Pit Marshall to stop his race and not let him back out."

"This is the Pit Marshall--understood."

"This is Turn 1. The corner is clear. Can you send the ambulance and the Jaws of Life?"

Turn 1 requested the famous "Jaws of Life" a hydraulic mechanism used to cut drivers from their bent and twisted cars.

"Roger, Rescue One on our way by the outside access road."

An access road for fans and track personnel completely circled the track, providing easy access to most parts of the track from the outside.

"Is the driver okay?" asked Andy Cobb, the Chief Steward.

"I think so. He's conscious, but his legs are pinned in, and he is in pain."

As they completed lap three, Marcoux received the open black flag telling him to come in. Poirier moved erratically through Turn 1 and 3, slowing Shannon and bringing Marcoux into a position where he could almost touch Shannon.

"He's on my tail," yelled Shannon. "I think he's trying to do the same thing to me as he did to TJ."

Turn 5 reported, "Car 34 almost hit car 44."

"Shannon," I said calmly. "Watch Marcoux. Watch your mirrors. If he's trying to take you out, he'll want to do it in the turns, by getting his front tire in front of your rear tire. If he does it, slam on your brakes. It's the only way to keep from ending up like TJ."

"Okay. Ohhh God, he--!"

I heard nothing else.

"This is Turn 8. Car 34 forced car 44 to take evasive action and drop two tires off the track. Both cars have continued on."

I squeezed my hands together, "If that sonofabitch takes out Shannon, I'm gonna break his durn neck."

"Turn 12, car 34 is moving in on car--they've hit! Metal to metal. One car is into the banking, the other has continued on. Request Turn 11 wave the yellow. Turn 12 is now waving yellow. We've sent two Corner Workers to the wreck site. Car 44 is off and in the embankment."

I dropped the scanner and started running down pit row as though I could do something, "God dammit, he took Shannon out. That little sonofabitch."

I could see Poirier round Turn 14, head uphill toward the start finish, and not far behind came Marcoux. I picked up a crescent wrench and was prepared to run to the track wall and throw it at Marcoux, regardless of the punishment--but wait . . . it wasn't Marcoux. Behind Poirier came Shannon!

The only explanation was the car in the embankment was Marcoux. I started jumping up and down, overjoyed to see Shannon.

"This is Turn 12, that's car 34 out of the race. The driver is out and uninjured. The car is away from the racing line, and there is no longer a yellow at Turn 12."

Not far behind Shannon followed Spratt, Dotson, Chappel, Augie, Hanna, Mercury, and Cruz. Shannon started to pull away and close in on Poirier.

Nine laps remained. Shannon caught Poirier at Turn 3 and passed him with ease at Turn 5, forcing Poirier to lock up his tires. At Turn 6, Poirier went off track in an effort to catch Shannon. He bounced across the Road America countryside, coming back on the asphalt track at Turn 7.

"This is Rescue One. We have the driver out. His left leg has a compound fracture. The driver is awake and alert. We are now in route to the hospital."

Well, at least TJ was alive and Shannon was in the lead, I said to myself. Quickly I made a mental calculation. Poirier was only 33 points behind TJ for the Points Championship and the $15,000 prize money. If Poirier kept his present 2nd position, which was most probable, he would only need a 13th place finish in the last race. In fact all he needed in the last two races was a 5th and a 6th. The championship was most assuredly Poirier's now.

Shannon flew past and I waited for Poirier. Poirier came around locked in a battle with Dotson and the others, more than six seconds behind Shannon. I surmised correctly that Poirier became too aggressive in his effort to reel in Shannon. "The temperature is climbing," said Shannon.

My heart sank. What now? I clicked the radio and asked, "What's the temperature?"

"Two-twenty and it looks like its climbing."

"Let me know what it does."

A minute later, Shannon streaked past on the main straight. The next group was battling fiercely among themselves and had dropped farther behind.

Les clicked the stopwatch, "Shannon's got eight seconds on Dotson."

Shannon was on the radio again, "Water temperature is two-forty."

I glanced to the heavens and mumbled, "Not now. Please not now."

"Is it serious?" asked Grant.

"Don't know yet," I said.

Tex started imitating the cars at the 24 Hours of LeMans, then pulled on my ear. Instinctively, I reached in my pocket and pulled out a sunflower seed, and gave it to him. Then I pulled the plastic bag out and took two lemon drops out.

Debris, maybe from Marcoux, I thought. I hoped the air ducts to the radiators were only blocked.

"Shannon, can you see if anything is blocking the pods to the radiators?" I asked.

Silence, then Shannon answered, "No--wait. Yeah, a piece of something is blocking the left front pod."

I smiled, "Good, good. What's the temperature?"

"Still two forty. No its two-forty-five."

Now it was time to take control, "Listen carefully. You must pull into the pits this time. Les and Marty will check the pods and clear them. If the radiator is not leaking, we'll send you back out. Hopefully, still with the lead. Don't leave the pits until I wave you back onto the track. Watch me and don't leave until I wave you on!"

As I finished my orders, Shannon rounded Turn 14, "I'm coming in!"

Moving quickly to the hand dolly, with the cabinet of tools should they be needed, I opened a drawer, pulled out two large screwdrivers and two long channel locks. I turned to Les and Marty and tossed them one of each.

"Marty, check the right side pod and look under the Swift for leaking coolants! Les, you take the left side and clear that crap!" I ordered.

Les and Marty put their hands on the pit wall and leaped over to take their positions as Shannon roared into the pits. At the entry to the pits, a worker sounded an air horn to warn of a racer coming down the fast pit lane.

Shannon came to a complete stop, looked directly at me . . . and waited.

I held my hand up toward Shannon as I watched Les and Marty. At the same time, I calmly repeated the same words over and over, "Hold it."

Marty stood and shook his head and yelled above the rumble of the engine, "All clear!" He had found nothing.

Dotson and the others were rounding Turn 14 and starting up the main straight.

Les jumped away from the Swift waving a piece of fiberglass high over his head, "Got it!"

I waved my hand and screamed, "Go! Go!"

The rear tires smoked as Shannon raced down the fast pits and toward the exit that would put him on the track and near Turn 1. Dotson and the others passed the start finish/line and charged Turn 1.

Most times, the corner worker at the end of the fast pits would hold up a car to let the traffic pass before letting it enter the track. But this time was different because Andy Cobb was watching, and radioed the pit worker to let car 44 enter the track.

Shannon entered the track at full speed only a car length ahead of the others, but he took Turn 1 as though possessed by a demon. He would not be denied at Turn 3 and at Turn 5, the uphill lefthander, he was four car lengths ahead of Dotson. Dotson closed at Turn 6 and 7 but Shannon pulled away at Turn 8 and 9.

"What's the temperature?" I asked.

"Two-twenty and dropping. Can't talk--it's busy here!" said Shannon rushing his last words.

Shannon started to pull away, and the next time he passed us, Shannon had a one second lead. Two laps later, Poirier had dropped behind Cruz and into 9th place. Poirier had problems and was faltering. Shannon was running away with the race and extending an already insurmountable lead.

The track commentator excitedly announced, "Shannon Kelly has set a new track record. In fact, his last three laps have been under the track record and all within a tenth of a second of each other. The last lap was his fastest."

Grant yelled before I could respond. Even Les and Marty whooped it up and hugged each other.

Poirier continued his charge to the rear. The next time he passed, his front wing was bent up on the right side showing contact with another car or another off road excursion. Poirier was pushing and had dropped to the 13th position.

With two laps remaining Dotson took over a solid second as did Spratt for third. The battle for fourth was between Chappel, Augie, Hanna, and Cruz. Mercury, Leclair, Reckert, Pollard, Pepin, and Tom Craig, old Patches, were less than a second behind. Dionne, having run well in the early going, was alone in 14th after passing his teammate Poirier.

Poirier continued to falter. Even Murf the Smurf passed him as old Murfy moved into 15th pushing Poirier to 16th.

Shannon crossed the finish line with a runaway victory. Dotson was second and Spratt third. Cruz and Augie came out of Turn 14 side by side. Hanna had laid back moving wide and cutting beneath both drivers. Three wide they raced to the finish line. Hanna took 4th, followed by Augie and Cruz. Only a few car lengths behind trailed Chappel. Old Moses took 7th. Mercury was next and all alone. Pollard and Leclair came across the finish line alongside each other with Leclair nosing out Pollard. Reckert, Pepin, and Craig followed in that order.

The first three proceeded to the podium near the tower. For the second time during the season, Shannon was on center stage, holding another tall trophy. A proud father stood to the side and watched his son revel in the moment's glory. Once again, Shannon humbly mentioned his father... and me.

This time in Impound, three friends found they had all made it. Hanna, Augie, and Shannon were ecstatic and continued to congratulate each other.

We talked about Shannon's runaway victory but the conversation continued to revolve around TJ's wreck and the close call Shannon had with Marcoux. Again, rumor around the paddock spread quickly. Word was that Marcoux was locked in a meeting with the Chief Stewards using Poirier as interpreter. LaForche quickly packed the PACE trailer and prepared to leave the track.

After the thirty minute Impound wait, the drivers went to their individual paddock area. Shannon, Hanna, and Augie opted to watch the more exciting Formula Atlantic race. After the Atlantic race, they each collected copies of the official race results. They learned Marcoux had been disqualified and suspended for the remaining season, with his license to be reviewed at the start of the season next year, should he request a renewal. He was also fined $2000.

Shannon and Augie returned to the PHAR trailer and gave me a copy of the final results and the current points standings after nine races:

```
                        SCCA/USAC
            U.S. Formula Ford 2000 National Championship
                    Official Points Standing
                      (After 9 of 10 events)
```

	Car No.	Name	Model	Team	Points
1.	(1)	TJ Benson	VanDiemen RF95	BRM	183
2.	(33)	Bob Dotson	Spirit	Dotson Racing	157
3.	(8)	Freddy Mercury	Reynard 95F	Dotson Racing	154
4.	(5)	Ian Poirier	Swift DB-8	PACE	154
5.	(44)	Shannon Kelly	Swift SE-3		150
6.	(71)	Gordon Chappel	VanDiemen RF95	MOSES	137
7.	(7)	Ron Leclair	VanDiemen RF95	TART	121
8.	(69)	Phil Spratt	Reynard 95F	Spratt Racing	107
9.	(11)	Alan Reckert	Stohr	TART	105
10.	(22)	Augie Zuehl	VanDiemen RF95	BRM	99
11.	(16)	Hanna Lee	Swift DB-8	Dotson Racing	98
12.	(47)	Darrell Pollard	VanDiemen RF95	BRM	96
13.	(27)	Roberto Cruz	VanDiemen RF95	Spratt Racing	92
14.	(21)	Rick Henry	Swift DB-8		49
15.	(43)	Jude Dionne	Swift DB-8	PACE	48
16.	(54)	Guido Pepin	Swift DB-8	GO Racing	48
17.	(55)	Cliff Roe	VanDiemen RF94	GO Racing	48
18.	(50)	Don Reese	VanDiemen RF95		42
19.	(30)	Bill Murfy	Swift DB-8	Smurf Racing	30
20.	(99)	Peter Hurst	Swift DB-8		29
21.	(19)	Maxwell Jordan	Swift DB-8		26
22.	(88)	Barton Springs	VanDiemen RF91		22
23.	(00)	Tom Craig	Swift DB-3	TC Racing	24
24.	(25)	Chase Wilder	Reynard SF90		20
25.	(3)	Will Jones	Swift DB-8		18
26.	(27)	Ben Cifelli	Swift DB-3		10
27.	(40)	Ernie Goolsby	Swift DB-8		7
28.	(74)	Mark McGrath	Swift DB-3	M & M Racing	5
29.	(13)	Steve Smagala	VanDiemen RF89		4
30.	(39)	Art Grindle	Swift SE-3		3

(34)   Claude Marcoux DSQ (Suspended)

Shannon had his first pole, his second victory, and another track record. I smiled, knowing Shannon could now give feedback on the suspension settings.

Shannon had moved to fifth in the points standings with Augie, and Hanna in tenth and eleventh, respectively. When our trailer was loaded, we helped TJ's crew load the wrecked Van Diemen, and Pollard's race car on the BRM trailer. After the trailer was on its way to Birmingham, we agreed to go to the hospital and see TJ.

```
             SCCA/USAC
    U.S. Formula Ford 2000 National Championship
             Official Race Results
                  August 27
                 Road America
               Elkhart, Wisconsin
                  (4 miles)

     Car     Name              Model            Time         Laps
     No.

 1.  (44)  Shannon Kelly      Swift SE-3        2:17.41**     13
 2.  (33)  Bob Dotson         Spirit            2:17.65*      13
 3.  (69)  Phil Spratt        Reynard 95F       2:17.74*      13
 4.  (16)  Hanna Lee          Swift DB-8        2:17.85       13
 5.  (22)  Augie Zuehl        VanDiemen RF95    2:17.87       13
 6.  (27)  Roberto Cruz       VanDiemen RF95    2:17.93       13
 7.  (71)  Gordon Chappel     VanDiemen RF95    2:17.95       13
 8.  (8)   Freddy Mercury     Reynard 95F       2:17.63       13
 9.  (7)   Ron Leclair        VanDiemen RF95    2:17.97       13
10.  (47)  Darrell Pollard    VanDiemen RF95    2:18.02       13
11.  (11)  Alan Reckert       Stohr             2:18.24       13
12.  (54)  Guido Pepin        Swift DB-8        2:18.55       13
13.  (00)  Tom Craig          Swift DB-3        2:18.62       13
14.  (43)  Jude Dionne        Swift DB-8        2:18.44       13
15.  (30)  Bill Murfy         Swift DB-8        2:18.88       13
16.  (21)  Rick Henry         Swift DB-8        2:18.42       13
17.  (5)   Ian Poirier        Swift DB-8        2:17.77*      13
18.  (50)  Don Reese          VanDiemen RF95    2:18.83       13
19.  (99)  Peter Hurst        Swift DB-8        2:18.75       13
20.  (40)  Ernie Goolsby      Swift DB-8        2:18.64       13
21.  (55)  Cliff Roe          VanDiemen RF94    2:18.57       13
22.  (3)   Will Jones         Swift DB-8        2:18.99       12
23.  (25)  Chase Wilder       Reynard SF90      2:18.78       12
24.  (27)  Ben Cifelli        Swift DB-3        2:19.23       12
25.  (13)  Steve Smagala      VanDiemen RF89    2:19.45       12
DNF  (1)   TJ Benson          VanDiemen RF95    2:17.85        3

DISQ    (34) Claude Marcoux   Swift DB-8

FASTEST LAP
Car      Time                Speed
44       2:17.41**           104.80 mph

**New Track Record
```

At the hospital, TJ appeared depressed but extremely grateful and happy to see most of his old crew. TJ told us he would be unable to participate in the season's final race. TJ was also genuinely happy to learn Shannon had won the race. We continued to talk about racing and the upcoming race in Atlanta. Finally the nurses forced us to leave and let TJ get some rest. As we started to leave TJ called me back. I turned around and walked back to his bedside.

I could tell the words were hard as he spoke, "I'm really sorry for all the problems I gave you."

"Aw, forget it," I said.

"No, I can't. I've been an asshole and I realize how good you are by what you've done with Shannon. He deserves it. It isn't the same without you." TJ laughed, "Hell, I even miss Tex."

A lump kinda swelled in my throat and I laughed, "Tex."

TJ laughed, "Yeah, Tex."

"Boy, howdy." We both laughed and then I knew there was still hope for TJ. I nodded and smiled to TJ, then caught up to the others.

As I walked away my thoughts filled with the championship and who could get enough points in the last race to beat TJ for the championship. Only three drivers could beat TJ in the points championship; Poirier, Mercury, or Dotson. For TJ to lose the points championship, one of those three needed to win the last race. A second would do none of them any good although Dotson could tie TJ with a second but TJ would win based on most victories. A win by Poirier, Dotson, or Mercury would take the championship away from TJ, and only one thing appeared to stand in the way of that happening--Shannon Kelly!

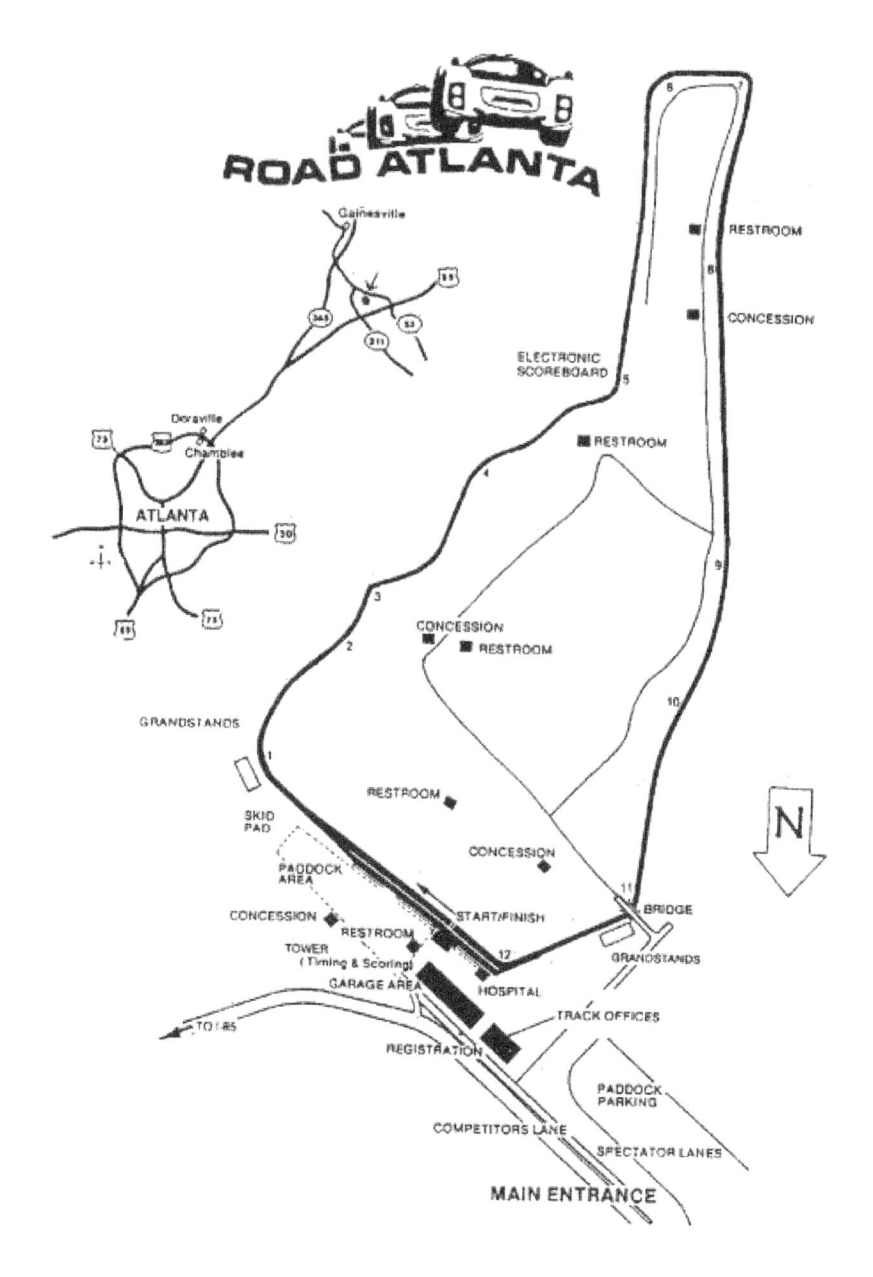

The final race of SCCA/USAC's U.S. Formula Ford 2000 National Championship series was finally here. Road Atlanta would be the last race and it would be a great event. The twisting, winding, Georgia road course would host four races over the September weekend and conclude two of those series.

FORMULA 2000, the Dream

Saturday, September 16, would bring the Shelby Can-Am series to an end. The Shelby Can-Am race would be followed by the highly touted Toyota Atlantic race. Sunday after lunch would conclude SCCA/USAC's U.S. Formula Ford 2000 National Championship series, and it would be followed with a 100-mile Trans-Am race.

All four classes would practice Thursday and Friday morning with qualification Friday afternoon and Saturday morning. Sunday morning would have a short warm up session for the final two races followed by a two hour quiet time before noon. This was an agreement between Road Atlanta and the local churches to provide a quiet time in the surrounding area for church services. After noon the final races would begin with the Formula 2000 racers scheduled first.

Road Atlanta's challenging road course was located Northeast of Atlanta and outside the small town of Gainesville off Highway 53. Immediately inside the track gate, a road to the right took a 90 degree turn downhill. It then climbed steeply back up to grandstands on the left and a bridge with car access to the infield of the track. Concession stands and bathrooms were conveniently dotted along the heavily wooded countryside that provided visitors with spectacular views of Road Atlanta. If one did not take the road leading to the grandstands and the infield but continued on, a one story office building housing registration and a souvenir shop were on the immediate right. Once again a visitor passed through another gate. The paved area dropped sharply down with garages and concessions to the right. Behind the garages and down a hill was the four story Timing and Scoring Tower, overlooking the fast pits and the main straight, with a view of the climbing, uphill Turn 1, and the bridge at Turn 11 dropping sharply to Turn 12. Off to the right was the hospital. Past the garages and down a gentle slope was a large paved area for the race teams. Still farther down the base of the hill and in front of Turn 1 were more grandstands and another large paved area for race teams.

The false Grid was on the lower area, above Turn 1, and fenced in to prevent spectators from wandering around before the start of the race. From the grid, the drivers went to the left, beneath the walk over bridge, then up the steep, right hand, 90 degree Turn 1. A road beside Grid went downhill to an unpaved area used by stock cars or those who arrived late. Across the road from the Grid, and slightly uphill, was the Tech Shed and directly to the left of Tech was a large paved area most teams used. Two-hundred feet down and leading to Tech was the PHAR trailer and motorhome.

All the teams were back for the final race with only a few faces missing. Claude Marcoux would not race, disqualified for the remainder of the season. TJ Benson would be unable to run, but he was in attendance and close to his BRM trailer not far from PHAR and Dotson. The three weeks since the wreck had allowed him time to practice with crutches. He had become quite adept. The hilly pit area would quickly exhaust him so he opted to ride as a passenger on what looked more like a one person golf cart, with a flat area for passengers. The cart was propelled with a gas engine that would start when the accelerator pedal was depressed. At Road Atlanta, very few bicycles were used for transportation as most teams used a variety of four wheelers. Qualifying had been uneventful and most of the trailers were quiet as the Formula Continentals were out on the track for Friday's first and only qualification.

The crews were stationed along the fast pits taking times for the qualifying sessions. Shannon streaked past and I smiled to myself when I saw yet another lap faster than any other driver. With another day of qualifying, it appeared Shannon might have the pole.

Shannon charged up the steep, right hand, 90 degree Turn 1, in fourth gear, leaving a quick spray of sparks on the newly paved track. Up the hill and without using the clutch, Shannon flipped the throttle, tapped the brake and down shifted into 3rd. A twist to the left comprised Turn 2, where the course flattened out, made a sharp 90 degree right hander for Turn 3, then arched to the left, and dropped downhill to Turn 4, a slight turn to the right and a part of the esses, a combination left, right and left. Some drivers downshifted to 2nd. Others stayed in 3rd and would go to 4th through the downhill and uphill esses. Shannon stayed in 3rd and shifted to 4th through the esses.

Out of Turn 4, the track rose back uphill to a 90 degree lefthander-- Turn 5, leaving another spray of sparks in the dip between Turn 4 and Turn 5. Not using the clutch, Shannon flipped the throttle and went from fourth, to third, to second. The road straightened and continued uphill, then dropped downhill where Shannon went into third then fourth gear. The track rose for Turn 6, a banked right-hander. Shannon downshifted to third, a short straight and Turn 7, another right-hander and the slowest point on the track where Shannon flipped the throttle and downshifted to second, then first. Exit speed was critical for Turn 7 as it led to the longest and fastest part of the track, Shannon accelerated through all four gears. Turn 8, 9, and 10 were in reality kinks taken under full throttle. Turn 8 kinked to the left, Turn 9 kinked to the right, then the track started a steep drop to Turn 10, a sharper kink to the left at the very bottom, where the high speed dip created a spectacular spray of sparks in the sudden steep climb to the bridge and the blind, right-hand, downhill Turn 11. Shannon made the turn blind in third gear, using only reference points, an eye on the corner workers to check for waving yellows and possible racecars directly in the drivers line of attack. All was clear as the Swift SE-3 slid out far to the left and downhill crossing the line for the fast pit entry. He gathered the car in and under full acceleration shifted to fourth and aimed downhill for Turn

12, the final turn, a right-hander. He flashed past us in front of the pits and the Timing and Scoring Tower.

Shannon completed another record lap.

I watched the stopwatch closely making mental count of the interval between Shannon, Mercury, Dotson, and Poirier--the ones to beat. By my count, Shannon was again the fastest with Poirier a close second. The atmosphere was relaxed and even Shannon talked more on the radio.

Les told me there was time for three more laps when Shannon roared past and charged uphill into Turn 1.

"Make one more lap then come on in," I said. "Your times are fine, and we want to get temps and pressures."

"Okay."

The seconds clicked off and just as I expected, Shannon shot out from under the bridge. Suddenly, the left front tire seemed to buckle, then the SE-3 slid off the course downhill and against the double tire barricade.

I watched and held my breath. The contact was hard but didn't appear severe . . . yet, the car looked sickly as though it were bent slightly forming a V.

A few minutes later, Shannon was brought back to the Paddock area and the PHAR trailer. Shannon was fine and intact, but not the same could be said for the Swift that had brought them so far, with a pole and victory at Road America. The frame was bent, something that could not be explained for the impact it sustained. I surmised the damage could be the result of the misuse from previous owners, time on the car, or possibly the wreck at Charlotte. The frame simply fatigued and twisted on impact. Spectators strolled past, pointing and talking about the bent race car. Some would even open their program to find a picture of Shannon, point to him, and the derelict Swift, shake their heads, and continue talking.

One dark haired spectator didn't do this. He ate jelly beans from a white paper bag, and when Shannon glanced his direction, he waved. Shannon and I walked forward to talk to the spectator.

"That's a shame what happened. I was watching from Turn 12. The car just seemed to let go," said the spectator.

"Yeah . . . I don't know what happened. Felt fine until the accident . . . say, isn't your name Pat?" Shannon asked.

"Right. How'd you remember?"

Shannon pointed to the bag, "The jelly beans."

Pat laughed, "Here, you can have the rest, I've had too many. How bad is the car?"

"Don't know yet," I said.

"That's too bad, I was looking forward to watching the race. You looked good. I heard about your race at Road America." Pat shook his head, "I hope you get it running. If you do, you can bet I'll be watching you. Well, good luck."

Shannon and I nodded to Pat, as he walked away, then I resumed my inspection on the Swift.

The Swift could not be repaired, and I knew it.

"Can't be fixed," I said, showing obvious frustration and anger at the turn of events after coming so far.

Tex squawked, somehow knowing something was wrong, "Squirt!" Tex pulled at my ear. I reached into the top pocket of my overalls and fished around with two fingers but unsuccessfully. No sunflower seeds. "This is not good," I muttered. I reached into a deep pocket and pulled out the plastic bag of lemon drops, looked at the plastic bag, and shook my head. Empty! "Boy, howdy! Got a broke racer. I'm out of lemon drops, and I'm out of sunflower seeds. Boy, this day's going to hell in a hand bag."

"What do we do?" asked Shannon rather subdued, knowing full well we would not make the last qualifying Saturday morning--and maybe miss the next day's race. All the preparation and all the work for nothing.

I squeezed my chin with my right hand, "Well, we don't give up. The race isn't until Sunday, and remember . . . until that flag drops, you're still in the race. The Swift is history as far as tomorrow's qualifying is concerned. We need a new frame, and it would take two days to outfit it . . . if we could find another SE-3. Right now, we need to find another car. Right now, we need some sunflower seeds and lemon drops."

Augie, Shannon, Les, and Marty were subdued and quiet. Like they had been beaten before the race had been run.

For a moment I thought, then quickly barked commands, "Augie, Shannon, see if anybody here has a spare racecar. Rent it if you must--but get it! Go to the office, see if you can get a list of local drivers racing Formula Continentals. Call 'em and see if you can rent one. Check with Dotson. I know Poirier has a car . . . ask him." Augie's eyes lit up, "Shannon can use my car!"

"Hey, Dude, no way," said Shannon. "You don't race--I don't race."

"Nope," I interjected. "I appreciate what you're doing Augie, but you race your car. You can help us find another car, and you will race tomorrow, and so will Shannon. Now, go find a car, while Les and I look at the damage."

I turned to Marty, "Go to town and get some Gatorade for qualifying in the morning. Get plenty, 'cause it's gonna be hot, and both Augie and Shannon are gonna need plenty for the race." I laughed, and Tex squawked, "But most important Marty, bring back two bags of lemon drops and a bag of uncooked and unsalted sunflower seeds--or don't come back!"

The four boys laughed and relaxed, confident with my ability to solve unbeatable odds.

I smiled, as they walked away to do their tasks--inside I worried!

* * *

Les and I stood over the Swift SE-3. While I contemplated my next move, Marty, Augie, and Shannon arrived almost simultaneously. None of us were smiling.

Augie and Shannon told me they asked Dotson, who was more than willing, but told them his spare car had a tweaked frame and he only used it for spare parts. If the frame could be straightened, it would take more than a day to transfer the parts. Poirier said he didn't have a spare car. He spoke quickly in French to Dionne, who closed the door to the PACE racing trailer so Augie and Shannon could not see it. But Augie had already seen the spare car when they walked up. Before they walked away, Poirier said something else to Dionne in French. Both Poirier and Dionne laughed when Shannon and Augie walked away.

Shannon and Augie called the locals, finding only one and the owner refused to rent it. They could do nothing.

"It's my fault," whispered Shannon.

"No, it's not," said Grant, putting a supportive arm over his son's shoulders.

I tried to cheer Shannon up with what little information I had. "I looked at the car. It looks like a suspension piece just broke. Those things happen-- and they'll happen again. The frame was plum tuckered out. You didn't hit hard enough to hurt the car this bad. The car was plain worn out. It can be fixed but not in time for the race."

Shannon nodded. Over the next hour, a slow procession of competitors came past our dejected group at the PHAR Motorsports trailer, where spirits reached a new low. Dotson and Mercury offered everything they had, but the one thing they lacked was the one thing Shannon needed. Smurf came as did Turtle and Patches. Patches even said he would buy a car if they could find one. Moses came and offered his car but Shannon refused his offer. Hanna came and stayed, giving all the sympathy she could.

"You coulda won," said Augie, more distressed than Shannon.

Shannon smiled, "Hey, those things happen like Charlie said. As long as we're here, we should have fun and help you win, Dude."

I wiped my eyes, pretending something had gotten in them. Well, that's one more thing the kid has handled well.

The four boys were trying to build each other's spirits up as was Grant. I was running out of ideas when BRM's mechanic drove up in the fancy golf cart vehicle, carrying TJ Benson as a passenger.

TJ pushed away from the cart and stood on his good leg. He reached across the cart, taking two crutches and placing one under each arm, then motioned his mechanic away. Slowly, he leaned forward placing his crutches ahead of him. He would let his legs swing forward and slightly ahead of the crutches, then he would repeat the slow arduous task, again and again, until he reached the small group watching his movements.

From habit, Tex yelled, "Squirt!" Then Tex repeated the familiar crashing sounds and brakes.

I twisted my head toward Tex so we were beak to nose, "Shut up." Tex opened his beak and spread his wings ready to fight.

Unexpectedly, TJ laughed, "Man, I've missed that bird." Then the smile disappeared. "I can't change what I did, but I want to try to be a better person. In the hospital, I realized I'm an arrogant asshole."

I nodded, "Boy, howdy, ya hit the nail on the head."

"I have a lot to learn. I also think Shannon is probably the best driver here, and I was just jealous of the attention Charlie gave you in the beginning of the year."

"You're the best. I've watched you race," Shannon said sincerely.

"I can't win without Charlie," said TJ.

"Don't underestimate yourself. You're a durn good driver." I added, "I might fix a car for a race but the drivers got to win it. You won races with your ability."

"Thanks, Charlie," said TJ, rather subdued, his voice cracking slightly. "I also realize I'm jealous of Shannon for another reason. He has something I'd die for. Grant takes great pride in him . . . I'd give anything if my father would watch me. If he would just say I did well. I'd give up all my victories if he would watch my races, like Grant watches Shannon."

Suddenly TJ started to cry. Both Shannon and Hanna moved to each side of TJ, putting arms around him. I also stepped forward to help.

TJ wiped his eyes, "Whew! What a pussy I am."

"Bull crap. You just had a reality check. I'm proud of you," I said. "How about we get you a drink, and you take a load off your foot."

TJ laughed, "Thanks, but first I have to tell you why I came here." Everyone became quiet when TJ paused. "If you don't have a car, I want Shannon to use my Van Diemen for tomorrow's qualifying."

"What?" chimed Shannon, Augie, and me simultaneously, while the others stood in shocked amazement.

TJ laughed, "There's more. If Shannon can beat Poirier, Dotson, and Mercury, I will win the championship."

Everyone was quiet.

TJ continued, "If he beats them he can have the $15,000 money I would win." TJ smiled, "But if Shannon breaks the car he has to fix it."

"Sure," said Shannon. "You don't know how much this means."

"Yes, I do," said TJ.

"I can't believe you're doing this," I said, shocked at the wonderful change in TJ's attitude.

Shrugging his shoulders, TJ added, "It's kinda selfish. My dad promised to move me to the next series if I won the championship. Shannon can win that championship for me." TJ looked to me, "I have a lot to learn, and I'm sure you and Shannon will find a sponsor and move to Formula Atlantics. I'd like to be on your team."

I took a deep breath, "This isn't BRM. This is Pepper's Haul Ass Racing and it will be run out of Atlanta."

"I understand," said TJ. "You better hurry to my trailer because I told my mechanic to take the Van Diemen out of the trailer and that you would come get it."

I snapped my fingers, "Marty, get the tow rope, Les pull out the four wheelers." I looked at TJ, "Why don't you go in the motorhome and relax."

TJ accepted the kind hospitality and was escorted by Hanna, Shannon, and Augie to the motorhome, while Les, Marty, and I hurried to the BRM trailer to retrieve our new treasure.

While Les and I worked on the Van Diemen, Shannon and his father cooked a meal none would ever forget. TJ remained for the dinner. Later in the evening Moses, Dotson, Mercury, O'Brien, Patches, Turtle, Smurf, and Guido came to join the party bringing other food, deserts, and drinks.

Les and I checked the electrical system, charged the battery, changed all the lubricants, replaced the filters, and changed all four gears in the transaxle. Then we checked the suspension and adjusted it accordingly for Shannon. I checked the bump steer and balanced the corner weights. I checked the total weight to make sure it would not come in over the maximum 1175 pounds. Les and Marty took time to eat and relax for an hour, then continued their work.

I dismantled the rear of the transaxle to change gears. Then checked the gears TJ supplied with the Van Diemen. I was careful to check the gears for wear and breakage, and he checked each of the four gears for the proper ratio; 1st-19:33, 2nd-21:33, 3rd-23:28, and 4th-23:24. With all the proper gears intact, I promptly started to replace them.

Just before midnight, we finished. I was satisfied the car was ready for the morning's qualification. The car was not the red, yellow, and blue familiar to all but the red nose, white midsection, and blue tail were close.

I smiled. The "jinxed" Van Diemen, as TJ called the new racer, was finally getting a chance to shine. The engine I had built would now be tested. Finished with my work I left Marty and Les alone. Both with mischievous smiles, but I was too tired to care. I drove home to Gainesville and waited for morning.

* * *

Saturday morning was cool, dry, and clear. A perfect day for racing I thought as I drove along Highway 53 toward Road Atlanta.

When I arrived, the smell of buttermilk biscuits and coffee hit me. I stuck my finger near the dashboard and Tex jumped on. Outside the car I saw the covered racer and felt good. I placed Tex on my shoulder, checked the top pocket for sunflower seeds and my hip pocket for the lemon drops. Everything was in order.

Shannon stepped from the trailer, "Thanks, Charlie. The car looks great."

"Yeah, sure," I said, rather confused. Looks great, I wondered. I walked over and removed the cover from the Van Diemen.

The mid-section was yellow. Not a perfect job, but it appeared someone had taken time to paint it and change the number from 1 to the familiar 44. Les and Marty, I thought.

"Where's Les and Marty?" I asked, as I seated myself in the motorhome ready for the coffee and biscuits.

"They went to mount new tires for me and Augie," said Shannon. He filled my cup and placed the biscuits on the table. "They said the cars are fueled and ready. The tires had fifteen pounds of air."

"Bless their hearts," I said, sipping the coffee.

Shannon seemed to fumble around, "Look, I'm going to thank TJ for what he did. I'll be back in a while."

"Sure," I said. Later I found out what he went to do at the BRM trailer.
* * *

Inside the air-conditioned room, at the front of the BRM trailer, Shannon found TJ to talk to him. They were alone in the trailer.

"You what?" asked TJ.

"I know it's crazy, but I was wondering if you would advance me $10,000 of the prize money?"

"What for?"

"It's a secret."

"What if you don't win?"

"You can have my Van Diemen. What I want to do with the money is more important than the race."

"Can you win?"

The confident smile said it all. "Yes I can win."

TJ pulled his checkbook out, "Being nice sure is crazy." He gave the check to Shannon, "Don't tell anybody I did this . . . and if you lose the race--I will take the Swift."

Shannon looked at the check, "Understood. Thanks TJ."

Shannon ran from the trailer and back to his pit area to prepare for the qualification.
* * *

Everyone on the grid was congratulating Shannon on getting a car for the last qualification and the race. All except Poirier who as the lead car for the session appeared to be pouting like a little kid.

Next in line to Poirier were Chappel, Dotson, Mercury, Leclair, Reckert, Hanna, Augie, and Shannon followed by Cruz, Pollard, and the others. This day there was no hacky sack. Shannon talked secretly with Hanna, while Augie seemed pleased and no longer nervous to be with Cindy. Cindy kept one ear on the headphones waiting for the signal for the start to the race.

Suddenly Cindy sounded the five-minute warning sending all racers to their cars. The one-minute warning sounded. Grant and Shannon gave their handshake to each other.

The drivers were ready. They proceeded in single file onto the track and up into the right-hander of Turn 1, for the second and last thirty minute qualifying session before the Sunday race.

On the first lap, Shannon did as I ordered, warming the tires and feeling the racer. Cruz and Pollard passed Shannon. Shannon held back and checked temperatures and oil pressure for another lap.

Happy with the feedback, I said over the radio, "Go for it, Shannon."

Shannon responded and in one lap was only a second off his previous day's record time. First, he passed Cruz and Pollard, then Leclair and Reckert who had been previously passed by Hanna and Augie.

The second lap under full speed, Shannon was within a few tics of his previous days' time in the new untested Van Diemen.

On the fifth lap, third under full speed, Shannon beat his previous days' time. He passed Chappel, Hanna, and Augie. Shannon was cutting a tenth of a second off each lap. Only three drivers were ahead of Shannon: Mercury, Dotson, and Poirier. The qualifying was like Sebring all over again--only it was dry! The only ones ahead were those drivers Shannon had to beat in order to get the $15,000 from TJ. Shannon was closing in! Shannon was in the Zone!

The spectators in the bleachers were on their feet at, Turn 11 and Turn 1 each time Shannon passed. His previous days' time of 1:21.73 was below the current track record. Shannon's times were in the low 1:21's. Only three other drivers were in the 1:21 range: Poirier, Dotson, and Mercury.

I looked at the stopwatch. Shannon had dropped below 1:21 with a high 1:20. On the next lap, with a time of 1:21.2, he passed Mercury and Dotson.

The next lap was again below 1:21. The next three laps were within two tenths of a second of each other, in the high 1:20's and low 1:21's. The track announcer called out the times to a thunderous cheering response from the racing fans.

Unlike Sebring, Shannon caught Poirier and jockeyed for position for one lap before passing him to the immense pleasure of the spectators. The checkered flag came out bringing the session to an end.

Every driver went to Impound to weigh in, where the Tech Inspectors checked tires to assure the correct "Spec" racing compound was being used. They measured front and rear wings for proper length and height, making sure they conformed to the rules. Satisfied all entrants were within the rules, the drivers and their cars were released from Impound and allowed to return to their paddock area.

As I walked to the trailer, I was extremely content with the Van Diemen and the motor I had built but had never been run. To think TJ thought the car was jinxed.

Thirty minutes later, Marty came running to the PHAR racing trailer with a copy of the final grid:

```
                        SCCA/USAC
            U.S. Formula Ford 2000 National Championship
                       Official Grid
                       September 11
                       Road Atlanta
                      Atlanta, Georgia
                       (2.52 miles)


       Car      Name              Model              Time        Time
       No.                                           1st         2nd

  1.   (44)   Shannon Kelly     Swift SE-3         1:21.73*    1:20.90*
  2.   (5)    Ian Poirier       Swift DB-8         1:22.05     1:21.65*
  3.   (8)    Freddy Mercury    Reynard 95F        1:22.46     1:21.71*
  4.   (33)   Bob Dotson        Spirit             1:22.35     1:21.75*
  5.   (22)   Augie Zuehl       VanDiemen RF95     1:22.76     1:22.13
  6.   (16)   Hanna Lee         Swift DB-8         1:22.89     1:22.21
  7.   (7)    Ron Leclair       VanDiemen RF95     1:23.25     1:22.54
  8.   (27)   Roberto Cruz      VanDiemen RF95     1:22.98     1:22.60
  9.   (11)   Alan Reckert      Stohr              1:23 40     1:22.65
 10.   (71)   Gordon Chappel    VanDiemen RF95     1:23.44     1:22.75
 11.   (69)   Phil Spratt       Reynard 95F        1:23.50     1:22.78
 12.   (47)   Darrell Pollard   VanDiemen RF95     1:23.25     1:22.94
 13     (50)   Don Reese         VanDiemen RF95     1:23.70     1:22.99
 14.   (43)   Jude Dionne       Swift DB-8         1:24.43     1:23.00
 15     (99)   Peter Hurst       Swift DB-8         1:23.75     1:23.10
 16.   (54)   Guido Pepin       Swift DB-8         1:25.83     1:23.40
 17.   (40)   Ernie Goolsby     Swift DB-8         1:24.75     1:23.42
 18.   (21)   Rick Henry        Swift DB-8         1:23.92     1:23.53
 19.   (30)   Bill Murfy        Swift DB-8         1:24.45     1:23.68
 20.   (27)   Ben Cifelli       Swift DB-3         1:24.45     1:23.76
 21.   (55)   Cliff Roe         VanDiemen RF94     1:25.51     1:23.87
 22.   (00)   Tom Craig         Swift DB-3         1:24.50     1:23.93
 23.   (13)   Steve Smagala     VanDiemen RF89     1:26.50     1:24.80
 24.   (25)   Chase Wilder      Reynard SF90       1:26.45     1:25.47
 25.   (3)    Will Jones        Swift DB-8         1:26.45     1:25.53

       *Below current track record
```

Shannon had broken the track record! So had three others--the three he had to beat to collect from TJ. But Shannon had not only broken the track record, he shattered it. Nearly three-quarters of a second in front of Poirier, who held the second position on the grid.

Sunday would be Shannon's day, his race.

Everyone seemed excited but Shannon, who hurriedly gathered up Hanna. He said they had plans for the day and would be back in time for the party at Dotson's trailer. Just as quickly as he announced his plans, the two were gone. And just as well.

Trouble was coming in the form of a Steward. I had seen it before and I would see it again. Another protest against Shannon.

Even Tex knew as he spread his wings, squawked, and screamed, "Butt breath." And Tex sounded just like me which got a quick glance from the Steward as I shook my head and pointed at Tex.

The Steward stopped in front of Grant, "Is Shannon Kelly here?"

"No," said Grant.

"Problem?" I asked.

Augie, Les, and Marty gathered near, all three of them knowing that Stewards seldom came for social calls. Only trouble beckoned a Steward to a driver's Paddock area.

"Poirier protested Shannon's qualification," the Steward told Grant. "You need to talk to the Chief Steward Andy Cobb."

"What did Shannon do?" asked Grant.

The Steward shook his head, "He didn't." The Steward pointed at the shiny, yellow, red, and blue Van Diemen with the double four's on each side of the tail wing and the nose. "Poirier is protesting the car."

Grant's shoulders drooped. My heart skipped a beat and the Steward walked away.

"Boy, howdy! We get TJ's head straight, and now we got to deal with that cocksucking French Dwarf!"

"Squirt!" screamed Tex feeling my agitation. Tex followed it with the familiar screaming breaks and crash.

Not long after the Steward departed, Grant and I arrived at the tall Timing and Scoring Tower and were soon standing before Andy Cobb.

Andy looked up when we walked in, and he held up his hand, "Don't say anything. I know how you feel. This protest sucks. Just between you and me, I'm gonna do everything to throw it out. But I have to listen to his protest because it was filed properly and has merit."

"What's it for?" I asked.

"Something about racing the car you qualified in."

"But Shannon qualified the Van Diemen."

"I know. But he qualified the Swift first. It's Poirier's challenge that Shannon must run the Swift."

"When will you reach a decision?" Grant asked.

"Later today. I'll let you know as soon as I find out," Cobb assured them. "Look, I admire Shannon for what he has done and how far he has come. I want to see him race, and personally, I don't think the protest holds any water. The wording of the rules are a little confusing, and I have to check it out first."

"What rule?" I snapped.

Cobb tried to explain the protest. "The rule states your position is determined by your qualifying time. If another car is used, you start in the last position. Poirier contends Shannon qualified the Swift, so he must start last in the Van Diemen."

"He qualified both!" snapped Grant.

"I know. I know," said Cobb. "That's the technicality, and that's why I think Poirier will lose the protest. All I'm waiting for is a clarification from headquarters in Colorado."

"This is a crock Cobb," I frowned.

"I'm trying." Cobb rubbed his chin and added, "Even if Poirier wins his protest, Shannon will still start the race. Even if it's at the back of the field."

"The back of the bus is the kiss of death," I snarled.

"At least, he'll start. That gives him a chance to win," said Cobb.

"Boy, howdy, some chance."

Cobb smiled, "I saw him at Road America, and believe me if anybody has a chance from the back, it will be Shannon."

"Damn," groaned Grant.

Tex squawked.

Cobb held both hands in the air with his palms toward the two angry men who were getting angrier by the second, "It's the best I can do if Poirier wins the protest."

Silently, Grant and I walked from the Stewards' room, in the Timing and Scoring Tower, and back up the hill to the railroad tie steps leading to the concession stand.

Grant snapped, "Damn it! Shannon's come too far for this. I'm gonna find Poirier and kick his butt. If Shannon can't drive, neither will Poirier."

I jumped in front of Grant and held him back with both hands. "Whoa, Grant! It's important for Shannon that you maintain control. Doing something to Poirier would only hurt Shannon. I know. I've seen crew and drivers do what you want to do. Hell, I want to kick the little dwarf's ass too." For a moment I thought about the wrench I was about to throw at Marcoux during the last race.

My words seemed to register on Grant and calm him down, "All right. I didn't think about it hurting Shannon. It's just that something always seems to pop up."

"Boy, howdy, I know." I chuckled, "Let Shannon kick his ass on the track tomorrow."

Grant laughed, then drew in a deep breath, "Look, I'm gonna walk around for a while and blow off some steam."

I nodded and shook a finger at Grant, "Now, no Poirier--promise?"

His smile reassured me, "Okay, no Poirier."

I watched Grant disappear over the wooden steps leading to the concession area.

With my hands in my pockets, I stood at the base of the hill. To my left I saw the little park-like area with tables and an octagon gazebo, all to the memory of Jim Fitzgerald. I walked across the steps and through the gate and into the picnic area.

Part of the hill had been cut away and railroad ties placed in the bank to form a 5 foot wall, 30 feet in length, with flowers growing from the top. Centered the length of the wall and five feet away was a granite column two foot square and five feet high with a bronze bust, with Jim Fitzgerald's likeness, topping the granite.

I stood before the bronze monument and reflected on the past. Tex pulled on my ear and I took out a sunflower seed, then the bag of familiar lemon drops, this time popping four of them in my mouth. Then I said.

"Hey, Jim, you'd be surprised at Newman's Indy team." I paused, "No, you probably wouldn't. These kids coming up are sure fast. Hell, even the slow ones are fast." I laughed. "I've got a couple of real fast "Young Guns" that would amaze you." I nodded my head, "Watch over 'em in the race, will ya?"

Slowly, I backed away, nodded in the memorial's direction, and walked quietly to the PHAR paddock area.

* * *

With a little more than an hour before sunset, there was no sign of Shannon or Hanna and no answer from Cobb. Augie, Les, and Marty went on to Dotson's trailer, and a little while later, Grant and I, with Tex, followed.

Grant and I intended to keep the protest quiet, but when we arrived at Dotson's party, we found word of the protest had already spread like a fire in the Santa Anna winds. Everyone knew and all gave condolences.

The more people offered solace, the angrier Grant became. Finally, calling aloud for everyone to listen.

Grant tried to smile but couldn't, "I appreciate the way all of you feel, but Shannon doesn't know about the protest. I'd like to keep it that way until a decision is reached by the Stewards. No reason to concern him until we know."

While most remained silent, some nodded their heads in agreement. The party continued. Atlanta's cool September weather provided the perfect opportunity to use Dotson's hot tub. The pleasing Jacuzzi spray churned the hot water and steam rose in the cool air.

Later, Shannon arrived with Hanna. They were both beaming from the day's qualifying session and the anticipation of the coming race. The two walked from group to group talking about the seasons last race. Grant followed like a concerned mother hen making sure nothing happened to her chick.

Not long after Shannon arrived, Andy Cobb was spotted walking from the Timing and Scoring Tower. In the darkness, we could not see his face, until he was upon us. Cobb's face told us everything. Cobb was smiling.

Cobb went directly to Grant, who stood next to Shannon. Augie, Les, Marty, and I moved toward Cobb.

"Good news," said Cobb. "The rules state you have to drive the car you qualified. It says nothing about qualifying only one like Poirier suggested. And obviously, you intend to drive the Van Diemen. You'll be glad to know, we kept his protest fee, since we felt his protest was vexatious with the intent to eliminate his competition."

"The Steward deserves a drink," yelled Mercury.

Dotson countered, "Come this way, Mr. Cobb."

"I'd think you'd be glad to be rid of Shannon," said Cobb.

"Contrary," said Mercury. "Shannon gives us something to work for. If we can't beat him on the track, then he deserves to win."

"Plus, he can beat Poirier," said Dotson with a chuckle. "I don't mind losing to Shannon, but it down right irritates me to have Poirier beat me."

Mercury and Dotson led Cobb to the food and drinks.

Shannon spun about to Grant, "Why didn't you tell me?"

"I didn't want you to be bothered. You were gone when it happened, and there was no sense in worrying you over it," said Grant.

A few more steps put Shannon beside his father. He put his arm around Grant's shoulder, "Thanks, Dad, but I'm a big boy. From now on, you can tell me."

Grant acknowledged his son, "Yeah, but you'll always be my boy and I'm sure proud of you."

Together, they walked over and got a drink. A few minutes later, Shannon and Hanna changed and went to the hot tub where Augie and Cindy waited.

Relaxed from the soothing waters of Dotson's hot tub, all four dressed and went on to the infield of Road Atlanta and the hill sloping down and toward the main straight between Turn 1 and the bridge at Turn 11. Splotches of red Georgia clay shown through the green grass. The cool nights forced them all to wear sweaters or wind breakers. Many campers made fires that dotted and lit the hillside. Cindy took Shannon, Hanna, and Augie to the Corner Worker's party at the top of the hill. Everyone celebrated, bringing the final race of the U.S. Formula Ford 2000 National Championship series to an end.

Some took turns going up in two hot air balloons, one rainbow colored, the other one was solid yellow with the large black letters, NTW, advertising a chain of tire stores. First, Augie went up with Cindy, where he surprised her with a kiss. A few minutes later, Shannon and Hanna repeated the trip. Only this time, Hanna gave Shannon a long, good luck kiss which he promptly reciprocated.

Late in the evening and completely exhausted, Hanna returned to her hotel dropping Cindy with the corner workers where she was staying. Shannon took Augie with him to his apartment and made a make shift bed on the couch in the living room for his friend to sleep on.

The only thing remaining was the race.

* * *

Sunday morning quiet time had arrived at Road Atlanta. Drivers and spectators all waited for noon and the first race.

With work completed on the Van Diemen the day before, our PHAR Motorsports team arrived near noon. Everything was checked one more time. At ten minutes till one, the brightly colored number 44 Van Diemen was rolled to the false grid for the race.

Located within the fenced false grid area was one huge oak, providing shelter for the workers. A wooden bench surrounded the tree and to one side of it was a portable blue toilet. On the bench was a cooler with water and a box of paper cups for workers and drivers. A few drivers sat beneath the stretching shade of the single large oak. One of the drivers was Pepin who could move up in the standings if he could beat Dionne, whose season had faltered drastically since mid-season and allowed Guido to catch up to him in the points.

Beating Cruz and Pollard would move Hanna and Augie into the top ten of the final standings.

The big move was Shannon. He could not win the championship, but he could be a spoiler. If he could beat Mercury, Dotson, and Poirier, he would move from 5th to 2nd in the final standings. Second in the standing was worth $7500 and third was worth $3000. The overall championship paid through the first ten positions.

Even without a win for Shannon, he, Hanna, and Augie, had made a spectacular comeback the last half of the season and raced like seasoned veterans.

Hanna seized the opportunity to talk to Shannon since he was not playing his normal pre-race session of hacky sack with Augie. Augie was near the front of the grid talking to Cindy. Cindy and Augie had been seeing a lot of each other since the Charlotte race.

Near the front of the grid, Poirier paced nervously, pounding his fist together and talking to himself.

To the side of Shannon's car, like the other drivers, was the ever present hand cart with tools, radios, and other items should Shannon need to come into the pits.

A whistle blew, alerting the drivers to the five-minute warning. The drivers went to their respective racers. Augie and Hanna wished Shannon luck. Shannon shook hands with Mercury and Dotson, moved directly to where Poirier was already fastened in, and extended his hand.

"Good luck," said Shannon.

Poirier was in utter shock but extended a limp hand and let Shannon shake it.

I helped Shannon in the car, and Grant plugged in the starter battery behind the engine. Similarly, Les and Marty did the same with Augie.

Shannon was fastening in when Cindy alerted the drivers with the three-minute warning. He started the Van Diemen. I turned the key behind Shannon's right shoulder, directing the power from the starter to the car's battery. Grant unplugged the starter battery from the engine. I checked the arm restraints, plugged in the radio, and pulled tight on the harness, while Shannon attached the neck brace.

With the one-minute whistle, Grant went through the handshake gyrations with Shannon. I stepped behind Grant and did the same handshake ritual with Shannon.

Grant and I backed away from the Van Diemen, as did all the mechanics and help from the other race cars.

The engines reached a deafening crescendo and the drivers raised their hands. All except Shannon who suddenly waved frantically!

Cindy pointed at Shannon but he continued to wave frantically.

Only I had the presence of mind to use the radio, "What's wrong Shannon?"

Suddenly, Shannon remembered the radio, "The throttle! The pedal feels like mush! I can't give it any gas!"

Duties as the Grid Marshall called, so Cindy could wait no longer. She signaled Poirier onto the track for the twenty lap race. Poirier pulled around Shannon waving his fist in the air victoriously.

Cindy waved Poirier to her left, giving Poirier the inside right pole. Mercury moved to her right. In perfect order, they alternated left then right.

Poirier led the group into Turn 1 behind the new Chevrolet Camaro pace car.

Without hesitating for a moment, I reached for the tool box, took out a screw driver and popped the fasteners covering the engine. Already alerted to the problem, Les and Marty ran in Shannon's direction to help if necessary. They reached the Van Diemen before the final car was on the track.

TJ's words suddenly haunted me, "The Van Diemen was jinxed." When the last fastener was undone, I pulled the cover away and handed it to Les. I was dumbfounded when I saw the problem. The throttle plate had come loose on the linkage. The same plate broken before the season's first race at Watkins Glen. It could be fixed but it would take fifteen minutes to take it apart, tap the holes, and put it back together.

"It's the linkage," I yelled, at the same time looking around for a quick fix, knowing the pace car would be back around in less than four minutes.

With radio crackling, Cindy stood in front of Shannon's Van Diemen speaking to the race Steward.

Then an idea struck me, "Les, give me a handful of Phillips screwdrivers, large channel locks, and a heavy steel cutter."

I took the screwdrivers and tried them until I found one to slide snugly through the hole where the missing bolt fit. I watched Cindy who was in contact with the tower, as I took the channel locks and bent the screwdriver in a "U" shape.

"Where are they?"

"They're at Turn 5," Cindy warned.

I knew they would be starting down the back stretch to the bridge, then Turn 12, and the green flag. I only had two minutes at the most. We couldn't hope for a wave off. The car had to be ready when they came past.

If only it worked. "Cutters!" I demanded, sticking my hand in Les' direction and not looking back.

I looked like a doctor operating on a patient. Only this patient was going to run and run fast when I finished.

Usually calm, Shannon's emotions ran rampant, when he screamed. "I'm gonna be a lap down!"

"Medium and small Vice-Grips!" I demanded. Suddenly my voice became calm and reassuring when I spoke to Shannon over the radio, "You will not be a lap down. You will be at the back of the pack. You're the fastest and the best I've ever seen. If anyone can win from the back--you can!"

"You don't understand," Shannon almost cried. "This race is for my Dad."

Les handed me the Vice-Grips. Suddenly, Shannon's words were lost under the pressure of the moment. I had trouble getting the medium size Vice-Grips in position to hold the plate. Finally, I found a place and squeezed, but it was not tight enough. I popped it loose, turned the bolt at the end of the Vice-Grips a couple of revolutions, and squeezed again. Too tight. I couldn't close it.

I looked at Cindy but she read my mind, "They're at the bridge."

"By God this better do it," I muttered.

With no more time for adjustments, I squeezed with all my strength and was rewarded for my efforts, when the Vice-Grips snapped closed. Quickly, I took the bent screwdriver piece and squeezed it in place with the small Vice-Grips.

As I pulled away, I could hear the roar of engines screaming closer. The green flag was out!

I didn't have to reach for the engine cover when I pulled away. Les was waiting and ready, literally throwing the blue engine cover in position, at the same time, handing me a regular screwdriver.

Poirier moved into Turn 1 with the lead. Neither Les nor I said anything, both knowing our jobs; the problem, the quickness of the moment! Half the field was through Turn 1 when we finished. We both stepped back waving our arms, and instantly Cindy waved Shannon onto the track.

Shannon smoked the tires, raced down the pit lane, and entered the track at the back of the pack, only a few car lengths behind Turtle and Wilder. As Shannon disappeared into Turn 2, it looked like he was already ahead of Turtle.

Les, Marty, Grant, and I raced to our positions in the fast pits where we found TJ on his crutches waiting.

"What happened?" asked TJ.

"My fault," I said.

TJ shook his head, "I knew the car was jinxed. I shouldn't have given Shannon ten thousand dollars. He can't win now."

I smiled, "Don't bet on it."

"Money for what?" Grant asked.

"Ten thousand dollars but he didn't say what it was for. He even gave me the Swift as collateral if he didn't win," said TJ. "It doesn't matter, I don't want his car but the money seemed important to him. This was a bad break for him."

Poirier came under the bridge and down the hill only a few car lengths ahead of Mercury, Dotson, Augie, and Hanna. The first five had pulled slightly away from the next group.

I started counting the cars as they came out from the bridge . . . five, six . . . Guido was 15th, then Goolsby. Rick Henry slid out from under the bridge next. Suddenly a red, yellow, and blue Van Diemen slid out and under Henry taking him before Turn 12.

"Oh, my God! It's Shannon!" yelled TJ.

Down the main straight, Shannon passed Goolsby, took Guido going up Turn 1, and disappeared into Turn 2.

"Boy, howdy!"

The announcer said, "Number 44, Shannon Kelly just ran the fastest lap at a 1:23 in traffic. Watch for him to be moving up."

On the next lap, Shannon was in 12th. On lap three, he was in 10th and moving up fast.

The top five had a two second lead over Cruz who had moved into 6th, stalked by Chappel and Spratt who had moved to 8th from 11th.

The announcer said, "The leader Poirier just ran a 1:21.9. The only driver under 1:22. Wait . . . Car 44, yes, Shannon Kelly has just run a . . . a 1:20.9! Folks, this is unbelievable, he's a second faster than our leader Poirier!"

Two laps later, Shannon moved up two places passing Chappel. Now, Cruz was three seconds ahead and Spratt two seconds ahead of Cruz. Two laps later, Shannon took Cruz and on the next lap he caught and passed Spratt for 6th position.

Twelve laps remained. The next four were six seconds in front of Shannon, and Poirier had five seconds over them. On lap ten, Augie worked past Dotson and Hanna followed, putting Augie in 2nd and Hanna in 3rd

As the leaders came past the Timing and Scoring Tower, the announcer noted, "We have three more drivers under 1:22, number 33, Bob Dotson; number 22, Augie Zuehl in second; and Hanna Lee in sweet sixteen. Listen to this fans, our leader Poirier has run under 1:22 the last six laps and car 44, Shannon Kelly, has been under 1:21 the last seven laps."

On lap thirteen, Shannon caught Mercury and passed him down the back straight. He caught Dotson under the bridge and passed him at Turn 1. He took Hanna to the inside left of Turn 5, closed on Augie's tail at Turn 6, lay back at Turn 7, and out accelerated Augie through the turn, making a clear pass. Augie and Shannon waved to each other, and Augie pointed ahead trying to tell Shannon to get Poirier. Shannon took second; only Poirier remained.

"Wow! Can you believe it! Shannon's in second!" screamed TJ over the thundering racecars as Shannon passed.

"I told you," I said calmly, containing my excitement inside.

Shannon completed lap fourteen, only six seconds behind Poirier. Like Sebring, the crowds were aware Shannon was catching Poirier and the chant began when Poirier came out from under the bridge. "One, two, three, four, five--" Shannon slid from beneath the bridge. The crowd roared its approval.

The next time around, TJ joined in the chant, "One, two, three, four--" Shannon slid under the bridge and down the hill, still maintaining his speed and momentum. Shannon was catching Poirier but Poirier refused to roll over and play dead as he also ran the race of his life, determined to deny Shannon of a victory

On lap seventeen, I noticed Poirier came out from under the bridge in third gear and would slide wide when coming down on the power. Shannon used fourth gear and was smooth and fast. I clicked the radio and told Shannon what I had seen.

The countdown continued. Poirier slid out from beneath the bridge almost sliding off the track and less than a second behind was Shannon. Poirier led Shannon across start/finish completing lap nineteen.

"Last lap," I said over the two-way radio.

Down the main straight, Shannon clicked the radio, "I saw it, Charlie, you're right. I have him."

Going up Turn 1, Shannon was less than a half second behind.

At Turn 5, Shannon came over the radio rather surprisingly calm, "He blocked me."

Shannon dropped back but caught Poirier coming out of Turn 7. Shannon moved right to pass. Poirier moved right. Shannon moved left, Poirier moved left.

"Poirier's blocking," yelled Shannon over the radio.

"Listen, Shannon," I interrupted. "Stay left but after the dip move right and stay. Force Poirier to the right. If he does, he'll go off the track when he goes under the bridge. Can you make it?"

"Yes."

Shannon moved left, then right, and Poirier continued to block. In the dip, Shannon stayed left. So did Poirier.

Coming out of the dip and heading up toward the bridge, Shannon jerked radically to the right. Again, so did Poirier to block which forced him off and away from the proper and fastest line through Turn 11.

Poirier downshifted to third and slid under the bridge as did Shannon. Third gears torque and the sharper off line turn broke Poirier's rear tires loose, forcing him to lift ever so slightly on the throttle. Still, his tires squealed down the hill and finally his two left tires dropped off the asphalt and into the red Georgia clay, filling the air with a cloud of red Georgia dust. In a micro second, the tires were back on the track, and Poirier was down hard on the throttle, charging Turn 12. Shannon stayed in fourth. His tires gripped and he slid out almost as far as Poirier but Shannon did not lift and when Poirier pulled off the throttle, Shannon moved his steering wheel slightly and moved slightly past Poirier. Poirier closed in on Shannon at the bottom of the hill but Shannon pulled away through Turn 12 and took the checkered flag to the cheers of the spectators and TJ Benson.

On the cool-off lap Shannon waved to the corner workers. When he came into the fast pits, we all mobbed him. TJ remained against the fence, unable to move across the fast pits on his crutches.

After the brief celebration Shannon along with Poirier and Augie went to the Winner's Circle for pictures and an interview, while Hanna, Dotson, and Mercury went straight to Impound.

Once again Jolit Torres was present for the awards and ready for the first interview. Again, Shannon thanked his father for all he had done, saying one day he hoped to pay his Dad back. And he thanked me--and TJ for the car.

Fifteen minutes later, Shannon, Augie, and Poirier arrived in Impound. The celebration continued when Hanna mobbed Shannon. Grant hugged his son, then quickly asked about the money he borrowed from TJ.

TJ, Les, Marty, and I stood nearby just as curious as Grant, wondering why he took the money.

Shannon smiled and pointed to Hanna, "She was in on it, too."

Hanna clapped her hands together, "You really will love it. Shannon was so sweet."

"What?" asked Grant.

Shannon reached in his pocket and pulled out a set of keys, "I put the money down for the house on Chestnut Mountain."

"But they sold it," said Grant.

"The people weren't approved, and it went back on the market last week. When I saw it, I had to get the money." Shannon walked over to Grant and handed him the keys. "For the best dad a guy could have."

Grant looked around and tried to talk but couldn't, "Uh, . . . I . . . " A tear rolled down Grant's cheek and his eyes reddened.

I wiped my eyes and mumbled, "Boy, howdy . . . whew."

Grant looked down, wiped his eyes and mumbled, "I don't know what to say Shannon."

"Hey, Dad, I kept a set of keys for me."

"Sure, but what about racing? What about next year?"

Shannon took another swig of Gatorade, "You've done too much. I need to find a sponsor on my own. I don't want to use your money anymore."

"Well, can I help you look for a sponsor?" Grant almost begged.

"Of course."

It was a happy group that left Impound . . . all except for Poirier. We took time to watch the Trans-Am race. When it was over, we walked back to the paddock area and started loading the trailer.

An hour later while loading the trailer, Marty brought back the official results and the final points standing. Although we knew the top five in the overall points, we studied the sheets enthusiastically:

FORMULA 2000, the Dream

```
              SCCA/USAC
     U.S. Formula Ford 2000 National Championship
              Official Race Results
                September 11
                 Road Atlanta
               Atlanta, Georgia
                (2.52 miles)
```

	Car No.	Name	Model	Time	Laps
1.	(44)	Shannon Kelly	VanDiemen RF95	1:20.47**	20
2.	(5)	Ian Poirier	Swift DB-8	1:21.51*	20
3.	(22)	Augie Zuehl	VanDiemen RF95	1:21.61*	20
4.	(16)	Hanna Lee	Swift DB-8	1:21.73*	20
5.	(33)	Bob Dotson	Spirit	1:21.78*	20
6.	(8)	Freddy Mercury	Reynard 95F	1:22.03	20
7.	(69)	Phil Spratt	Reynard 95F	1:22.14	20
8.	(27)	Roberto Cruz	VanDiemen RF95	1:22.37	20
9.	(71)	Gordon Chappel	VanDiemen RF95	1:22.55	20
10.	(7)	Ron Leclair	VanDiemen RF95	1:22.25	20
11.	(11)	Alan Reckert	Stohr	1:22.54	20
12.	(47)	Darrell Pollard	VanDiemen RF95	1:22.62	20
13.	(21)	Rick Henry	Swift DB-8	1:22.22	20
14.	(54)	Guido Pepin	Swift DB-8	1:22.75	20
15.	(43)	Jude Dionne	Swift DB-8	1:22.84	20
16.	(99)	Peter Hurst	Swift DB-8	1:23.00	20
17.	(30)	Bill Murfy	Swift DB-8	1:23.88	20
18.	(3)	Will Jones	Swift DB-8	1:23.45	20
19.	(00)	Tom Craig	Swift DB-3	1:24.22	20
20.	(40)	Ernie Goolsby	Swift DB-8	1:22.44	10
21.	(50)	Don Reese	VanDiemen RF95	1:23.13	19
22.	(25)	Chase Wilder	Reynard SF90	1:22.46	19
23.	(13)	Steve Smagala	VanDiemen RF89	1:24.45	19
24.	(55)	Cliff Roe	VanDiemen RF94	1:23.15	19
25.	(27)	Ben Cifelli	Swift DB-3	1:24.54	19

FASTEST LAP

Car	Time	Speed
44	1:20.47**	110.37 mph

**New Track Record
* Below Previous Track Record

```
                        SCCA/USAC
          U.S. Formula Ford 2000 National Championship
                    Official Points Standing
                      (After 10 of 10 events)

      Car      Name              Model           Team            Points
      No.

 1.   (1)      TJ Benson         VanDiemen RF95  BRM              183
 2.   (44)     Shannon Kelly     Swift SE-3      PHAR Racing      180
 3.   (5)      Ian Poirier       Swift DB-8      PACE             180
 4.   (33)     Bob Dotson        Spirit          Dotson Racing    175
 5.   (8)      Freddy Mercury    Reynard 95F     Dotson Racing    170
 6.   (71)     Gordon Chappel    VanDiemen RF95  MOSES            149
 7.   (7)      Ron Leclair       VanDiemen RF95  TART             132
 8.   (22)     Augie Zuehl       VanDiemen RF95  BRM              122
 9.   (69)     Phil Spratt       Reynard 95F     Spratt Racing    121
10.   (16)     Hanna Lee         Swift DB-8      Dotson Racing    118
11.   (11)     Alan Reckert      Stohr           TART             115
12.   (27)     Roberto Cruz      VanDiemen RF95  Spratt Racing    105
13.   (47)     Darrell Pollard   VanDiemen RF95  BRM              105
14.   (21)     Rick Henry        Swift DB-8                        57
15.   (54)     Guido Pepin       Swift DB-8      GO Racing         55
16.   (43)     Jude Dionne       Swift DB-8      PACE              54
17.   (55)     Cliff Roe         VanDiemen RF94  GO Racing         49
18.           (50) Don Reese     VanDiemen RF95                    43
19.   (30)     Bill Murfy        Swift DB-8      Smurf Racing      34
20.   (99)     Peter Hurst       Swift DB-8                        34
21.   (88)     Barton Springs    VanDiemen RF91                    22
22.   (19)     Maxwell Jordan    Swift DB-8                        26
23.   (00)     Tom Craig         Swift DB-3      TC Racing         26
24.   (3)      Will Jones        Swift DB-8                        21
25.   (25)     Chase Wilder      Reynard SF90                      21
26.   (27)     Ben Cifelli       Swift DB-3                        11
27.   (40)     Ernie Goolsby     Swift DB-8                         9
28.   (74)     Mark McGrath      Swift DB-3      M & M Racing       5
29.   (13)     Steve Smagala     VanDiemen RF89                     4
30.   (39)     Art Grindle       Swift SE-3                         3

      (34)    Claude Marcoux (Suspended)
```

We put away the sheets and continued loading the trailer.

Standing near the rope, holding the spectators back, stood a man with a bag of jelly beans. Pat waved to Shannon, and we walked over and took the jelly beans.

"That was one fine race," said Pat.

"Thanks," said Shannon.

"Where do you go after this?" Pat asked.

"Formula Atlantic," I said.

Pat asked, "What does that cost?"

I rubbed my chin, "About two hundred-fifty to three hundred

thousand."

"Formula Atlantic. Don't they race at Long Beach?"

Shannon smiled, "Yep, you know anybody who would like to sponsor a team?" Shannon looked at me and laughed, "I better start now."

I laughed, but Pat didn't.

"How much would you need to start?" Pat asked.

Tex pulled on my ear and I responded with a sunflower seed. "About a hundred thousand for the car and rig."

Pat pulled out a business card and handed it to me. "Start looking for a rig. I'm sure you'll find a competitive car. Then I'll purchase it for our team."

My mouth dropped open. Shannon seemed equally stunned.

"Boy, howdy."

"I want you to get with me next week and we'll iron out the details. I'll show you what I'm looking for in a team. Although, you have most of what I'm looking for."

"I don't understand," said Shannon.

Pat smiled, "Easy. I've been wanting to do this for a year. So I started watching this series. I like your team's attitude and I think you can best represent my company. You see, I own an oil exploration company, and I want to advertise that fact--on the side of a racecar. Get the car and the setup, and I'll pay you on a per race basis."

We were speechless. Pat handed us each a business card and talked to us for a few more minutes. Shannon was elated

Shannon was quick to tell his father, Hanna, and Augie. I told Les and Marty.

"Hey, Dudes," Shannon said to Augie and Hanna. "It's Formula Atlantic."

"Oh, wow!" said Hanna.

Shannon did a double high five with Augie who responded, "Awesome, Dude!"

"Unbelievable! A dream come true," mumbled Grant.

"Boy, howdy!"

Shannon had a sponsor. Next year, the road to Indy would continue in the much faster Formula Atlantic series with the first race at the Long Beach Grand Prix. Now more than ever, the quest--the dream of Indy--seemed possible!

Hot Laps – Video Links
for
Formula 2000 the Dream

For your enjoyment here are links to hot laps for each of the tracks described in Formula 2000 the Dream. As you read you can click on the links to watch what it is like on these tracks. My son and I have on all of these tracks.

For those who don't race these videos will give you an excellent idea of speeds and track layouts. These are an excellent way to better understand the story and see visually what the drivers see.

I can't even begin to tell you the thrills you feel when in a racecar. Like Jim Fitzgerald once said, "When you do and you do it right it is the greatest turn on in the world!"

WATKINS GLEN
https://www.youtube.com/watch?v=tgYGw3yFP04
https://www.youtube.com/watch?v=-pmskfWfDf4
https://www.youtube.com/watch?v=DzUVzDF-l4c
https://www.youtube.com/watch?v=QHtwPewMxF8

MOSPORT
https://www.youtube.com/watch?v=UTxJdI32suQ
https://www.youtube.com/watch?v=BsNWZD25NjI
https://www.youtube.com/watch?v=yTujQ9_ag6E

INDIANAPOLIS RACEWAY PARK (IRP)
https://www.youtube.com/watch?v=jerZNmfBRZs
https://www.youtube.com/watch?v=xNaOA_xAvpQ
https://www.youtube.com/watch?v=2ic-WvVsD3w

DALLAS GRAND PRIX
https://www.youtube.com/watch?v=KVkD5wVX-Z4
https://www.youtube.com/watch?v=1Fp890l-oMo

SEBRING
https://www.youtube.com/watch?v=s1P2D3-0CVs
https://www.youtube.com/watch?v=YDIm3UZ1Ap8
https://www.youtube.com/watch?v=Ovp9n-vXMSY

MID-OHIO
https://www.youtube.com/watch?v=1hN8_ZajhvI
https://www.youtube.com/watch?v=iSlx8ZOL63Q
https://www.youtube.com/watch?v=OECh5HgWATc
From Last to First
https://www.youtube.com/watch?v=4gVk_lvsWG4

CHARLOTTE
https://www.youtube.com/watch?v=yN08-ARctjk
https://www.youtube.com/watch?v=VEWU2UsHr5U
www.youtube.com/watch?v=Ip86HsiEXqA

RUAN GRAND PRIX
https://www.youtube.com/watch?v=64T_Tv9_JA8

ROAD AMERICA
https://www.youtube.com/watch?v=1hN8_ZajhvI
https://www.youtube.com/watch?v=nnpUpOlwt7U
https://www.youtube.com/watch?v=-SVh8zNKRjw

ROAD ATLANTA
https://www.youtube.com/watch?v=bvU7FTaj0pw
https://www.youtube.com/watch?v=waeRPxx-et8
https://www.youtube.com/watch?v=LnESk5C70TY
https://www.youtube.com/watch?v=-cOxRoJMvu4
https://www.youtube.com/watch?v=-E8Bb8-Tses

LE MANS
Probably one of my favorite road courses. For your enjoyment
https://www.youtube.com/watch?v=GnDZXBZluIY

ABOUT THE AUTHOR

The author has led an adventurous life. He was married at midnight in a jail in Mexico when he was eighteen. Often he has said raising his children has proved helpful in his writing. His other activities include racing cars professionally, even winning the 6-Hours of Sebring, scuba diving, weightlifting and building houses. On a wild adventure to Cali, Colombia, twelve years ago, he met his wife Lucia. He started writing fifteen years ago and says, "For me writing has solved all the problems I couldn't in real life."

Connect With Me Online

My Webpage
www.jbarfield.com

SMASHWORDS
www.smashwords.com/profile/view/thecajun

AMAZON
www:amazon.com/author/joebarfield

See the Live For Today Trailer
http://goo.gl/Oesoxd

See the Moon Shadow Trailer
http://goo.gl/NSN4Ho

...About the Author's Son

Beaux Barfield was born November 15, 1971 in Houston, Texas. At an early age he started racing Go-carts, moved to Spec Racer, did well in Formula Continental. In 1995 started his first Indy Lights race at Phoenix, where at one point he was 17th but with a push in the final half of the race finished 8th. Of the ten race tracks mentioned in this novel Beaux has raced professionally at all but IRP, although he has raced at numerous oval tracks in the Southeast. Currently, Beaux works for IMSA.

OTHER BOOKS BY JOE BARFIELD AVAILABLE IN PRINT

AND AS EBOOKS

Link to eBooks:

https://www.smashwords.com/profile/view/thecajun

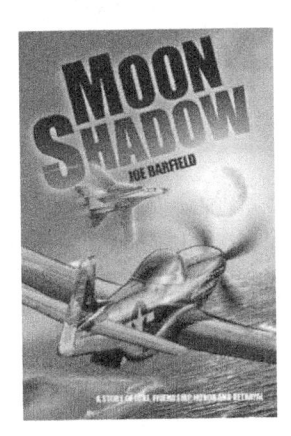

MOON SHADOW THE LEGEND - (Book 1)
MOON SHADOW – (Book 2)
MOON SHADOW'S REVENGE – (Book 3) Available in July

Action-adventure - by Joe Barfield

In 2016 the Muslim Brotherhood has infiltrated America rising in numbers from three million in 2008 to over twelve million in 2016. They have established more than 45 jihadist camps across America determined to take over America and install Sharia law. Members of the Brotherhood attain key spots in the government and military. Hundreds of thousands are granted amnesty, while tens of thousands walk freely across the border of Mexico with the help of America's liberal adminiistration, the Department of Justice and the President of the United States. Unmolested they roam freely across America doing Allah's work. Muslims control the Department of Homeland Security with unlimited weapons and billions of rounds of ammunition. With men in key positions, Christians have been labeled traitors and the debt is given no limit with the express intent of bankrupting America. The United States is destroyed, not so much from outside forces, but rather from the greed within. Unable to pay what remains of the military they simply go home. Along with the President, the Department of Homeland Security and the Muslim Brotherhood control America. The invasion that began in 2008 takes America down. But the Coalition as they call themselves run up against American Civilians armed and deadly. A handful of pilots try desperately to take back America. Against insurmountable odds the future of America depends on its best pilot defeating an F-14 at night but all he has is an antiquated P-51 Mustang and an old Indian Legend; Moon Shadow.

Written in 1996, **Moon Shadow** has become eerily historical with each passing year.

Moon Shadow, the Legend

Considered a traitor and murderer, Beaux Gex, with the help of military friends, is determined to return to America and warn her leaders, but he soon learns they are the problem. Could America's top secret, Aurora Project save or destroy America? Will he be too late? Will the old Indian legend, Moon Shadow, save him or destroy him?

Moon Shadow

Trapped behind enemy lines, a handful of America's best jet pilots, led by ace Beau Gex, discover a dozen old World War II aircraft that they can use in guerrilla-type warfare against the invaders—their enemy. But when the invaders find one of the SR-71 Blackbirds—and intend to use it to destroy the space station, Starburst—Beau and his men are forced to fly one last deadly mission.

Now America's future depends on Beau, its best pilot, defeating an F-14 Tomcat at night. But all he has is an antiquated P-51 Mustang and an old Indian Legend, Moon Shadow.

Moon Shadow's Revenge

America has collapsed but Beau Gex, and Krysti Socorro have found love and they are safe. Their peace is destroyed when Krysti is kidnapped. Beau swears revenge even if he must kill them all to find her. But before he can rescue her it will be a long journey and he will need to deal with the "Crazies," and the Sand People."

For the not-faint-at-heart, *Moon Shadow* begins with one of the edgiest torture scenes since *Marathon Man*. And for those looking for love mixed in with their adventure, *Moon Shadow* satisfies as a tender romance between Beau and Krysti Socorro, an exquisite doctor. Will the betrayal of another tear them apart forever? Can a child save their love or is it too late?

THE CAJUN

(action-adventure) by Joe Barfield

A little Crocodile Dundee and a little Rambo. With a million dollar reward on her head, Kelli Parsons hides in the treacherous Atchafalaya Swamp where living or dying depends on one man--the Cajun!

FORMULA 2000, *the DREAM*

(action – based on a true story) by Joe Barfield

Hoosiers on Wheels.

Keeping a promise, a father enters his son, Shannon Kelly, in the Formula 2000 race series with only a dream and a prayer. When things go from bad to worse it takes a crusty old mechanic, Charlie Pepper, to show them how to win. They soon learn that with Pepper almost anything is possible.

URBAN KILL

(detective thriller) by Joe Barfield

Ex-policemen are taking wealthy men on the hunt of their lives—human prey! The only two witnesses have already been murdered. To solve the case, the lead detective must find a pimp called The Rat and the drug addict Pinky, because they have the answers. But the Rat and Pinky are trying to kill each other. The only people who can help him are a gay bar owner, a hyper, absent-minded forensics expert from India, and his one-eyed, three-legged dog, Lucky.

CHEM STORM

(action – chemical disaster) by Joe Barfield

A reporter and an engineer race to save Houston from a disaster worse than a nuclear explosion—a chemical storm!

Jean Alexander, a reporter for The Houston Post, is young and inquisitive and has gained unauthorized access to an area, where she finds five dead bodies. She wants to know why but a spectator alerts the guards to her presence and she is removed.

The following day a Civil/Chemical Engineer, Travis Selkirk, approaches Jean. She learns he is the spectator from the day before that alerted the guards. He points out the foolishness of her adventure and how the chemicals could have killed her. Jean baits Travis and gets him to agree to show her the dangers that exist on the Houston Ship Channel.

WORDS THAT DON'T OFFEND LIBERALS
(Satirical humor) by Joe Barfield

A humorous look at words that don't offend Liberals. The book will probably offend Liberals. This is meant for the entertainment of open minded people. This a book to keep notes. Check it out before you purchase your printed copy. Fun gift for your Liberal friends. They may never forgive you.

PALABRAS QUE NO OFENDEN LIBERALES
(humor satírico) Joe Barfield

Una mirada chistosa en palabras que no ofendan liberales. El libro probablemente ofender a los liberales. Esto es para el entretenimiento de personas de mente abierta. Este es un libro para guardar notas.
Compruébelo usted mismo antes de comprar su copia impresa. Regalo de la diversión para sus amigos liberales. Es posible que nunca perdonará.

The Single Male Parent's Cookbook and Short Stories
by Joe Barfield

The Single Male Parents' Cookbook, is a delightful combination of food and humor, two subjects everyone will enjoy. As a single parent, the author raised his children from the time they were four and six, and soon became an expert in the kitchen. As he said, "My cooking must have been good, because both are adults now and still alive, which only attests to culinary skills... or luck!"

The Single Male Parents' Cookbook combines recipes with humorous anecdotes of things that did and didn't work in the kitchen (and in the author's life). Joe includes lots of fun cooking ideas along with some that were not so good, and even a few you don't ever want to try at home! He shares everything from his Friday Night Special to his Motel Doggy (the electric hotdog). And let's not forget the ROC (Roaches on Chocolate).

Each recipe is followed by a short story about his childhood antics or raising his children. Not everything always ran smoothly. There was that time his boiled eggs blew up all over the ceiling. Oh, and that grease fire… don't ever pour water on a grease fire! But they say experience is the best teacher, and they are right. It wasn't always easy in those years, but Joe managed to retain his sense of humor.

He once heard George Carlin say that although he's over sixty, he never stopped being ten. That describes the author perfectly. In fact, Joe says, "I've been ten six times over, and my life is as fun as ever."

His final comments are, "Are you curious about my recipes for rattlesnake, rabbit, squirrel, and armadillo? I think you'd enjoy the rattlesnake. Can you picture me cooking the Roaches on Chocolate (ROC) on Rachel Ray's show?"

Don't let the cookbook confuse you. Joe is just a normal type of guy. Well, maybe except for the time he got married at midnight in a jail in Mexico. But that has nothing to do with cooking. Neither does the time he almost got kidnapped in the mountains of Colombia when he met his second wife. He's just a wild and crazy guy from Texas.

FORMULA 2000, the Dream

A Life in Time, My Story – non-fiction
by Joe Barfield

Remember lying on the grass in your front yard and watching the stars? Your best friend was beside you, and neither one of you uttered a word. Then a meteor flashed across the sky and both of you got excited and pointed to the sky.

Our lives are like a flashing meteorite. Often the moments go unnoticed, but we do manage to brighten and touch the lives of those around us. Although we are not all famous or well-known, our stories are important. Each of us has a life in time. These are a series of short stories about my life. From the past comes comparison I'm sure you have heard before, so let me ask you again: Who won the Super Bowl last year? Who won the Indy 500? Who won the last game of the World Series? Who were the Best Actor and Actress at the last Academy Awards? You might remember one, but you probably don't know the others.

Now ask yourself these questions: Do you remember the names of some of your teachers? What teacher helped you in high school? What valuable lessons did your mother and father teach you? And who was your best friend? They may not be famous, but they brightened your life just like that flashing meteorite. I believe life has been an adventure and that we learn from all the things that have happened to us.

The one thing I try to do is look at things in a humorous way. As a child I was called Tiger because I was always into things. I thought I was just curious. As a teenager the death of my father weighed heavily on me. We began to move around. I became angry—a "Rebel," as some of my close friends called me. I had conflicts with religion. When my children were four and six I became a single parent. I learned a lot from them. Most of the stories, I hope, will keep you laughing. There are some that are sad, but that is life. And that is what *A Life in Time* is all about.

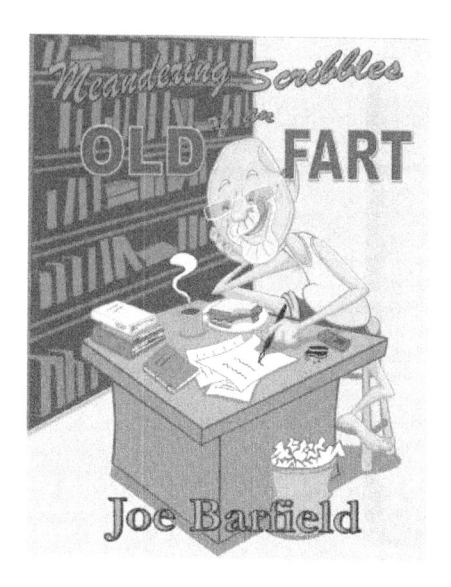

MEANDERING SCRIBBLES OF AN OLD FART – (Political essays) by Joe Barfield

People need to look at their government. I have written articles for over 20 years; from the first Bush to Obama. We have problems we need to face and quit sticking our head in the sand. It's okay to be a liberal or a conservative, but neither exists in our government today. Our politicians do everything but what they were elected to do: Represent the People.

If you are open minded you will enjoy this. If you've only voted one party all of your life then don't download this book. Stop to look at what our politicians are doing today. If you are an open minded Christian you might enjoy this. And if you are you must admit God is probably not too happy. Atheists are offended. Everyone should be offended that they are offended. When talking about being Christian in the military becomes an act of "treason," then we have bigger problems.

America has spent so much time protecting each individual's rights that no one has any rights. Throughout history every great empire has collapsed; there have been no exceptions.

WARNING!

This is for mature audiences so if you're a Democrat or Republican who always voted the same ticket, this is not for you, because it means you are incapable of thinking on your own, so I'd rather you not buy it. If you are a frustrated American upset with the current administrations then you may find these scribbles quit enjoyable.

Should I Forget

A simple reminder, since I might forget. These are scribbles of an Old Fart and you may find repetitions. This is due to "Oldheimers."

DISCLAIMER

Any resemblance to political persons in office is purely intentional.

FOR PETA'S SAKE!
For your peace of mind let it be known that NO animals were injured during the making of these meandering scribbles.
GIVE ME A BREAK!
I'm not a racist, and I'm not a terrorist, I'm just trying to be funny and open your eyes to other solutions. If you have better ideas then you write a book.
FINAL WARNING!
Before you read this I must remind you that you have three choices. You can only pick one so be careful. You are a Democrat, a Republican or an American.

If you picked one of the first two then don't get this book and if you do then don't complain. Americans tell the truth, the other two don't.

Offended yet? You will be; unless you're an American.
FOR OBAMA I'M AMERICA'S BIGGEST THREAT
I'm a white, Christian, heterosexual, and I believe in traditional marriage.
I am America's Biggest Threat.
Get Over It!

A Short Story Collection – fiction
by Joe Barfield

These short stories are based on actual events, and parts from some of my novels, and children's stories. *Sebring, the Rainman* is based on a race my son, Beaux, actually competed. What a race it was!

Night of the Virgin is a combination of events that happened to me in high school. I eventually married her in a jail, in Mexico at midnight. Some of the dialog from *Flight 223* actually occurred. You see I was on flight 223 from Seattle to Houston during the 911 attack. A very strange and chaotic event I will never forget.

I hope you enjoy these as much as I did bringing them to you.

Made in the USA
Middletown, DE
23 December 2023